DIVINE DESTINY

Linda Lindsay & Jane Johnson

PublishAmerica
Baltimore

Hardcover 978-1-4512-6178-3
Softcover 978-1-4512-6179-0
PUBLISHED BY PUBLISHAMERICA, LLLP
www.publishamerica.com
Baltimore

Printed in the United States of America

DEDICATION

To our children: May you be blessed with lives guided by faith, the abundance of family, and friendships that last a lifetime. Believe in your self-worth, strive for integrity, always hope and dream; and live your life looking forward—no matter what the geography is. But above all…love deeply.

ACKNOWLEDGEMENTS

We would like to thank our parents for bringing us up in Christian homes and instilling in us the values that have guided us throughout our lives. We would also like to thank Linda's husband, Walt Lindsay, for his understanding and patience through the ten years it took to write this book.

CHAPTER 1

The French doors were open to the balcony in the guest room on the upper level of Mon Amie Famille. A gentle breeze blew through the sheer curtains and rustled the bouquet of fresh flowers centered on the oak table next to the bed. The aroma of bacon and fresh baked bread called from the kitchen as the morning sun flowed into the room. John came from the shower softly whistling, dressed quickly, and went down the stairs with a spring in his step. Sliding his hand over the antique wooden hand rail, he marveled at the craftsmanship of old. The hallway led past the library with the cream and mauve cabbage rose wall paper, and into the dining hall where the cheery fireplace cast golden shimmers on the fine china and crystal settings on the dining table.

Muffled noises came from the country kitchen just beyond, coupled with the tantalizing aromas that had wafted up the stairs. This brought a smile to his lips and a gleam to his soft brown eyes. As he opened the French doors into the kitchen his smile broadened and his eyes brightened. Even though the woman was standing with her back to him he recognized her. Time appeared to have stood still, her figure was still trim and her long blond hair curled softly on her shoulders.

The warmth of an old friendship flowed through the kitchen, heavier than the scent of the fresh cinnamon rolls that just came out of the oven.

"Hello," he said, in a deep penetrating voice.

Karen turned from the stove, her faced slightly flushed from the heat of the oven, becoming even rosier as she recognized the tall gentlemen standing before her. For a moment she was speechless. She had seen the name from the Internet registration, but was sure it couldn't be him. No, what were the chances he would come back into her life? Just as she opened her mouth to speak, the doors leading onto the patio, where they often served breakfast, burst open.

"Karen, that handyman you hired is killing my roses," said Lily.

At the look on Karen's face, Lilly turned toward the tall man standing in front of Karen and memories began. Oh so long ago. Warm summer nights spent slow dancing on the banks of the river to soft music playing on a car stereo, while stars twinkled brightly in a clear sky. The memory was so strong Lilly could almost smell the wild dogwood that grew along the banks of the Columbia River back in Washington State where they all came from.

The moment was priceless. So much time had passed, but the connection between the three of them was still alive. They had made memories that last a lifetime. And the thirty plus years since they had last seen each other melted away.

John's strong arms brought both women to him. Nestling his cheek against Karen's soft hair he felt complete with a feeling akin to coming home after a long absence.

Quickly brushing the tears from her eyes, Karen reminded Lilly that they had a business to run and guests to care for. Breakfast was ready to be served, so they moved out to the patio, each carrying a tray full of artistic masterpieces. The fresh fruit was arranged perfectly on the oval shaped platter and looked like a rainbow with the colors of watermelon, cantaloupe, honeydew, grapes and pineapple. The scrambled eggs were steaming hot. The biscuits were arranged around containers of butter and home made jelly. The French roasted coffee was hot and fragrant.

There were so many things to talk about, but conversation was difficult as the first of the sleepy guests arrived for breakfast. The food at this Bed and Breakfast is world-renowned. Visitors travel there just to taste the food and experience the hospitality of these two most charming women.

Soon the guests were satisfied and set about their daily business. Some went back to their rooms to pack and be on their way, others set out on strolls through Lilly's Rose Garden and down the path that led to the Gazebo on the banks of the lazily flowing river.

"What on earth are you two up to now?" asked John. "I was planning this business trip down to New Orleans and there you both were—smiling at me from my PC monitor, telling me to visit and taste the best food at the best Bed & Breakfast in the whole U.S. of A. And I couldn't resist, as if I ever could resist either one of you, and here you both are—Lilly you haven't changed one little bit. And Karen, you're as beautiful as you were the night we said goodbye. Karen, do you remember that night? Dear, dear Karen…"

Karen blushed, and gently said, "You're in my heart forever, and it would be impossible to forget anything at all about you."

John looked satisfied at this comment, and settled into his comfortable padded wicker chair. He smiled, and said, "I haven't forgotten a thing either," with a twinkle in his eye.

Just then, a familiar country music tune could be heard from the radio in the kitchen. Seeing their obvious delight at the song John told them that the singer, Dylan Wyatt, was a client and fishing buddy of his. He then told Lilly and Karen how Dylan had mentioned that he would like a great get-away spot, and he had noticed that they have taken great care to give their guests privacy if they desired. John said he would make the contact, and he bet they could expect a special guest yet this summer.

Lilly laughed with joy and excitement. Meeting Dylan was at the top of her dream list.

Karen was already planning in her head, how could they get him to do a private concert? What were his favorite foods? Of course he would bring his wife…the roses should be in full bloom, along with the heliotropes, and the many other flowers in the garden. They would have all of the water fountains running.

"Oh Lilly," Karen said coming out of her daydream, "What is it that the gardener is doing to your roses? What were you so upset about earlier?"

Karen had really hired the gardener for his looks, as much as his gardening skills. She knew that their daily life would be much more exciting when she could watch Lilly keeping her eye on him, and he had a fun sense of humor to spice things up a bit also.

"Well, I no sooner have a beautiful rose blooming, when all of a sudden it's gone! I wonder if he has a sweetheart in town. Maybe that's where all my beautiful blooms are going. At this rate we will have to have the florist deliver flowers for the guest rooms. But I will give you credit, that gardener may be destroying my roses but he certainly has improved the scenery in the garden as far as I'm concerned." Lilly smiled, "Anyway I think I know what you're up to, and I know I haven't been the best company since Waldo went on that extended fishing trip up to Alaska with Engelbert. But I married the man knowing fishing was his first love. I guess I can't blame him. We are so busy here with the business. Karen, he just hasn't had much to do since we forced an early retirement on him and moved so far away from Washington. John, you said you do some fishing? Maybe you could interest Waldo in one of your fishing trips and then maybe I would get to see him this year? And if you can manage to get Dylan here for a while I know Waldo will come home for that."

Lilly's excitement was barely contained as she continued talking, "We can set chairs up around the Gazebo and spread blankets on the river bank; it will be just like the concerts we used to go to down by the Columbia River when we were teenagers. I'll bet Dylan would enjoy a good southern barbecue! My son, Jamie, and Karen's son, John, built us a wonderful pit barbecue when they visited with their families last year. Karen makes the best ribs with her special Jack Daniels sauce. And since Waldo quit drinking, most of the Jack Daniels actually goes in the sauce. Of course that depends on how much fun we're having when we start cooking!"

Lilly got up to refill the coffee cups, since Karen couldn't seem to take her eyes off of John, then settled back into her chair. "John, tell us about your life—the last we heard you had returned from Vietnam in 1975 and joined the Peace Corp. Did you marry? Do you have children? What is your work that brings you to New Orleans?" Lilly chattered on, not noticing the tightening of John's lips at the mention of their children.

In a quiet voice John spoke, "Karen, you have a son named John?"

Karen jumped as the phone rang. She felt relief at the interruption and said, "Excuse me just a minute. I'll be right back."

10

It was just a call about the grocery order to be delivered later that day. Hanging the phone up Karen slipped into the office, where she knew she could be by herself for a few moments.

Karen was anxious to get back to John, but her heart was beating so fast, her senses were at a peak, and she was unsure of how she would answer his questions about her son.

Karen was wearing her Levi's, and her new lavender cotton shirt was crisp and reflected the spring fever she had been feeling. She quickly flipped her long hair up onto her head with a clip, and slipped her glasses on as she settled herself into the comfortable computer chair. She was very anxious to see John's computer registration. Yes, Lilly had taken the registration. Had she known it was him? She quickly looked for more information, but it really didn't tell her much. His employer was paying for his room with a credit card, but the name on the card didn't give her very much information either. She quickly prepared some checks for the bank, thinking that she may be able to get away later, and possibly invite John along so that they could talk alone.

Karen was so lost in thought that she didn't notice the door to her office open and the tall man step quietly inside. John liked the advantage of studying her profile while she was lost in thought. He loved every line in her face and especially the way her blond hair curled in tendrils around the soft spot at the base of her neck. How many times had he seen that dear face in his dreams? It was that memory that kept him alive in Vietnam. And that memory that brought him home. Oh how heartbroken he had been when Lilly told him of Karen's marriage to Dunston. He always wondered why, just at the time he needed her most, she had turned to someone else.

John didn't regret his life. He had been married for twenty years to a wonderful woman. Even though they didn't have children because her heart condition left her in frail health, they did have a great life together and when she died he had thrown himself into his work as a music producer and began traveling. Did fate bring him here? Was it destiny?

Karen had never meant to deceive anyone, but by the time she knew for sure, John was already missing in action in Vietnam. It didn't help matters that her father was a minister and it would break his heart if he

11

knew what she had done. And Dunston was there, always there, begging her to marry him. Lilly didn't like Dunston and had even run over his foot once when he refused to move away from her car. Lilly was a kind, gentle soul but she was fiercely protective of people she loved. When Dunston was killed in an accident with another woman, it was Lilly who had been there for her and even though Karen knew how she felt, her dear friend had never said, "I told you so."

After the death of her husband, Karen turned to her friends, Lilly and Waldo to help raise the children. Waldo was a great father figure and often took John on fishing trips with their son, Jamie. While the guys were out fishing; Karen and Lilly shopped on the Oregon coast with Karen's daughter, Heather. Now the kids were grown. Lilly and Waldo's son, Jamie, was twenty-nine. Jamie and his wife owned a very profitable horse breeding ranch back in Washington State. Karen's son, John was now thirty and as tall and handsome as his father. He had rapidly worked his way up through the ranks of the Newport, Oregon Police Department and had just made detective. John was now married with two kids of his own. Karen's daughter, Heather, had followed her mom and Lilly to New Orleans where she owned the local "what not" shop just a few miles away from the B&B.

Finally John spoke, "Hey, you and Lilly have a great business here."

Karen looked up and then paused for a long moment as her eyes wondered over his tall, lean body. She longed to touch him, but knew it wouldn't be appropriate. She was anxious to talk with him, and yet not sure if she was ready to answer all of his questions. She felt that she needed time to think about how she would tell him about all that had happened in her life. It needed to be graceful and kind; she didn't want to just blurt it all out.

When she finally stopped staring at him, Karen invited John to go into town with her that afternoon to do some errands. This would give her at least a couple of hours to think, and hopefully be able to talk about this with Lilly. Lilly always had a lot of good sense, and Karen was sure she would be able to give good advice and the confidence she needed to tell John about their son.

John sensed that Karen was a bit uncomfortable with conversation and decided he would let her off the hook for now. Besides, if John Jr., as he had just started thinking of him, was really his son, he needed some time to comprehend the impact this would have on his life. His heart welled up within him at the thought of actually having a son, and knew that he would love him as if he had known him all of his life. And what if he wasn't his son? How would he handle the disappointment?

John told Karen he had some very important business calls that he had to make yet that morning, and they agreed that they would meet at 2:00 to go into town. Karen would do a few errands, and perhaps she would take him to meet Heather. Karen was very relieved that she would have some time to collect her thoughts, and find Lilly.

As Karen started to think about what she would say to John, the memories flooded into her mind. She hoped that John had noticed the flagpole they had put in last fall. The large flag rippled majestically in the breeze. Tom, the gardener, was faithful to raise it every morning, and lower it in the evening. The flag was very important to Karen; it represented a time of innocence lost and great sacrifice for her country. She felt this sacrifice must be honored and remembered every day.

When they first got the news that John was missing, Waldo and Lilly had helped her search for information. John's name on a missing in action list was all they were ever given. It was difficult for Karen to go through her pregnancy while she was grieving, but yet the baby was the connection to John that held her life together.

Dunston had been there, and he wanted to be a father and to have a family in the worst way. Karen knew that Lilly didn't really like him, and even though she had a lot of respect for her opinion, in the end she didn't feel that she had a choice. Karen knew for sure that she would keep this baby no matter what, and dreaded the disappointment the truth would bring her parents. Dunston was the financial support she needed, and she really did like him and enjoyed his company. Karen knew successful marriages could be built on friendships. Sometimes the best way to start out a new life was with someone you trust and are comfortable with. How could she have known that Dunston was the last person she could trust? And time was of the essence! Karen not only had to think of her own reputation but the feelings of her parents and most of all not wanting her child to be born without a father. The 1970's were the beginning of the sexual revolution but that did not include girls from good families.

Karen finally gave up hope that John was still alive. If there had been any hope at all she would have weathered any storm her unplanned pregnancy might have caused just to be with him once more. So after Lilly and Waldo had searched and searched through their many connections, the wedding was planned. Even though it was quickly put together the wedding was beautiful. Karen's father married them in the little country chapel at the camp where Karen and Lilly spent many happy summers as teenagers. The wild dogwood was in full bloom along the creek bank and the air was filled with the aroma of spring. Lilly had prepared a picnic style luncheon for the wedding guests. After the reception the bride and groom left for a brief honeymoon in Canada, and then settled down in the Seattle area to start their life together. Their first son John was born six and a half months later. John was the joy of her life; so much like his father he could charm anyone, especially his mother, with just the slightest of smiles. Two years later, Heather was born and Karen loved her no less than her brother, but there was a distinct difference in their personalities. John was tall, handsome and self-assured, and Heather was sweet, shy and somewhat delicate.

Karen loved her children with a passion and when Lilly came up with this Bed and Breakfast idea it almost broke Karen's heart to leave John in the Northwest. But if Lilly was willing to leave Jamie, then Karen could do no less with John. It was time for their children to live their own lives. They did visit often and at least Heather had made the move with them, opening her what-not-antique store just down the road. Yes, life was good. The B&B had grown beyond their wildest imaginations and they were now booked a year in advance reserving only one suite for very special, last minute reservations. Karen grew quiet at this thought, if they were booked out that far, how had John gotten a reservation with just a month's notice? What was going on here? Karen got up and swiftly moved to the French doors opening into Lilly's rose garden, "Lilly, can I see you for a moment?"

As Lilly came into the office, Karen blurted out all of her questions, "What do you know that I don't know? Should I just tell him everything? You knew he was coming didn't you! When did you talk to him? How many times have you talked to him? "

"Calm down, Karen, I admit I knew he was coming. A few months ago John ran into Waldo in Alaska and Waldo told him all about Dunston. John's wife had passed away a few years before and he wanted to come here immediately. Waldo told him to call me and I would arrange it. But I didn't tell him about John Jr., and neither did Waldo. And at the look on the poor man's face, you totally blind-sided him with that one. And about time too! The man has a right to know his son. He always did. Oh, Karen, I understand but honestly, the two of you were meant to be together."

Karen turned from the window where she had been staring out at the garden. "Maybe you're right Lilly. He does have a right to know his son. But what kind of a can of worms are we opening? John grew up thinking Dunston was his dad. What will he think of me?"

Lilly gently patted Karen's arm and said, "John Jr. loves you Karen, and this can't be all bad. One day John thinks his dad is an insensitive, cheating jerk, and then finds out the next day that he's this wonderfully kind, successful man. Only good can come from this."

Karen took a deep breath and turned back to the window. "OK. Well what's done is done. I'm taking him into town at 2:00 to run our errands and meet Heather. I'm sure we will have a heart to heart sometime today and from the looks of the pruning job Tom is doing, you better get back out there and see if you can salvage some of those roses for the tour today."

Lilly rushed past Karen onto the Patio, "Tom, where did you learn to prune roses? Honestly, were you hired by the florist in town to sabotage me?" As Lilly flew past the window, she tripped over the wheelbarrow that had been left too close to the patio steps and landed in a not so graceful heap at Tom's feet. Lilly's shorts came up even further on her slender thighs and she attempted to pull everything back into place as Tom's strong arms picked her up in one fluid motion and set her back on her feet.

For a moment, Lilly was speechless and as Karen fought back laughter, she thought to herself that this might be just what was needed to bring Waldo home once and for all.

Glancing at the clock, Karen realized she had to hurry if she wanted to take a quick shower before going to town. There was so much between them to say; the anticipation caused her heart to flutter.

Back in her bungalow, Karen undressed and choosing the gardenia shower gel that Lilly had gotten her for her birthday she took a quick shower, then applied a little bit of make up and ran a brush through her hair. Going to her closet she picked out the new spring dress she had bought last week. Stopping briefly to admire the dress in the mirror, Karen remembered that Lilly had pushed her to buy the new dress when they went shopping last week. All that Karen really wanted was the lavender shirt, but Lilly had insisted that she buy the dress. I'll have to remember to thank her later she thought.

Karen walked quickly around the house to the front yard, looking for Lilly again to get approval on her quick do. As she came around the corner, she saw John standing under the big oak tree. He was watching the flag, and the look on his face told her that he was remembering a painful time of his life. Hearing her approach, he looked up and said, "It's beautiful, isn't it?"

"Yes," Karen replied, with heartfelt emotion. She longed to know every detail of his experience in Vietnam. She had seen movies that depicted some of the horrible things that had happened there, but she was the type of person that wanted to know all of the truth, even if it was painful.

"John, tell me about your experience in Vietnam. I want to know everything, and what has happened in your life."

John firmly replied, "First, you need to answer my question that I asked earlier this morning! Please tell me about your son. "

Karen's memories went back to the beginning, the day before John had left for Vietnam. She had always had tremendous respect for the values her parents had instilled in her and at first just being friends with John was easy. In the beginning of their relationship they were like most teenagers and had no concept of time slipping away. Even though they were always active; hiking, church camps, and just hanging out with their friends, they became very close. And then John was drafted and they were forced to say good-bye for an indefinite amount of time. They had talked about marriage, but Karen's dad influenced them by insisting that if they were meant to be together, they would still love each other even more when he got back. Then they could build their lives together.

On their last day together, they had taken a picnic lunch to a private spot on the riverbank. It was a hot summer day, and the breeze from over the water was refreshing. They talked and dreamed and shared their fears. They laughed, and cried together. They had spread a blanket out in a grassy area, wanting to be together for every minute they had left. All caught up in their emotions and passions it was a beautiful, natural experience that took place. When night came, they had dared each other to going skinny-dipping. They had fun playing in the water as the moonlight shimmered on the surface. When the night air got cool the rest of the night was spent in John's truck. In the early dawn they went to a 24-hour restaurant for breakfast, and then they kissed good-bye for the last time. Karen had cried the rest of the day. When she finally came to her senses, she called Lilly of course, and poured out her heart. More than a month passed before Lilly took Karen to the local health clinic for a pregnancy test. Lilly had been her constant companion during this difficult and confusing time. Faced with the need to tell her parents, Karen's guilt was heavy as she thought about her relationship with her father. She knew it would break his heart but she also knew he loved her with a father's unconditional love and would stand beside her no matter what. But it was exactly this unconditional love that made it impossible for her to tell him. And Dunston made it almost too easy. He had always been a bit of a pest, according to Lilly, but Karen knew that Lilly loved John as a brother and wanted desperately for them to be together.

"Karen, are you OK?" John asked softly, bringing Karen out of her daydream.

"John, I promise I will answer all of your questions before the day is done, but can we please leave here for a short time? I really do have to get to the bank before it closes, and I want to introduce you to my daughter, Heather. And it's impossible to have a quiet conversation here while Lilly is trying to train that new gardener. Of course it probably would be very entertaining to stay and watch."

John laughed and said, "Oh no, we're not going to stay and watch Lilly and her gardener. Whose car are we taking—yours or the Cadillac I rented at the Airport?"

Karen moved towards the garage and answered, "Let's take my car; I think you'll enjoy it."

The surprise in John's eyes, as the garage door went up and he spied the 1964 cherry red Mustang convertible, was just as she had dreamed many times. As he turned to her she smiled and gently said, "Yes, John you can drive."

"Oh boy, where did you find this car, it's exactly like the one I had just before 'Nam. I always regretted selling it before I left."

Karen couldn't help the laughter bubbling out, "John, it is your car. Waldo found it about ten years ago and he and Jamie and John restored it for me. I wanted so badly to find you and give it to you, but I couldn't. I didn't know if you were married or had a family and besides this way I had something that belonged to you."

Sadness crept into Karen's voice as she turned toward him, her green eyes met his deep brown ones and for a moment time did not exist.

Knowing the time had now come to have his question answered, John softly said, "Karen, did you have something else that also belonged to me?"

Karen slipped her hands into his and drawing a ragged breath said, "Yes, we have a son."

John pulled her close to him, and held her tightly. With tears in her eyes Karen pulled back from him, still holding his hands, and asked the dreaded question, "John, is there someone else in your life?" He softly replied that there was not, and the burden rolled off of her shoulders.

Lilly had been helping Jennifer clean and prepare for the next morning in the kitchen. She happened to walk by the window and catch a look when she had heard the garage door open, and was hoping the security camera was on to catch the moment on tape so that Waldo could see it too. Lilly's attention turned to the camera just in time to see the look on John's face when he saw the car and even though she could not hear the conversation, when John took Karen in his arms, Lilly knew that her mission was a success. Moving swiftly to the control panel she turned off the garage camera. What happened now was between Karen and John and that's the way it was going to stay. Besides, Karen would tell her all about it when she was ready. And now she could call Waldo and tell him. He had been so excited when he ran into John in Alaska, and it was actually his conspiring with Lilly that had brought John here. He was really an old romantic softie at heart. She was still smiling to herself thinking about it, as she returned to the kitchen.

Jennifer was washing the china by hand, as Lilly had served tea to some guests earlier. Karen and Lilly had done all of the work themselves in the beginning, but hired Jennifer part time three years ago and now that they were so busy she put in quite a few hours. Jennifer was in her early twenties and she always had a lot of energy. Just before graduation from high school, she had found herself pregnant and when the father discovered how much responsibility was involved, he split. Jennifer's mother lived in town and had taken a leave of absence from her job for the first year when the twins, Jill and Allie, were born. Jennifer was a very hard worker, and they could always count on her to do a complete and through job. She had earned their trust, and was always welcome to bring the girls when she had work to do outside of their school schedule. The twins were five years old now, and Lillie and Karen loved having them around. Karen missed her grandkids and having the twins around helped fill that void. Besides, they were so well behaved they rarely had any problems to deal with.

John and Karen had all afternoon and evening to talk, so John turned his attention to the Mustang. He ran his hand over the hood, "Let's put the top down...you said John...wow, our son...he helped to restore my car?"

Karen was so excited she could hardly hold still, "Yes, Waldo thought it was good for the boys to learn how to do that kind of work.

So he involved them in every part of it. Jamie and John searched for months before they found a 289 stock engine, and they all spent hours and hours sanding and painting. They wanted to keep it a secret but it was just too much and of course Lilly knew and we all know she can keep a secret from anyone…except me! I didn't know until it was all completed that the car was yours. I'm sure that Waldo knew though; remember how much he loved the car when you had it? And I know he would have loved keeping it for himself, but Lilly had her heart set on a Karmann Ghia. When they were finished with the Mustang they restored her car."

John turned toward the beautiful baby blue VW in the garage stall, "That doesn't surprise me. Lilly always had a soft spot for VW's. Remember we used to say she loved Waldo for his Super Beatle! "

"Karen, are you ready to go? We have a lot to do and you still have questions to answer." John opened the passenger door and Karen slipped gracefully inside, "Yes, John, I'm ready." There was a promise in her voice and peacefulness in her lovely green eyes that had been missing for the last thirty years.

John parked the car in front of the bank and stayed in it to check it out further while Karen went in to make her deposit. A minute later she came back and asked John to go into the hardware store with her. Tom had asked if he could put up two swings for the twins in the big tree the other side of the rose garden. Waldo would have taken care of it himself if he were here, but Karen thought this was a perfect opportunity to find out how handy John could be. He turned out to be an expert, and in no time at all they had the rope and supplies they needed.

As they came out of the store, John eyed the little grocery store across the street, and suggested they get something to drink.

Karen hesitated, knowing Etta Kelly would be there. Etta had worked there for years, Lilly thought it was at least a hundred, and Karen knew she was the source of most of the town gossip. Karen would have liked to avoid anyone knowing about John just yet but she really was thirsty. Entering the store they went past the produce, and back to the coolers where they picked out their drinks.

On the way back to the register, the bookrack caught Karen's attention. "Hey, this romance novel is the new one that just came out. It's Lilly's favorite author, and we just have to get it for her! I know she always wants to have the latest book as soon as it hits the rack. She really is lonely when Waldo isn't here, even though there is always a lot to do and a lot of people around, and Tom to watch."

Karen started to take her wallet out as they came near to the check out counter, but John already had a twenty-dollar bill outstretched to Etta. Etta Kelly picked up the book, held it in front of his face, and asked, "So what do you think of this kind of book?" Karen's insides churned and she searched her thoughts for an idea, something that would put the old busy body in her place. Quickly her mind went to at least a dozen retorts for Etta's rudeness. However, she refrained and was glad she did when John responded to Etta's question. In a cool, business like, voice he said, "I like these books just fine, and by the way, you have some rotten apples over there you better take care of." Karen could hardly contain her giggles until she got out of the store.

Now her thoughts turned to Heather. Karen was having second thoughts about having John and Heather meet, but it was a little late now. Mrs. Kelly would have rumors going within the hour, and if Heather heard about this through the grapevine, her feelings would be hurt. Heather was sure to notice how much John looks like her brother, and there would be more explanations to be made.

They drove the five blocks to Heathers what not shop. As they entered the store a chime went off above the door but there was no one in sight. Karen suggested that Heather was probably in the back in her studio and they could look around the shop for a few minutes if he liked. The store was divided into three sections. One was full of antiques, furniture, kitchen gadgets, and everything else you could or couldn't think of. The second room contained a variety of interesting newer items such as modern collectibles and jewelry. The third room was an art gallery where Heather's paintings were displayed. The back room was used for deliveries, storage, and had a sunny corner where Heather painted. John asked if there was a restroom, and Karen directed him up the back stairs to Heather's apartment.

The apartment above the store was just four rooms. The kitchen was neat and clean, the small living room looked like the cover of a home interior magazine, and the bathroom a department store catalog, but it still felt comfortable. John's eyes skimmed over the layout of the small apartment, and then focused on the framed picture on the small end table.

The picture of Karen, Heather, and John Jr. had been taken the summer before. He stared for a long time drinking in everything the picture told him about his son. The young man was tall, standing head and shoulders above his mom and sister, his dark wavy hair and soft brown eyes framed the mischievous smile on his lips. Oh I'll bet Karen had quite a time raising him, he thought. John could hardly wait to hear every little detail of his son's life. And strangely enough there was no remorse in his mind. He felt badly that he had not been there for Karen, but you can't change the past and the past is a part of who we are in the present. Had he married Karen before he left for Vietnam like he wanted to, he probably wouldn't have accepted the dangerous mission in 'Nam that sent him to the POW camp. And without all those years in that hellhole he would not have been the strong man with the moral values that he has today. No you can't go back—from where you are today you can only go forward. Now it was time to meet Karen's daughter.

John quickly washed his hands and hurried down the stairs. Karen was standing at the door of the artist's studio watching a lovely young woman paint. The artist was so intent on her work that she had not heard the two of them come in. Putting one arm lightly around Karen's shoulders, John urged her silently forward.

"Heather, dear, I have someone I want you to meet," Karen said quietly.

Heather put her brush down and began wiping her hands on the back of her faded Levi's. "Hi Mom, I was hoping you would stop by today. Aunt Lilly called and said you were coming into town." Turning towards John, Heather stepped into his arms without hesitation and softly said, "May I call you Dad?"

"Wait…Wait…How did you…You didn't…" Karen stuttered.

"Oh Mom, when I was about twelve I found the love letters you kept in that little mahogany chest. I didn't mean to pry, but you left the chest out one day and I wanted to know what was in there that made you so sad. I grew up listening to you and Aunt Lilly talk about your wild teenage years, even though I knew neither of you were really wild." Heather put an arm around her Mother and pulled her close as she continued to speak. "I also sensed there was something different about my brother, John. Dad didn't treat him the same way he did me, and besides I saw this gentleman's picture in your old albums. The first picture I saw I thought it was John, until I saw the date on the back. Honestly Mom, give me a little credit, I grew up knowing John and I didn't have the same father. And don't look so embarrassed. We're all adults here."

Karen felt as if a huge burden had been lifted from her shoulders, "Did Lilly tell you he was coming?"

Heather laughed gleefully, "When I guessed the truth and confronted her, she would only say that if I had questions I should ask you. That told me right there that I was right! So when are we telling John? And don't worry I never told him my suspicions."

Karen sighed, "Well in a way I wish you had. I just don't know how I'm going to explain…"

John was delighted by this turn of events. After the warm welcome from Heather it took him a moment to regain his composure. "What a day this has been, I woke up this morning far away from New York City in the most beautiful Bed and Breakfast in the world and by 3:00 PM I not only have my one true love back in my life, I also have a son and a beautiful daughter. Heather, I would be honored if you called me Dad."

It was Friday night, and Karen knew her son would not be home from work yet. The time was three hours earlier in Oregon, so they couldn't call for a few hours. Heather was close to her brother, and she obviously wanted to be involved. Karen was anxious to tell John Jr. about his dad, so to pass the time she asked, "What would you two think about getting a bite to eat together? By the time we're done, John should be home from work, and we can call him."

John replied, "Sure, I'm famished. It's been a long time since breakfast!"

Heather wanted to change before they went, so John and Karen looked around the store while Heather got ready.

They looked at all of the interesting merchandise, and then John found the paintings. There was a painting of Karen and Lilly sitting in the gazebo, with the rose garden around it. He was quite taken with it, and slipped his large hand over Karen's while he studied it. Finally he asked, "Is this one for sale?"

Heather had just come around the corner and said, "No, that one I can't part with!"

"Ok," he replied, "but maybe I could have a print?"

"Maybe," she answered with a smile.

As they left the shop Heather noticed that John went immediately to the driver's side of the Mustang as if he had been driving it every day for the last thirty years. "Is there something special about this car too?" she asked.

Karen explained to her that it had been his originally. Heather thought about the hours Waldo, Jamie and John had spent on the car. John was really going to be excited, and she couldn't wait to see his reaction. They went to the family restaurant down the street, and sure enough Etta Kelly's daughter was in the restaurant with her husband. She kept staring, but Karen ignored her. The conversation was easy and comfortable, and Karen was pleased, and relieved, that Heather liked John so much.

After dinner they returned to Heather's apartment, and Karen dialed John's number. John answered immediately, "Hey Mom, how are you? I just got home from work, and getting ready to e-mail you like I do every week. Is something wrong?"

"No, nothing is wrong," replied Karen. "We're here at Heather's apartment, and there's someone here I think you'd like to meet. I should have told you year's ago that Dunston was not your dad. Your Aunt Lilly and Uncle Waldo have done a lot of searching for your father, and they've located him." She paused to take a breath, but before she could continued, John was already asking questions.

"Where is he? Mom, I always suspected Dunston wasn't my real dad. To be perfectly honest, I'm glad I wasn't related to that jerk!"

Karen was surprised at this, but asked, "He's here, John. Would you like to talk to him?"

John Jr. was excited and apprehensive at the same time. "Of course, put him on."

John picked up the other phone, he was completely confident, and immediately they were talking up a storm. Karen learned a lot by listening. "Where do you live? What do you do? When are we going to meet?" John Jr. asked.

John Jr. told his dad all about his wife, Melinda, and their two children, Tyler and Kristin. He went on to say that he was just getting ready to send their school pictures in an e-mail. They talked about his job as a detective.

John Sr. told him about his home in New York, his work in the music industry and his late wife, Sarah. These two talked liked a father and son who had been in contact every day of their lives, not two men who had just met long distance over the phone, there was a bond here that made the years disappear.

Finally the phone connection was broken with the promise of more phone calls to come and a reunion as soon as John Jr. could arrange to take time off of his busy schedule, and when the kids were out of school.

Karen could not have been more pleased with the way her day had turned out but she did have responsibilities that couldn't be ignored. "I'm sorry to break this up you two, but if I don't get back to the house Lilly will have my head. This is Friday night and the house is booked solid. I have to get back and start the dough for cinnamon rolls for breakfast. Lilly will have her hands full with the last minute requests from our guests and we try to give Jennifer Friday nights off. After all she is a young woman and needs a social life. Heather, dear, goodnight—sleep tight—and thank you for being the most wonderful daughter a mother could hope for."

25

Heather hugged her mom tightly, "Goodnight Mom, you two have a good evening."

Turning to John she hugged him also, "Goodnight Dad, welcome home."

"Goodnight Heather, my darling daughter," John said hugging her gently, "sleep well."

John and Karen returned to the Mustang. He asked if she was chilly, did she want him to put the top up on the car? Karen said no, the evening was mild and she liked the feel of the wind in her hair. He opened the passenger door for her and was pleasantly surprised to find her sitting in the middle between the bucket seats when he got into the driver's side. Sliding behind the wheel and pulling away from the parking place at the antique store, John put his arm around Karen and pulled her close with her head resting on his shoulder for the return trip to the Bed and Breakfast.

John asked, "Do you think Lilly would mind if we stopped for just a couple of minutes?"

Karen knew there was a lot of work to be done, but agreed to stop. Following her directions, John pulled over to a rather private spot by the river, got out, and then opened Karen's door for her.

He had been thinking about kissing her all day long… when he first saw her this morning, when he walked into her office and she was sitting at her desk, when she had confirmed that they had a son… but he knew that the timing had to be just right. He knew the time was now. The moon was bright in the sky, and it reflected off of the water, just like their last night together. He led Karen to a smooth spot of ground, took her in his arms and began humming softly. For a few minutes they danced to the tune of an old love ballad. It was like a wonderful dream. Karen reached up and put her hand through the curls of hair at the base of his neck. As their lips met the kiss went through their bodies like electricity. It was full of passion and tenderness. Karen caught the smell of his clean t-shirt as she laid her head on his chest to listen to his heartbeat.

Karen finally pulled back as she said, "We really should get some sleep tonight, and tomorrow is going to be another big day. I will get out all of my photo albums and show you the pictures of the kids as they grew up as soon as we're done with the breakfast guests."

"OK," said John, "but are you sure you wouldn't like to come to my place for breakfast? I would cook your eggs any way you wanted!"

Karen laughed, and said, "Don't tempt me."

Driving back to the Inn, Karen's head rested on John's shoulder and she thought how easy it would be to follow John to his room. But that was not the way she wanted their relationship to turn. It was suddenly important to her to do the right thing for herself, and for her children. Karen's dad had passed on several years before, but she was still very determined to do what was right in his eyes as well as following her own morals.

Karen knocked on the door of her bungalow. John opened it with a very surprised look on his face. She had made it quite clear that they would not be spending the night together. John had on a deep blue robe, and looked like he was ready to get into the hot tub out back. He also looked like he belonged on the front cover of a magazine. His body had filled out nicely in thirty years, and Karen could not resist. She sweetly asked if she could please have her eggs sunny side up? Karen was wearing a black lace negligee that flowed around her ankles as he pulled her towards the hot tub...

Karen woke up with a start from her dream. She had forgotten to set her alarm, and Lilly would be doing all of the work by herself. She hurriedly got dressed, and practically ran to the house. Lilly and Jennifer already had breakfast ready for the guests, and Tom was helping too. He had just come in from taking the garbage out and was asking Lilly if there was anything else she needed him to do. Karen looked at Lilly to see if she was mad. "Lilly, I'm so sorry, you were already in bed when we got in last night and I found the cinnamon rolls rising on the shelf above the stove, and the fruit was all cleaned, there was nothing for me to do, so I went to bed."

At these words Lilly smiled, and Karen continued, "Alone!"

Lilly laughed gleefully, "Oh Karen, I was writing a letter to Waldo when you came in and I saw you go off to your bungalow alone. But you should know I had three phone calls last night, all from the Kelly clan. Honestly those people don't know how to mind their own business. And what's this about John buying some kind of porno book? When Old Lady Kelly told me that, I asked her what she was doing selling porn, and she hung up on me. So it was worth it!"

Lilly paused for a moment and took a long look at Karen, "Karen, you're absolutely glowing. I want to hear everything but if you don't want our guests to know all about it we better wait until after breakfast." Lilly smiled and grabbed a platter of artistically arranged fresh fruit and headed for the patio, "I'm so glad this weather is allowing us to serve out here, everything tastes so much better out of doors."

"Good Morning everyone," said Karen, "did you all sleep well? Matthew, I'm so happy to see you, I had forgotten you were visiting us this weekend and how is Annie and the baby?"

Matthew Denali was an old dear friend of theirs. He grew up with John, went away to college and in his spare time developed an extremely successful computer software program that was used by businesses worldwide. Matthew was now one of the richest men in the world, but he had not forgotten his old friends and had even installed the computer programs in the house, putting a terminal in each room so the guests could have access to e-mail.

Matthew rose from his seat as Karen approached and he kissed her on the cheek, "Karen, it's so good to see you, Annie and Maggie are fine. Annie sends her love and said to tell you she hopes to visit as soon as Maggie is a little older. I wouldn't have left them, but felt I really needed to overlook the installation of my software at that new aircraft plant being built just the other side of New Orleans. And what's this I hear about a certain gentlemen visiting from New York?"

Karen smiled, patted him on the cheek, and said, "We'll talk later, but now I have to see to my other guests." As she turned back to talk to Mr. and Mrs. Adams from Colorado, she suddenly caught sight of the tall, bare-chested man, adjusting the faucet on the side of the garage. Distractedly she excused herself and followed him around the house.

John was out front washing the mustang in the morning sunshine…his wet chest glistened in the sun. His muscles rippled, and his damp hair was curlier than usual. Karen stared for a moment before she could get the words out. "Good morning! Did you sleep well?"

He looked up from the shiny red car, smiled and said, "Good morning to you…want to help?"

Karen paused as she pondered the consequences of once again playing in the water with John. She also wasn't sure if her faded blue t-shirt would hold up under a good hose drenching.

"I think I'll have to wait until my work is done before I can play in the water with you," she said as she put her arms around him and gave him a big long kiss. "Ok, I can go to work now, did Lilly already feed you?"

"Yes, she's a great cook. Where were you?" he teased.

Karen ran back to the kitchen and started on the morning dishes. She felt like she needed to work hard to make up for the slack time she had taken, and she was capable of doing a lot in a short amount of time. She joyfully swished her hands back and forth in the water creating bubbles in the trails her fingers left. Not even Lilly could fully know how grateful her heart was for her answered prayers.

Lilly was entertaining the guests just outside the door. She really did have a lot of class, Karen thought. Lilly had medium length dark curly hair and was rather petite in build. With her trim figure anything looked good on her, and Karen admired the way she was always ready for whatever came her way. She somehow knew just the right thing to say, or not to say, as the case may be. Karen was certain Heather and John Jr. wouldn't be quite the great kids they were if Aunt Lilly hadn't had a part in their lives. Waldo adored her with all of his heart, and Jamie had turned out to be a productive, kind man as well as extremely handsome. He and his lovely wife, Kelsi, were very hard workers, loved their animals, and were happy in Washington. Lilly and Waldo were both very proud of the way their son turned out and secretly hoped someday

Jamie and Kelsi would have children to care for along with the assortment of animals on the ranch.

Finishing the last of the dishes, Karen hung the dish towel up to dry and slipped out the front door to go for a quick walk before more chores came her way. The mid-morning air was still cool and refreshing on Karen's face as she walked down the road to the little country chapel that sat back in the woods a quarter mile from the main road. She knew the door would be unlocked, and usually there was no one there this time of the morning. Reverently she entered the small building and once again the stained glass windows were a breath taking sight for her. She sat towards the back where she had a view of most of the windows, and started talking out loud. "Oh Lord, thank you for the many blessings in my life, thank you for my children, for Heather's sweet spirit and John's loving kindness to everyone in his family. Thank you for enriching my life all these years with the long and lasting friendship of Lilly and Waldo. Thank you for bringing John back into my life. If it is truly your will Lord that I have a life with this man then please let it be so. And...Dad, if you can hear me, thanks for your care and unconditional love." Karen's spirit was saturated with peace. She knew in her heart and spirit that she was doing the right thing this time.

Karen walked back to the Bed & Breakfast very light hearted. When she got there, John and Tom were just getting ready to put the swings in the tree, so she found Lilly. "Come talk to me while I shower and find something decent to wear."

After letting Jennifer know where they were going, Karen and Lilly went to Karen's bungalow where Lilly immediately became comfortable on Karen's antique settee.

"So tell all, and don't leave out one little detail."

Karen laughed, "Let me get a quick shower, then I'll fill you in." With that she disappeared into the shower stall. Soon the steam and aroma of the fragrant shower gel filled the air.

Lilly was quickly lost in thought, back to the night she and Karen had met John. It was that Ford Mustang that first attracted them. You could hear the roar of the engine for two blocks and the squeal of those oversized tires as he turned corners. One night they followed him, just to see what he looked like. When he parked at a local all night breakfast cafe and unfolded his 6'3" frame from the bucket seats, they both sighed. He was the most magnificent thing they had ever seen and both of them squealed with delight when he walked towards them instead of inside the restaurant. John went to Lilly's driver side and bending down he asked them if they would like to come inside for a cup of coffee. They both fell immediately in love, but it was plain to see that Karen was the one he was interested in. Not wanting to interfere in her friend's happiness, Lilly never actively pursued him.

The three of them had wonderful times, often John would invite a friend along for Lilly, but most of the time it was just the three of them until Lilly met a young sailor named Waldo. Those were wonderful times, they were so young, not afraid to try anything and so terribly in love. They went to dances and parties on Friday nights and swimming on warm Saturday nights in the river. In the winter they had sledding parties and went to movies. John even started going to church with them on Sunday because he knew how important the church was to them and he loved them for their beliefs, and wanted to be a part of everything in their lives.

Lilly reluctantly left her daydreams behind as Karen came from the dressing room and started speaking. "It was more wonderful than I could have ever imagined. The last thirty years just disappeared, there was no awkwardness. Heather and John both accepted him without question and I feel like I've given them the father they always deserved."

Lilly got up to adjust the collar on the powder blue cashmere sweater set that Karen had put on with her Navy washed Levi's. "Karen, he is the man you've always deserved. You never asked for the life that Dunston gave you, but you raised the kids to respect their "so called" father anyway. You never ran him down in their eyes, even though you could have. And now, you need to accept the happiness that life is offering you."

Karen gave her friend a quick hug and said, "When he kissed me goodnight last night and held me in his arms, I felt like I had come home. I won't let him go this time. Now we better get back to the kitchen before Jennifer fires us both. It's Saturday and I know she wants to do some shopping and then bring the twins back to try out the swings. That is if the guys have them hung."

Karen gave Lilly the book they had gotten for her the night before and they laughed at old lady Kelly calling it porn. They were still talking as they left the bungalow about the night before and the phone calls from the nosy Kelly clan. Giggling and laughing, they agreed that they really felt sorry for her. Karen told her all about the dance and the first kiss, and described Heather's reaction to John, and his phone conversation with John Jr. as they made their way to the house.

"How is Tom doing on the roses? I think they're looking better," Karen said, "You've done a good job with the training. You haven't fallen over any more wheelbarrows lately have you?"

They were still giggling when they got to the kitchen. Jennifer asked, "What's all the levity around here? That John guy sure is good-looking! What are we making for lunch? "

"Well," said Lilly, "I think we'll make chicken salad in wheat pita bread, and serve some fresh fruit with it, and for dessert we can have that apple crisp I made with pecan, walnut, raisin crust. I already told John and Matthew we would have lunch in the gazebo, and we can take all of the photo albums out there. Tom has set up a table, so we'll have plenty of room."

They all busied themselves putting lunch together. Lilly made the chicken salad, and who knows what her secret ingredient was this time, she was always adding something that made it spectacular, but usually didn't share her secrets. Maybe because they really were a secret or maybe because she really didn't remember since she varied her recipes every time she made something. Jennifer left to do her shopping and pick up the girls, promising to bring them back to play after their naps.

Lilly and Karen placed the food and table supplies on the big serving cart, and luckily Tom was close by to push it out to the gazebo for them.

Leaving Tom to put the food out, they both went to find John and Matthew. Tom had told them they were in front admiring the Mustang. As they rounded the corner of the house, a car pulled into the driveway. John and Matthew were watching it intently and barely noticed that the women had come up beside them. Karen strained her eyes to see who was driving and her heart leapt with joy as she recognized her only son. He barely got it into a parking gear before she practically pulled him out to hug him. She had been feeling badly that he wasn't here to take part in this.

John Sr. turned to Karen, "Karen, you didn't expect me to wait any longer than necessary to meet my son did you? And I wanted to surprise you."

Karen was so overwhelmed it took her a moment to catch her breath, "Are Melinda and the kids coming?"

John Jr. smiled and said, "Mom, aren't I enough?"

"Quit teasing me John, you know how much I love you. It's just…"

John Sr. was laughing at this exchange, "Don't worry, my love, the whole family will be here tomorrow."

The father and son turned towards each other and hugged without hesitation. After a brief moment they pulled Karen into their embrace.

"Hey, wait a minute there's another member of the family here too." No one had noticed Heather ride up on her bicycle. She hopped off and wrapped her arms around both men. "Heather did you know he was coming?" Karen asked.

"John called me last night after the arrangements were made," Heather replied.

Karen turned toward Lilly. "Lilly did you…"

John laughingly said, "Now Karen, you know Lilly can't keep a secret from you. Besides, has anyone noticed that there is someone else in the car?"

With that they all turned towards the vehicle sitting in the driveway just as Waldo got out of the front seat and started towards Lilly. Lilly screamed with delight and threw herself into his arms. John just stood back with his arms around his family and smiled as he said, "It really didn't seem right not to share our happiness with everyone."

To John Jr.'s surprise, Matthew stepped up to give him a hug, and Karen thought she saw a hint of a tear in his eye. "I didn't know you would be here too, it's great to see you!" said John Jr.

Lilly disentangled herself from Waldo and gave John a quick hug, "I don't suppose you have my son in the backseat do you?" she asked wistfully.

"Nope, but he and Kelsi will be here on Tuesday. That's the quickest I could arrange it. Waldo chartered a plane in Alaska and had it stop in Newport and pick up John Jr. The rest of the families have to fly commercial. But we'll all be together soon. And I don't know about anyone else, but I'm starved. Waldo, I'll bet these women of ours have fixed quite a spread for lunch, what do you say we sample it?"

Waldo laughed and said, "Every time I go out on a fishing trip I lose twenty pounds and it takes Lilly about a week to put it back on me. Let's go."

So with arms around each other they all proceeded to the Gazebo where Tom had efficiently arranged the food on the buffet built into the side of the Gazebo. Lilly and Karen looked at each other in surprise.

"You ladies didn't know my former experience at Camp David was in the dining room, you just assumed it was in the garden didn't you?" Tom said, stepping forward to shake hands with John Jr. and then Waldo. Waldo quietly sized him up and then turned to Lilly. Lilly said lovingly, "Honey, Karen hired him, not me."

Karen leaned forward and whispered in Waldo's ear, "Lilly has been training him." Waldo looking shocked and said, "What, the…" Waldo didn't even finish his sentence, but he knew he would be asking Lilly about it later.

"These sandwiches are great!" Waldo said taking another bite. "I sure missed your cooking, Lilly. It's good to see you, love of my life." He winked at her and then continued, "We're just lucky we're here safe and as soon as we are. John Jr. spotted a criminal at the airport, but he had the proper authorities there to help, and handcuffs were on the guy before we knew it."

Karen looked her son in the eye and found total confidence mirrored back at her. There didn't seem to be anything he couldn't accomplish.

Heather and Matthew were soon telling everyone stories about John Jr., "Remember when he was about five years old and rode his little plastic horse into the blackberry bushes? Then he walked home, crying all the way, with blackberry stickers stuck all over him. And then when he was about thirteen, he crashed on a bike jump and didn't remember walking home at all that time."

Just then Jennifer walked up with Jill and Allie, and introduced them to everyone. They were dressed in matching pink shirts and jeans, with pink ribbons in their braided, long blond hair. "Can we play on the swings?" They asked excitedly together.

"You have swings?" Waldo asked.

"Yes, Mommy said her friends fixed them up for us." Jill answered as Allie looked hopefully at her Mother. Tom laughed and took Allie's hand as Jennifer took Jill's and off they went to find the new swings.

Karen's heart swelled as she thought of seeing her own grandkids tomorrow. Tyler was seven, and Kristin six, and they would all have a great time playing together.

The group spent several hours reminiscing, and pouring over each picture. John was pleased and felt very blessed that he was now part of the family he didn't even know he had a few days ago.

John moved away from the table and sat on the steps of the Gazebo gazing at the reflection of the sun setting over the water. The kids were so involved in their reminiscing they didn't notice Karen join him on the steps. John reached out and took her hand, "Karen, this has been the most wonderful day of my life."

Karen squeezed his hand, "John, I'm so sorry you weren't part of his life growing up. I never meant to deceive you, but by the time you came back there were too many feelings to consider if the truth came out. And here I was trying to protect the two people I love most in the world and they knew all the time. How can I ever make it up to you?"

John put his arm around her slender shoulders and pulled her close. "Shhh, my darling, don't ever feel you need to apologize. What will be will be, we had no way of knowing thirty years ago how the story would end, and we have no way of knowing now. All we can do today is seize the moment and make it last as long as possible. No regrets, Karen."

Karen sighed, gently resting her head on his broad shoulder as she thought about his kind words, and remembered their dance the night before.

Behind them Waldo was entertaining with the story of the first time he took Jamie and John Jr. on a deep-sea fishing trip and how sick they both had gotten, in spite of the seasickness medicine. Waldo had not only caught his own limit, but he caught theirs as well. After that particular trip Karen, Lilly, Heather and Matthew had met them on the dock and they had all gone to the Casino where Lilly, not usually a gambler, had won enough to pay for everyone's lunch.

John spoke softly in Karen's ear, "Sounds like you all had lots of fun while the kids were growing up?"

Karen replied, "Oh we did. Lilly and Waldo have been the best. Waldo made sure the boys grew up with knowledge of cars, boats, hunting and fishing. And now John will have the influence of a great dad as well."

"Ok, let's clean up this mess," said Lilly, "and everybody helps"

They loaded the cart, and Waldo pushed it up to the house while everyone else carried the remaining items. John Sr. started in right away putting dishes in the dishwasher as Matthew was handing them to him. John Jr. and Heather were taking care of the leftovers. The kitchen was spotless in no time, and all of the preparations for the morning were done. Lilly looked around her spotless kitchen and smiled, "Just like Mama always said, many hands make light work."

Waldo and Lilly said goodnight while Karen, John, and the grown kids retired to the living area of the house. John asked Heather more about her life, and she told him about her love for kids. On Wednesday evenings you could always find her at the library with a group of children around her, listening to her read a story. They talked more about her store, how she got it started, and her paintings. Matthew pulled out his pictures of his daughter, Maggie, and Karen and Heather begged him to bring her for a visit.

As Karen listened to them, she realized that the last two days had been so busy; she hadn't even had a chance to think about the reality of John living so far away. Fear gripped her heart for a moment as she dreaded a long distance relationship. This was something they hadn't had a chance to talk about yet, let alone think about. As a matter of fact, she didn't even know if he likes his toilet paper to roll over or under. I must be getting tired, Karen thought.

It was getting a little late, and John Jr. looked very tired. So Karen suggested that if it was okay with them, John Jr. could sleep on the couch in John's room, and tomorrow they would work on another arrangement for all of his family. John Jr. went into the office to call Melinda even though it was late, as he knew she was waiting for him to say goodnight.

John, Karen, Matthew and Heather visited quietly for a time, Matthew filling them in on the success of his software. It turned out that his were the programs that John had installed in his new offices in New York and Nashville. Finally looking at his watch Matthew excused himself and went to his room. He had promised Annie that he would call each night. Heather yawned and said it was time she started back to her place; she had an early showing of one of her paintings and still needed to tidy things up. John didn't want her riding her bicycle after dark and insisted on driving her home. Karen chimed in and said she would ride along.

After delivering Heather safely to her door, John asked Karen if she would like to stop for coffee somewhere. Karen responded that the only thing open was the local nightspot called "The Huddle" because that's where the college and pro football teams hung out.

"What I would really love John is another moonlight dance, is that option available?"

John pulled the car expertly out of its parking place and headed towards the same spot they danced in last night. "You bet, but I need to warn you this time I may not let you out of my arms."

At this Karen only smiled, "Somehow I think you'll do the right thing. You don't have my dad to contend with this time, only my children."

John parked the mustang and went around to Karen's side of the car. Opening the door for her John took her lovingly in his arms and began dancing to the soft music coming from the car radio, "Our children, my love, our children." As Karen rested her head on his shoulder, John hummed softly and their bodies melted together.

It was like heaven on earth...John was so graceful and smooth...Karen's fears melted away with the years as their bodies meshed together and swayed to the music. Pulling away from her slightly he searched her green eyes before their lips met in a kiss such as neither of them had experienced in the past thirty years. He kissed her like he had never kissed before in his life. All of his heart and soul was in it, and Karen knew this without a doubt. She responded equally...her knees weakened and as the kiss lingered she clung to him. "John, what are we doing? Are we moving too quickly into an impossible relationship? I don't mean to pressure you, and I don't have any right to ask, but..."

John stepped back slightly without releasing her and smiled, "Why Karen, did you just propose?"

Shyly she said, "I guess maybe I did. But if I remember right, you did that first thirty years ago. Does your offer still stand?"

"Absolutely my darling" John said covering her mouth softly with his, "And is your answer the same as it was thirty years ago?"

"Yes, John, I will be your wife, now and forever until death do us part." With that he pulled her close again and they continued to sway together letting the soft words of the song speak of their love for each other.

As the song ended, Karen raised her head from his shoulder. "John, where are we going to live? What about my business? What about your business?"

John placed one finger lightly across her lips, "Shhh, my darling, don't worry, love will find a way. There is nothing in my life more important than being with you and seeing as much of our children as their lives will allow. Everything else will sort itself out." He kissed her passionately once more and she was again lost in the sensations of the moment, but all too soon he moved away and said, "We have to go back, do you remember who's sleeping in my room?"

Karen laughed, "Putting John Jr. in your room was the only way I could make sure that I wouldn't be there tonight. Do you mind terribly if we wait? I want everything to be perfect this time."

John groaned, "Well I can't hardly go to your room and have him know I didn't come back. My gosh Karen, this reminds me of when we were kids. We have gone from sneaking around behind our parents back to sneaking around behind our son's back! But if this is the way you want it then this is the way it will be. Let's go home."

For the second night in a row John drove home with Karen's head resting on his shoulder. Pulling into the driveway of the Inn he took her in his arms. "Let's set a date tomorrow and it better not be too long. John Jr. won't be sleeping in my room forever." With that John kissed her goodnight and returned to his suite.

Karen opened the door to her bungalow and walked in, throwing her bag on the kitchen table. She looked around at her living space that she had created for a single person. It was fairly simple; the living room walls were painted a pale rose color. Her antique settee covered in print fabric with ivory roses sat in one corner, and an over stuffed chair in the other. An entertainment center took up the space on one wall. Towards the back were a kitchenette, pantry/storage area, and patio doors leading out to a private deck with a hot tub. The privacy walls had large wooden windows that opened up to provide shade and create an open outdoor atmosphere. In the evening Karen liked to sit at the patio table where she could read, write, or catch a view of the sunset over the river. The bedroom was decorated in pale lavender and silver. The walls were painted a silvery sage green. The bed was accented with purple pillow shams. It had a white cotton eyelet bed ruffle, and the flower print duvet cover matched the valance over the window, with white sheers that flowed with the breeze. One of Heather's paintings, the hibiscus flowers, hung over the antique dresser. The dresser matched the armoire and headboard. Heather had found the furniture set when she was searching for merchandise for her store last summer. A vase of fresh lilacs sat on the bedside table and an antique wooden rocker in the corner. But Karen's most favorite place in the whole bungalow was the walk in closet. It was huge, and Heather had helped her organize it from top to bottom. On the opposite side of the room was the bathroom, decorated in blues and greens with seashells and fish.

Karen looked around, and realized that tonight her life had changed dramatically. She had thought her bungalow was the one thing that would always remain stable in her life, and now it would change. She didn't know how or to what extent yet, but for sure she would be sharing her living space, wherever that may be, with John. She went in and lay on the bed, drifting off to sleep as she remembered the feel of his arms around her, and his kiss on her lips.

Not wanting to disturb his son, John opened the door and quietly stepped inside, "Dad, can we talk?"

John Sr. stopped short just inside the door, "Waiting up for your old man, son?" John Jr. laughed and said, "Well I was beginning to think you might be a no show and that brings me to a question I need to ask. I don't quite know how to phrase it though."

"Let me see—you want to know if my intentions towards your mom are honorable, is that right?"

John ducked his head shyly, "Yes. It's just that she is so fragile I can't stand the thought of her being hurt anymore than she has been."

John stared at his son earnestly for a moment, choosing his words carefully, "Son, you don't have to worry about your mom anymore. I promise I will take care of her. You know I have loved her for three quarters of my life and I'm not letting her go this time. I'm not bragging, son, but I have managed to put away a great deal of money, and as soon as I can liquidate my holdings in New York and Nashville I am prepared to live whatever kind of life she wants. I would be happy to live here and help her and Lilly run this business, maybe I can be the new gardener or take some fishing trips with Waldo. Or perhaps we can move to

Newport and be near you and your family for a while. Or maybe she will want to retire and travel a bit. John, I will lay the world at her feet if she will allow me to. And as far as my intentions being honorable, I want you to be the first to know—your mom proposed to me tonight and I've accepted. Tomorrow I'm buying the biggest diamond I can find in New Orleans and we're going to set a date. That is if we have your blessing, John?"

At the end of this speech, John Jr. was grinning broadly, "Shall I give the bride away or do you need a best man?"

"I would be honored for you to be my best man. I think maybe Waldo can give the bride away. We better get some sleep now. What time does your family fly in? Would you like to go shopping with me tomorrow?"

John Jr. glanced at the clock yawning, "The plane lands at 11:47 AM so we will have plenty of time to shop before that. Good night, Dad. I will be thanking God in my prayers tonight for bringing you back to our family."

John moved to the adjoining bedroom and softly closed the door. He crossed to the antique wardrobe and began undressing. As he was doing this he couldn't help but admire again the matching 4-poster bed with the cross-stitch sampler of the Lord's Prayer hanging above it. Gazing at the cross-stitch John said a silent prayer of his own thanking God for bringing him to this place and this time, and remembering all the blessings in his life. Ever since leaving the POW camp in 1975 he had not missed a day being thankful to his Creator for his very life and now he had so much else to be thankful for. His eyes welled with tears at the thought of all the things the last two days had brought him. Slipping under the down comforter he was soon asleep dreaming of Karen's luminous green eyes and shining blonde hair.

CHAPTER 2

Karen was the first one to the kitchen. The sun was up and it looked like a wonderful day! Lilly was probably still sleeping, after all it was her turn. Karen busied herself with the preparations for the Sunday brunch. She was very excited, not only was John and John Jr. right here in the house, but she would get to see Melinda, and best of all Tyler and Kristen today. She couldn't wait to see John with his grandkids for the first time. Then she realized that there might not be very much room in the car. Maybe she would need to sacrifice and let the men go to the airport without her.

The scones were in the oven, and the coffee was brewing. The kitchen smelled delicious. Lilly and Karen had designed the remodel together when they opened the B&B. They had installed a large commercial refrigerator, and big ovens. There was plenty of counter space, including the island in the middle. The sink was close to the back door where they could take care of fresh fruits and vegetables right from the garden, and another smaller sink was in the island. Pots and pans hung from large metal hooks over the island. The far wall showcased a massive natural rock fireplace with the large braided rug made by Lilly's grandmother in front, and two rocking chairs sat on either side. Occasionally they would roast meat or nuts on the roasting rack there. The room was filled with natural light from the big windows, and there was a view of the river.

Waldo and Lilly came in with a burst of energy. Karen briefly caught the scent of sandalwood as Waldo walked by to the coffee pot. "Good morning," they all said at the same time.

Waldo was obviously in a very good mood, and poured coffee for Lilly and himself. "I see you have everything in order here, what flavor are the scones?" asked Lilly.

"Lemon/blueberry, raspberry, and poppy seed, they'll be done in ten minutes," replied Karen.

"How was your night last night?" asked Lilly.

Karen updated them on everything they had missed the night before. "John's business uses Matthew's computer program, and have you seen the pictures of Maggie yet?"

The update was interrupted as John and John Jr. came into the kitchen. John walked up to Karen and gave her a big kiss. "Did you tell them yet?" he asked.

Karen replied, "No, I wanted to wait for you."

"Tell us what?" asked Waldo.

John grinned and replied, "Karen popped the big question last night…"

With a slightly urgent tone in her voice, Karen interrupted, "John we need to talk. Lilly, Waldo, would you mind finishing up here?"

"Of course we will," replied Waldo as he grabbed the hot pads to take the scones out of the oven. Lilly already had the hot pot filled with coffee, and handed it to John. "Don't worry about a thing," she said.

"Thanks so much, Lilly. John, you haven't seen my bungalow yet, come on and I'll show it to you." Karen took his hand and led him out the door.

John loved the cozy little bungalow. It was full of light, and the place reflected Karen's spring fever. "Let's have our coffee at the patio table," said Karen as she took two coffee cups out of the cupboard, took them to the table and poured. They sat down, and as she contemplated the concerned look in his eyes she reached across the table and took John's hands in hers. "I just need to share with you what I'm thinking and feeling. What I really want to do right now is to take you into the bedroom and make mad passionate love to you. However, when I check with my common sense, it looks like we're moving awfully fast. I know it's asking for problems when you base a relationship on sex, or other physical circumstances. I don't want those kinds of problems, and it just seems like in thirty years time, our life experiences have changed us. Do we really know each other? I love you so much it hurts; every cell in my body loves you. But what if you get bored with me in a year's time?"

"Oh Karen," he said as he pulled her over into his lap. He put his strong arms around her and pulled her close. He kissed her forehead and said, "I'm sorry that you have had so much pain in your life. I have loved you for so long, I can't imagine anything else." Karen cuddled into his neck to smell the scent of his clean t-shirt again.

"I need to tell you about Sarah," he continued.

Karen pulled away and sat back in her chair again, taking a sip of her coffee. The thought of another woman touching him made her insides churn, even though she knew the circumstances. John continued, "I believe God gave Sarah to me to help me make it through life. When I found out you were married, I was devastated. Sarah was a nurse in the VA Hospital in Virginia where I was sent after the liberation of the POW camp. It was Sarah that pulled me though, not only taking care of my physical body but my spiritual one as well. Her faith was what drew me to her at first; she was the only person I ever knew whose belief in God ran as deep as yours. She knew about you from the beginning. I tried very hard to never treat her as "second choice" and in the end I think I succeeded. Her physical heart was diseased and finally took her life, but it was her loving, generous heart that kept me living. We had a very happy, contented life together. And she died knowing that I truly loved her."

Karen couldn't help the tears running down her cheeks as the jealousy melted away, "I wish I had known her," was all she could manage before laying her face on her arms and sobbing quietly.

John eased her from her chair and brought her back onto his lap, "Shh, my love, don't cry. She's in a much better place now. Free from the pain she had carried for many years. And if there is one thing I learned from her it is not to look back—only forward—regretting the past will cloud the future, and my darling Karen, we have a bright and shining future before us."

As his words ended, their lips met in a kiss salty from the tears that streamed from Karen's eyes. Karen's arms curled about his neck as John's arms curved around her waist and hips.

As the kiss ended Karen looked at him shyly, "The bedroom is right through that door, John."

Picking her up effortlessly John carried her towards that open door, but stopping at the threshold he gently put her on her feet. "Don't tempt me woman, there is nothing I would rather do, but I promised our son I would go to the airport with him and I have a small errand I need to run on the way. And to be perfectly honest the smell of those scones has left me weak with hunger. I'm not sure I have the strength to make love to you. So wipe away those tears, fix your face and feed your man!"

Karen laughed gleefully and skipped to the bathroom, "Yes sir! Oh, by the way, do you like your toilet paper to roll over or under?"

John laughed and said, "I don't really care which way it comes off the roll as long as we're sharing the bathroom."

Karen came out and stepped into his arms for just one more kiss, "This could be habit forming. Come on, Lilly doesn't believe in room service."

Karen was amazed at the relief she felt. She had brought him here to talk, needing reassurance that they weren't rushing into something one, or both, of them would regret. Somehow he had said exactly what she had needed to hear.

Joining Waldo and Lilly on the patio, John couldn't make up his mind which kind of scone he wanted, they all looked and smelled delicious, so taking a platter Karen cut wedges of each kind and they ate their fill followed with large mugs of strong, black coffee and freshly squeezed orange juice.

Just as breakfast was ending John Jr. and Matthew came back from a walk down by the river, "Are you ready, Dad? We have about an hour to spare. Will that be enough time for your errand?"

"Should be, son, I have something in mind. I guess we better take the Cadillac, it has quite a bit more room than my Mustang, even though I hate leaving it."

"Your Mustang?" John Jr. asked.

John Sr. suddenly realized that even though they had talked a lot about cars, John Jr. had missed the part about the Mustang being his years ago. "Come on, you tell me about refurbishing it and I'll tell you about buying it the first time."

Waldo went off to check on the irrigation system and Karen and Lilly were busy cleaning up the kitchen while Jennifer was upstairs cleaning rooms. Karen asked, "Lilly, part of me wants to get married right now today, and another part of me says I need to wait a reasonable amount of time. What do you think? You always have such good sense about things. You know we could put it together. We have the perfect place here, and all we need is a dress and some flowers." Karen paused, "What am I thinking? I don't even know where we'll live, or very much about his job, or anything else for that matter. He might want me to live somewhere bazaar like the North Pole, and I'd need to prepare for that one! Besides, getting back to the reality of the moment, we better think about where everyone is going to sleep tonight. Hey, I bet Tyler and Kristen would love to camp in the tent. Let's see if Waldo will set it up back of the bungalow, and I'll sleep with them. Those air mattresses are really pretty comfortable, and I need strength to keep from sleeping other places, if you know what I mean. That would give John and Melinda a little privacy. With the hours he works I don't think they get a lot of alone time." Karen rattled on, sounding slightly nervous.

Lilly touched her friend's arm lightly. "Slow down, Karen, you don't have to make all those decisions today. And as far as where you'll live—what does it matter as long as you're together? If you want to wait a few months to get married, that's OK, or if you want to get married next week, that's OK too. What really matters is that he is back in your life, where he always belonged. And as far as the lodging goes, the Miller's are leaving today and the Hamilton's called and cancelled for next week. I didn't pull any names from our on call list so the Rose Room is vacant, why don't we put John and Melinda there. With Melinda coming John will lose his chaperone, but you will have your grandkids with you. Do you think you can handle that? Jamie and Kelsi can stay with Waldo and me in our apartment. Oh, I can't wait! It's been so long since we've all been together."

Karen laughed excitedly, "Now, who needs to slow down, you sound as excited as I am. But seriously, what will happen if he wants to live in New York or Nashville, what about our business?"

Lilly looked at her friend solemnly, "Your happiness is what matters here. This is just a house; the business is just a business, when you take a good look at it—its just geography. Loving and being loved is what matters and as much as this business means to me, maybe it's time I did a little traveling with Waldo—get out that old fishing pole he gave me for a wedding present. You know Jennifer can run this place and if you had been paying attention you would have seen that Tom will probably be helping her. When Waldo and I came in to start breakfast early yesterday morning we saw Jennifer leaving Tom's bungalow."

"Really?" Karen sounded shocked.

Lilly laughed and said, "Don't sound so shocked, Karen. If it wasn't for your Quaker background and surrounding yourself with chaperones you would be in her shoes. Now admit it, wouldn't you?"

Karen blushed, "Forget the Quaker background and chaperones, I tried to drag John into the bedroom before breakfast this morning, but he was too hungry. Can you imagine that?" Lilly laughed and Karen quickly changed the subject, "Come on, we better get down to business, what's for lunch? Do we need to call for a grocery delivery?"

"We do need groceries," Karen answered her own question. "If anyone is hungry at noon we can make some sandwiches or soup. No, I know why don't we barbecue? When the guys get back with Melinda and the kids we'll make a big potato salad, then we can barbecue hamburgers, and fix strawberry shortcake. Sound good? Or would you rather have a watermelon? We're about out of onions and tomatoes too, and we can make home made buns, I'll get the dough started, and you know, I'm not sure I could really leave this wonderful place, do you think John could live here for a while? At least until we have a chance to make some plans?"

Lilly laughed at Karen's energy and said, "It sure is good to see you happy." She went into the office to order the groceries on the computer, and then went out to find Waldo.

"Do you think we could set up the tent behind Karen's bungalow? She thinks the kids would like to camp out, and it would make for some extra sleeping space. Those air mattresses are in the shed too, and I know Tyler has been asking if his uncle Waldo is going to take him fishing. He sent Karen a picture last week of you two fishing together."

"One step ahead of you, Lilly my love, I've got one of Jamie's old rods ready for the little guy," Waldo answered.

Karen came out to join them and help get the supplies out of the shed. "Hey, Waldo, there's an old box up on that top shelf, can you get it down for me?" Karen and Lilly opened the box and there was John's lettermen's jacket, his class ring, the mahogany box of letters, and his senior graduation picture. "What does it say on the back?" Lilly asked. "Karen, it's been a groovy year…let's go swimming in the river again this summer."

Karen's voice caught as she finished reading the back of the picture. "We did go swimming—one more time—August 30, 1973—the night before John left for Vietnam. The weather was unusually warm so we went to the river." Karen turned away so her friends couldn't see the sudden tears in her eyes. "Anyway let's take this stuff inside, I'm sure Tyler and Kristen will want to see their Grandpa's Letterman's Jacket. My goodness did I say "Grandpa"? How strange is that?"

Waldo laughed, "Well hopefully I'll be called that someday. We're all getting older Karen, even though both of you seem to have defied time. You both look just like you did when I first met you."

Lilly glowed at his words, "Waldo, we already decided on barbecued hamburgers for lunch, you don't have to butter us up."

Waldo picked up the box and headed for the house, "And Apple Pie?"

Lilly ran after him, "Nope—strawberry shortcake—no time for pie."

"Oh, all right." Waldo said grudgingly.

CHAPTER 3

John pulled the Cadillac into a parking place at Tiffany's in New Orleans. The trip into town had passed quickly with the story of the first time John had seen his Mustang and couldn't resist buying it. It was the first car that had ever beaten Lilly's brother, Ray, and his 1968 Pontiac GTX. Hearing about Waldo and the boy's restoring his car reminded John Sr. that he needed to thank Waldo for that. Entering the store, John Sr. immediately asked for the store manager, then giving his name was shown a remarkable one caret, princess cut, sapphire surrounded by quarter caret flawless diamonds. John Jr. whistled softly, "Holy cow, Dad, just how rich are you?"

"I have my share, son, do you think your mom will like it? Sapphires used to be her favorite stone. Are they still?"

"Well, uh yeah I think so. A few years ago Heather and I gave her sapphire studs for Mother's day and she wears them constantly. But how did you find this ring?"

John Sr. laughed, "Connections, son. I called Tiffany's in New York and had it shipped to this store. Earlier this year I was shopping for a watch and saw this ring. Immediately I was reminded of your mom. It must be destiny, don't you think?"

John Jr. put his arm around his dad lovingly, "Call it what you want, Dad. You were meant to be a part of this family and I think mom will love this ring."

While John Sr. was paying for his purchase John Jr. was admiring the Ruby jewelry.

"John, would you pick out something for me to give my new daughter-in-law and granddaughter?"

John Jr. shook his head, "Dad you don't need to do that."

"But I want to. I feel like I've missed so many birthday's and Christmas's. I know I can't make up for all those years, son, but I would like to get them something. Does Melinda like rubies? How about this bracelet, and look, they have a matching one for a little girl."

It was exactly what John had been wishing he could afford, "They would love it," he said.

John Sr. asked the clerk to add it to his bill, along with an amethyst necklace for Heather. "And just so Tyler doesn't feel left out, I saw a sporting goods store down the block, let's stop and pick up a new fly rod for him."

Moving towards the door, John Jr. warned, "We better hurry, Dad, I want to be at the airport when the plane lands."

"So do I, son, so do I." John answered.

The airport was busy with long lines. They viewed a lot of personal belongings spread out on the counters, and the security level was high. By the time they arrived at the gate, they only had about ten minutes before the plane arrived. John Jr. loved the bustle of the airport, and watching the people. "It never ceases to amaze me that those heavy planes can fly. You can explain it to me a hundred times, and it's still amazing," he marveled.

It wasn't long before the plane landed and passengers started unloading. Spotting their daddy in the crowd, Tyler & Kristen broke free of their mother and ran toward him. "Daddy, Daddy, we missed you," they cried, throwing their arms around his legs. Coming right behind them Melinda gave John Jr. a hug and a kiss, and said, "We sure are glad to be on solid ground again!" She turned to John Sr. and her husband introduced her to her father in-law. Melinda gave him a big hug, which he returned.

"I am so happy to meet you. And you probably figured out that these are your rambunctious grandchildren," she said proudly.

Their new Grandpa squatted down to their level, and they hugged him like they had known him all of their lives. "I made you a picture of us," said Tyler as he pulled out a rolled up paper from his pocket. "It's you, Dad, Uncle Waldo and me, fishing. And I caught the biggest one!"

"That's really good Tyler, we'll have to see if we can find a fishing pole for you while you're here." As they started down the walkway he softly said, "You've done very well son!"

The luggage was found easily on the lower level, and they finally made it back to the car. Melinda spotted the Tiffany's package in the trunk, which roused her curiosity, but she didn't say anything, she just looked at John Jr. and he winked at her. The kids talked a mile a minute, "Grandpa, is this your car? We don't have to go to school all of this week and Cindy Adams got a new cat...How far is it to Grandma's?"

Waldo, Lilly, and Karen all worked quickly to get everything done. The potato salad was made and in the fridge, all of the meat was on a platter ready to be put on the cart, and the condiments were arranged neatly on a round platter. The buns were still on the cooling rack. "Let's go into town to see Heather for a bit. The truth is I want to stop and get one of those bridal magazines," said Karen.

Lilly was ready to go, she hadn't been out driving her VW for several days now. Waldo and Tom could finish setting up the eating area, and get the barbeque pit going.

Lilly and Karen rode with the windows down and the breeze in their hair. As they got to Main Street, they didn't say anything, but that old feeling of dragging the avenue was there. They smiled at each other as they stopped at a red light next to two young men in a shiny black corvette and Lilly couldn't resist revving the VW engine just a little. The two women burst into laughter as the local police officer passed in front of them.

Lilly expertly pulled into a parking spot as she said, "Let's go buy one of those magazines and start a rumor."

Entering the grocery store, Lilly paused in front of Etta Kelly, "Good morning Mrs. Kelly, how are you today?" she asked cheerfully, "Have you ever seen such lovely weather? How are your beautiful daughter, Charlotte, and the grandkids?" Mrs. Kelly looked slightly shocked at this enthusiastic greeting from Lilly. She had heard that these two called her "Ole Lady Kelly" behind her back and she made no secret of the fact that she didn't approve of these two middle aged women wearing Levi's and T-shirts like teenagers, no matter if they did still have the figures for it. It just wasn't seemly. And she had her suspicions about what went on at that bed and breakfast when Lilly's husband wasn't around. Charlotte had told her about seeing Karen and Heather have dinner with a handsome stranger. It was probably the same one that had bought that smutty romance novel from her.

"Humph, everyone is fine. If you're looking for more of those trashy novels, I took them all off the shelf," Etta said spying Karen at the book and magazine rack.

Lilly laughed slyly, "Nope, just checking out the "Bride" magazine. Have a nice day."

Etta Kelly waddled after Lilly, "Who…who…who's the bride? Is Heather getting married? I heard she dates that David guy that owns the nursery, or is it Jennifer? You know I have some lovely cake toppers in the back, would you like to see them?"

Karen turned from the rack with the magazine in her hand, "Good Morning, Etta, just the magazine please." Karen laid the exact change on the counter and strolled out of the store. Lilly couldn't help the smirk on her face. "Have a nice day, Mrs. Kelly," She said following her friend out to the car.

Once inside the VW the two bent over in hysterical laughter. "Oh, Karen, have you ever seen her move so fast? I thought she was going to find a way to get past me in that isle. I think I have a bruise on my hip where I hit the canned vegetables." Lilly wiped the tears from her eyes and started the car.

Karen finally composed herself enough to talk, "We are soooo cruel. But she deserves it. We're about two minutes from Heather's do you think that's enough time for Old Lady Kelly to call Charlotte and Charlotte to call Heather?"

Lilly stepped on the gas, "Let's see if we can set a record."

In Just under two minutes the VW pulled into the driveway at the antique store. Heather opened the door, as the two friends came up the walkway, "Ok, what kind of mischief have you two been up to?" Just then the phone rang and the caller ID showed it to be Charlotte Munchie. Groaning Heather reached for the phone, "Oh, man, what does she want?"

Karen stopped her daughter's hand in mid air, "Don't answer, we'll fill you in. Melinda and the kids will be here in about an hour and we're barbecuing this afternoon, do you want to come over?"

Heather grabbed her keys, "Let's go. Have you two been pestering Etta, again?"

"No dear, just buying a magazine," Lilly said innocently.

"Honey, I think your bicycle is still at the B&B…do you want to try to squeeze into the VW with us, or are you ready to show up in your pink Subaru wagon?" asked Karen.

"OK, I guess I'll drive, riding with you two could be trouble," Heather laughed.

Lilly pulled out, and thinking about all there was to do yet, her foot was still heavy on the pedal. "I think we have company," said Karen, just as Lilly noticed the red and blue lights in her mirror.

"Oh no, and in front of Heather too…this won't be a secret for long."

"Yes, officer, thank you officer, thank you again officer," she said as she gazed into his deep blue eyes. Fortunately it was just a warning this time.

"I won't tell Waldo if you don't want me to, but I can't vouch for anyone else," said Karen, still snickering.

When they finally got back to the B&B, Waldo and Tom had the barbeque pit ready, the gazebo area prepared, and the big cart ready to go. "What took you so long?" asked Waldo.

Lilly stepped forward and gave him a quick kiss, "Oh just dawdling, you know how we can be. Is everything ready? What do you think of the pit our boys made us?"

Waldo didn't seem to notice that Lilly was drawing the conversation away from her. He had been married to her long enough to know whatever she was up to would come out eventually. "They're pretty talented when it comes to metal works, aren't they? Have you heard that the iron silhouettes Jamie and Kelsi have been making are being featured at the Horse & Tack Warehouses in Washington, Oregon and Alaska? Better hang on to everything those two designs, could be worth a bunch of money some day. That reminds me Jamie called, they plan on being here Tuesday afternoon. I think the plane lands at 3:15."

"Thanks, honey, can't wait to see them," Lilly said as she grabbed her purse out of the VW and started towards the house. "I need to check on the guests, you know I almost forgot we have three couples staying here."

Tom was gathering up the tools as he informed her, "Don't worry about them Lilly, Jennifer is still here, she has made all the beds, refreshed the flower vases and put clean towels out. I think she said the Morgan's are leaving today, so actually there are only two couples left and they are both touring New Orleans today. The Martin's are leaving on Monday and the Johnson's on Tuesday."

Lilly smiled at him, "Tom, you seem to know quite a bit about what's going on here and even more about Jennifer."

Tom blushed, "Just trying to help out, Ma'am."

"Yes, you certainly are," Lilly softly replied.

Waldo took Lilly by the arm and steered her towards the house. "Lilly, did you know they are seeing each other?" he whispered.

Lilly squeezed his arm, "Yes, remember when we saw Jennifer coming in to make breakfast the other morning? You did notice where she was coming from? Did Tom tell you about it?"

Waldo paused opening the front door for her, "He sure did. He's pretty smitten with that little girl too, not to mention the twins have him wrapped around their little fingers. I wouldn't be a bit surprised if we didn't have two weddings this summer."

Just then Karen came running past them headed for the driveway, "I think I hear the car," She said excitedly.

Waldo quickly turned around and opened the door for her, "You two women have me so mixed up I don't know whether I'm coming or going. I wonder if John wants to go to Alaska with me."

Lilly grabbed his arm and they followed Karen out, "Don't you dare take him away right now."

Just then the long black Cadillac came to a stop in the driveway under the portico. Two small children came tumbling out of the back, "Grandma, Grandma, did you know Grandpa was going to be here too? Why haven't we met him before? Why didn't he ever come to visit? What's for lunch?"

Karen met them with outstretched arms and hugged and kissed them both. "My you've grown!" She said. "And Kristen, your hair is so long, just like your mommy's. I think you've both grown at least a foot since I've seen you." Then she gave Melinda a good hug, "It's so good to see you, I've really missed all of you." She turned to John and gave him a big hug, "I missed you, Grandpa," she said softly with a wink.

The kids gave Aunt Heather, Aunt Lilly, and Uncle Waldo big hugs and kisses. Then Karen took them by the hands, "I see you've met your Grandpa. We'll have lots of time to answer all of your questions while you're here. Let's all go back to the gazebo and we'll get you some cold drinks. Tom, would you please help with the luggage, you can take it to the Rose room. How was your trip with the kids, Melinda?"

"Grandpa, will you give me a piggy-back ride?" asked Tyler. John came up beside her and popped Tyler onto his shoulders.

Melinda spoke up, "The trip was fine Karen, and a very nice steward kept the kids entertained and the flight wasn't booked fully so we had room to spread out. Tyler, take it easy on your Grandpa, he probably isn't used to lugging big boys around on his shoulders. Although his shoulder's certainly look like they can handle it."

Melinda glanced at Karen with a wink in her eye. Linking her arm with her mother-in-laws and speaking softly she said, "Wow, what a hunk. I see now where John got his looks."

Karen had always half-teasingly told John Jr. that he needed to give her a good daughter in-law, and he had done exactly that. Melinda had long golden brown hair, and brown eyes like John's, so of course the children also inherited the gorgeous eyes. She was a very loving wife and mother, and Karen knew she couldn't have done any better. When they got married the only reason Karen could bear for him to leave home was that he was marrying the only other person alive that loved him as much as she did. Melinda had never been jealous of Karen's relationship with her only son, and now that she had a son of her own she fully understood that special mother/son relationship. She never seemed to mind the little slips of the tongue when Karen would call John "Sweetie" or insist on making a special dinner for his birthday. And now after almost ten years of marriage Melinda was just as much a daughter to Karen as Heather.

Karen laughed back at Melinda, "Not bad for a Grandpa, huh? Oh, Melinda, if it's OK I'm going to take the kids off your hands while you're here. Waldo and Tom set up the big tent behind my bungalow and I'm going to stay out there with the kids. You and John will have the Rose Room Suite all to yourself."

Melinda started to protest, "No, Karen you have too much going on to be saddled with those two, and besides after all these years, you and John have just gotten back together, you must be wanting to spend time with him. No, Karen, as good as it sounds I can't let you do it." Melinda's voice dwindled off longingly.

"Oh yes you can, Melinda, and to be perfectly honest, I need the chaperones, if you know what I mean?"

Melinda laughed, "OK—you twisted my arm. But if you change your mind send them to me."

Karen started for the kitchen, "I will, darling, I promise. Right now we need to get the barbecue going. Where is that Lilly? Honestly when Waldo's home I can't get a lick of work out of her."

"For heaven's sake Karen, I'm right here and the meat is already on the grill, and I wouldn't be complaining about me not working if I was you," Lilly laughed.

Karen joined the laughter, "OK, ok what do I need to do?"

Lilly shook her head, "Nothing, go join your family in the gazebo, Waldo and I have it all under control. Tom has gone to pick up Jennifer and the twins. The salads are made and the meat is cooking."

The hamburgers were especially good, and everyone was hungry. Karen wondered what extra seasoning Lilly had used. "Lilly, did you use hickory chips in the barbeque?"

Lilly replied, "Yes, hickory chips and that new steak seasoning sprinkled on the meat. The relish is green chili, onion, tomato and green pepper. And the cheese is pepper jack."

Everyone ate until they could eat no more and then settled back to visit. The men told a lot of fishing stories, some new, and some old that Lilly and Karen had heard at least a hundred times. Melinda was doing well with her part time job in Real Estate and the extra money she made was being saved for the kid's college educations. It also helped out on little things like family vacations. Lilly and Waldo answered questions about Jamie and Kelsi. Everyone could tell they were excited about having their son and daughter-in-law visit.

It wasn't long before Heather had the kids running and playing games in the yard. As Karen sat next to John, with his arm resting lightly on her shoulders and all of her family around her, a peace and contentment came over her that she had never felt before. This was where she was meant to be. Oh, not in the Gazebo on the lawn of the Bed and Breakfast she owned jointly with her best friend, but in the presence of the people she loved most in the world. It was at this moment that she realized how much she wanted to get married. I don't want all of the fluff and puff she thought, I just want to be with the people I love. Lilly and I will give Jennifer the fancy wedding. She hoped Jennifer and Tom would want to be married here on the grounds of the B&B. They would spare no expense on the reception. Oh and how adorable the twins would be as flower girls. Karen was deep in thought planning Jennifer's wedding when her mind drifted to her own. Just a simple ceremony she thought, maybe right here in the gazebo, or the little church with the stained glass windows.

Karen got up to go get the strawberry shortcake and Lilly and Melinda were right beside her. Karen asked, "What do you two think, should John and I get married in the gazebo, or the little church down the road?"

Melinda and Lilly spoke at the same time, "Definitely the church." They all laughed and Lilly continued, "You know how I feel about church weddings. I know God will bless your marriage to John, it just seems more lasting to have it in a church."

Then it was Melinda's turn, "You remember John and I wanted to elope and you wouldn't hear of it? You practically preached a sermon about the sanctity of marriage and how our life would be off to a much better start with a church wedding. And there is something about promises made in a church. Remember, "Promises made in a church can never be broken", you said that."

Karen laughed, "Ok, ok you two, you convinced me. But I'm getting ahead of myself. We haven't even set a date. Let's get these shortcakes out to the guys, Lilly have you done something different to the cakes? They don't smell like they usually do."

Lilly replied, "I think I'll wait until everyone tastes them before I confess."

The cakes and fresh strawberries were a big hit and Lilly did admit that she had added just a tiny bit of lemon and poppy seed to her shortcake mix. As usual her creations were wonderful. The only problem with Lilly and her recipes was she could rarely remember what she had done. Karen was constantly after her to write it out. In the back of her mind she secretly wanted to publish a B&B cookbook some day.

Melinda announced that she wanted to lie down and rest for a while and John Jr. quickly said he would join her. Heather had spread a blanket under the Oak tree next to the Gazebo and was quietly reading to all four sleepy kids. Jennifer and Tom had wondered away and Lilly and Waldo went to their quarters to rest.

Karen leaned her head on John's shoulder, "Well Grandpa, what do you think of your Grandkids?"

John's arm tightened slightly around Karen, "They're just wonderful, I couldn't be happier. Well, maybe I could…"

Karen laughed softly, "Now, now you know we agreed to wait."

John smiled, "I know, my darling, and that's not what I'm talking about." John put his free arm into his pocket and pulled out the small Tiffany ring box. Popping it open he presented it to Karen and softly said, "Will you be my wife…soon? I really don't want a long engagement."

Karen's eyes suddenly filled with tears, "John that is the most beautiful ring I have ever seen. And I don't want a long engagement either. I love you with all of my heart. I always have and I always will." She put her arms around his neck and hugged him tight. John pulled back far enough to place the ring on her finger and taking her in his arms he kissed her from the very depth of his soul.

Karen sat back, still nestled into John's side, occasionally glancing at the new ring on her finger. "If it's alright with you, I would like just a simple ceremony in the chapel down the lane. The stained glass windows are gorgeous, and it's one of my favorite places. We can have the reception here and Lilly can make the cake. As long as our family can be here, I'll be happy with anything, but what would you think about Saturday? John and Melinda don't go back until Sunday, and Jamie and Kelsi will be here. Do you think it would be too soon? I know we just got back together, but it's not like we don't have our roots. Not only are they roots that have been established for over thirty years, but we also have our family, and I've never been so sure about anything in my whole life. Maybe we can have a big party later when you get Dylan to come, and we'll celebrate again."

"If it's Saturday you want, then Saturday it is," he replied, "The sooner the better."

Karen saw the relief in his eyes, no longer worried about the waiting time.

Heather came up to the gazebo and asked, "What are you two love birds up to now? The kids are getting hungry again."

Karen turned to her, and holding out her ringed finger she said, "This is what we've been up to."

"Wow, Mom that is some rock, and it's beautiful! Dad, you're spoiling her already," Heather said as she admired the ring.

Karen continued, "That's not all, we're going to get married on Saturday."

"OK, I'm ready," Heather replied, "I'll close the store for the rest of the week if you want me to help."

John quietly pulled the Tiffany box from his pocket and handed it to Heather.

"For me?" she questioned.

"Yes, I thought it might make up for some of the birthdays and Christmas's I've missed," he said.

Heather gasped when she opened the box to find the amethyst necklace. "It's absolutely beautiful," she exclaimed. "Thank you, Dad."

Karen knew that this gift was about more than just birthdays and Christmas's. A missing piece of Heather's life was being filled, and emotional healing was taking place. She squeezed John's hand in appreciation.

The kids were calling for Heather and as she went to them, Karen turned back to John, "Oh, by the way, we have the tent set up back of my bungalow and I'm planning on staying there with Tyler and Kristen tonight. Would you like to go camping? Of course I would understand if you would prefer a real bed, but it would be fun."

John grinned at Karen's words, "Karen, you are amazing, not only have you figured out how not to sleep with me tonight, you've also figured out how to sleep with me, and I have slept in a tent with you before, do you remember? You and Lilly snuck Roger and I under the back flap of your tent when Mr. and Mrs. Hobart were giving the rest of the kids a lecture about sneaking around the campgrounds after lights out. I'll never forget that night, the tent was barely big enough for you two and there we were sandwiched between you. I would be honored to share your tent again. Although I would prefer it to be just you and me, but having the little munchkins there will be lots of fun."

"Just don't trip over the tent ropes this time and collapse it on us," Karen said as she remembered the night he was talking about.

John perked up, "Do we get a weenie roast and marshmallows too?"

Karen laughed delightedly, "How did you know that's what we had planned for dinner? And speaking of dinner I hear Lilly rummaging around in the kitchen. Will you excuse me, darling, I really want to show her my ring and tell her our plans?"

Pulling her close for one more kiss, John said, "Of course, you run along. I saw Waldo headed down to the river a few minutes ago. I think I'll see what he's up to."

Karen found Lilly in the kitchen making an apple pie. "So Waldo's going to get his pie, huh?"

Lilly smiled, "Yes, you know how he loves it. So what's happening with you? How is your hand staying on your arm with that enormous rock weighing it down? Let me see, let me see."

As Karen held her hand out the fire from the diamonds, surrounding the sapphire, danced off the bottoms of the copper pots hanging above the island where Lilly was working. "My gosh, Karen, that is the most beautiful ring I've ever seen."

Karen smiled softly, "Yes it is, isn't it. And there's more. Do you think you can have a wedding cake and reception luncheon put together by this Saturday? I know it seems sudden but it also seems so right. What do you think, Lilly? Are we rushing into something we know nothing about? Am I about to make another huge mistake like the last time I rushed into a marriage?"

Lilly put her arm around her friend, "No, Karen you're not making a mistake. And the first time was not a mistake either. It was the only choice you had at the time. And poor old Dunston, he never really had a chance, did he? At least you got Heather out of that relationship. And now you're going to spend the rest of your life with the person you were meant to be with all along. What can be wrong about that? The wrong would be if you didn't take this chance at happiness. Now what are the plans for dinner? Have you checked the registration log? Are we going to have guests for your wedding? Oh there's so much to do, I can make my special pecan cream cake. Would you like that?"

Karen was always amazed at her friend's capacity to do so many things at one time. Lilly seemed to thrive on being busy and cooking. She was happy when she was cooking for a house full of guests, but was happiest when she was cooking for her family. This brought Karen to the question she hated to ask, "Lilly, what's going to happen to our business? John and I haven't really talked about where we'll live, but I can't promise it will be here."

Lilly shook her head, "Hey, no regrets, remember? We started this to do something for ourselves. Now it looks like our lives may be taking us in different directions. I have something to tell you too. Waldo wants us to start a branch of the B&B in Alaska. He would like me to run the kitchen and take care of the Lodge and he will become a fishing guide. What do you think of that?"

Karen replied, "What will we do with this one?"

"Let's keep it, Tom and Jennifer can run it for a percentage of the profits, that way we can still visit. And maybe you and John can run the one in Alaska every once in a while so I can get to Washington and back down here. Oh, Karen, it will work. We'll be twice as busy and I know I can't ask you to work full time, but things will work out, you'll see. Now I have to get this pie in the oven and how about some apricot and banana salad to go with the hotdogs for dinner? Have you talked to Pastor Jim to even see if he's available this Saturday? What about a marriage license? What's the waiting period in Louisiana? What will you wear? Oh, there's so much to do."

"I saw a dress I like in that magazine, we'll have to make some phone calls, and you're right, there's a lot to do. Right after dinner we'll start a list." Karen said excitedly. "Heather can do my hair and you'll take care of the reception and what about a ring for John? Lilly, you know a lot about jewelry, Waldo is always buying you something, help!"

Karen took an arm load of paper plates and napkins out to the gazebo just as John Sr. had called Melinda and Kristen over. As he presented them with the ruby bracelet set, Melinda gasped and Kristen's eyes got big. "My birthday isn't until next month," said Kristen as her Grandpa explained that he was making up for lost time.

"That's okay," he assured her. "We'll get to celebrate next month also."

"You're spoiling all of us," insisted Melinda.

"I just want you to know how much it means to me to have my family. Having a son is incredible, and I'm very proud of him. I'm impressed that he chose such a fine wife, and the grandchildren are definitely a bonus and a precious gift I never thought I would have!"

It wasn't long before they were all together again roasting hot dogs over the coals. Karen had her pen and paper beside her, and she would write down every item and chore as they thought of them. "Melinda, what sizes are the kids wearing? We'll pick up something tomorrow morning. I think I would like some gardenias in the flowers. How about lavender and pale blue for the color scheme with a slight touch of pink or rose? What do you think Lilly?"

Lilly replied, "I love it. Don't forget Kelsi will be here. That girl could make beautiful arrangements out of weeds and dandelions if she had to. And I know she will want to help. She can make your bouquet and the boutonnières and corsages. And since Tom here has been too preoccupied to kill roses lately, I should have some good blooms by Saturday."

Everyone was tired from a long day, and it wasn't long before everything was cleaned up for the night. Heather went home right after dinner and Tyler and Kristen were excited about camping in the tent. Waldo was helping them to find some flashlights. "Are you going to go snipe hunting tonight?" Waldo asked.

"What's that?" asked Kristen, and Waldo replied "You get paper bags and look for the snipes out by the bushes. Then when you shine your flashlight on them they'll run right into your bag. However, it is getting a little late for snipe hunting, we just might have to wait until tomorrow night."

Lilly spoke up, "Waldo, what are you trying to do to those kids?"

"Oh, Lilly you remember how much fun Jamie, John and Heather had snipe hunting when they were this age. I haven't done a lot of research but I'll bet the snipes in Louisiana are just as big as the ones in Washington."

Tyler's eyes got big. "Really, Uncle Waldo, how big are they?"

Waldo laughed, "Well you remind me tomorrow, and if it's OK with your dad and mom, we'll see if we can find some of those Louisiana Snipes. Now goodnight you two, sleep tight."

After a round of hugs the two kids slipped into their sleeping bags. They were exhausted after their full day of travel, good food and games, and it wasn't long before they were fast asleep.

Their Grandparents were cuddled up in a lounge chair just outside the tent. Karen said, "I haven't had my moonlight dance yet tonight."

"Well, we can fix that," John replied, as he led her out onto the lawn and taking her in his arms their bodies melted into one as they swayed to the music coming from Waldo and Lilly's bungalow.

Melinda was enjoying her time alone with her husband, and she knew that her children were safe and in good hands. However, out of habit, she stepped out onto the balcony to gaze in the direction of the tent. "John, come here!" she called, "Look, your parents are dancing in the moonlight, isn't it beautiful and romantic?"

John Jr. was totally amazed. "Wow, you know when you have one of those déjà vu moments, and then something happens in reality that you know you have dreamed before? This was my dream!" He almost had tears in his eyes as he watched. "This just completes the happiness in my life. I have you and the kids, and now I have my dad too. Melinda, do you realize that my dad has a lot of money? What do you think we should get them for a wedding gift? I can't imagine anything they need at this point." They paused for a few moments as they continued to watch, and then John Jr. took Melinda's hand, put his other hand on her waist, and they danced along. "I know what we could get them, how would you like to try for another baby? My dad has missed out on all of the babies, including me, and it's something we have talked about and considered."

Melinda smiled at him, and went into the room. She took a small gift bag from her suitcase. "I haven't had a chance to talk to you in private for several days really, but I brought you a present."

John eagerly dug to the bottom of the bag, and pulled out a positive pregnancy test. "So this is why you're glowing!"

As the song ended Karen and John's bodies became still for the kiss that followed. At long last John peeled himself from her embrace, "Are you sure the kids can't sleep out here by themselves?"

"Nope, I promised their Mom," Karen replied.

"Well in that case, my love, we had better get into our separate sleeping bags while I'm still willing to let you go."

Entering the tent Karen and John were careful not to wake the sleeping kids. Crawling into their sleeping bags side by side, Karen laid her head on John's shoulder. "This is where I want to be for the rest of my life," she said softly.

John replied teasingly, "In a tent?" they both laughed as quietly as possible and then he said, "Shh, go to sleep my love, we have a million tomorrows ahead of us."

CHAPTER 4

John Jr. quietly slipped out of bed trying not to disturb Melinda. After all she may need more sleep now and she had an awfully big day yesterday. He dressed and went down stairs to find the kitchen buzzing with excitement and aromas.

"Good morning, John," Lilly greeted him, "Because you're so special I'll make you anything you want for breakfast, do you want bacon and eggs, pancakes? Or does something else sound good?" Aunt Lilly had always spoiled him with his breakfast desires. She had gotten up early many times to be sure he had a good breakfast before he started his day, and he always looked forward to it. Turning to Tyler and Kristen he said, "Well, I see you two have already taken advantage of Aunt Lilly's breakfast skills, do you recommend the bacon and eggs?"

They both responded enthusiastically as they were devouring their food, "Yes, yes!"

John woke up to the sound of the kids whispering, "Can we wake him up yet?" Tyler asked, and Kristen replied, "Grandma said to let him sleep."

"But, Kristen, I want to go fishing and Uncle Waldo said we had to wait for Grandpa."

With that John leaped to his feet, "Fishing? Did someone say we were going fishing?"

Tyler and Kristen giggled at the sight of their tall Grandpa trying to stand upright in the tent. "Uncle Waldo is going fishing down at the river, he said to come and get him as soon as you were up. That is if you want to go too?"

John sat down attempting to put his shoes on as he answered, "You bet, but where's your Grandma?"

Kristen replied, "Her and Aunt Lilly are fixing breakfast for the guests. She said to tell you to come and get breakfast and they'll make a lunch for us to take to the river. She said they are going to be real busy shopping and making plans today."

John crawled out of the tent and grimaced slightly as he attempted to stand straight. "Not used to sleeping in tents. OK, kids let's go."

He was just in time to join his son for the bacon and eggs Lilly was fixing. Karen took a break from arranging the fruit platter to give John a kiss and then returned to her work. "So how did you sleep?" she asked.

"Well, I'm not exactly used to sleeping in tents, but the fresh air is good. Waldo, are we going fishing?" Karen knew his thoughts were about sleeping with her, and she sensed that he was just a tad grumpy about it.

"You bet," answered Waldo, "If you want we can try for catfish? Ladies would you like a mess of catfish for dinner?"

Lilly wrinkled her nose slightly, "OK as long as we cook them outside, I don't want my kitchen smelling like fish."

Waldo laughed, "I know, dear, you always want me to practice "catch & release", but since Tyler's going he might want to eat his fish."

Tyler was jumping up and down excitedly, "Really Aunt Lilly can we eat them?"

Lilly smiled at him tenderly, "Of course we can darling. I'll cook everything you catch."

John finished his breakfast and followed Karen out to the patio where she was arranging napkins and silverware. There were only two couples still left at the B & B but they had to be well taken care of. This was no time to let their reputation slide. Coming up behind her, John slipped one arm around her slender waist and dropped a quick kiss on the nape of her neck, "Do you need me for anything today? I should have checked with you before I told Waldo I would go fishing."

Karen turned in his arms, "No, you can go fishing. You would probably only be in the way here. Besides your son and grandson are going too. Have fun." John kissed her quickly on the lips, and then left to talk to Waldo about borrowing fishing gear.

Karen finished setting the tables just as the guests came down. Mr. and Mrs. Johnson, from Michigan were old friends of Karen and Lilly's. They knew the two friends when they were teenagers in Washington State and never missed coming to see them for their yearly visits that were booked two years in advance. As they sat down Mrs. Johnson commented, "Karen, what is that on your finger?"

"Do you remember John from our youth group? Over thirty years ago?" Karen asked. "We have just gotten back together, and actually we are getting married this Saturday. Will you still be around? We would love for you to attend the wedding, and it would be so nice to have you."

Mr. and Mrs. Johnson beamed back at her, "We always thought you should have married him, dear. Well, better late than never, so they say. If we stay will we be able to help? We don't want to be a burden."

Lilly had overhead this exchange, "Oh you two would never be a burden and we would be more than happy for you to stay if you don't mind not having the extra service you're used to. Jennifer will still be around but the rest of us will be busy with wedding plans and we are canceling everyone else for next weekend. My son and daughter-in-law will be here tomorrow. But we won't need your suite. They are going to stay in the bungalow with Waldo and me. Now if you'll excuse me I need to get dressed, Karen and I are going shopping."

Karen was in the kitchen getting more coffee when John Sr. came in. "I just wanted to give you this before we take off fishing. Here's my credit card, and the phone number of my personal shopper. I don't know where you intend to go today, but if you don't find what you want just call the number and she will arrange anything you ask for. If you have any problems at all, just call my cell phone. And there is no limit on the charge card."

Karen looked at him in surprise, "Really?" She asked with wide eyes.

"Really!" he answered.

She kissed him all over his cheeks, and he kissed her once more on the lips. "You two have fun and stay out of trouble," he said teasingly as he left.

Karen found Lilly in her bungalow and told her about John's personal shopper and the credit card. Lilly was impressed and asked her friend, "What do we wear for that kind of shopping?"

Karen laughed and answered, "Levi's of course, what else do we ever wear shopping. This is us remember? Our finances might have changed drastically from when we used to buy a new top at the discount store in the Mall every Saturday. But we really haven't changed!"

"Levis it is then. But I think I'll wear my new emerald green cashmere sweater that Waldo brought back from Alaska. That should give my confidence a little boost."

Karen answered, "You wear your emerald green and I'll wear my new yellow silk shirt. We will look like a spring garden. Meet you outside in ten minutes, OK?"

Karen went to her own bungalow to change as she reflected on Lilly's comment about her self-confidence. She wondered if she was so caught up in herself that she was neglecting her best friend. All of a sudden it dawned on her that she hadn't even asked her to be her maid of honor yet. Maybe this was all just too much stress and extra work, maybe she should have waited, and after all quick marriages were against her beliefs. She had never advised them, and her life experience had taught her that they usually don't turn out well. She thought about her friend Janet Andrews, she had re-married after just three months of dating, and seemed happy at first, but now it was obvious to Karen that Janet was very depressed and unhappy. Oh, she had a job and her flower garden, but her husband was nothing more than a lump on the couch. Karen felt panic creeping in. She was doing everything opposite of the way she had always believed it should be, and had also preached to her children for a quarter of a century. She could call it off…Confusion began to spiral in Karen's mind as she tried to review her thoughts and feelings. Is it the way we choose to handle life's circumstances that influences the outcome, or does it just happen anyway? And why is it that the physical relationship has to wait? It really doesn't seem to make much sense; after all you need to know what you're getting into. But there must be more good reason otherwise it wouldn't be a biblical rule. And was this the only reason she was rushing into this? And the shopping, Karen knew very well that happiness is not found in money. Happiness you make for yourself with the attitudes you have, and the choices you make, and the people you love and are loved by. The pain we go through enhances life, and doing what is right, what you know is right. Karen was so confused at these thoughts that the tears were running down her face. She had loved John for so long, it was heartbreaking to think of the possibility of making a big mistake, and she knew the last thing she wanted to do was to make a mistake to cause people unhappiness. And if Lilly didn't really approve, she wasn't sure she would actually tell her so, because you usually can't tell people those things. And Lilly honestly wanted her to be happy and have the life she felt she deserved.

John Jr. knocked on her door as he walked in, "Mom, I'm glad you're still here, do you want me to take your camera with us?" He stopped short as he saw her tears. "What's wrong?" he asked.

Karen took a long look at him. Her son had turned out to be as handsome as his father, and he looked happier than she could ever remember. It was this moment that her spirit knew that being with his father was the right thing for both of them, and loving him was the best gift she could give or be given.

"Oh, I'm just having a case of "cold feet," she replied honestly.

He put his strong arms around her and hugged her for a moment, "Mom, I know it's unusual, but I also know that it's the right thing to do. And that's what you've always taught us, to do what we know is right. If you believe that too, which I think you do, then everything is going to be alright."

"You're right, and you've warmed my feet!" She smiled and hugged him so tight he thought he might pop.

Waldo, John and their sons were busy in the shed putting together all of the fishing tackle. Waldo was quite the expert at choosing the best tackle for the task ahead. Tyler was right at their heels, asking questions.

Not giving Tyler a chance to question what rod he would be using, John said, "These rods all look a little big for you Tyler, what do you think we should do about it? I think I have an idea, I'll be right back."

Tyler said, "Dad, what is Grandpa doing? Which rod am I going to use? Will I have a reel on it? I need a big one if I'm going to catch a big fish."

"Just be patient, son," his dad replied. He smiled as he remembered the fishing fever they used to get when he was younger.

It wasn't long before Grandpa returned with a big package, "Here you go Tyler, open this." Tyler was so excited he almost fell getting into the packaging, and John had to help him a little bit. "This is so cool!" Tyler proudly said. The rod was black and red and shiny. They had all of the pieces put together within minutes.

"Looks like you're about to get your first fly fishing lesson Tyler," his dad said.

Waldo was checking out the rod, and he was quite impressed with the quality. He then chose some special lures for Tyler to use, and got out an old fishing vest of Jamie's for him to wear. "OK guys, looks like we're ready. Let's check out this hole and then if it produces we can come back later in the week with Jamie."

CHAPTER 5

Karen and Lilly headed off to town in Lilly's VW. Melinda and Kristen had planned on spending the day with Heather at her shop. Kristen loved the antique dolls on display and Melinda was looking forward to spending time with her sister-in-law. They could catch up on each other's lives and Heather could bring Melinda up to date on Karen and John.

It was a beautiful spring day and a gentle breeze blew through Lilly's dark hair. She loved driving this car with the top down. Lilly and Karen had put in a lot of miles together and even though Lilly was terribly happy for her friend, a part of her was sad too. They had spent many years living in different states while the kids were growing up, getting together for summer vacations and whenever else they could manage and it had been a great adventure starting this business with Karen. Lilly hated the thought of not seeing her every day but she also knew it was time to go on to another phase of their lives. She needed to be with Waldo and was happy that Karen and John had found each other.

"What did you have in mind for a wedding dress, Karen? Do you think we will find one at Mademoiselle Jane's? You know she was featured in a well known bride magazine last month, I can't remember which one."

Karen answered, "Hopefully we'll find all of the dresses there, but first of all, there is a matter of business that should have been taken care of long ago. Well, at the pace I'm going at least hours ago. Will you be my maid of honor?"

"Of course, I would be honored," replied Lilly. Lilly had a casual tone in her voice, but Karen knew it meant a lot to her.

"Are we going for a total matching look, or do you think my dress should be a different style than Heather and Melinda's? Did you want Kristen to be the only flower girl or did you want Jill and Allie to have a part too? Oh, there are so many decisions to make—are you sure you want to do this?"

Karen laughed softly, "I'm surer than I have ever been in my life. And I was thinking maybe all of the girls could carry flower baskets and Tyler can be the ring bearer. Peach maybe for Melinda and Heather? And maybe mint green for you and the girls? Anyway at this late date we may just take what they have that fits! By the way, your emerald green sweater looks absolutely gorgeous on you, and did Waldo buy you an emerald ring also? I'm impressed! "

Lilly held her hand out for Karen to admire the square cut emerald stone set into a delicate gold band. "He gave it to me the first night he was home. We've been so busy I didn't have a chance to show you. He does have good taste doesn't he? It's a perfect match for the bracelet he bought me for our anniversary and the earrings from last Christmas."

"Lilly," Karen said, "you know I almost cancelled the wedding plans about twenty minutes ago...I had a bad case of "cold feet." But then John Jr. came in, and he was standing there...the spittin' image of his father, and he made me realize how much a part of his father we all are. Obviously my feet have warmed up now, and I just want to thank you for all of the support you've given me through the years. I would never have had the good life that I do without you and Waldo. And like you always say, I wouldn't be the person I am if I didn't have my life experiences. And who knows what would have become of my children without you two! I've been kind of wrapped up in myself lately, and I want to apologize for that. I know I have a jewel of a man that's come back into my life, but that's no excuse to neglect our friendship. And you know, no matter where we live, we'll always be best friends, and we'll visit and call and stuff."

Lilly was both glad and sad that Karen had said these things. It sealed their friendship even closer, but it was also the start of a separation for them. "Yes," she replied, "we'll always have our friendship. But you weren't the only one that got support from our friendship. I never would have had the confidence to start this business without your encouragement in all my catering jobs. And you were the one that taught me how to make a melon basket and the fine art of arranging fruit and veggies. And as far as Waldo's involvement in your kid's life I always felt bad I couldn't give him more children. This way he had two more to tease and take fishing. But we won't be separated long, thanks to this business Waldo and I are fairly well off, that mean's you are too, even without marrying a gorgeous, rich, hunk! So we'll see each other often. Have you talked about where you're going on your honeymoon? "

"You can't go on my honeymoon with me," laughed Karen, "and that reminds me, how much time are you going to let me have off?"

Lilly laughed with her, "As much time as you need, then we'll see if you want to work at B&B South or help me run B&B North! But we'll work that out later. B&B North is still just an idea and we are leaving the one here in capable hands."

Karen's mind went back to the wedding plans. "There are so many decisions to make, let's go to Mademoiselle Jane's, and take it from there. Do you think there are enough peach colored roses in the garden to focus on the color? Lavender just doesn't seem quite right for John's bride. We need to create a theme here."

Lilly answered, "I'm sure there are plenty of ivory and peach roses, now that Tom is too preoccupied to prune. And if we don't have the roses, we'll call a florist. I think your dress should definitely be ivory, perhaps tea length? Heather can do your hair in a French braid and intertwine peach roses and ivory ribbons." They were both deep in thought as the wind blew softly through their hair, and then Lilly turned the radio on. An old rock and roll song blasted through the speakers. The two friends grinned to each other and started singing along at the top of their voices.

The time flew by and soon they pulled into the parking lot of Mademoiselle Jane's. Lilly expertly swung the little VW into the small space in front of a handicapped parking stall, "Look they have parking just for VW's." The two laughed at this, just as they always did, and started toward the door of the elite shop.

Stepping inside Lilly said, "Don't look back Karen but Old Lady Kelly and Charlotte were just across the street. I think Charlotte is scraping her mom's jaw off the sidewalk, her mouth fell open that wide." They attempted to stop giggling as Mademoiselle Jane, herself, stepped from behind the Counter and approached them. "What may I do for you ladies today?"

Lilly was the first to regain her composure enough to speak, "Please excuse us we just saw the funniest sight outside and were laughing. My friend here is getting married and I'm afraid we don't have much time. The wedding is this Saturday."

Looking slightly shocked Mademoiselle Jane couldn't help glancing at Karen's trim figure and slight amount of gray in her blond hair.

Karen laughed, "Oh no, not what your thinking, it's just the love of my life has reappeared and I'm not letting him go this time."

Jane was a consummate professional and in her many years of successful business had seen it all. She smiled, "Whatever you wish, Madame, I am sure I can fit you in anything you desire, I have a full staff of seamstresses standing by. If you would like to be seated in the Salon I will have a selection brought out to you. And are we looking for attendant dresses as well?"

Karen answered, "Yes, my friend here will be the Matron of Honor and then I will have two attendants, one a size five and one a size seven, and three flower girls, five year old twins and a six year old. And do you take the tuxedo orders or can you recommend?"

"What exactly did you have in mind?" asked Mademoiselle Jane.

"I'm not entirely sure," Karen answered, "Maybe something tea length, elegant? I think we would like the main color to be peach and we plan to use peach and ivory roses, and either a mint green or a powder blue as a secondary color."

Jane studied the two quietly for a moment and then replied, "I have just the dresses for both of you."

Disappearing behind the mauve velvet curtains she re-appeared a few moments later with the most beautiful dress Karen had ever seen. The skirt was ivory satin with the bodice and overskirt of antique ivory lace. Embroidered along the scalloped hem and neckline were tiny peach roses. The dress took Karen's breath away. Then following Jane was her assistant Angelique with almost the identical dress in Peach with Ivory embroidered roses. The two dresses were Victorian in style, tea length and the epitome of elegance. The Bride's dress had a heart shaped neckline and long sheer lace sleeves while the attendant's dress had a rounded neckline and short capped sleeves. The dresses brought tears to Karen's eyes.

Mademoiselle Jane spoke, "I see you like them. I created these dresses myself and until now I haven't shown them to anyone. However, I have a feeling about you two and would be honored if you chose them for your wedding. I can show you several options for the other attendants. We have a lovely princess style in both powder blue and mint green. The blue has antique ivory lace accents, and with the lovely sapphire ring you are wearing, I think I would recommend the blue."

"Blue it is then," said Karen after suddenly realizing that Jane was right.

The morning passed quickly and when Karen and Lilly left the shop they had purchased their dresses and decided on a style for Heather and Melinda and the flower girls. They had also made appointments for all of the men to be fitted for tuxedos. When Karen had presented John's charge card, Mademoiselle Jane had looked intensely at it and Karen was under the impression that John's name was well known.

Feeling very good about their morning they headed towards the market to pick up a few things for dinner.

"Do you feel like barbecuing again, Karen? We could probably get Tom to do most of it. Or we could order pizza for dinner and make some salads. What do you think?"

Karen answered, "Doesn't really matter to me. Either one sound's good. The kids would probably like pizza, and that would be quick and easy. Let's just pick up some fresh veggies while we're here, but we have a couple more stops to make first. And what did you have in mind for tomorrow night? I'm sure you're thinking about Jamie's favorite foods."

Karen led Lilly down the street to the Lingerie by Linda shop. "You know, we need to buy you something new too," Karen said. "How about this red lace, didn't you say Waldo likes red?" It wasn't long before Karen had both black lace, and a more elegant ivory lace picked out, along with a red satin for Lilly.

"I hope ole lady Kelly isn't still spying on us," said Karen, "Not that it really matters, she just doesn't need to see my lingerie."

Next they stopped at the Walter Lindy jewelry store. Lilly was the expert in jewelry, and she was able to lead Karen right to a perfect band with five diamonds in it. It was a good match with Karen's ring, and the diamonds sparkled in the light. As Karen paid for the ring with her own card, she marveled at the reality of what she was doing. Just last week she wouldn't have dreamed she would be doing this today, and she was amazed again at how fast her life was changing. If John had come back into her life earlier, she probably wouldn't be able to afford such a classy ring.

"This ring is the symbol of the unbroken circle you know," said Lilly, "I don't think your circle has ever really been broken."

Karen smiled, "I don't think so either. I mean I haven't seen the man for over a quarter of a century, he shows up in my kitchen and I walk into his arms as if I have been there every day for the last thirty years. He completes me. Does that sound strange?"

Lilly had tears in her eyes as she answered, "No, there's nothing strange about your relationship with John. You two were always meant to be together. And now I can quit feeling guilty about my happiness."

Karen quickly turned to her friend, "You should never have felt guilty. What happened was never your fault. And if your life had been a mess too then you couldn't have helped me. And my life wasn't totally ruined, after all I have two of the best kids in the world."

Lilly smiled, "You bet you do and I have the other one. Now let's quit sniveling and get to the store so we can feed those kids of ours."

They continued on to the market. "By the way, did you ask Jennifer to cancel everyone out for the rest of the week and week-end?" asked Karen.

Lilly replied, "Yes, I believe the only guests left are the Johnson's, and you know I saw Mr. Johnson talking with Tom just before we left. I think he's going to insist on helping, he always was a hard worker."

Karen rambled on, "What time are Jamie and Kelsi supposed to arrive tomorrow? Should we order the pizza now and pick it up on the way home? Or should we have it delivered?"

Lily answered, "I think the plane lands at 2:35, so I was thinking of lasagna for dinner, Caesar salad, parmesan garlic bread of course. And if the market has fresh rhubarb I'll make their favorite strawberry rhubarb pie. And why don't we wait and have the pizza delivered. We don't know what time our men will be back. Besides doesn't Ronald Kelly deliver for Antonio's?"

Chattering away the two friends almost knocked Old Lady Kelly down as they went through the door. "Well what have you two been doing all day? You certainly look excited."

Karen smiled kindly, "Just doing a little shopping, Mrs. Kelly. Lilly's son and daughter-in-law are coming for a visit and we need a few supplies."

Mrs. Kelly turned to Lilly and said, "So your son and his wife are coming, and isn't Karen's son and his family here? Are you two having a family reunion?"

Lilly smiled, "Nope, just our kids here for a visit. No big deal."

Grabbing a shopping cart and pushing it towards the produce Karen added, "Have a good day, Mrs. Kelly."

Lilly grabbed Karen's arm laughing uncontrollably, "Did you see her face, she's about to blow a vein! If we don't tell her something soon she's going to have a stroke."

Karen answered, "I'm not going to tell her anything, let her read it in the paper."

The fishing trip had gone well, and yes, Tyler caught the biggest fish. Tyler was especially excited that Uncle Waldo had insisted on paying him $2.00, one dollar for the first fish caught and one dollar for the biggest. This was Waldo's tradition and all of the kids had worked hard to earn those dollars. Lilly and Karen knew that they would still need the pizza even though Tyler was planning on a fish dinner, and Tom already had the barbeque pit going when they got back to the B & B.

The grounds around the Gazebo showed that Mr. Johnson had been hard at work. Tom explained that the elderly gentleman had insisted on being shown where the tools were kept and he suspected that Mrs. Johnson had been making pies in the morning after she helped Jennifer with the dusting and then the two women had brought lunch out to Tom and Mr. Johnson. Lilly wondered briefly if the retired couple might want to relocate to Louisiana and help run this place.

Melinda and Heather worked on the salad and Karen asked them to order the pizza when they were ready. Finding everything in such good order Lilly and Karen took their purchases to their bungalows. Karen met John as she went out the back door. She really had missed him, "Would you like to see what we got? And I have a receipt for the damages on your credit card."

He dropped a quick kiss on her lips and took the packages out of her arms, "Lead on, woman."

Once they got inside the bungalow he dropped the bags on the couch and took her in his arms, "I can't believe how much I've missed you. It's only been about five hours but I feel like it's been at least five days. How are we going to live through this week?" Kissing her tenderly, Karen's arms went around his neck and he pulled her deeper into his embrace. The moment was broken by the sound of two youngsters giggling. Reluctantly John turned toward the door to see Kristen and Tyler peeking around the corner.

"What are you two up to?" Karen asked moving out of John's embrace.

"Grandpa, can you come out and play catch with us?" Tyler asked. John's face lit up, "Sure can, Tyler. Why don't you two run along and I'll be right there." This time John closed the door firmly behind them.

"My fault" he murmured, "should have shut the door the first time. Now where were we?" He pulled Karen close again.

However, she dropped a quick kiss on his lips and spun out of his arms. "Oh, no you don't, you told the kids you would play with them."

"But I'd much rather play with you," John chuckled. Karen was already moving toward the bedroom with her packages when one of them fell. John moved swiftly to pick it up for her and saw a bit of black lace and ivory satin peeking out from the top. Hooking one finger through a strap he drew the negligee from the bag. "Didn't you say you wanted to show me your purchases? Does that mean you'll model them for me?" he asked hopefully.

She moved back into his arms and teasingly nibbled his neck, "You bet I'll model them for you…on Saturday!"

Karen handed John the receipt from Mademoiselle Jane's, "John, the bill for the dresses was quite a bit. Are you sure it's ok? I know you said that there wasn't a limit, but there has to be some kind of a limit, and I have some savings now."

John smiled at her, "I really meant that there is no limit Karen. Work has been my life for the last few years, and I really don't think we have anything to worry about. And there is something I want to ask you. I've been able to keep up with most of my work thanks to the Internet, but there are some things that I need to personally attend to soon. I know you have a lot to do, but there are a lot of working hands around here. Would you go with me to New York on Wednesday? The plane is a four seater so John Jr. can go with us. I know you'll want a chaperone if we spend one night. Or we can just make it a day trip if you want. I've been able to see where you live, and what you do here. I think it's also important that you see what I've been doing. I've been sensing that New York is the missing piece for you."

"I would love to go," said Karen with enthusiasm, "we'll just have to make sure everything is in order around here first. And you're right, I had a bad case of cold feet this morning, and John Jr. is the one that brought reality back to me. Oh John, it's so right to be with you, but I do need to know who you've been and where you've been. I want to know everything about you."

John went to play catch with Tyler and Kristen, and Karen walked over to Lilly's as she reflected on the events of the day.

"Guess what Lilly! John has invited me to go to New York on Wednesday with him for a day trip. We would take John Jr. with us. He has some business that needs his attention, and I will be able to see where he lives. Do you think everything is in order enough for me to go? I'll work on the list of things to do tonight to be sure, we can assign jobs."

Lilly answered, "Of course you can go. We'll be fine here. Actually I wanted to talk to you about offering Mr. and Mrs. Johnson a position here. Those two did so much work today. Maybe they're ready to come out of retirement. And just think, New York City, how exciting. But promise me you won't go into any skyscrapers?"

Karen laughed, "We'll be safe, don't worry. And I'm not sure how much sightseeing we'll get to do anyway. But I am excited about seeing his world. And I don't know about you, but I'm starved, we haven't eaten breakfast. Let's see how the girls are coming on the salad and if the pizza's been ordered yet."

Karen and Lilly strolled slowly to the big house, pausing at the side lawn for a moment to watch John playing catch with his grandchildren, on past the barbeque pit where Tom and Mr. Johnson were overseeing the fish, past the gazebo where Mrs. Johnson and Jennifer were setting tables for dinner, past the oak tree where Jill and Allie played with their dolls, past the carriage house where Waldo was cleaning his fishing equipment and entertaining John Jr. with Alaska stories. Pausing on the back steps, Lilly and Karen surveyed the beauty of their world.

Lilly turned to Karen, "Just look at all this, Karen! God has given us this wonderful family, this beautiful old house and grounds, these amazing friends. He has blessed me with a friend that left her comfortable home to travel completely across the country on a harebrained scheme that turned a ramshackle old mansion into a world famous bed and breakfast. I have been blessed with a loving husband for almost twenty eight years now and tomorrow my son and daughter-in-law will be here and my life will be complete. And in a few days you will be joined forever to the love of your life. My heart is so overwhelmed with joy at this moment, I feel like I might burst."

Karen smiled at Lilly, "It is wonderful isn't it. And from here on out, my friend, it's only going to get better. Now let's check on dinner."

Lilly and Karen found everything to be in order, and the pizza would arrive any minute now. "I'm sure glad we didn't miss Ronald Kelly, he has the best buns," Lilly whispered to Karen. They giggled as Karen went to the office to get cash. By the time she came back Ronald was there. Lilly was asking about the "buns", and he was blushing a bit when he shyly corrected her, "These are your free bread sticks."

Karen joined them and handed him the money. "Thank you for coming, we really enjoy your pizza," she said as they both took a long moment to watch him leave.

"This place always has attracted a little spice," Lilly said with a giggle.

Everyone gathered in the gazebo once again. Tyler was the first to have fish on his plate. Melinda wasn't sure that he really liked it as well as the pizza, but he devoured it with pride. And there was no way that Kristen was going to try it at all! The rest of the men all had their share and raved on and on about it.

Their group was growing, and tomorrow it would be even bigger. "We need to have a family meeting," said Karen, "John and I are making a trip to New York on Wednesday, so we need to be organized. I've brought my pad of paper here, and since we are doing this on such short notice, let's figure out who's doing what.

"Who wants to volunteer something specific?" asked Karen.

John Jr. perked up, "You're going to New York?"

"Yes, and you're invited," said his dad.

"I'll set up the awnings," said Waldo.

"Do you think we could put up some of the clear Christmas light strings?" asked Karen.

"Sure," he replied, "Jamie can help me with that."

John Sr. said, "I'm in charge of the music and the honeymoon."

"What's a honeymoon?" asked Kristen.

"I'm going to make rum flavored chocolate truffles tomorrow morning," Heather cut in. "Melinda, do you want to help?"

"Sure," she replied.

Lilly piped up, "I'm in charge of the cake and I know Kelsi will be in charge of the flowers."

Karen turned to look at Lilly, "Are your mom and sister going to be able to be here? My goodness, we haven't sent out any invitations, John! Tonight we will have to come up with something on the computer."

"We should be able to do that," he replied.

Karen turned to her son, "Have you talked to Matthew? It just wouldn't be right if he wasn't here."

"Yes, Mom, he's on his way and Annie and the baby are coming too."

"I saw an ad for an ice sculpture, have you thought about a theme yet?" asked Lilly.

"Do you have an organist yet?" asked Mrs. Johnson.

"No, and we would absolutely love to have you play, and I think I'll ask Jamie and Kelsi to sing. They sang at John and Melinda's wedding, and it was beautiful!" responded Karen. "Tom, are all of the water fountains working properly? Will you need some help in the garden? Oh my goodness, I forgot I ordered annuals from the nursery in town."

Mr. Johnson spoke up, "I'd be glad to plant them for you, and help with the fountains or anything else in the yard."

Karen turned to Waldo, "Waldo, would you do the honors of giving me away?" She almost had tears in her eyes as she thought about her own father, and treasured Waldo's presence in her life at the same time.

"Of course, I'd be proud to," he replied. "But do I have to wear one of those monkey suits?"

Lilly answered, "Yes dear, but you would have had to wear one anyway to go with my dress. And that reminds me, all of you men, including you, Tyler, have an appointment at 11:00 AM tomorrow to be fitted. Melinda and Heather can pick out their dresses then too. We thought we could all go into town and then Waldo and I will pick up Jamie and Kelsi at 2:30. And Karen, I already told my family about the wedding. LaWanda and Robere' are bringing Mama on Saturday morning. They are combining the wedding and reception with a trip to visit the rest of the family in Alabama. So they will spend Saturday night at a hotel near the airport and fly on down there on Sunday. What's next Karen?"

"Well, I want to work on a little printed invitation so that we have something printed up to keep. John, will you work with me on it?"

"Sure will," he replied. "I will leave the list on the back kitchen counter, and if anyone thinks of something that we've forgotten or needs to be done, just add it to the list and we'll work on it."

Kristen had been playing in the tent with Jill and Allie. Tom and Waldo had supplied them with various boxes and items to set up house with, and every doll they could find was in their bed taking a nap while the girls ate dinner. They returned to the tent when they were done eating to continue their play. "I want to play too," said Tyler.

"Ok, you can be the daddy," said Kristen.

"No, I want to be the grandpa," He replied.

It wasn't long before they had their roles worked out. "Grandpa Tyler" was soon stuck babysitting, and he changed his mind about playing house with the girls.

Tyler suggested that they all play school, and the girls wanted to but they couldn't decide who was going to be the teacher as they both wanted the position.

Melinda joined them and said, "I'm glad you're playing school, because you do have some homework to do. After all you are missing a whole week of school. Kristen, run and get your books out of mommy and daddy's room."

Kristen took Allie with her, and they were back shortly. Heather decided to play the teacher. She was good with the kids, and made their learning fun with stories and imagination skills. They all looked forward to the story she was going to read right before their imaginary recess.

The Johnson's helped Tom and Jennifer clean up, along with John Jr. and Melinda. There were so many hands at work that there wasn't much left for Lillie and Waldo to do so they decided to go for a walk by the river.

John and Karen went to the office to work on the computer. Karen took control of the keyboard, and before long they had their design worked out. "At least we can give these to our family for a keepsake," said Karen as John massaged her shoulders. "I hope this is something you make a habit of doing," she said.

"Ok, your turn," John sat in the chair and continued to fine-tune the document as she massaged his shoulders.

"Hey, you have a brother! I almost forgot, that means I'll have a brother in-law. Where does he live? Have you invited him?"

"As a matter of fact I have. Dan is single, he lives in North Carolina and he'll be flying in on Saturday morning. I just heard from him right before dinner and didn't have a chance to tell you yet. He went ahead and reserved a room close to the airport, since he didn't know what the accommodations were here, and he needs to fly back early Sunday morning.

"And your parents are…?"

"They passed on a few years ago," he finished for her. "We'll talk more about that later. But if you know anyone that needs to know about the five steps of grieving, I can probably help."

"It sounds like you've worked through an awful lot. I wish I would have been there for you," she said with an ache in her heart.

"Me too," he replied. He finished the invitation and e-mailed it to the list they had selected, and also printed several copies.

Karen slid her hands down onto his chest and nuzzled her nose into his neck. "You know, I love the smell of your t-shirt, and I love to hear your heart beat," she said.

He slid his arm up around her waist and pulled her into his lap. "You can smell my t-shirt and listen to my heart any time, you just might look a bit funny in public," he teased. "How are you doing Karen, are you stressed with all there is to do?" he asked.

"No, I'm used to being busy, and I'm having fun, how about you?"

"Oh I'm fine, just a little anxious for Saturday night if you know what I mean," John teased.

"I know exactly what you mean, and I plan to make it well worth your wait," Karen said with a smile.

CHAPTER 6

Lilly and Waldo strolled along the banks of the river until they came to a grouping of large rocks. Waldo helped Lilly up on a flat rock and then settled in beside her. "What are you thinking my love?" He asked gently.

She smiled at him, "Oh, just thinking about life and the direction we're heading now. I can't wait to see Jamie and Kelsi tomorrow. But at the same time I want to slow things down. This week is moving too fast."

"Don't worry, Lilly, Karen and the kids will still be a part of our lives no matter where John takes her."

"I know," she answered, "but it won't be the same. And it's not just that, you know I'm terribly happy for her and I love John like a brother. It's this house too. I'm sure going to miss it."

Waldo looked hopeful, "Miss it?"

Lilly laid her head on his shoulder, "Is Alaska as beautiful as they say?"

The grin on Waldo's face was at least a mile wide. "It will be even more beautiful with you in it. Do you honestly mean you would leave all this and come back with me?"

"Of course I will, and we're not going to give this place up. We're going to see if Jennifer and Tom will run it for us. And I think we can talk the Johnson's into staying on to help. So, have you found that fishing lodge for me or do we have to start from scratch with that one too like we did here? Do you remember what a mess this place was? Look at it now," She said wistfully. "Mon Amie Famille has become famous and we have become wealthy. Do you remember that shy little girl you married? What happened to her?"

He laughed softly, "She's sitting right here beside me. She is still the sweet, kindhearted and fun loving girl that stole my heart. I'm only going to ask this one time. Are you sure you can give this up?"

Lilly snuggled in closer, "What will we name it? Let's see the native language in Alaska is Aleutian. What does "My Friends and Family" translate to in that language?"

Waldo grinned, "The place I have in mind is in great shape but it has been vacant for about five years. It has ten bedrooms and a great dining hall and needs just a little work on the kitchen. It already has a name "Wolf Creek Lodge" but we can name it anything you want."

When Waldo and Lilly arrived back from the river, John and Karen were just coming out to the gazebo where the Johnson's were still talking and waiting to watch the sunset about to happen. Lilly's eyes met Karen's, and they both knew instinctively that this was the time to talk with the Johnson's about staying. Lilly nudged Waldo, and he also knew what was about to take place.

"Come and watch the sunset with us," said Mr. Johnson.

John replied, "We would love to."

"This is a beautiful place," said Waldo, "we've all worked hard to make it into the Mon Amie Famille, which means "My Family and Friends" in French. Jed and Louise, have you ever thought about staying here?" This was the first time anyone had used the Johnson's first names, Waldo had moved from the professional level to the personal level.

Louise's eyes were wide with amazement. "We were just talking about how we would love to live in a place like this. Are you serious? John…Karen, are you going to be living here?"

Waldo explained that they were opening another B&B in Alaska, and they would be asking Tom and Jennifer to run this southern business while they started the northern.

"As far as John and Karen, I don't know what their plans are yet," he said, looking at John.

"We haven't really had the time to talk about it yet," John replied as he checked the expression on Karen's face.

"I don't think I'm ready to give it up yet," said Karen. "Perhaps we'll do some traveling or something, but I think I would like to stay involved." John squeezed her hand and she knew immediately that he approved, and also wanted to participate. "But it could be quite some time before John and I are ready to "settle" any place. So until then Lilly and I would love it if you two could stay on here and help. This place is so special and it needs the special touch that you two have. Part of the charm of Mon Amie Famille is that the people running it honestly care about the guests. The guests are the friend part of the name. And I know you two would carry on the tradition."

Jed and Louise looked at each other for a moment and then Jed spoke, "We would love to stay here as long as you have work for us to do."

Waldo laughed, "Don't you want to know what the salary is?"

Louise answered, "Oh, there is a salary? We don't have to pay you anymore?"

The whole group laughed at that, and Lilly answered, "We will work out the salary part later and I think we can throw in some profit sharing also. Now look at that sunset." Each of the men slipped their arm around their wife (John his soon-to-be wife), and the three couples gazed at the red, gold and purple painting that God had created.

Jennifer took the girls home, and John and Melinda took Tyler and Kristen in to give them a bath and have a little bit of family time. The other two couples retired, and John asked Karen, "Do you want to go for a drive? I haven't driven Little Red all day."

"Sure," she replied, "besides, I'm not ready to break our tradition of the nightly moonlight dance yet. Just let me get a sweater, it might get a bit cool tonight."

They slipped into the car and John drove to their spot down the road by the river. The bright stars twinkled in the clear, dark sky and with the radio playing softly Karen stepped into John's arms and nuzzled his neck. At the end of the song, their bodies stopped swaying and John's arm tightened around Karen's back and molding her body to his he tenderly kissed her. When Karen pulled away, John said, "I know, I know our chaperones are waiting. It's way past their bedtime and we have to get up early too."

Karen smiled gently, "You read my mind."

Karen sat close beside him on the short ride back to the house. "I love being here at your side John," she whispered softly.

He pulled her in closer and said, "This is your place now, and you're welcome to be in it any time you want." Karen was overwhelmed with the feeling of being loved. Never before in her life had she felt like this.

Karen went straight to her bungalow to get ready for bed. When she returned to the tent John was already inside reading a story to Tyler and Kristen. Karen slid quietly into her sleeping bag and studied John's face as he added his own animation to the kid's favorite story. The kids were fast asleep by the time John put the book away and turned off the flashlight. As John settled down beside her, Karen whispered, "I'm so sorry you never got to do that with John, or with any other child of yours. How can I ever make it up to you?"

John pulled her close, "Shhh from now on no looking back, we're only going forward. Go to sleep, my love, tomorrow is a busy day."

CHAPTER 7

Karen rose early the next day. She wanted to get breakfast started before Lilly beat her to it again. But when she walked in the back door of the kitchen, just before the sun came up, she was greeted with the mingling smells of fresh brewed coffee and strawberry rhubarb pies baking in the oven, and Lilly and Waldo sitting at the breakfast nook. "Good morning you two, what are you doing up so early?"

Lilly giggled, "Can't sleep, our kids are coming home today, remember? Besides, Waldo's used to getting up at the crack of dawn and I decided to join him today. Karen, I'm so excited, there's just so much to do. The pies are in the oven already and right after breakfast I'm going to make the lasagnas and put them in the fridge. Oh, I almost forgot, you have e-mails. They're probably about the wedding so I left them for you."

Karen moved to the computer station set up at the end of the country kitchen. She typed in her personal password and found eight e-mails. Opening the first one she smiled with delight, "Deirdre's going to come. Oh I had so hoped she could make it. She was so kind to me after Dunston died, even though he was her only brother. It will be good to see her again. And look Lilly, your brother Ray and his wife, Lynn, are coming too." Karen continued working at the computer and quickly entered the wedding chores and who was doing what into the spreadsheet program. She also made a list of things yet to be done. "We don't have a photographer yet," she suddenly said, almost in a panic. "What if we can't get anyone on such a short notice?"

"I think Mademoiselle Jane has some contacts, let's ask her this morning," replied Lilly calmly. "Besides, we can put some of those disposables out and I'm sure quite a few of us will have our cameras available." Karen added film and disposables to the list.

Heather arrived, ready to start on her truffles. "Good morning everybody, you sure are up earlier than I expected." Waldo jumped up and helped her unload her supplies onto the counter, which then enabled her to give her mom a quick hug. "What is your favorite flavor, Uncle Waldo? Do you want me to make some Irish Cream? Mom, look at these new candy molds I got. There's wedding bells, and swans. Do you like them? Lilly told me she ordered the swan ice sculpture. It sure is beautiful in the picture!"

"They're just perfect," answered her Mother, "and I know your truffles are always a big hit. Maybe I'll hide some so that John and I can have some later. I'm sure they'll be all gone before we get back from our honeymoon. And that reminds me, I still don't know where we're going.

Lilly was taking the pies out of the oven and stated, "Wow this is really going to be some family reunion. I hope the Airport Inn has lots of empty rooms! Waldo would you hand me that tray of rolls so we can get breakfast started?"

Karen jumped from the computer station, "Oh no you don't. I'm doing breakfast today. You guys go get yourselves ready. I have your lasagna recipe Lilly and I'll get that started. Don't worry I won't let anyone see the secret ingredients."

Lilly laughed at that, "It's not really a secret, but I guess Jamie won't mind who actually makes the lasagna as long as there's plenty of it."

The group turned as John opened the back door and stepped inside, "Hey what's going on here? I smelled the coffee way back at the tent and is that pie I smell too? What kind is it?" Karen stepped close for a quick kiss and replied, "Lilly's famous strawberry rhubarb. She makes it just for Jamie and Kelsi and if you touch it you won't live long enough to be a groom."

John turned to Lilly, "Is that true?"

Waldo laughed, "Karen's exaggerating, Lilly wouldn't really kill you, but you probably wouldn't enjoy your wedding night very much."

Lilly quit laughing long enough to get the words out, "Stop it you guys, there's plenty of pie. We just can't cut it until after dinner tonight. Now Karen, if you're sure you can handle this alone I think I'll get a shower?"

John answered, "You run along Lilly, you too Waldo, I'm helping with breakfast this morning. I better start learning the ropes so I can earn my keep around here."

Lilly and Waldo returned to their bungalow and Lilly quickly undressed and got into the walk-in-shower. Waldo had installed the shower especially for her; he worried about her lifting her bad knee over the side of the tub when he wasn't home. The tempered glass was etched with golden hummingbirds and teal roses and had been manufactured in France. Foaming herself luxuriously with the shower gel Jamie and Kelsi had sent her for Christmas, Lilly relaxed for a moment and let the warm water pulsate on the back of her neck. Stepping from the shower she wrapped herself in an oversized terry cloth robe and sat down at the small vanity. As she began brushing her hair she was not surprised when the door opened and Waldo stepped inside. Waldo took the hair brush from her, laid it down and began to massage her neck and shoulders. "Waldo, remember when we were newlyweds?"

"Of course," he replied.

Lilly reminisced, "I was so disappointed that Karen wasn't around to help plan the wedding. She was at college then, and I had to do most of it by myself. And the loneliness was unbearable when you were out at sea, but I survived. We made up for it though when you came home. We had the little three room apartment that came furnished with wonderful antiques, and Jamie was born there."

Waldo continued, "The first jewelry I gave you were the little pearls nestled into the silver leaves. You cried when I gave you those. And I think I only had $250.00 in saving when you took over my finances. We did spend a lot though on the weekends."

Lilly spoke again, "We saw a lot of movies, ate out a lot, and we loved Seattle. The hours fishing in your boat can never be replaced. And you always volunteered me to cook when we went to your dad's. The music was different then too. There was always country, but there was also the soft rock. Those were good times, and good memories, and I love you more now than ever."

He kissed her tenderly as he assured her that many, many memories were yet to come.

CHAPTER 8

The lasagna was prepared and stored in the refrigerator and the breakfast preparations ready. During the preparation, Heather entertained her parents with stories about her customers and the three of them worked comfortably together.

John Sr. went back to the tent to wake the kids for breakfast, but found them sleeping soundly so he slipped into Karen's bungalow and crawled into her bed between the down comforter and pillow top mattress just to doze for a few minutes. When Jennifer arrived for work a few minutes later Karen asked her to finish the preparation while she went to look for John and the kids. Finding Tyler and Kristen still sleeping in the tent she went in search of John and found him in her bungalow sleeping in her bed. "Hey, are you awake?" she asked softly. She moved closer to get a better look at his face, and he suddenly reached out and grabbed her, pulling her onto the bed with him. "There's something you should know my love, I like to sleep next to nature."

Karen's eyes got big as he laughed his deep whole-hearted laugh. Matching his smile she wondered if he was bluffing and was relieved to hear the back screen door open. "Grandpa, what are you doing sleeping in Grandma's bed?" Tyler asked. "I guess I just wanted something a little softer," he replied with a twinkle in his eyes.

Tyler and Kristen both jumped up onto the bed and cuddled in. "Will you read us another story tonight Grandpa?" asked Kristen.

"Yeah, and we're going to go snipe hunting with Jamie tonight too," said Tyler.

"Ok you two, run along and put in your breakfast order. Jennifer and Heather are in the kitchen. They'll be fixing your breakfast this morning and don't bother Aunt Lilly. She has too much to do today to cater to your wishes."

"Kristen, what are you going to have for breakfast?" asked Tyler. "You know Aunt Lilly will make us anything. Do you think Heather will too? How about we try for chocolate chip pancakes? Mom won't let us have those very often."

Gathering up her clothes and robe Karen started for the bathroom, "Come on sleepy head, get back to your room and get yourself together. Lilly and Waldo aren't going to wait for us. Not when it comes to Jamie and Kelsi."

John just lay there grinning. "Isn't your shower big enough for two?"

Karen smiled back, "I wouldn't know. It's never been tried."

John laughed and jumped from the bed. Karen stopped still and admired the muscles rippling down his back and his well formed legs. John quickly slipped on his sweats and she was slightly saddened by the loss of her view. When John straightened and turned he caught the glimmer of desire in her eyes. Starting towards her she met him and was caught up in his embrace.

"John, I must be out of my mind. Why are we waiting? Why are we wasting one precious moment of this second chance that God has given us?"

John held one finger slightly over her lips, "We're waiting because it is the honorable thing for me to do. We're waiting out of respect for our parents, even though they are now gone. But the biggest reason we're waiting just left the room. What kind of signal would we be sending those kids if they grew up knowing we had slept together before we were married? And as bright as they are they would pick up on it right away. I will never regret what we did that night before I left for Vietnam. In fact that memory probably kept me alive, but that doesn't mean it would be right now. Besides you're worth waiting for and the woman that comes to me on our wedding night will still be the sweet, shy girl I knew so many years ago and oh so much more."

She kissed him softly, "Ok, get going before I try to change your mind."

They all gathered on the patio when it was time to leave. "We'll take the Cadillac and the Mon Amie Famille van," said Waldo. John and Waldo had decided that Waldo and Lilly would take the Cadillac to the airport and John would bring everyone else back to the house in the van.

Getting the group together and on their way was a monumental task, but finally both vehicles were underway. Pulling in the parking lot of Mademoiselle Jane's, Karen couldn't help looking up and down the street to see if anyone was watching and sure enough there was Old Lady Kelly coming out of the beauty shop. Grabbing Lilly's arm and pulling her aside she whispered, "Old Lady K at about one block and closing fast."

Lilly just laughed, "She can't move that fast." Hustling the kids along, the group made it just inside as Etta Kelly came huffing and puffing up the street. Waldo was holding the door open to the group and said, "Good morning, Mrs. Kelly," just as he shut the door. Winking at Lilly he chuckled, "I kind of enjoyed that."

Jane and her assistant came from the back and taking the gentlemen in tow they started their expert measuring and soon had every one taken care of. The dresses Lilly and Karen had picked out for Heather and Melinda fit perfectly and so did the dresses for the flower girls. Jill and Allie were so excited with their baskets they were practicing strewing their petals all over the shop. When Karen attempted to apologize to Jane about the unruliness of the bunch, Jane pooh pooh'd her away, "This is what I live for. A wedding should be a truly happy occasion and when I see whole families and extended families involved I feel very blessed. It is I that should thank you for allowing me to be a part of it."

Very soon it was time for Waldo and Lilly to leave for the airport. Jane had fitted Waldo in a beautiful gray cutaway coat and matching trousers. The color accented the premature gray in his hair and he looked very much the proud father. Lilly could tell he was pleased with the fit even though he continued to grumble about the monkey suit. John and John Jr. were extremely handsome in traditional cut black tuxedos with peach silk cummerbunds.

Karen had the list that Kelsi had e-mailed detailing the types of flowers she would need for the arrangements and her group was headed to the florist next. Making arrangements to meet later at the house for dinner they went their separate ways.

Karen, Melinda, and Heather stopped at the variety store. Picking out supplies was fairly easy. They purchased large ribbon for the pews, ribbons for hair and trimming, and all of the extra floral supplies for Kelsi. Melinda found some round twelve-inch mirrors and the perfect candles for centerpieces. Heather found swans that fit nicely next to the candles, and in a variety of sizes she thought Lilly might like to use decorating the cake. They were able to purchase disposable cameras, and extra film for their cameras. And thank goodness they walked by the nylons, or they might have missed buying them because they were not on the list.

"There, we have everything on the list," said Karen with a look of satisfaction on her face. "We do need to pick up the annuals from the nursery though. I guess we can do that while we're here in town instead of coming back."

Karen and Melinda bought sandwiches and met the rest of the group at the city park where they were keeping the kids entertained with games. After eating the ladies headed off to the local nursery while the men treated the kids to ice cream.

"Mom," Heather said as she pulled her away from the group. "There's something I need to tell you. I've been dating David. He owns the nursery you know."

"Really?" said Karen in a surprised voice. "How long has this been going on?"

"Oh, about four months now, he's really nice and we go to dinner and the movies a lot. I just thought you should know before we run into him."

"I'm glad you told me honey, and I'm really happy for you. I'm looking forward to meeting him."

Heather had been hurt badly right before they moved to Louisiana, and it probably was the final push for her to move out here with her mom. The guy she had dated for a year turned out to be a two-timing jerk and Heather hadn't been the same since. Karen had worried that she hadn't completed the grieving process after her father's death, and really hoped for her happiness.

Arriving at the nursery, Karen tried to be nonchalant and at the same time thoroughly check David out. Oh how she wished Lilly were here, she would manage to get a lot of information about him. Oh well, Karen thought, better start functioning on her own.

Lost in thought and staring off into space, she didn't hear the young man come up behind her, "May I help you Ma'am?" he asked.

Karen turned and was immediately lost in the deepest sapphire blue eyes she had ever seen. The man's blond hair was wispy across his forehead and Karen had to stifle the urge to brush his hair back from his eyes. Smiling at him, she apologized for daydreaming.

He smiled back and said, "Now I know where Heather gets her beauty."

Startled she asked, "Oh, are you David?"

"Yes ma'am," he drawled. "I knew who you were when you walked in the gate. And Heather tells me congratulations are in order."

Blushing and slightly flustered Karen replied, "Thank you. I do hope you will be able to join us on Saturday, I'll tell Heather that she must bring you. By the way, have you seen her? I seem to have gotten lost from the group."

"Right this way, ma'am, they're in the hot house checking out the Lilies."

"Oh David, you don't have to keep calling me ma'am, please call me Karen."

Smiling he replied, "Thank you ma'am. Uh, I mean, Karen."

The two laughed together like old friends and taking her arm he ushered her into the hot house where her group was admiring the hybrid lilies on display.

It was only a brief moment before John Jr. realized that Heather had an interest in David. Her brother had always been very protective of her, and Heather knew she had better introduce them. David made a good impression, and Heather was a little more at ease as they conversed about the lilies.

The van was full with people, not leaving much room for plants, so Heather arranged for David to bring them out to the B&B later when he got off work. After quickly checking with Heather, Karen asked, "David, why don't you plan to stay for lasagna tonight?"

"I would love to ma'am, uh Karen," he replied. "I've heard a lot about the food out there but I've never had the chance to check it out."

"We'll see you after while then," she said in a matter of fact manner. He briefly put his hand on Heather's shoulder as he helped her into the van.

John Sr. and Karen squeezed into the back seat with the kids. "It's been a while since we were in a back seat," John whispered in her ear. Karen snuggled into her place beside him, and tired Kristen leaned her head on Grandma's shoulder. "Wagons HO!" shouted John Jr. as he pulled out of the parking lot.

CHAPTER 9

Lilly's anticipation was at a peak. The airport wasn't as busy as other times she and Waldo had been there, and it was easy to make their way to the gate. After complaining that the plane was never going to land, it finally did, and her eyes were set on the end of the ramp. She was thinking that enough people had come off the plane to fill three planes, when finally she saw them. She couldn't fight back the tears any longer as she finally was able to hug Jamie her tightest. When she managed to pull herself away she turned to hug Kelsi.

Kelsi and Waldo had greeted each other with a big hug and Waldo's usual question, "How's my favorite daughter-in-law?"

Followed by Kelsi's usual reply, "I better be your only daughter in law."

It was so good to see these two and as usual Lilly was amazed at how strong they both looked. Jamie was tall and well built and had Lilly's father's dark hair and eyes. Kelsi had inherited Indian features from her father with honey colored skin and golden highlights in her long brown hair. But it wasn't just an outer appearance, they both had so much self confidence that people were instantly struck with how capable they appeared to be with everything they undertook. Kelsi was a tall girl, actually only about an inch shorter than Jamie and when she hugged Lilly she always gave the appearance of hugging a small fragile doll.

As usual, Jamie was eager to get moving. Grabbing the bags off the baggage carousel, he headed for the parking lot, "Let's go. Mom, what's for dinner?"

Lilly told him what she had planned and could see the anticipation in both their eyes. On the ride back to the house Lilly and Waldo brought them up to date on what was happening. Jamie and Kelsi likewise filled them in on the newest happenings in their lives. They reassured Lilly that they would be able to stay until Monday and seemed very pleased about the plans for the B&B in Alaska. Jamie loved to go fishing up North and thought this would be a great getaway for him and Kelsi. "Hey you two, when you get that one established, think about a dude ranch on our property. That way, Mom, you can come and cook for us all the time!"

Lilly smiled tenderly at her only child, "There's probably nothing I would rather do, but let's get the Alaska business up and running before we make plans to start another. Oh I almost forgot to tell you, Englebert and Angie will be here tomorrow and they'll be staying until Monday also."

Karen, Jennifer and Louise were in the kitchen preparing dinner. The lasagna was in the oven, the bread was ready for the broiler, and they were working on the vegetables. Karen had decided to eat inside tonight and Melinda and Heather were setting the table with the regular blue and purple ceramic dishes.

David knocked at the back door. "Your plants are here ma'am," he announced. Jed was right behind him.

"Jed, will you please show him where you want them? Perhaps they could sit by the shed for now," Karen requested. Heather went out to help as soon as she heard their voices.

When Karen went out to check on them, they had placed all of the containers out where they were to be planted. "I just wanted to get your approval before I get started planting," said Jed. He showed her the planting design he had in mind. Jed had placed red geraniums, white pansies, and blue lobelia around the flagpole. The lobelia continued all along the front driveway. They already had the hanging plants spaced evenly around the front porch, and were ready to finish hanging the back planters.

"Everything looks absolutely lovely. Lilly will be so surprised when she gets here!" Karen said as she noticed that Heather and David were in the gazebo. She so hoped that things went well for them. He seemed like a very nice young man and it was good to see Heather happy.

Just then she heard car doors slam from the front of the house, the front door of the house slam shut and the kids shouting, "Jamie, Uncle Waldo says you'll take us snipe hunting tonight. Can you please?"

Jamie picked both kids up in a giant bear hug, "Snipe hunting, huh? Dad, what have you been telling these kids? I didn't know there were snipes in Louisiana, but let me tell you some stories about the snipes in Washington State. I caught one last year in a bear trap!"

Tyler and Kristen's eyes were like huge saucers, "Really, Jamie? Are you teasing us? Is that true Kelsi?" Kristen asked.

Kelsi laughed and said, "Oh no you don't, I'm not getting involved in any snipe hunts. That's Jamie and Waldo's department."

John Jr. and Melinda had followed their children out on the porch and were greeting Jamie and Kelsi. Living only about six hours away from each other they got together fairly often. Jamie always said John and Heather were the brother and sister he never had.

Karen saw John Sr. standing in the doorway of the house, he was taking in the sight of all these beautiful young people, laughing and talking all at once. Going to him and taking his hand, Karen led him to Jamie and Kelsi. After getting her hugs she introduced John and as he stepped forward to shake hands with Jamie he said, "I'd like to hear about those snipes too."

Kelsi laughed and hugged him, "Oh I'm sure you will, when Jamie and his dad start telling stories there's no end. Where's Heather?" she asked turning to Karen.

"She's in the gazebo with a new boyfriend," Karen whispered.

Kelsi smiled, "That's nice, let's get the bags to our room and you guys can tell me all about him."

Jamie and Kelsi were amazed when they entered the "Western Room." Lilly and Karen had decorated since the last time they had visited, and with the cancellations they were able to give them their own room.

"Whoa, it looks like our bedroom at home!" exclaimed Jamie. All of the furniture was made out of pine logs, and the log cabin quilt on the bed complimented the room. Lilly had collected some of Jamie and Kelsi's metal art, and it hung on the walls among other western prints. Two large antique wooden rocking chairs with denim cushions sat out on the balcony next to a matching couch. Lightweight denim colored curtains hung at the windows, and hand made braided throw rugs accented the area in front of the couch. There was a small desk area with a computer, and an entertainment center also made of the pine logs. They immediately loved the room, and felt right at home.

After unpacking, Jamie and Kelsi went out to visit with their family. Everyone had gathered in the gazebo and relaxed in the comfortable chairs. Heather seemed to have a glow about her as she introduced David.

Jed had found an old dinner bell in the shed earlier that afternoon. Louise had polished it to a shine and Jed had hung it on the back porch. To everyone's surprise, she rang the bell and called for dinner.

"This is a new tradition," remarked John Jr.

"It has a beautiful tone," commented Lilly as they all filed into the large dining room.

John Sr. and Karen lagged behind a bit as he took her hand and whispered, "We need some alone time tonight, I just want to hold you for a while."

Karen looked up into his brown eyes and almost melted right there. "We can go for a drive after dinner," she promised.

As the group settled in around the huge dining table, Waldo rapped his spoon on the crystal goblet. "Attention everyone, I know you're all hungry, especially you, son" he looked tenderly at his only child and continued, "But I think under the circumstances it is only fitting that we thank the Lord for bringing us here today." As the group murmured their agreement they all joined hands and bowed their heads, "Heavenly Father, thank you for bringing John back into our lives, thank you for bringing Jamie and Kelsi safely to us today, thank you for our new friends and family gathered with us, for Jed and Louise and their willingness to stay and help out here, and for our newest friend, David. We ask that you watch over the rest of our family and friends traveling to be with us on Saturday and that you keep John, Karen and John Jr. safe on their trip to New York tomorrow. And Lord, thank you for the years of friendship that you have blessed us with and please continue to bless us in our ventures for many years to come. Amen."

Jamie's head popped up with a big grin, "Woops Dad, you forgot something." Bowing his head Jamie spoke, "Thank you Lord for the best lasagna in the world."

The group laughed as Lilly swatted her son. The salad, fresh vegetables, lasagna and garlic bread were enjoyed by all. Jamie sat back finally satisfied, "Mom I think that was the best you ever made."

"Oh no, Jamie, I didn't actually make it. Karen and John did."

Karen spoke up, "But it's your recipe Lilly and how many years did it take for you to finally trust me with it?"

"I've always trusted you Karen. I never gave you the recipe because I never make it the same way twice. But now that it's written down I probably will. And now, who wants pie with whipped topping or pie with vanilla ice cream?"

Most everyone wanted ice cream except Jamie and Waldo, who wanted both. "I knew that", Lilly said, "and that's why I offer both. Those two can never make up their mind which they like better."

Karen went to the kitchen with her friend to help with the promised dessert. "What do you think of David? Is he a doll or what?" asked Lilly as she placed generous slices of pie on dessert plates and Karen added the requested toppings.

"I liked him right off the bat." Karen answered.

"Oh good, I did too. Heather seems so happy. I just hope he's everything he seems to be," Lilly paused and then continued, "He certainly seems sincere and John and Jamie liked him and you know how protective they are when it comes to their "little sister."

"John and I are going to take a little drive after dinner and catch up on the wedding plans," Karen said.

Lilly laughed, "Yeah right, I'll just bet you'll be catching up on wedding plans."

Karen joined the laughter, "How well you know me."

The two carried trays of pies out to the dining room and got there in time to hear Jamie filling Tyler's head with stories of giant snipe. "Jamie, that boy's going to have nightmares," admonished his wife.

"That's OK, Kelsi; he's sleeping in the tent with his grandparents. We'll let them worry about him," said Lilly.

Karen briefly helped to clear the table, and then she and John stole away in Little Red. She expected him to head for their spot by the river, but to her surprise he turned the other direction. 'Where are you taking me?" she asked.

"I think Waldo had the right idea tonight," he explained, "we need to be thanking God for our blessings, and I was wondering if you would show me the little church we're going to be married in."

"Of course, absolutely," she answered.

They pulled into the back of the parking lot to view the scene. The sun was setting and the glow surrounded the little church building and highlighted the steeple. "This is perfect," John exclaimed. Karen cuddled up beside him and they sat, observing the scene in awe for some time.

As they entered the front doors, there was still enough light outside to show off the stained glass windows. Once again, they were both in awe and they instinctively knew this was a moment that would live throughout time.

John took her hands in his and said, "In front of God, Karen, I love you with all of my heart."

"I love you with my whole being," she responded.

"Shall we write our own wedding vows?" John asked.

"I think we just did," she replied. They held each other in silence, knowing that what they had together was extraordinary, and that these moments were more precious than words could describe. Finally Karen pulled away and looked into his deep brown eyes. Her heart felt like it would burst with her emotions. "I just hope I can control the tears on Saturday, you touch my heart so deeply."

"You'll be fine," he reassured her, and held her close again. "I don't want to let you go, Karen, but we have to be at the airport at 7:00 AM if we're going to make this a day trip. Are you sure you don't want to spend the night?"

She laughed lightly, "There's probably nothing I would rather do, but John Jr. is counting on coming back tomorrow and there's so much to be done here."

"Very well, we'll be back tomorrow night."

They got back in time to see Tyler sneaking around the side of the house carrying a large pillow case held out in front of him. John laughed, "Look at our grandson. He's a natural born snipe hunter. Did Waldo really do this with John and Jamie when they were that age?"

Karen replied, "Of course he did, and Heather too. She wouldn't let the boys do anything without her. But you know I think she caught on long before they did. He had those boys out during the summer for two years looking for snipe." Karen laughed delightedly and snuggled in closer under John's arm. "Let's just sit and watch for a while."

As soon as Tyler spotted his Grandparents, he had to explain the whole snipe hunting procedure to them. He was getting quite good at holding the flashlight and having the pillowcase ready at the same time, and thought he had seen a few actual snipes. They listened to him intently and enjoyed every moment.

"Ok, I think it's time to call it a night," said Karen. "Maybe the snipes will be out again tomorrow night."

John needed to do a little work on his computer, and really needed a good night's sleep, so they agreed that he would stay in his room tonight and the kids would stay with their parents. Karen was relieved to actually sleep in her own bed, even though she wouldn't be next to John. They were tired and would have a big day tomorrow. When John said goodnight at the door to her bungalow he kissed her tenderly and left, each of them longing to be together.

Karen awoke, feeling refreshed and full of energy. She could hardly wait to see John again even though it had only been hours since they had been together. However, she lingered in the shower just a bit to enjoy the hot steamy water. Quickly she packed a bag with supplies to freshen up later in the day, and a change of clothes as John had said something about going out to dinner. She was anxious for this day, having no idea what she would learn about her beloved hunk of a man.

When she entered the kitchen, Lilly already had breakfast finished, and John was sitting at the end of the counter with a cup of coffee in his hand. His words greeted her with a big grin on his face. "I need you like coffee needs a cup."

Karen laughed and kissed him as she replied, "Like flowers need the rain."

He answered, "Like salad needs dressing."

She grinned, "Like French fries need ketchup."

Laughing Lilly stepped in, "Enough you two. You could go on this way forever."

Just then John Jr., Melinda and the kids came through the door. Tyler and Kristen were asking for chocolate chip pancakes again and Lilly said it was OK with her if it was OK with their parents.

John Jr. was excited and ready to start on the day's adventure. "Are you two ready?" He asked his parents.

It was a beautiful day to fly, and to their surprise John Sr. was the pilot. He was very informational and pointed out various sites along the way. "First, I'll show you two where I live, and then we'll go to the office," he instructed. "Karen, I want to get your opinion on some things before I make some decisions that will affect our lives together."

Karen was full of anticipation and couldn't wait to see the world that he lived in. The landing was very smooth, and it was apparent he was no stranger to the big city. Not only was he strikingly handsome with a magnetic personality, he had an air of confidence that she loved and it made her feel like she owned a gold mine. He expertly guided them to a waiting taxi, which took them to his penthouse apartment across from Central Park.

Karen was halfway in shock as she entered this new world. She looked around the clean and classy surroundings to find leather furniture, and dark cherry wood accents. It had a very masculine feel to it. She and John Jr. were immediately drawn to the painting above the fireplace. "John," she exclaimed, "Is that an original?

"Yes it is, darling. It's one of my favorites and now that I know you like it too, it will definitely be one of the things we'll keep. And we don't have to decide everything right now. In fact we can keep the apartment until we decide where we want to live."

Karen looked concerned as she turned to him, "Are you sure you want to give up your life here? How can you go from the excitement and glamour of New York City to a little Bed and Breakfast in Louisiana? How can I ask you to do that?"

John looked quietly at Karen for a moment and then walked over to the entertainment center and flipped a switch. Dylan Wyatt's mellow voice filled the air with one of his first hits, a ballad about a man that would give up every material thing he owned to spend a lifetime with the woman he loved. Taking Karen in his arms John began to dance, "Listen to the words, Karen. Having you in my life is all that matters, where ever we go from here will be home and being together and seeing as much of our family as possible is all that matters."

As they continued to look around the apartment, John Jr. found his dad's collection of coins, and they spent some time looking at some of the rare ones before John excused himself to dress more appropriately for the office. Karen liked the apartment, and was thinking about specific plans of how she would put a "woman's touch" in it as she rearranged the items on the hearth. She turned around at the sound of his footsteps on the stairs.

John had changed his clothes, and Karen could barely breathe as she watched him skip down the stairs. He had on dress slacks and a royal blue cotton shirt, topped with a sports jacket. The fragrance of his cologne made her knees buckle, and the sight of him aroused everything in her that she loved about him.

"Let's go to my office," he said. John Jr. was there to steady her, and she was grateful that he was because there was no telling what would happen if he wasn't.

As they entered John's office building, John greeted the front desk person and headed for the elevator. His secretary, Jill, was very excited to meet them, almost jumping up and down in her chair. "It's so good to meet you!" she exclaimed.

Karen noticed right away that she wore a wedding ring, there was no reason to be jealous but she found herself feeling protective.

The office also had leather furniture, and was decorated with fishing memorabilia. John Jr. looked around, finally feeling like he was learning to know his father.

John sat at his desk and started going through the papers left there for him. He signed a few letters, and dictated a memo to his secretary advising her that he would be unreachable for at least a week after Saturday. He grinned at Karen as he finished the memo. "I think they can do without me for awhile, maybe even indefinitely."

Karen smiled back. "Whatever you say, dear."

John's secretary knocked on the door. "Come in," called John.

"I have a little something for you," she announced with a big smile on her face. She held out a large beach bag full of items for a sunny vacation. "I thought since you two are going to the Bahamas, you would need some of these things."

"The Bahamas?" asked Karen in surprise. She excitedly started pulling out the items. A laminated map of the Bahamas, his and hers beach towels, sun glasses, tanning lotion, body lotion, flip flops, lip gloss, a make up bag, a shaving bag, water bottles, gum for the airplane ride, and post-card stamps.

"Are we really going?" she asked John as she gave him a big hug.

"Yes my dear, I hope you still like the sun like you used to. Jill, are the tickets here?"

"Yes," she replied. "You're flying out Sunday morning at 10:05, and your accommodations and dinner reservations are also confirmed."

Karen was exuberant, and she found herself hugging Jill and John Jr.

Gathering up some unfinished work John said, "Let's get freshened up and have a little dinner, then head back."

They went back to the apartment and Karen went into the dressing room adjoining the bathroom to change. John had told her that they would be going to dinner and she couldn't resist bringing the dress she had bought on an impulse when shopping with Lilly and Heather in New Orleans last summer. It was an awful extravagance but the dress really was incredible. Coming out of the dressing room Karen blushed slightly as John whistled. "Wow, you look fantastic."

Karen knew then that the dress had been worth every penny. It was aquamarine and silver lame' with a shawl collar that dipped low between her breasts. The hem barely skimmed her ankles and was slit on the right side midway up her thighs. Silver strappy sandals completed the look.

"There is something missing though," John said twirling her around and pretending to study her entire body. Reaching into his pocket he pulled out a burgundy Tiffany jewelry box. Opening the box he revealed a flawless one-carat sapphire necklace surrounded by baguettes of quarter caret diamonds, matching earrings and bracelet.

The set took Karen's breath away. "John, they match my ring. But you shouldn't have done that, they're so lovely."

John replied, "Not as lovely as you. Your beauty only enhances the sparkle in the diamonds."

John Jr. interrupted, "Sorry folks, the desk just called and said our car is waiting."

John had reserved a table at a very luxurious New York restaurant and enjoyed watching Karen and John Jr. exclaim over celebrities they recognized. All too soon the evening came to an end and the three returned to the airport. John turned the controls over to his private pilot on the way home and while John Jr. sat in front, John and Karen snuggled into the seats behind. Dozing off and on, the trip back to Louisiana passed rapidly. They were back at Mon Amie Famille by 11:00 pm.

Getting up early the next day, Karen hurried to the kitchen to start breakfast. Jennifer and Louise got there just a few minutes later, and they proved again that many hands make light work.

Karen was full of excitement. There was so much yet to do, and they only had today and tomorrow to finish. Checking the list on the computer, she felt relief as a lot more was done than she had thought.

Lilly came in and cheerfully sang, "Good Morning!"

"Lilly," Karen said, "You all must have worked like busy bees yesterday. Almost everything on the list is checked off. I'm impressed!"

"Yes, we did get a lot done," she replied as Heather burst into the kitchen in full-blown excitement. "Mom, guess what!" Jamie, Kelsi, and Melinda had talked her into trading in her pink Subaru. Karen went outside to find an Expedition, and it was a normal color too, blue. It was perfect for hauling around the things she did, and it was plain to see that Heather was relieved to be driving a nicer looking vehicle, even though she did have a special place in her heart for the pink Subaru.

They were still checking it out when John Sr. came out. "Dad, look at my new wheels." Heather was elated, and she drank in every bit of attention he gave her. He thoroughly checked out the vehicle and gave his approval.

The morning went fast with test drives and whispers of secrets. Lilly was suspicious by now, and was starting to ask questions. Heather had just returned from a trip to her apartment, and she was all dressed up. John Sr. gave a little whistle. "Wow, you really look nice, do you have a date tonight?"

"Where are you going?" asked Lilly.

"Just felt like dressing up today," she responded.

The plans for Lilly's surprise birthday party were almost complete. Karen was sure Lilly thought they had forgotten about her birthday with all of the wedding commotion, and the trip to New York, and Waldo confirmed this. He had told Lilly that they would just have a private celebration, and he would take her out to dinner with Jamie and Kelsi, and maybe whoever else was available. Jamie and Kelsi came every year for her birthday, and this was just how it would be this year.

John Sr. had secretly arranged for Dylan Wyatt and his band to play at the wedding reception, and had also talked him into arriving on Thursday afternoon to surprise Lilly for her birthday. Dylan had just turned fifty also, and he and Norma needed a little get-away. Dylan and John Sr. had become good friends on their fishing trips and he was looking forward to being a part of this happy occasion.

Karen had arranged everything with Heather, Jennifer, Melinda and Louise. They were all sworn to secrecy. Heather was hiding the party supplies at her place. They would make Lilly's favorite meal. Tom and Jennifer had filled all of the helium balloons and had them hiding in the shed. They were bright rainbow colors with a special bouquet of black.

"After all, you have to tease a little when someone turns fifty. I sure hope she keeps her sense of humor," said Karen as she arranged the "old" items in a black gift bag. Among the gifts were a hearing aid battery, a clapper key chain, a magnifying glass, hemorrhoid cream, support hose, and a bottle of "memory pills".

Waldo caught a glimpse of the limousine pulling into the driveway and took Lilly's arm, leading her out the front door. Karen was right behind, and John Sr. quickly joined them. Lilly's eyes were bigger than silver dollars. She held her breath as the door opened, and out stepped "the man." She had never seen him in person before and almost fainted when he gracefully helped his wife out of the car.

"Welcome," said Karen, "we are so privileged to have you here at Mon Amie Famille. Tom, will you please help with the luggage?" Mr. Johnson was right behind Tom, helping with the over flow. John Sr. shook hands with Dylan, and then Norma. He introduced Karen first as his fiancé (this was the first time she had heard herself referred to as a fiancé), and then Lilly.

"This must be the birthday lady," Dylan said in his beautiful deep voice, taking both of Lilly's small hands in his much larger ones.

Waldo had to support Lilly as she was about to faint, and still couldn't find words.

"How's the fishing around here?" Dylan asked.

"You will be staying in the Southern room," instructed Karen taking Norma's arm and looking worriedly at her friend who appeared to be in a catatonic state. "We will show you your room, and then you're welcome to join us for lemonade in the gazebo if you like."

"That would be very nice," answered Norma.

Lilly followed the group up the stairs and Karen whispered to her, "I've never seen you so speechless. Happy Birthday!"

Heather, John Jr., Melinda, Jennifer, Tom and the Johnson's quickly put the party plans in action. The kids were having dinner at Jennifer's mothers. Melinda and Jennifer had decided they were too young for the dinner they had planned. It wasn't long before the four couples were in the gazebo visiting, and they were able to work secretly in the kitchen.

Lilly dressed for dinner wearing a black dress that came just below the knee. The neck was low cut, which enabled her to show off the diamond and emerald pendant Waldo had given her earlier that day. She really was strikingly beautiful tonight, and she had a glow about her that Karen hadn't seen for quite some time.

Finally Mrs. Johnson came out to the gazebo. "Dinner is served," she announced. They all followed her to the house. Karen was watching Lilly's surprised expression as they entered the dining room. They had added the extra leaves to the table, and it was set perfectly with the fine china. A bouquet of red roses graced the middle of the table on the lace tablecloth, and each place setting had a rose print fabric napkin in a gold napkin ring. The delicate place cards directed them to their seats. Waldo pulled out the chair for Lilly and announced, "For the guest of honor."

Tom entered with a small cart. He was dressed elegantly with tails and a bow tie. He expertly made fresh Caesar salad with a theatrical flair to everyone's delight, and topped it with hand grated parmesan cheese. Then he served a fine white wine with a towel draped over his arm. Dylan and Norma were absolutely delighted and impressed, along with everyone else. Lilly still seemed to be still slightly in a state of shock, but finally was able to talk a bit.

Jennifer and Louise had the cart re-loaded with the main course, and it was served as soon as the salads were finished. They had baked the potatoes in the oven to perfection. Jed was an expert at grilling the steaks, and he also had a platter of salmon in case someone would prefer it rather than the Texas beef. They passed a large bowl of steamed vegetables, and hot garlic parmesan bread right out of the oven.

"Whose bread recipe is this?" asked Lilly.

"It's Mrs. Johnson's," answered Jennifer.

"It must have secret ingredients, it's wonderful, everything is wonderful!" said Lilly delightedly. Jennifer kept the water glasses full, and continued to make sure everything was perfect.

Dylan and Norma found they had a lot in common with Jamie and Kelsi. Both couples were in the thoroughbred horse breeding business.

Heather had brought David. He was no longer shy and could tell a good joke. Heather looked lovely in her lavender sweater with her amethyst necklace, and she seemed to glow a bit.

The men were planning fishing trips to Newport, Oregon, and Alaska. Dylan announced that he was writing a song about the fishing trip he and John had made, and he would get their opinion on it later.

Tom and Jennifer were obviously having fun putting on this dinner. Not only was it for friends they loved and respected, they loved working together and creating a masterpiece. They worked well with the Johnson's, who also were having the time of their lives. The four were looking forward to running the bed and breakfast themselves in the near future.

Coffee was served as Tom wheeled in the little cart again with the birthday cake. It was pink champagne, and Mrs. Johnson had decorated it with miniature roses and ribbons. They all sang Happy Birthday with Dylan's voice highlighting the occasion.

"This is the best birthday, ever!" said Lilly. She made her wish and blew out the candles.

When the cake was eaten, Jennifer gave Heather the signal that everything was ready. Heather announced that their presence was needed back in the gazebo again. The group trailed out the back door to find the back yard full of balloons and lights. Mr. Johnson had worked all day on the speakers mounted on the gazebo, and music played softly. The clear lights were strung along the rose garden paths, around the water fountains, and around the gazebo. It was incredibly beautiful and Lilly gasped in amazement at the sight before her eyes.

Jamie led Lilly out to the rose garden to find a new trellis hand crafted and designed by Jamie and Kelsi. "It's absolutely gorgeous, how in the world did you get it here?" she asked.

"Happy Birthday, Mom." Jamie said as he gave his mom a big hug.

"There's more," Heather said excitedly. The table in the gazebo was covered with gifts.

Lilly was seated in the wicker chair of honor, with helium balloons and ribbons tied to the back. Everyone laughed as she pulled out each "old' item from the big black bag.

"You're so kind, Karen. It won't be long before I can get even with you!" Lilly said. Karen was relieved that she seemed to take it well.

Karen also gave her a fifty year photo album with memories from their past. She had worked secretly for many months and Lilly never knew what she was working on. Many of the pictures had been sent from Lilly's sister and mom. Karen had also given her a wooden memory box of letters that Lilly had written her when she was at college. They had a lot of fun reading the letters and Waldo especially enjoyed the parts about him.

From Heather she received a beautiful china doll with a sweet face that looked so real it made you look twice.

John and Melinda gave her a music box with a bouquet of roses engraved on a wooden lid.

Dylan and Norma gave her an autographed CD.

Karen had received several UPS packages without Lilly's knowledge. Lilly opened the largest one to find an afghan that her sister had made; the colors were beautifully intertwined of variegated blues and purples. There was a gardenia bush full of blooms from David, and the Johnson's gave her a crystal dish with roses in the pattern.

Tom was still dressed in his tails, and came out to the gazebo with a big boom box under his arm. Lilly looked up in surprise, and then looked at Waldo's face to see what his reaction was. Then she turned to look at Karen, who shrugged her shoulders and held her hands out, palms up. "I have no idea what they're up to! Really!!!" she pleaded.

Tom laughed at them, and then announced; "Tonight for your entertainment, we present the best and most awesome group you've ever seen... The Eight Raisins!" They all came single file from the kitchen as the onlookers clapped enthusiastically. Melinda and Heather came first, then Tyler, Kristen, Jill, Alley, and finally Jennifer and David. They were all wearing large black plastic garbage bags with holes cut out for their arms and legs and the top draw strings around their necks. They all filed in front of the group in the gazebo and started lip-syncing and dancing to an old tune from the 70's. As the song ended, John Sr. yelled, "Play it again!" This time everyone got up and danced along. Waldo and Lilly danced like professionals.

"I'd forgotten that they won first prize once in a dance contest," John Sr. said to Karen, "they dance so well together!"

And they were quite the graceful dancers, not quite as limber as they were thirty years ago, but only Karen could tell that Waldo was supporting Lilly's bad knee.

It wasn't long before Jamie tapped his dad on the shoulder to have his turn with his mother. Waldo took Kelsi by the hand and swung her around as they danced together. Then Dylan was tapping Jamie on the shoulder to dance with the birthday lady. Lilly ended up dancing with just about everyone, including a group dance with the kids.

Tom and David were taking charge of the music, and experimenting with the new speakers. They had the radio on, and when one of his songs came on, Dylan picked up his guitar and started singing along with himself. Norma sat beside him with her arm on his shoulder as the other couples danced.

With the exception of her wedding and the day her son was born, Lilly thought this was the best day of her life. How blessed she was to have friends and family that would go to this kind of extravagance to make her birthday special. As her head rested on Waldo's shoulder, she thought back through the years to other birthdays. The birthday when she turned eighteen and her girlfriends had ripped off a toilet paper dispenser from their high school and gift wrapped it for her. This was no doubt masterminded by Karen. Then there was her twenty first, when her brother had bar hopped her and Karen all over town and made Lilly go into each tavern and buy beer for them. Some birthdays early in their marriage money had been tight but Waldo and Jamie had always managed to get her a really nice gift, especially on her forty second birthday when they bought her a Mother's ring. The ring was beautifully crafted from Black Hills Gold with her emerald birthstone and Waldo's diamond birthstone on the outside and Jamie's garnet in the middle. Then there was her forty fourth birthday. Her party that year was held in her dad's hospital room and early the next morning he passed away. It was as if he was waiting for her special day to be over before he went on, not wanting to mar her birthday with everlasting sadness. Now here she was on her fiftieth birthday and life just seemed to be getting better. She was in the arms of the man she loved, surrounded by her family and closest friends.

Raising her head and looking around Lilly's eyes met Karen's and they smiled at each other for a moment before Lilly snuggled her head once again under Waldo's chin.

CHAPTER 10

Karen and John woke up to their last day of being single. They had crashed in the tent with the kids after dancing most of the night away. They took turns in the shower, and John watched as Karen laid out some of the items she would be packing for the honeymoon.

"You can't see me tomorrow morning you know, how are we going to handle that?" she asked with a sneaky little smile.

"I guess I'll just have to hang out with the guys then," he responded.

"That's good because I plan on spending the morning with Lilly. We have to make ourselves beautiful you know."

John smiled and answered, "That should take about 2 minutes, my love."

Kristen came in, looking sleepy and rather upset. "Grandma, Tyler got sick all over the tent!" she wailed.

John ran out to the tent and scooped up Tyler, while Karen took Kristen in her arms for a comforting hug. "Let's go find your mom," she said.

John handed Tyler to her and said, "I guess it's time I had my share of these things. It's really not all that bad. You go ahead and take him to his mom and I'll clean this up."

Karen looked at John with love in her eyes. She hadn't seen this side of him before, and frankly she liked what she was seeing. Karen took Tyler and Kristen to their parent's room. Melinda thought it was probably just too many marshmallows the night before and tucked Tyler into the little rollaway bed.

Karen went to the kitchen to see about breakfast and found everyone already there eating the biscuits and gravy that Dylan had requested the night before. Just as she was settling in to have a bite and listen to Waldo and Dylan tell their slightly "tall tale" fish stories a car pulled in the drive and Engelbert and Angie got out. They had arrived late the night before and not wanting to disturb anyone they had stayed at the Airport Hilton. Lilly told them what nonsense that was; they could have come at any time, and then went on to tell them about the lovely room they had prepared.

This was the latest restored room at the house and Karen and Lilly called it the Antebellum Room as it was decorated entirely in antique furniture the two had discovered at an estate sale at one of the oldest mansions in Louisiana. The furniture was priceless and the locals had told them it was nothing short of a miracle that those "Damn Yankees" hadn't destroyed it during the Civil War. Not only was the furniture amazing, Lilly and Karen had gone all out to decorate with hand made quilts, embroidered laced edged table runners, hand woven rugs, and various items of interest. The pitcher and bowl set that was found in Karen's Grandparent's farmhouse in Ohio sat on the stand under the window, and the pictures on the walls were all found at antique stores. They were mostly of children and Karen's favorite was one with whispering and giggling little girls.

Lilly and Karen took Angie upstairs to see the suite, leaving the bags for Jed to bring up later. Engelbert was drawn to the other fishermen like a magnet. Having a few fish stories of his own to tell he was soon entertaining the group with tales of fishing in the wild waters of Alaska, the land of the midnight sun.

When the women returned to the kitchen the men were practically foaming at the mouth at the prospect of dipping their lines in the water.

Taking pity on them and looking forward to a peaceful day to complete the wedding plans, Lilly suggested they take a little fishing trip just across the river. The men were so excited they jumped from the table and had their gear gathered up in no time. Melinda didn't think they should try to take Tyler and Waldo wasn't too keen on the possibility someone would get sick in the B&B Van.

So off they went—two fathers, two sons, a professional fisherman and a country music super-star. You would have thought they had known each other all their lives the way they were chattering and carrying on.

Norma was helping Louise clean the kitchen and having more fun than she had in ages. Lilly apologized for expecting her to work on her vacation and she told them how much she was enjoying this getaway and thanked them for allowing her and Dylan to be a part of their family for a few days.

Jed had taken Engelbert and Angie's bags upstairs and then joined Tom in the garden to make sure the grounds were perfect for tomorrow's reception.

Heather had arrived in her new car and went to find Kelsi to go hunting for the wild flowers she needed for the arrangements. Knocking on the door, Heather was surprised to find Kelsi looking a little peaked, "Are you OK? Do you think you're getting the flu? Maybe it wasn't the marshmallows? "

Kelsi smiled wanly, "No I'll be OK. I just have a hard time in the mornings."

Heather's eyes grew big, "Are you…"

Kelsi grinned and again assured her that she was OK. "Now let's get going. Is Melinda going with us, how is Tyler?"

When they got to the Rose room they found Melinda ready and Tyler much improved and irritated because the men had went fishing without him. Trying to appease him Melinda asked if both kids could come on the flower hunt with them. "Of course," said Kelsi, "the more the merrier. I'll bet these two are first-rate flower finders. Now let's get before this Louisiana sun bakes all the good ones."

Angie had joined Norma and Louise and they were starting the salads and veggie trays for the reception, so seeing everything was under control, Karen and Lilly snuck off to Karen's bungalow to begin their own preparations.

It had been a whirlwind week and the two hadn't really had a chance to visit. Getting out the manicure set they chose the colors, mauve and rose tones, they wanted for their nails and decided to go all out and do their toes as well.

Karen filled Lilly in on New York, ground zero, John's honeymoon plans and the movie stars they had seen at dinner.

Lilly told Karen about the Lodge in Alaska and the dreams Waldo had for that business and what Jamie had said about opening a Dude Ranch on their property in Washington.

"Wow, Lilly, we're going to be a chain! But doesn't it seem like we're going too fast? Maybe we had just gotten used to the slower pace in the South, and all of a sudden here we are heading at breakneck speed towards different lives. You're moving to Alaska, I'm going "God Knows Where" with John, but what's happening to us? You and me?"

Lilly was quick to reassure her friend, "Nothing's happening to us! We're still you and me and no matter where we go we'll always be connected. Besides, we'll always have Mon Amie Famille and when our husbands drive us crazy we can come here and get each other back on track."

A strange silence struck the bungalow and Karen's eyes met Lilly's. They were unsure if the sick feeling in their stomachs was because of the sudden changes in their lives, the expectation of going their separate ways, or maybe it was the marshmallows. Trying to shake it off Karen asked Lilly if she wanted to get something to drink and they returned to the kitchen, hoping their maudlin moods would lift.

They heard a car pull in the drive as they walked to the house, "Oh, that must be Matthew and Annie, I can't wait to see them and little Maggie", Karen exclaimed. Coming around the side to the driveway they saw it was the company they were expecting but were greeted with somber faces.

"What's going on, Matthew? Why the long face? Annie, what is it?" Lilly's voice was beginning to sound panicked.

Putting his arm around Lilly and drawing Karen into his embrace also, Matthew spoke, "Have you had the TV or radio on? We just came through a roadblock just outside of New Orleans. Something happened to the Arkansas River Bridge. The authorities don't know if it was terrorism or just what happened, but they do know that the bridge has collapsed and at least ten vehicles went in the water."

Gasping, Lilly pulled away, "No, no you're not going to tell me that Waldo and Jamie were involved. No, I won't accept that. They left too long ago; they would be well on the other side. Karen, you don't..."

Karen grabbed her friend, "Calm down Lilly, you'll make yourself sick. We don't know anything yet."

Still gasping for breath, Lilly clung to Karen, "But Karen, if Waldo and Jamie are gone then so are John and John Jr. Oh, my goodness Engelbert and Dylan were with them. Where are Angie and Norma?"

Once more Karen told her friend to calm down and turned to Matthew for reassurance. Panic was thick in the air and they desperately needed his calming demeanor. "OK, Matthew, exactly what happened?"

Matthew knew the reality of the situation and the adrenalin was feeding his ability to function. "All I know is there was an explosion, fishermen saw about ten vehicles go in the water, and I'm sorry Karen and Lilly, but one of them was the B&B van. Trooper Larry Kane had just seen your guys filling up at the station on the way to town and knew they were going fishing. He was on his way out here to tell you all when we came through the roadblock. They're all over the place looking for survivors and I volunteered to tell you so he wouldn't have to leave the scene. Now you two, don't give up, the van was empty when they found it."

Karen spoke, "All six of them are missing?"

Matthew looked startled, "Six, don't tell me Tyler was with them?"

"No, Dylan Wyatt!" Karen answered.

"Dylan Wyatt, you mean that guy that plays guitar and sings the corny country music?"

"The one and only. He's a friend of John's and he and his wife came for Lilly's birthday and the wedding. We better find Angie and Norma and tell them."

Matthew asked Karen to help Annie and Maggie get settled so he could set up his computer database in the office and monitor the rescue efforts. He felt he could gain more information there, and this was reassurance to both Lilly and Karen because they knew without a doubt that he had the knowledge and tools to get anything he wanted from his computer.

Going straight to the kitchen, this room that was central to the Mon Amie Famille, Karen tried to compose herself.

Norma could tell immediately that something was wrong. Holding her hand up Karen asked for silence. "Please, we'll tell you what's happened in just a moment. But first, Louise would you please ask Angie to come down? I don't want to have to repeat this too many times." Going to the back door Karen called to Tom, "Do you know which direction the girls went?" As he nodded, she continued, "Please find them as quickly as you can, we need a family meeting immediately."

While they waited for everyone to gather Lilly was pacing by the door, "I've got to go, Karen. You don't understand my husband and son need me. I've got to go to them."

Trying her best to retain her composure Karen replied, "You've got exactly the same people out there that I do, Lilly. I know what you're feeling but even if we went out there the authorities wouldn't let us anywhere near the river. Matthew will keep us updated. If there's anything we can do Matthew will tell us."

Turning away from her friend Karen saw the look on Norma's face. "Hey you two, what's happened?"

"Oh Norma, there's been an accident."

"Karen, it wasn't an accident" Lilly interrupted.

"OK, so we don't know what it was, but our men are missing. The important things are to stay calm and pray."

Tom arrived back with Heather, Melinda, Kelsi and the kids, just as Angie and Louise returned. Jed had also come in from the garden to find out what was going on. Karen asked Matthew to come and repeat to the group what had happened. Norma was not only concerned for her husband's safety but also worried that the scene could be turned into a media circus and further hamper rescue attempts.

Matthew reassured her that no one knew Dylan Wyatt was in the van. Tyler and Kristen clung to their mother not completely understanding what had happened, they only knew their father and grandfather were in trouble. Wanting to protect them as much as possible, and not being able to, Karen grieved for their pain.

Throughout the rest of the day the air was heavy, not only with the humid Louisiana heat, but also with the pain of the friends and family gathered in the country kitchen. They waited, somewhat impatiently, for Matthew's reports.

Lilly still insisted periodically that she had to go to the river. Somehow she felt she could single-handedly rescue her husband and only child.

Kelsi continued to work on the flowers to keep her hands busy and her mind away from reality and wouldn't allow herself the luxury of going down the same panic road her mother-in-law was on.

CHAPTER 11

No one in the van was prepared for the shock of finding themselves upside down in the muddy river. It was only a matter of seconds between the explosion and the crash into the water below. John Jr.'s training in the police department kept his senses intact and thanks to Waldo's foresight and unwillingness to leave his wife unprepared, the vehicle was equipped with an emergency kit containing flashlights and rope.

The men released their seat belts and Jamie grabbed the emergency kit as John Sr. and Dylan kicked out the back door. Raising to the surface all six men escaped unharmed. Swimming to the shore they realized there were other vehicles in the water and without a second thought they returned to the water.

The first vehicle they found was an older model Volkswagen. The man behind the wheel was unconscious, there was a woman screaming in the passenger seat and a baby crying in the back. The water entering the car was almost over the baby's face. Taking a chance and deciding glass cuts may be better than drowning, Jamie smashed in the back window with the flashlight. Entering the car John Jr. used his knife and cut the baby free. After handing him out to Engelbert he swiftly moved forward and did the same with the woman and man. Waldo and John Sr. carried the man and Dylan supported the woman as the team rose to the surface. Depositing the family on the rocky shore of the river, the rescuers paused briefly for air, and then returned to their efforts leaving Engelbert to care for the baby and the parent's in the capable hands of Dylan.

Jamie and John Jr. had already located another vehicle. Time was of the essence as water was flooding into a Chevy pickup. The water pressure was too great to break a window this time. Using sign language, John Jr. was able to instruct the occupants to roll down the window. As soon as it was cracked they forced it down just as Waldo and John Sr. arrived and relieved their sons. John Jr. and Jamie returned to the surface for air and their father's continued the rescue. This time they delivered the couple from the pickup to the shore unconscious. John Sr. and Waldo started CPR procedures and soon had them breathing again.

They responded to the yells of paramedics that were making their way over and down the rocky terrain, and would eventually be able to take over the care of the victims. The men viewed the activity on the other side of the river as emergency teams were arriving, scanning the river area for signs of life. But at this point they were still the best hope that any survivor had. The professionals were still too far away and without a word the fathers and their sons returned to the water.

Jennifer had heard the news, but had no idea what had been happening at the B&B. She arrived planning to help with the last wedding preparations, but stopped short as she entered the kitchen full of crying and praying women. She had never in her life experienced anything more dramatic than her pregnancy.

Jed appeared to deliver the latest report. There were only three survivors found so far and a dive team had just arrived at the site. Matthew now had direct e-mail connections with his friend and officer Larry Kane at the sight.

Their hearts sank with each moment that passed without news that their men had been rescued. Karen seemed to be in a bit of a daze. Jennifer pondered the scene for a few moments; she had never seen them like this before. Everything she had learned from Lilly and Karen automatically kicked in as she started to make coffee. Many times she had watched the two women climb out on top of their challenges in life.

They would determine the facts of the situation, and then work with what they had whether it was a piece of fabric or a creative design, or some muscle and determination. She knew there weren't any words that she could say to make things better as she put all of her effort into making the strong black Louisiana coffee.

Kelsi was finally able to calm Lilly a bit, knowing within herself that she had a gift that would live on. "You know we'd both be there if there was anything at all that we could do, but right now our prayers are the best tool we have, and we have first hand information right here."

Angie and Norma didn't really know each other very well, but they sat close together as they sipped their coffee and fought back the tears and fear. Little did they know that the bonds being built in the heart of the B & B would change their lives.

Melinda and Heather didn't know what to do with Karen, but they knew from experience that time would bring her around. Melinda subconsciously held her hand on her stomach, knowing that her children were a part of the strong man she loved. She had always been aware of the dangers of his career, knowing that tragedy was able to strike at any time, but they had both decided at the beginning that they wouldn't live their lives in fear of the unknown. John Jr. had given her love and a life that she wouldn't trade for anything, and she was confident that he was able to conquer anything. He had always come through before.

Heather was feeling angry that God would even think about taking away her brother, and the father figure that had just come into her life. These were the two people in her life that seemed to be the glue to hold her together, and aunt Lilly was such a mess, never in her life had she seen her like this. As she looked around the room, her eye caught Kelsi's and she realized that everyone there was fearful of losing the people they loved.

Jed came back from the office exuberant this time, "They've spotted some survivors on the South side of the river," he announced. "Actually there appear to be at least a dozen people on the rocks over there. Which is strange since the bridge girder broke at least a ¼ of a mile in and the rescuers haven't gotten that far yet."

Lilly rose from the chair at the table where she had been frozen in time for the last several hours. "It's them. I know it's them. Karen, how do you feel? Remember how sick we both felt earlier today, I've been thinking, that had to have been when it happened. But since then I've felt fine. If our boy's were gone we would feel it. Don't you think? Kelsi, remember when Jamie got stepped on by a horse and almost lost a finger? I was waiting by the phone when you called from the hospital. I knew he was in trouble."

Karen smiled, "You're right Lilly, remember when they were just little boys and John Jr. dropped a hammer on Jamie while they were building a tree house? We were out the back door and running toward them before he even started bleeding. They are OK. And if Jamie and John are OK then so are Waldo and John Sr. and so are Dylan and Engelbert, because those four would never give up on a friend."

The group was startled out of their reverie as the phone rang. Karen and Lilly grabbed each other's hand and stared at the ringing phone. Norma was sitting closest and with trembling hands she picked up the receiver. "Hello" she said.

The voice on the other end was one she knew well, "Hey darlin' is everyone there OK?" Norma almost dropped the phone at the sound of her husband's voice, and spoke to the group suddenly huddled around her; "Shh, it's Dylan," then went back to the phone. "Are we OK? What about ya'll? What's going on?" In the background she could here Waldo asking to speak to Lilly, the love of his life, as he always called her.

Dylan spoke again, "Darlin', we're all just fine. These two young men and their dad's have been saving lives right and left and ol' Engelbert here has a baby tucked up into his coat and even I've been helping a little. I would have called you sooner, but couldn't take the time if you know what I mean. But now that the real rescuers have come we're going to try to get out of here. Just tell everyone that we're all OK and we'll get back as soon as we can."

Replacing the receiver, Norma turned to the group, "They're all OK. It seems they've been rescuing people all day and just now got a chance to call."

Matthew burst into the room, "They've been found. Larry just sent a message that all six of them have been found on the south shore."

Karen spoke up, "We know, honey, Dylan just called Norma, but would you find out if we should send someone to get them?"

Lilly piped up, "I'll go. I'll go."

Karen tried to calm her friend again, "Settle down Lilly. We know you want to go but I was thinking more of sending Tom in Heather's car, something big enough to bring them all home at once."

Lilly argued back, "Oh no, we're not sending one more man away from this house. I couldn't stand to go through that again."

Matthew spoke up, "Let me find out what I can and then I'll take Lilly in Heather's SUV, if that's OK with you Heather?"

"Sure, just bring them all back please," She replied.

Karen's heart was full as her fear lightened. Not only were they all safe, but also her love for John was stronger than she could describe or comprehend. It was okay with her that Lilly was the one to go with Matthew to pick up the men. It just seemed like the additional three hour wait was a lifetime, and she didn't want to waste a minute of her remaining lifetime without him. She started pacing back and forth by the front door, listening and watching intently for them.

It had been about an hour after they heard their men were safe before Larry had let Matthew know that the guys had been airlifted by helicopter across the river and could be picked up on the North shore. Matthew practically had to wrestle the keys away from Lilly. He would have let her drive but her driving scared him under normal circumstances and he wasn't about to ride with her now.

Arriving at the scene, Lilly was out of the SUV and running toward her husband and son before it had come to a complete stop. Grabbing them both together she hugged them like she would never let go. Finally pulling away she extended her happiness with hugs to John Sr. and Jr. and Engelbert and then finally planted a huge kiss on Dylan.

"Let's get you guys home so you can get out of those wet clothes," she said.

"And get some food in us too, Mom. I'm starved," said Jamie.

Dylan chimed in, "What have ya'll been cooking for us today, Lilly?"

"Dylan, Jamie, I'm ashamed to say I haven't been cooking. I haven't been able to concentrate on much today. But I'm sure we can find something for you to eat," she said as she snuggled into the back seat under the blanket with Waldo.

When the SUV pulled down the drive the women waiting at the Inn could hear the men singing "Amazing Grace."

"Yes, yes," said Karen softly. She knew that some people had died in today's tragedy, and her heart went out to the unknown people that had lost loved ones. As the doors opened, she fell into John Sr.'s arms and her tears rolled down her cheeks as she pulled her son into her grip also. There were so many people hugging and weeping, it was quite a site.

They returned to the kitchen to find a small buffet style feast. Louise and Jennifer knew that they would all be hungry and would want to visit before they settled down. They all gathered at the dining room table. The pause was awesome as their overflowing thankful hearts joined Waldo's voice in giving thanks.

When their hunger was satisfied and with a little encouragement the men started telling their stories.

Angie's heart was full of love as Dylan described how Engelbert had taken charge of the tiny baby in the first car. After they arrived at the shore he had stripped the baby down, removing all of his wet clothes. Then ripping the lining out of his expensive raincoat he had fashioned a diaper and blanket for the baby, and then placed him inside his own coat keeping him warm next to his heart.

Matthew had discovered that the authorities suspected terrorism. Why they would pick a bridge in Louisiana was a mystery. There was also talk that it could be a copycat bombing.

The exhausted extended family finally retired to their rooms.

Karen led John to her bungalow as she adamantly informed him of her plan. "There's no way I'm letting you out of my sight ever again. I don't care about my ole beliefs I'm going to be next to you tonight."

"Ok, but tomorrow night is still our night. We've come too far to change that now," he replied. It was only minutes before he lay sleeping in her bed. Karen snuggled in close and ran her fingers through his hair, listening to his heartbeat until she fell asleep.

Jamie had been as exuberant as the rest of the men while sitting around the table revealing the events of the day, but as soon as he was alone with Kelsi he grew unusually quiet and Kelsi could practically see a dark cloud over his head. When she came out of the bathroom she found him standing on the balcony staring out at the dark river. Coming up behind him and encircling his waist with her arms she said, "Come on to bed, honey. You're exhausted."

A strangled sob escaped from Jamie's chest, "There are still people down there, Kelsi. There are still children down there. They shouldn't have made us come back; they should have left us out there to keep trying. At least John and I could have stayed. We were needed there."

Kelsi looked deeply into the eyes of this man that she had loved since she was fourteen. It was exactly this stubborn determination that had attracted her to him in the first place. Jamie never left a job half done and it irritated him to no end when circumstances didn't allow him his own way. She felt this was the time to share the secret she had been carrying since leaving home and chose her words carefully. "You did your best, Jamie; it was time to turn it over to the professionals. And you all were exhausted. To keep going back in the water was endangering all of you. And besides, honey, there is a baby right here that needs you too." With that she turned him around and placed his palms on her flat tummy.

He smiled slowly, "Really? Did you tell Mom?"

"Nope, I'm going to let you do that. Besides, she had already gone through the ceiling several times today, I didn't think she could handle anything else. Now let's get to bed, tomorrow's going to be quite a day."

Lilly lay in the dark bedroom and listened to Waldo's soft snoring and once again thanked God for bringing him back to her. It really was time for the two of them to be together permanently. He had been so understanding of her need to start this business with Karen and now it was time to give herself back to him totally and forever. Karen was going to be OK now that she had John; and Jamie had Kelsi. Snuggling deep into the down comforter Lilly smiled. God was in his heaven and all was right with her world.

CHAPTER 12

Karen woke up in the comfort of John's arms. She really didn't want to move, but thinking about the day before her and feeling very hungry, she quietly slid out of the bed leaving him to sleep.

In the kitchen she found Jennifer making waffles and Lilly was sharing some of her secrets with her as they added cinnamon and lemon juice to the batter. They were full of excitement and acting rather silly after the relief from the events of the previous day.

Heather appeared with her large fabric bag filled with beauty supplies, prepared to work her magic on her already beautiful mother.

"Are you ready to start Mom? What about you Aunt Lilly, are you going to let me do your hair too?"

"I don't know honey, there's not much you can do to help this hair. But you can try if you want."

Tyler and Kristen came bursting in clamoring for breakfast, followed by their parents and Jamie and Kelsi. The room was getting crowded and Karen asked Lilly if she wanted to go sit in the hot tub with her before getting their hair done and maybe John would be out of their room by the time they got out.

Lilly suggested that she send Waldo to check on John, "But don't even think about leaving these grounds until time for the wedding. You two aren't going anywhere today. And don't even think about fishing from the shore of the river down here. I don't think my heart could take anymore." Planting a quick kiss on Lilly's cheek Waldo promised they would be good.

The events of the previous day could not be forgotten, but the mood lightened as Lilly and Karen reviewed the highlights. Because of who they were, the men had survived and also saved lives that would have otherwise been lost.

"I can't wait until your mom and sister get here," said Karen. "If there's one person in the world that understands the importance of family, it's your mother. You know, it feels like we're the center and beginning of this family, but really we're just the next generation repeating the same thing, and before you know it our children will be in our places repeating the pattern again. I bet your mother felt the same way when she was our age."

Karen stopped short to check the expression on Lilly's face and wished she had chosen her words a little more carefully. "I know you've always felt bad about not being able to have any more children, Lilly."

Lilly smiled at her friend, "Oh, but look at the one I did have."

Karen spoke again, "I wonder how many children John and I would have had together if we had married before he went to Vietnam? I may have given him a son, but I regret not being able to give him a baby."

"Karen, don't beat your self up over this again. You did what you had to do at the time. And I'm sure you'll have more grandchildren."

Karen answered, "Oh, I do think Heather will have kids. At least I hope she will, she deserves to have a family and be happy but I know it's going to be hard for her to trust again. I like David though. Maybe that will work out."

The two grew quiet for a moment, contemplating their lives and the directions they had turned. They had come a long way from the two young girls who met in the little church in Washington State to the two strong, independent women they were today. Together they had experienced love, the birth of their children, the loss of Karen's first husband and parents and the death of Lilly's father.

Finally Karen broke the silence, "Here we are on my wedding day and we're still trying to solve the problems of the world. Today is going to be filled with happiness and laughter. I won't allow any sadness today. OK, Lilly? Promise me you won't cry?"

"I promise, Karen, no tears today. Well, how about a few tears of happiness?"

"OK, maybe just a few. But there probably will be more than a few laughs, we're doing this without a rehearsal remember?"

The missed rehearsal for the ceremony wasn't important at this point, and Karen really wasn't concerned. "What happens, happens," she said. "Pastor Jim will be able to handle the ceremony, and Jennifer is going to coordinate everything else. I'm really not worried, I just want to relax and have a good time."

"I agree," said Lilly. "We better get out of here now so that Heather can get started on your hair and I can finish up the cake decorations."

Karen returned to an empty bungalow. Remembering her vow to never let him out of her sight again she brushed off the empty feeling, knowing that John was well taken care of. She was relaxed after her long soak in the hot tub, and took her time in the shower. As she slipped into her robe she could hear Heather setting up beauty shop in her little kitchenette. Karen took the cover from her wedding dress and hung it out so that she could see it. It seemed to be even more beautiful than she had remembered, and she knew for sure that the sapphire blue really was the right color. Mademoiselle Jane had added little blue pearls to the tiny peach roses on the dress to match the color in the other dresses.

Going into the kitchenette she remarked to Heather, "Work your magic, dear. Make me a beautiful bride."

Heather surveyed her mother quietly, "Mom there's not a thing I can do to enhance your beauty. We'll just make you a little more presentable for company. OK? You already do look like a blushing bride," she said with a sad note in her voice.

Karen moved swiftly to her side and taking her daughter in her arms she said, "What's wrong, Heather?"

"Nothing Mom," Heather answered brushing a tear away, "I'm just so darn happy for you. After everything you've been through you're finally marrying the man you should have married over thirty years ago, instead of my dad."

"Heather, don't ever think for a moment that I regret marrying your dad. After all, look what I got out of that relationship. I never could have hoped for a sweeter, kinder child than my darling little girl. And you're made up of all the best your dad had to offer. So even though John may have been the true love of my life, the way things worked out were part of a much bigger design than any of us could imagine. So dry your tears. There will only be happiness today."

Lilly burst into the room, her words tumbling out. "The airport limo just arrived. My family is here and John's brother Dan hitched a ride with them from the airport. What shall I do with them Karen? Mama's already complaining!"

"Oh just tell her to take a walk Lilly," Karen said laughingly.

"Is that anything like telling her to take a hike?" Asked Heather.

Karen and Lilly burst into laughter at the thought of Lilly telling her still active 84-year-old mother to "Take a Hike."

"I know, let's put Mama to work in the kitchen and give LaWanda a break. Maybe she and Robere' will want to get away for a few hours by themselves. I'll even let them take my VW. OK, thanks Karen." Lilly flew out of the room as quickly as she had come in, giving Heather only a second to instruct her to be back in an hour for her turn.

Heather looked at her mom and remarked, "Is she going to be OK, Mom?"

"Of course, she'll be fine. Lilly does her best under pressure, but most people don't see it, they only see the end result. Now let's get going on this hair and makeup."

Heather's artistic hairdressing abilities were amazing. Peach colored satin ribbon was intertwined through the braids and twisted into a French knot held in place by antique combs adorned with tiny peach roses and blue pearls.

They just finished putting the base makeup on when Lilly returned. "Ok, so what do you want to do with me Heather?"

Heather replied soothingly, "I know just the perfect thing."

As Heather worked her magic, they asked Lilly about her mother and her family. "Yes, she's calmed down now. Actually Jed volunteered to take her for a walk, and since she knew him it worked out great. Lawanda and Robere' were ecstatic to get away after their long trip with her, and I think they finally solved their little fight about who was going to drive."

To Lilly's amazement she found a smaller version of the braids and ribbons when she looked in the mirror. "I never knew I could do anything like this with my hair!" she exclaimed. "How do you do it?"

Lilly was still admiring her reflection in the mirror when Jennifer came in with sandwiches. "You two need to eat. I know you only nibbled at breakfast."

Lilly answered, "We were saving our appetites for the reception. Those ribs Jed and Tom are barbecuing smell wonderful."

Jennifer being a typical southern girl remarked, "Now you know it isn't seemly for a lady to stuff herself in front of people. You eat a little now and then you will be too full to do any more than just nibble at the reception. That's the way it's supposed to be."

Karen and Lilly looked at each other and burst into laughter. "Thanks Jennifer, but we're from Washington. We'll eat a little now and a lot later, OK?"

Jennifer went away grumbling something about manners and proper etiquette. Karen and Lilly quickly devoured the avocado, bacon and tomato wrapped in spinach flour tortillas.

"I do feel better now," Karen remarked, "I think I have a few butterfly's hatching in my tummy, but they've calmed down a little."

Lilly glanced in the mirror again as she replied, "Well it's certainly worth it all to have my hair look like this. Heather, where have you been all my life? Talk about hiding your light under a bushel! Is there anything artistic you can't do?" Heather blushed and busied herself putting her beauty supplies away.

They could hear the band setting up in the gazebo and Dylan was warming up on his guitar.

"Did you know that Dylan asked Angie to sing with him today?" Lilly asked Karen.

"No, I didn't. I knew that she could sing though. Wasn't she a singer in the Golden Nugget saloon in Alaska when Engelbert met her?"

"She sure was, and what a knockout too. The first time Waldo saw her with all that blond hair and those beautiful brown eyes I thought I was going to have to peel his tongue off the floor. It's a good thing that she is as sweet as she is pretty, otherwise we would have had to kill her long ago," Lilly said jokingly. They all knew that Angie was totally devoted to Engelbert and had given up a budding singing career to follow him around the globe on fishing trips.

The rose room was crowded with the hustle and bustle of getting ready. Melinda was trying to get Tyler dressed, Kristin's hair braided, and the men organized all at the same time. Fortunately for Dan and John Jr., John Sr. already knew how to put on the cummerbunds. Melinda helped them with their collars and then stood back to view the sight. "You four are the handsomest men I've ever seen!" she exclaimed.

There was a knock on the door and Melinda let in the photographer. The mood was light, and they all turned into clowns showing off with poses of masculinity and goofiness. It was obvious that Dan was going to be a fun uncle, he already had Tyler and Kristen wrapped around his little finger. Although he lived a very different life than his brother, he fit into the group like a glove.

The photographer wanted to take some outdoor shots, and suggested they all gather by the river.

"You all better stay away from the river!" instructed Melinda in a firm tone. "If anything happens you'll have Lilly and Karen to answer to! And don't let Tyler get dirty."

John Jr. gave her and Kristen a quick kiss, "We'll be fine and you two beautiful ladies don't need to worry."

Tyler was pleased as punch when Uncle Dan popped him up on his shoulders and jogged down the stairs. There was no way he was going to get left behind again like yesterday.

Melinda finished getting Kristen and herself ready and then they went to find Grandma. They found Karen and Lilly in Karen's bungalow finishing the pedicures that had gotten cut short the day before. Heather had gone to help Kelsi put the finishing touches on the flowers. Karen was bubbling with excitement and trepidation, but still seemed to be slightly calmer than Lilly.

"Hey, you two, can we join you for a little while?" Melinda asked.

"Of course you can, honey. Look at you Kristen. You're going to be just as pretty as your Mama," Lilly said pulling Kristen onto her lap. "Where are your brother and daddy and grandpa?"

Kristen answered innocently, "They went to the river."

Lilly almost dumped the little girl on the floor in her haste to get up. "The river! What are they doing at the river? Are Waldo and Jamie with them?"

Melinda laughed, "Calm down Aunt Lilly. The photographer wanted some outdoor pictures of the three generations. Dan is with them. The last time I heard Waldo and Jamie were in the garage checking out what's left of their fishing gear after the accident."

"Well that's bad enough. I can't handle any talk about rivers, or water, or fishing, or boating right now. Let's just get through this day." And off Lilly went to find her husband and son and hustle them into getting ready.

Lilly returned to the bungalow after getting her men in order, and everyone was busy finding the right shoes and applying the finishing touches.

Karen was feeling a bit more nervous, there was only half an hour before they would leave for the church, and even though everything seemed to be perfect she looked around to find something else to do.

Angie entered the room, giving Lilly a big hug. They had been friends for many years, and Angie knew how important this day was to Lilly.

Karen turned her attention to Angie, who took a moment to admire the sapphire creations. "You told me about the dresses, but I never imagined this! And your hair, where did you have it done?" she exclaimed.

The phone rang and Karen picked it up to find John's deep voice at the other end. Her heart melted, her knees became weak, and she wanted to run out to meet him.

"I know I'm not supposed to see you yet, but is it okay if I talk to you?" he begged.

"Oh yes," Karen said.

All Lilly could hear Karen saying was "Oh yes, oh yes, oh yes…"

As soon as she hung up, Lilly asked, "Is everything okay? Or were you making a shampoo commercial?" Everyone laughed and Karen blushed.

"I can't wait to see him in a tux," swooned Karen. "John Jr. had to catch me when I first saw him dressed for work, so maybe we should make sure I have something to hold onto this time."

"Do you have something borrowed?" Angie asked. She pulled out a hankie with blue tatted lace around it. "This was my great grandmother's, and it went down the isle with her, my mother, with me, and also Lilly. Now it's your turn Karen. And may this beautiful hankie bring as much happiness to you as it has to the brides that have carried it before you."

Karen took the hankie and examined the delicate lace edging. "It's just beautiful, and I'd be honored to carry it," she said with a tear in her eye as she hugged her friend.

"Now, now," said Lilly, "we're not going to start crying now. I've made it this far and we have to keep it together. Besides, I don't think this mascara is waterproof. And don't forget to put on your garter."

With help from Angie and Lilly, Karen slid the white lace garter up her slender thigh.

"Just think, when this thing comes off, it's going to be John taking it off," She remarked.

Lilly answered with a sly look in her eye, "That won't be all he'll be taking off."

"Oh no, I don't think he'll have to take it off. I will probably rip it all off and throw myself at him as soon as we're alone. So if we disappear during the reception, don't go looking for us!" Karen replied in a silly sexy voice.

Heather popped in just then and announced that David was here and she was going to go ahead and go to the church with him and Jamie and Kelsi.

"OK, darling, we'll be along soon," her mother replied and they began gathering up a few essentials in case they needed to touch up hair and makeup before the ceremony.

After Lilly had been assured that John had already left for the church, she and Angie ushered Karen out. John had left Tom instructions to drive the ladies to the church in his rental Cadillac, but when he went to start it they discovered the battery was dead. Everyone had already left for the church and with the B&B van out of commission Karen, Lilly and Angie stood staring at each other in panic for a moment before Lilly took charge.

"OK, there's nothing left to do, we'll have to take my Volkswagen," she instructed.

Angie answered, "That will work. You two go ahead and then send Engelbert back for Tom and me."

"But Angie, you're singing with Dylan before the ceremony. I'm not taking a chance on you missing an opportunity like that," Karen said.

Lilly had other ideas. "Come on, we've done it before and we'll do it again. All of us into the VW. And I'm driving." So putting Angie in the back with Tom and Karen folding her dress around her and squeezing into the front seat with Lilly, off they went. And like they used to do when they could squeeze three girls in the front and three boys in the back, Karen tucked her arm and hand under her full skirt so she could shift when Lilly hit the clutch.

Arriving at the church, Karen was actually feeling rather relaxed having to think about shifting, and laughing all the way. Ray, Lynn, and Lawanda were cracking up at the sight of the four arriving in the VW, and the photographer was busy getting shots of the commotion.

They entered the familiar building from the side door this time and went into a small room to wait.

Jennifer was very organized, and was busy giving instructions as the preparations had been so minimal.

"Whatever happens, happens," soothed Karen. "We're making memories and I trust everyone here will make it happen just the way it is meant to be."

Karen looked at her best friend Lilly for just a moment. There was no way she wanted to start crying now, and they both knew they had to concentrate on the ceremony.

With Jennifer's signal to start, Lilly and Heather slowly made their way down the aisle, one at a time, taking time to enjoy the faces of the quests.

Jennifer gathered Jill and Allie to be the next ones down the aisle as the music signaled them to start. The girls were adorable in their matching sapphire blue dresses, and you could hear the sighs of delight from the guests as they were guided to their places by the bridesmaids.

Following the little girls were Tyler and Kristen. Kristen was very particular to get an even spread of petals throughout the aisle, and Tyler carefully carried the rings on the pillow Kelsi had created. They were the best-looking grandchildren in the whole world thought Karen peaking in from the back to see. From her vantage point she didn't have to miss anything at all. Suddenly she was hit like a bolt of lightening with the reality of what she was doing. She looked out over the guests, all of them family and friends, and then focused on the love of her life. The stained glass windows that she had admired so many times accented her mood of reverence. Not only was she doing what was right for herself and her beloved, she was also doing this for John Jr. and Heather. She was giving them the dad they had always deserved, and also a grandfather for their children. They probably couldn't comprehend it yet, but she knew this was a precious gift that could only be given once.

She caught her breath as she saw the love of her life holding out his hand to Tyler to come stand by the men, and was grateful for Waldo's steady hand on her arm.

Everything was perfect, everything was beautiful, and she was ready to present herself to her husband. She bowed her head to catch the scent of the gardenia in her bouquet, and then said, "Okay, Waldo, let's go."

Looping her arm through Waldo's, Karen slowly started down the isle as everyone rose to their feet. Knowing that this ceremony would join them for a lifetime, she glided down the isle with a smile, being careful to step on some of the petals, as she knew Kristen was watching for it.

Looking around Karen met the eyes of Dorothy, Lilly's mom, and smiled lovingly at her. Karen was reminded of her own mother, lost to her now, and how much this elderly woman had meant to her growing up.

Sitting just the other side of her was Lawanda, Lilly's sister. Lawanda and Robere' had allowed Karen and Lilly to borrow their car to run around in on Saturday nights when they were growing up and even allowed them to have a few parties at their house.

Sitting in front of them was Ray and Lynn, Lilly's brother and sister-in-law. Ray had been like a brother to Karen growing up and she still called him when she needed advise on cars.

Sitting next to Ray and Lynn were Jamie and Kelsi. This young man, the son of her best friend, had been raised with Karen's children and she couldn't be more proud of him if he was her own son. And his wife, Kelsi, was just as dear to her as her own daughter-in-law.

On the opposite side sat Matthew, Annie, and sweet little Maggie all dressed up in peach lace and ruffles. Karen had been a second mom to Matthew, and he had always been like a son to her. He and John Jr. had been best friends as they grew up, similar to Lilly and herself. His friendship was so very valuable and important to her family.

Continuing to look around as she slowly walked down the isle she was reminded of how blessed she truly was. Engelbert and Angie, Dylan and Norma, Jed, Louise, Deirdre and Nikki all the way from Washington gathered here to share in her happiness.

Finally Karen's eyes went to the front of the church and once again she thanked God in her heart that all of these men were home and safe. Her entire life was gathered at that alter. Everyone she loved was there to see her married to the true love of her life and sitting in the audience was the rest of her life, the people from her childhood who had helped mold her into the woman she had grown up to be, and the local people who had befriended her and Lilly when they came south.

With a few feet left to go Karen's eyes met Lilly's and she knew that Lilly was quickly losing her resolve not to cry. Hoping her smile would communicate to her friend that it was OK to cry, OK to be happy for her, OK to be sad at the coming changes in their lives, Karen turned her attention to John and without Waldo's arm she no doubt would have fainted.

John's eyes told their own story. They told of heartache and trials and faith that had brought them here together today. As the music ended John stepped forward and Waldo placed her arm in his.

Pastor Jim gave a welcome to the guests, and then spoke of love for a few minutes. He continued, "now for the vows," and Karen started speaking when he paused. The vows hadn't been prepared other than the standard words that Pastor Jim had in front of him, but Karen knew she didn't need them now. "John, I promise to love you for the rest of my life, and I know that we are strong enough to make it through tough times. I thank God for bringing you back to me, and I'm so glad we'll be living the rest of our lives together. I love you with all of my being and I present myself to you as your wife."

The groom was very surprised to see the diamonds in his ring as she slipped it onto his finger and it left him speechless for a moment. Then his eyes met hers as his vows flowed from his lips. "Karen, I promise to love and take care of you for the rest of my life. Thank you for giving me children and grandchildren." He paused as he searched for words and composure of his emotions. "I accept this ring as a symbol of your unending love and by the way, you are more beautiful today than ever. And I'm proud to be your husband. I pray that I will enhance your life as much as you do mine."

John Jr. handed him the band that fit snuggly against her diamond and sapphire ring, and John Sr. placed it on her finger. Karen was so happy she thought her heart would burst, and a tear ran down her cheek.

The music had been playing softly, and now changed to the song John had chosen to sing to his bride. When the song ended Pastor Jim continued with the traditional part of the ceremony. "By the power vested in me by the State of Louisiana I now pronounce you husband and wife. John, you may kiss your bride." John bent and placed a tender kiss lightly on Karen's lips and was totally unprepared when her arms wrapped tightly around his neck and she kissed him back with a passion rarely seen in wedding ceremonies. Karen finally released him when people in the audience giggled, and she thought she heard a "yahoo" from Jamie and Kelsi.

As John and Karen turned to face their audience Pastor Jim said, "It is my privilege and great honor to be the first to introduce, Mr. and Mrs. John Worthington."

The audience clapped and cheered as John and Karen walked down the isle as man and wife. When they reached the front steps of the church John caught Karen up in his arms. "You're finally mine. And my darling I'm never letting you go." With that he kissed her back answering all the passion of her earlier kiss in the church.

Their kiss was finally interrupted by the clip clop of the Clydesdale horses pulling an antique buggy. Karen's eyes were still wide with surprise as John helped her up into the seat and then climbed in beside her as everyone threw confetti and blew bubbles towards them. With Jamie guiding the horses, they slowly made their way back to the Inn with a trail of guests behind them.

Karen was elated, sitting close to her new husband, still kissing him periodically, and enjoying the ride.

Waldo and Lilly were right behind them in the VW, and were almost run off the road as they passed Etta Kelly and Charlotte, stretching their necks to see the sight.

When they arrived at the B&B, everything was in order. "Waldo, it's just amazing," said Lilly. "We haven't even left yet and the Johnson's and Tom and Jennifer have everything running just about like Karen and I would do. It partly makes me sad, but mostly leaves me relieved. We've accomplished so much, and I know that our lives wouldn't be complete without everything we've done here. Not only have we enhanced geography, we've made a difference in a lot of people's lives. I love this place, I hope it lives on forever, and I really think I have the ambition to start our B&B in Alaska."

Waldo took Lilly's hand in his as they circled the grounds. They appreciated the flowers and smelled their fragrance, they took in the scent of the barbeque and walked through the trellis that Jamie and Kelsi had given her, briefly touching the water in the waterfalls. As they stood by the rose garden they observed the children playing on the swings, and the busy hands filling the long table with various foods. The swan ice sculpture was regal, and the food relished to perfection. In the background was the river with lily pads blooming close to the bank. And to top it all off Karen and John stood visiting with the guests, looking the happiest they had ever seen them.

Dylan and Angie were warming up with one of his first hits. Engelbert came over to Waldo and Lilly, "What do you two think? She doesn't know it yet but right here in my pocket are two round trip tickets to Nashville," he said patting his left hand breast pocket. "She's given up enough for me, now it's her chance. After our little dunk in the creek the other day, Waldo, I realized how selfish I have been. That little gal gave up everything for me, now I'm going to try to give some of it back. Dylan has offered to introduce her around town if I can get her down there. So we're off tomorrow."

Waldo shook hands with his old friend, "Well, Engie you know Lilly's giving up this place to come north with me. We'll look after your place in Alaska. Don't worry, Angie's gonna make it big, I know it."

Lilly hugged Engelbert and then excused herself to check on the progress in the kitchen. There was nothing in the kitchen that needed her attention but she was still having a hard time keeping those tears in check. She felt like she was on an emotional roller coaster that didn't have any signs of stopping. And as usual the only way to slow it down was work, and Lilly worked best in the kitchen.

Tom and Jed were anxious to take the wedding cake out on the cart, but Jennifer couldn't find the cake top anywhere. "Lilly," she said in a panic, "do you know where the top to the cake is?"

"No," she answered. "I haven't even been in the kitchen today except for this morning when it was here. I left it in the fridge. Do you think it was moved to the back?" They went through everything again, not finding even a crumb of the special pecan praline top layer. Lilly had made the cake different from the other layers because it would be the cake the bride and groom would eat on their first anniversary. She had then decorated it beautifully with spun sugar peach roses and pink swans.

"Well, we'll just make do with what we have" said Lilly as she took charge again, secretly pleased that things didn't go quite as smoothly without her personal attention. "Let's see, what do we have…"

Kelsi had joined them by now, and expertly put together flowers borrowed from one of the arrangements to fit the top of the cake. Lilly placed it on the layer of cake that remained, and then added some china swans that were in her china cupboard.

"There, that looks good," she said as she stepped back to view it. They added a few curly ribbons and strings of pearls, sticking them on with the extra frosting, and soon found a masterpiece in front of them. "Wow, we're good," said Lilly in approval. "You'd never know that we didn't plan it this way."

"Now, be careful, you guys!" she instructed as they wheeled the cart out. Her admonition was almost too late as Tyler and the twins chasing a butterfly almost ran into Jed.

Jennifer squeezed out past them after the kids, "Don't worry Lilly, I'll take care of them. They can play the other side of the Gazebo."

Kelsi and Tom laughed at the look of horror on Lilly's face as the cart had tipped slightly when Jed turned to make sure the path was clear. "Don't do that to me Jed, I might be able to re-decorate a top but I don't think I could re-invent an entire cake."

Following the cart Lilly made sure that the cake was placed in its proper place on the refreshment table. Kelsi quickly arranged extra flowers around it and the entire table looked picture perfect.

"Come on, Kelsi, I think we've fussed enough over the cake, if something happens to it now it's out of our control." The two laughed together and then seeing that John and Karen were still busy visiting guests they went to join Jamie who was entertaining his Grandma Dorothy.

Lilly asked her mother, "Are you having a good time, Mama? We're going to have cake pretty soon, but can I get anything for you now?"

"No, I'm fine. There sure are a lot of people here. How do you know so many people down here? Why didn't they come back to Washington to be married?"

Lilly was used to her mother being slightly difficult, she had become increasingly so since the death of Lilly's father. Knowing the loneliness and pain her mother felt, Lilly tried to ignore the complaining and steer her into a more pleasant conversation. "I'm so glad you came, Mama, it means a lot to Karen for you to be here. Have you seen the cake?" she asked attempting to lead her to the refreshment table.

"I saw it earlier, it's pretty enough, I guess, and it doesn't taste too bad either. I hope you don't mind, I ate the little piece you left in the fridge. That was the only lunch I could find. You call this place a bed and breakfast, does that mean you only serve breakfast? A person could starve around here!"

Lilly's eyes widened in horror, "You ate the cake in the fridge?"

"Yep, it was the only thing I could find." Dorothy said defensively.

For the second time in two days Lilly was completely speechless. She was brought out of her daze by a hoot and giggle from Kelsi. Turning to her daughter-in-law she saw tears of laughter streaming down her face. Grabbing Jamie by the hand Kelsi ran toward the house leaving Lilly alone with her mother.

"Mama, I'm glad you enjoyed the cake. Would you like for me to make you a sandwich?"

"Nope, don't need one now."

"OK, why don't you go and visit with Louise. I need to speak to Lawanda." With her head held high and her back straight Lilly walked away from her mother. She desperately needed to compose herself before she saw anyone.

Knowing that this would be something to laugh about later, Lilly was able to talk to Lawanda and go on with the evening.

As Lilly viewed the guests, she knew they were pleased with the food, decorations, and entertainment. There was excitement in the air, and Dylan was giving his band some last minute instructions for requests he had already been given. Several people that John Sr. worked with had arrived just in time for the wedding, and now were asking about future reservations.

John and Karen moved to the wedding cake. As they passed Lilly, Karen whispered, "Was there a problem with the cake?"

"I'll tell you about it later," Lilly whispered back.

John Sr. already had the knife almost touching the frosting when John Jr. came up beside him to do a toast. "I just want to thank everyone, on my parent's behalf, for coming on such a short notice," he said with a grin on his face and pride in his tone. "A lot has happened in the last week...I've been united with my father, which has been the dream of my life. And it's not everyone that's able to attend their parent's first wedding. I wish you two much happiness for years to come. Welcome to this family Dad, and I'm so glad you're around now to be a Grandfather to my children. And Mom, it's really good to see you so happy, I couldn't ask for more."

Lilly wasn't sure what she was going to say, she'd just have to wing it. But it was obviously her turn, so she just started talking. "It's taken thirty years for you two to get together, and finally you've made it! Our hearts were broken when you were missing in action John, and we had to face life without you. But now you're found and back in our lives where you belong. Karen, our friendship could never be replaced, you mean so much to me, and I hope you're happy for the rest of your life." She stopped at this point, choking back her tears, and Karen wrapped her arms around her. "Thank you for being my best friend, life wouldn't have been this good without you," Karen said.

"Is it okay to cut the cake now?" asked the groom. He bent over to Karen's ear and whispered, "Maybe if there's some extra frosting we could take it with us on our honeymoon."

"Behave yourself for a couple more hours," she whispered back as she looked at him with a twinkle in her eye.

"I'll try. How long do we have to stay anyway?" He asked and she replied, "We haven't danced yet. I'm not leaving until I dance with my husband."

"Well I can arrange that right now."

"Slow down, John, we're married now and we have the rest of our lives to spend together and I don't want to miss one minute of this day. Besides we have presents to open too."

John groaned and rolled his eyes, "OK, I'll try to be good. But after that kiss you gave me in the church are you sure you can restrain yourself?"

She grinned at him slyly, "I'll try not to drag you off to the bushes."

John's deep brown eyes sparkled as he replied, "Little Red's parked in the garage, no one would look for us there."

The photographer, wanting to get pictures of the happy couple cutting the cake interrupted their banter. John and Karen held the knife together and then gently fed each other a small bite. There would be no cake smearing with these two, they would always treat each other with loving kindness and gentleness.

As the guests began lining up for cake and punch, Lilly found Waldo and told him about the top cake layer. By that time it was beginning to seem funny and Waldo thought it was hilarious. Feeling better, Lilly wandered away and sat on the steps of the gazebo feeling the closeness of the crowd and the love that seemed to envelop everyone there.

Jamie saw her sitting there and came to sit beside her. "Hey, Mom, is everything OK? You look a little down."

She smiled at her only son and patted his hand, "I'm fine. You know how I get when I can't control everything. I have felt the last week like everything is moving too fast and I don't know how to stop it. And Jamie the funny thing is, look at Karen and John, see how happy they are? I wouldn't stop it for anything in the world. Oh listen to me, mumbling and grumbling. Cheer me up, Jamie. Say something to get me out of this funk."

He looked at her solemnly for a moment and then grinned, "OK Grandma, what would you like me to say?"

"Oh anything at all, just tell me funny stories about the ranch or the horses. How are the barn kitties?"

Jamie sat and stared at her for a moment and then finally saw a glimmer of the light bulb over her head.

"What did you call me?" Lilly questioned.

He smiled again, "I called you Grandma. Didn't you like that? Do you think you could get used to it?"

"Don't tease me Jamie!"

He took her hand and looked seriously in her eyes, "Mom, I'm not teasing. You and Dad are going to be Grandparents in about seven months."

Lilly's hooray could be heard above the band and chatter of the crowd. After calming down just a bit, she said, "I knew as soon as you figured out you could get power tools for father's day you'd come around," in a teasing tone. "Waldo, Waldo! Come here!"

Waldo and Kelsi joined them at the same time and the buttons on Waldo's tuxedo almost popped as he listened to the news. Kelsi was glowing, dreaming of pink and blue lambs and soft blankets to swaddle her baby in. The smiles on the four faces remained for the rest of the evening, and nothing could even begin to dampen their complete happiness.

Lilly couldn't wait to tell Karen. She pulled her aside and whispered, "I'm going to be a Grandma!"

"Really? Is that what all the commotion was about?" Karen asked.

"Yes, but don't say anything because I don't know who they've told yet. I just couldn't wait to tell you." They both hugged and would have and jumped up and down like a couple of teenagers if not for Karen's wedding dress.

"What's all the fuss about?" asked John.

"I'll tell you later," promised Karen.

Heather and John Jr. approached their parents. "Why don't you open your presents? Come on, we've set a couple of chairs over there for you, and I'll make a list for you," said Heather.

Karen was amazed at the generosity of their friends, and on such a short notice they had all come up with amazing gifts.

Heather brought out a large package, and it was easy to guess that it was one of her paintings before they even ripped the paper off of it. "Be careful," she instructed. "It may be a little tacky still."

John Sr. stopped and stared in amazement and shock. Heather had painted a family portrait of the four of them with the Mon Amie Famille in the background. "I don't even know what to say, I'm speechless," he choked out around his emotion.

"Of course I didn't have much time, you two are so fast! I think I'll add some more of the rose bushes if you don't mind."

"It looks perfect like it is Heather, but I'm sure you'll make it even better if you have it in your head," said Karen proudly.

Heather was very proud and feeling more complete in her life than she ever had. Karen had known about the painting, and encouraged her to finish it in the short time that they had before the wedding. Actually, she had completed most of it the night before after the men returned from the river. Being all wound up, she stayed up most of the night working on it.

It was plain for Heather to see that her newfound dad loved the painting, and she didn't need words to know it. "I'm glad you like it," she said as they made eye connection.

"It's beautiful, and way beyond anything my imagination could have come up with," he said softly. "We'll always treasure it."

John Jr. and Melinda now stood in front of them, presenting a card. They both had big grins on their faces, and all of a sudden Karen's curiosity was at a peak. What in the world could these two have in an envelope to bring such an expression? "What have you done?" she asked. John handed the envelope to his father. "Open it."

As he opened the card, little baby graffiti fell out onto the ground. The card was hand crafted with baby roses, and he read out loud; "The best present we could think of was to make you Grandparents again. Dad, you missed out on the first two babies, but now you'll have a chance to be a part of this child's birth. If we've figured correctly, this son or daughter will be arriving with the New Year. Please visit often, we're looking forward to having you both in our lives."

This time a tear rolled down John Sr.'s cheek as he swallowed hard. Both he and Karen were speechless now, and their hearts were so full they didn't know how to express themselves. "Wow," said John Sr., "Somebody better pinch me to make sure I'm not dreaming!"

It's real," assured Karen as she put her arm around him. "Now, how about that dance?"

Dylan was right on queue as he started singing his latest hit and Angie was singing back up like she had been doing it for years.

John swung Karen around gracefully. "This is a perfect moment," she said.

"Yes my dear, a perfect moment to be followed by a lifetime of perfect moments," he replied as he dipped her.

When that song ended and Dylan's mellow tenor and Angie's sweet soprano voice joined together in a ballad, Karen had a chance to look around at the people gathered for her wedding. Lilly and Waldo were dancing, as were Jamie and Kelsi, and John Jr. and Melinda. Jed had led Dorothy out onto the dance floor against her wishes and Lawanda and Robere' sitting with Ray and Lynn were laughing at the sight of their elderly mother dancing. Karen could see Heather and David sitting close together on the steps of the Gazebo watching Tyler dance with Jill and Allie. Her heart swelled with joy at the sight of her family and friends gathered here on her special day.

Pulling away slightly and looking deep into John's brown eyes she spoke, "John, have you ever wanted to freeze time? I have never in my life been as happy as I am right now. Until this very moment I have always felt like something was missing from my life. But today, right now, I am complete."

John pulled her tight against him once more. "Always look ahead, my love, never look back."

The evening ended way too soon for them to do all of the visiting Karen would have liked, but they would have to make time for all of that later. And they would, travel was definitely in their future.

But now it was time for John and Karen to leave the B&B, and finally they were free to love without holding anything back.

"John," asked Karen, "which car are we taking? Did you know the Cadillac battery is dead? And where are we going? Do we have reservations for tonight?" She had assumed he was taking care of all this, but all of a sudden the unknown made her a bit fearful. The idea of spending their first night here wasn't what she had in mind, and the hotel by the airport was booked with all of their friends.

"Karen, I had planned on surprising you, but I guess I can tell you now. We're staying with the competition." John laughed at the shocked look on Karen's face. "It was Lilly's idea. I've rented Twelve Oaks, that Plantation just the other side of New Orleans that was turned into a B&B last year."

Karen smiled, "John, did Lilly tell you that I've always wanted to stay there? But darling, don't you mean you've rented a suite at Twelve Oaks?"

"No, Karen, I rented the whole house."

"But, John, that house has forty-two rooms!"

"I know, my dear, and you get your pick of which one you want to stay in. Personally I think you'll like the Scarlet O'Hara suite." John lowered his voice and whispered in her ear, "We can try more than one room and we can make as much noise as we want."

Karen blushed and whispered back, "How soon can we leave?"

John laughed, "Now who's getting impatient? We need to start telling people goodbye and then we can go."

At his words Karen grew solemn and looked in Lilly's direction. This was not going to be easy.

Karen and John quickly changed into more comfortable clothes, and John took the suitcases to the car while Karen went to find Lilly.

The best friend's eyes met, knowing that this was the moment of separation. Not only for just a couple of weeks, but the close daily relationship they had had at the B&B would never be quite the same again. Each of them knew in their hearts that they had prepared for this moment of moving forward in their lives by being sure the other was taken care of. Even so, their hearts were full, and they knew that their bond of friendship would never be broken. Geography would not change a thing about the way they felt about each other, and it was the way they lived their lives that would influence their children for generations.

"I hope you two have a good time tonight," said Lilly with a twinkle in her eye and a smile on her lips.

"Frankly my dear, I expect we'll have a grand time," replied Karen in a theatrical tone and with a big grin on her face. "I think I'll wear the ivory lace, no, the black, when I gracefully walk down the staircase to meet my husband as he comes out of the parlor where the fireplace glimmers..."

"You are a romantic Karen, and here he comes, hush we don't want to spoil the surprise," Lilly laughed.

There was a lot of hugging, and Tyler and Kristen were smothered in love and kisses.

"Mom, Dad," said John Jr., "Have a good time, and don't forget to send us post cards, that is if you're not too busy...eehhhh." Heather joined into his "eehhh," and also reminded them that they had better hear from them.

Turning once again to Lilly, Karen's eyes welled with tears, "I don't know how to do this," She sobbed, "I don't think I can…" Suddenly feeling John's strong hands on her shoulders she turned and buried her face in his chest. Lilly had likewise turned to Waldo and her slender shoulder's shook from her tears.

Looking over the top of their wives heads Waldo and John smiled at each other and shook their heads and then Waldo spoke, "They sure are getting upset over being apart for two weeks aren't they John?"

"I'll say, Waldo, maybe I should go fishing with you and let Lilly go to the Bahamas with Karen."

Pulling away suddenly Karen searched her husband's face, "Two weeks? What's happening in two weeks?"

John smiled tenderly at his bride and wiped the tears from her cheeks, "I thought we would help Waldo and Lilly get the new business started in Alaska. That is if you want to?"

Karen turned to Lilly and grabbed her hands, "Want to? Want to? Oh my goodness there's so much to do. Lilly, you need to start working on the layout for the kitchen. This will be a perfect opportunity to try out some stew and chowder recipes."

Lilly was so excited she was practically dancing, "And I've been anxious to invent a new chili recipe for the longest time, but it's too darn hot down here."

John interrupted the two friends, "Can we go on our honeymoon now?"

Smiling brightly Karen answered, "Of course, darling, let's go."

Giving her friend one last quick hug she grabbed her husband's hand and the two ran to the red Mustang parked in the drive as their family and friends cheered.

PART 2

ALASKA

Built entirely of rough-hewn lodge pole pine, the enormous lodge, known as the Wolf Creek Lodge, was an imposing sight in the otherwise bleak Alaska wilderness. Tall pine trees lined the driveway leading to the house, creating a path of invitation for visiting family and friends. Dark pungent smoke rose from only one of the five chimneys the inn boasted.

Inside the Lodge, basking in the warmth of the wood fire, Lilly was curled up next to Waldo on the new sofa that had been delivered earlier in the week. She was exhausted from the many hours she had cleaned and scrubbed in the last five days. It had been all she and Waldo could do to get the kitchen in working order and two of the bedroom suites suitable for sleeping in before John and Karen would get here. Lilly was very anxious for their arrival, and the last two weeks seemed like a year. So much had happened without Karen there to share it with. Waldo had been a great help but it wasn't the same as the fun Lilly and Karen had when they worked together.

As Lilly gazed out the frosted windowpane at the sunlight, typical of Alaska in the late evening, she sipped her hot chocolate and thought about what needed to be done next. "Waldo, it feels so good when you rub my feet like that," she crooned, "we haven't been alone like this since we first got married thirty years ago."

"Your chowder was delicious, and now that my stomach is full…"

Lilly moved closer into his arms, "Yes? What's going to happen now that you have a full tummy? Did you have anything in particular in mind? Or are you going to go to sleep like you usually do when you over eat a little?"

Chuckling lightly Waldo replied, "Sleep was what I had in mind, but maybe not for at least a half an hour." Pulling her into his arms, Waldo kissed his wife lightly on the lips.

The couple on the couch was interrupted suddenly by the barking of a dog.

"What's that puppy up to now?" Waldo grumbled. "Honestly, I love the little guy but he's going to get swatted this time."

"Now, honey, be gentle. He's only six months old. Jamie and Kelsi didn't have much time to train him before sending him up here, so just be patient."

Moving toward the door Waldo was startled to hear a solid knock. "Oh! Well maybe this time he had a reason to bark."

Waldo opened the door and the wind and snow blew John and Karen inside. For a moment the four were speechless as Waldo and Lilly took in the sudden arrival of their friends and John and Karen gazed with wonder at the great room of the lodge.

"Well, look what the snow blew in," exclaimed Waldo.

Lilly ran to Karen to give her a welcome home hug, and they jumped up and down like teenagers. By their actions and appearance it was hard to tell they were both "fifty-ish." They hadn't aged much over the years, and still had the figures to look good in anything they wanted to venture trying. It had only been a little over two weeks since they had all been together at John and Karen's whirlwind wedding in Louisiana, and the two best friends had lived and worked together at their Southern bed and breakfast for several years now, but they now acted as if they had been separated for decades.

"It's quite the difference in temperature here after being in the Bahamas," remarked John. "It's a good thing we stopped at the Mon Amie Famille and found some warmer clothing to bring with us."

"The place is absolutely wonderful and perfect," said Karen excitedly. "It has massive character, and it's so romantic."

"Maybe it's romantic because you're still in your honeymoon mode," teased Lilly. "But then on second thought, I do have to agree with you. This is the perfect place for our friends and family."

It wasn't long before the four were visiting in front of the fireplace with hot chocolate cupped in their hands. The aroma of mint lifted to their senses.

"This really feels like home," remarked Karen. "Lilly, your reputation for adding extra ingredients to your cooking masterpieces lives on, and it's wonderful."

Lilly smiled, "I have experimented a little. Have you two eaten? I made seafood chowder for dinner with corn muffins, and there's fresh blackberry cobbler with vanilla ice cream? You know how I cook; even Waldo can't eat it all. But he does try."

Waldo patted his slightly bulging middle, "I don't know what I'm going to do. I use to come up here to lose weight now I may have to go back to Louisiana every once in a while."

John and Karen laughed and John replied, "Thanks anyway, Lilly, but we ate at the airport. We weren't sure how long it would take us to get out here. But I could take you up on some cobbler."

Karen lovingly patted John's middle and said, "Come on Lilly let's see if we can fatten this one up a little."

Waldo spoke as Karen and Lilly left for the kitchen, "Lilly, Love of My Life, I can't let John eat alone. Maybe just a little bit of cobbler for me?"

Laughing, Lilly agreed that Waldo could have just a little.

Waldo and John put on their coats and went out to get the luggage and check on the dog.

"Did the seaplane over there come with the place?" asked John.

"Yes, I was hoping you would be able to look it over. I don't think it's been used for a year or so. This place was kind of like a ghost town when we first got here; Lilly claimed the dust was a foot deep throughout the house. And one of my first projects will be to restore that shed over there for the fishing gear."

They rounded the corner and Waldo opened the gate to the dog run. "You sure are excited to have visitors; maybe we'll have to get you a roommate," Waldo spoke to the puppy.

"He's a fine one," said John. "What's his name?"

"We don't know yet, Lilly said that Karen should name him. So we've been calling him "the puppy" for now."

Once in the kitchen the two friends began chatting and catching each other up on the events of the past two weeks.

"Lilly, everything is great at the Mon Amie Famille. I can't quite believe that it runs without us, but I guess it just goes to prove that we can be replaced. Tom and Jennifer want to expand to serving dinner in the evening in the formal dining room to the locals and tourists. I told them I would talk to you about it. Their idea is to have Jennifer do breakfast continuing with our tradition of fresh fruit, rolls (still your recipe) and scrambled eggs or breakfast casserole and Tom would take over the cooking duties in the evening with Prime Rib and some local seafood dishes and Louise wants to try her hand at a full dessert menu for the dinners. What do you think?"

"Wow! I thought we were ambitious. Sure, it's fine with me, as long as they promise to charge the Kelly clan twice what they would charge anyone else. You know Old Lady Kelly has been trying to get a peek inside that house ever since we renovated it. And it's not like we're losing our connection," replied Lilly. "Matthew is working on the computer network so that we have access to both places here. He's scheduled to be here next month to evaluate the situation and make the plans for terminals in the suites. Angie called," she continued, "Did you know she's been writing her own songs for some time now? They love her in Nashville and she's been recording in the studio for the last week. Dylan got her connected with a good manager, and who knows what will happen next. She insisted that she and Engelbert have the very first reservation here. Dylan and Norma want to come up too. I told Angie I needed to remove a foot of dust first, but we would let them know when we're ready for business. Maybe they can all come up before we're officially open to the public."

"I can't wait to have a complete tour," said Karen.

"Well, we only have two of the bedroom suites cleaned, and as you can see we have our work cut out for us. I can feel it in my bones…we're going to be mail order experts."

"You must have talked to Heather, because she sent a bunch of catalogs with me. David was with her when we visited her, and we all had dinner together. They seem to be quite the happy couple. Heather just glows when she talks about him. And Tom and Jennifer were never far from each other. There's definitely romance in Louisiana."

"Oh, I miss them already," said Lilly. "I was hoping we could all have Christmas here this year. After all it's been a while since we had a white one, and with only one reservation so far we can plan it any way we want."

"Christmas lights," said Karen excitedly. "Lots and lots of Christmas lights, all over the lodge and the trees in the driveway. This place will be unbelievable. And snow sculptures, and a big tree in the front window. We'll decorate each of the suites too. Oh, we'll miss Jennifer big time. Have you had a chance to meet any locals? Does anyone actually live up here?"

"There are a few families. The O'Callaghan family lives just on the edge of the village. Mr. O'Callaghan is from Ireland and his wife, Nona, is a Native Aleutian Indian. She is very lovely. They have five children and the oldest, Lanie, will be coming home from college next week. I haven't met her yet, but Nona said she would be looking for a job. If she's anything like her Mother we would be lucky to have her even just for a season. Now, enough about this place how was the Honeymoon?" Lilly asked slyly, "And tell me all about Twelve Oaks, the B&B where you spent your wedding night. Or did you even get a look at the house?"

Karen laughed, her cheeks turning rosy, "Twelve Oaks was beautiful, but didn't have the charm that Mon Amie Famille has, and the Bahamas were wonderful, and I'm more in love than I ever thought possible. And that, my dear friend, is all I'm saying about that! So when is Kelsi's due date?" continued Karen, changing the subject. "Was she sick at the wedding? I thought she looked a little peaked, but with all of the turmoil, I really didn't think much of it. Have you knitted any booties yet?"

Lilly answered, "You know I can't knit. But maybe I'll do some quilting. What do you think? We could do one this winter when the roads get too bad for people to travel. The baby is due the first of December, should be about a month before John and Melinda's baby. Do you suppose the little mothers will want to travel that close to their due dates to be here for Christmas? How is Melinda feeling?"

"Pretty good," Karen said, "I think she's trying to sell as much real estate as she can before she needs to quit work. They're hoping she won't have to go back to work for a while after the baby's born. We stopped by on our way here. They made it back to Oregon okay, and the kids were tired and didn't want to get up for school that first day back, but they survived. Grandpa talks about them constantly, and he's really excited about the new baby on the way."

Lilly chattered on, "We received a letter from one of the couples the men rescued at the bridge bombing. We answered his letter and they have a reservation for this fall at our Southern B&B. Dylan and Norma sent a thank you note too and said they'd never forget us. How could they! They had a blast at my birthday party, and if Dylan would have died at the river, the whole world would have known and mourned. I think Norma and Angie are best friends now. We really should have a reunion on your wedding anniversary."

Waldo poked his head in the back kitchen door, "You two want to say hi to our new puppy?"

Karen was elated. He was the most adorable Alaskan Wolf Husky she had ever seen. All furry and fluffy, he had gray and tan coloring, and more energy than a toddler. She picked him up to cuddle.

"Jamie and Kelsi bought him from a breeder in Seattle and sent him to Waldo. He's to protect us up here in the wilds and you get to name him," explained Lilly.

After a brief moment of thought Karen responded, "How about Tyson? He looks like a Tyson to me; do you all like the name?"

"Tyson it is," said Waldo. "That name will be perfect."

The two couples returned to the warmth of the great room in the lodge and enjoyed Lilly's berry cobbler and talked into the evening. It would have been hard to say which they enjoyed the most, the ambience of the lodge, each other's company or the wonderful cobbler.

The four rose early the next day, ready for work. Mainly out of habit, Lilly and Karen had a big breakfast ready in no time. The men wolfed it down, anxious to see Tyson and get to work on the old shed.

The two-story lodge had ten suites, each having their own fireplaces. A large dining hall was located on the west end of the main floor, next to an enormous kitchen. There were plenty of storage areas, and nooks and cranny's to satisfy anyone's imagination. Three separate staircases led to the upstairs. The decorating possibilities were endless, and ideas were brimming in both Lilly and Karen's heads.

"Are you ready for some heavy duty cleaning?" asked Lilly.

"Sure am, I'm anxious to get started. I haven't had my hands in the dirt for quite a while," answered Karen.

They turned on the radio, and wearing jeans and old t-shirts, Lilly and Karen vacuumed, mopped, and wiped the walls down. The lodge smelled of disinfectant and cleaning solutions and things were looking much brighter. They didn't even realize it was past noon when the men came in to find some grub (as they put it).

"We're starving," complained John. "What's for lunch?"

"We weren't really thinking about food yet," replied Karen. "Let's see what there is."

A package of hot dogs was the quickest and easiest to satisfy their stomachs, and it felt good to sit and relax a bit.

"I bet Tyson would like one of these hot dogs," said John.

"Ok, let's take him a treat," replied Waldo.

Karen and Lilly followed so that they could check out the progress on the shed.

Tyson seemed to think he had been ignored for most of the morning, and was hungry and anxious for attention. Waldo opened the gate with the plate of leftovers in his hand. "You don't look like you're starving, but you sure act like it," he soothed.

Tyson was very excited, and could smell the hot dog. Before Waldo had a chance to break them up for him, Tyson attacked the plate and wolfed down an entire hot dog. The hot dog stuck in his throat, and it became obvious within seconds that he could not breathe. He was unable to cough it up, and soon was not moving.

"He's dead!" cried Lilly.

"Get the hot dog out," instructed Karen.

Keeping his cool, John gave instructions. "Just keep calm, get the hot dog out, and then you can do CPR."

Waldo quickly tried to remove the food, but it was stuck. Knowing he had to get it out to save his life, he swept his finger harshly down his throat, firmly removing it after several tries. However, Tyson was not breathing at this point.

"CPR can't be that different on an animal than it is on a human," he said as he quickly placed his mouth over the dog's mouth and nose. He gave him a couple of quick small breaths, knowing that it would be easy to burst his small lungs. It seemed like several moments before Tyson finally gasped in some air. His tongue had already begun to turn white for the lack of oxygen.

Looking up from his endeavor, Waldo saw Lilly hugging herself with tears streaming down her face, "He's going to be OK, Lilly. I guess we forgot he's just a baby and shouldn't be eating things like hotdogs."

John slapped Waldo on the back, "You did it buddy, you saved that little puppy's life."

Waldo's grin was a mile wide, "I sure couldn't tell Kelsi that I had lost the little guy. At least not until I had done every thing I could to save him."

Karen added her thoughts, "I can't believe you did that. You gave him CPR without even thinking twice."

"Of course he did," said Lilly moving into Waldo's arms, "he is the kindest, most caring man in the world. And he's all mine." With that she planted a big wet kiss on the lips that had brought a helpless little animal back to life.

"You two now officially have dog germs," teased Karen. "You better go use the mouth wash."

It was plain to see that all four of them were now very attached to Tyson, and they were all feeling like they belonged in this new world.

"We're planning on making a trip into the village in the morning," announced John. "So you two might want to make a list."

"Oh, we already have," replied Lilly. "And it will be fun to see just what the place has to offer. I better get back to the house. I know we just ate lunch but thought I would make a beef stew for dinner and I need to put the meat on to cook. Karen, would you like to make apple dumplings for desert? Come on, I'll talk you through it while I'm doing the meat."

"You two go ahead, Lilly. I'm going to stay out here and work on the shed for a little bit," Waldo said. Lilly knew he didn't want to leave the little puppy just yet.

"I'll stay and help Waldo. Can Tyson run loose out here while we're working?" John asked.

"Of course he can. We need to get him used to the place and teach him where he can't go. Eventually I would like for him to be out all the time," replied Waldo.

Returning to the house Lilly and Karen became immersed in cooking and enjoying each other's company as they always did. The kitchen was warm and cozy in spite of its massive size. A fire burned brightly in the fireplace large enough to cook an entire quarter beef, and cast flickering shadows on the copper bottoms of the pans hanging above the island where the friends worked side by side. The radio softly played the latest country songs and the two were comforted by the sounds of hammers and laughter coming from the back of the house, and an occasional bark from Tyson.

"Just when we thought life was perfect in the south, we moved here and now it feels perfect in the north," commented Karen. "Happiness is who you're with and what you're doing in life, not the geography. I know we've already learned this lesson, it's just right in front of us again."

The two friends spent the rest of the afternoon in the kitchen organizing cupboards, making lists, and finishing the meal preparations. They were still basking in their happiness when Waldo and John stepped in the back door to find their nostrils filled with wonderful aromas.

"I didn't know anything could smell so good, I'm famished," said John.

Waldo had moved to the stove where his wife was ladling bowls of fragrant, steaming beef stew. Wrapping his arms around her slender waste, he planted a kiss at the nape of her neck, "Have I told you lately how much I love you?" He asked.

Lilly playfully swatted him away, "Love me or my cooking?" She asked.

Waldo replied with a pretend hurt look on his face, "You of course, I would love you even if you couldn't boil water! But the cooking doesn't hurt a thing."

Lilly laughed, "You two get washed, and we're putting it on the table."

Karen had already set the rough pine table in front of the fireplace in the kitchen. There was no need to eat in the formal dining hall. The four would be lost at that table that would seat forty comfortably. The firelight reflected off the iron stone dinnerware and joined the candles on the table in creating a homey atmosphere.

The two couples ate the savory stew and biscuits followed by apple dumplings with fresh cream. After they had eaten their fill Waldo and John helped Lilly and Karen wash dishes and clean the kitchen.

After the kitchen chores were done Waldo brought Tyson in and he played with a ball contentedly basking in the warmth of the fireplace for most of the evening while the two couples watched him and laughed at his antics. Lilly thought Waldo would have taken him into their room for the night to keep an eye on him but he was afraid of the puppy becoming overheated. He was, after all, a Siberian Husky and in spite of the close call that day his place was outdoors where someday he would stand guard over the massive lodge and its beloved occupants. Besides, Tyson seemed to have recovered fully.

CHAPTER 2

Lilly and Waldo woke to another wonderful day. "Are we taking your new truck today?" she asked.

"Definitely," he answered.

Waldo was very pleased with his new Ford diesel pickup. He had chosen a red one for easy visibility in the snow, with an extended cab to hold extra passengers comfortably. They would undoubtedly need it to haul supplies, transport guests, and get through the snowy weather to come. He wasted no time getting dressed, being motivated by the thought of driving it, and wanting to spend a little bit of time with Tyson before they left.

After a breakfast of pecan waffles and maple sausage the two couples left to run their errands in the village. Waldo was driving his shiny new Ford truck with John riding shotgun and their wives in the comfortable back seat of the new pickup.

They drove along the gravel road that led out of the valley, and Waldo pulled over to a viewing spot. The view was beautiful; John and Karen hadn't seen it yet from this perspective. The spring breakup had recently thawed the surface, melting the creeks and the river, and land could be seen in the snow on the hills. The valley was wide, and about a mile deep which provided protection from the harsh winter winds. It was full of large trees, still accented with a little snow. After the warmer weather of the last few days a promise of green meadow and wild flowers could be seen here and there. The airstrip lay at the far end of the valley, and the enormous lodge sat in the midst of the south side, creating a perfect picture.

The four stood breathless on a large rock overlooking the scene. "Look! There's a bear over there in the clearing," exclaimed Waldo.

"And there's her cub right behind her," added John.

The wilderness held more wildlife than it did humans, and fences, poles, and telephone lines did not mar it. The beauty breathtakingly made time cease to exist as they took in the view.

As they gazed at the majesty of the wilderness and marveled at the closeness of nature and the wild, they were all speechless with awe at this raw, incredibly beautiful world they now called home.

Lilly startled them all by excitedly asking, "Waldo, did you bring your gun? What if that mama bear comes over here and charges at us?"

Waldo laughed and drew Lilly close, "No, Lilly, I didn't bring my gun. And I don't think I could bring myself to shoot one of these beautiful animals. After all this is their home, we are the trespassers here."

"But Waldo, what would we do if it did charge us?" Lilly persisted worriedly.

"She won't, Lilly, we're too far away to be a threat. See, she's moving her baby farther away from us. Come on we better get to town."

Waldo and Lilly turned to see that Karen, looking a little worried herself, had moved into the protection of John's strong arms.

Waldo chuckled softly, "We'll turn these two into wilderness women eventually John."

John pulled Karen to him tightly and replied, "I don't know Waldo. I'm kind of enjoying this."

It quickly became evident that they would not be making quick trips to town whenever they were out of eggs or milk. The road was rough and long, and the tundra seemed to reach endlessly into the distance.

The giggling two in the back seat decided to give the men a hard time…"What time is it? How many more miles? I'm hungry. When are we going to get there? I have to go to the bathroom. She hit me."

"Are you sure we'll be able to make these two into wilderness women?" asked John. "It seems they're rather spoiled with the amenities they've become used to."

As they neared the village, the scene before them was of slightly run down buildings, older cars, and people of various types and races.

"Oh no," said Karen in alarm. "They're going to think we're rich snobs in this truck!"

"No", explained Lilly, "the people that originally homesteaded on Wolf Creek found gold in the under layer of the creek, and they made a lot of money. People up here tend to live very simply. But don't let the run down appearance of the town fool you; there's plenty of wealth here. Our main customers will be coming from the States anyway, but we do need the cooperation of the natives to be successful. We've already talked to the mayor of the village, and I think we'll get along just fine. You'll see. And now we have to start thinking like pioneers to make the purchases we need, because I don't think we'll be making this trip again for a while."

Pausing on the boardwalk in front of the trading post/mercantile store Karen and Lilly felt like they had stepped back in time. However, once they crossed the threshold into the store they were in for a pleasant surprise. An enterprising man by the name of Edward Bjorn owned the business. His grandfather was one of the first men to find gold in Wolf Creek and had chosen to stay in the village, marry a local girl and raise his family. Edward's coal black hair and high cheekbones told of his Aleutian heritage as much as his name and blue eyes told of his Norwegian roots.

The shelves were well stocked, there was fresh produce, and towards the back of the store clothing and other merchandise could be seen. It was a great relief to Karen to see the selection.

"Hello, Mrs. Lansford, how are you today?" asked Mr. Bjorn.

"I'm fine this sunshiny day, thank you, and I would like to introduce my friend Karen Worthington."

"Glad to meet you," he replied in a slight accent. "I understand you are living at the Lodge with the Lansford's now.

Karen was wondering whether his accent had more Indian origin or Norwegian as she greeted him with a friendly smile. "Hello, yes we are living at Wolf Creek Lodge, and I'm glad to meet you. You have a great store here. Are the eggs fresh?"

"They certainly are, pulled them out from under the hens this morning myself," Edward chuckled.

Karen smiled and turned to ask Lilly how many dozen she thought they would need when her path was blocked by a rather large woman in a flowered print house dress that had definitely not come from the same decade as the rest of the people in the store. Her little squinty eyes peered at Karen from her chubby face, and she asked, "So, where did you come from? Are you from the south too? What kind of business are you two thinking of running up here in our area? You need to know we won't put up with no nonsense, even if you are twenty miles out!"

Karen was so startled that for a moment she couldn't speak.

During that brief span Lilly came quickly to her friend's aide, "Hello Elma. This is my friend Karen; her husband John is the tall handsome man checking out the fishing gear with Waldo. And yes, we were in business together in New Orleans and we will continue that here. And for your information, our business…"

Lilly was just heating up to tell Elma what she thought of her rudeness when Waldo, seeing what was going on, interrupted.

"Why hello, Elma, how are you this beautiful day? My, that is a lovely dress you're wearing and I didn't know there was a beauty parlor in town, but there must be and you must have come straight from there."

Elma Smith was so taken aback and flustered by Waldo's charm that she forgot she was on a fact-finding mission. Allowing Waldo to guide her away from Karen and Lilly she finished her purchases and left the store with a smile on her lips.

Karen was laughing at the look of disdain on Lilly's face. "Oh, Lilly, you should see your face. And why didn't you warn me that Etta Kelly had a sister in Alaska?"

Lilly had to laugh with her friend, "There was no way to explain her and I knew you would meet her eventually. I just didn't expect her to be so rude right off the bat. And Waldo, why didn't you let me finish her off? She needs to know she can't treat people that way."

Waldo replied, "Calm down, my love, we don't want to upset the natives just yet. And remember she is Nona O'Callaghan's aunt and if you want Lanie working for you we better not rock that boat."

Lilly grumbled back, "OK, but some day I'll really tell her what I think of her. And I wouldn't be surprised if Nona doesn't feel the same way. Now where were we, Karen?"

"I think we were about to purchase some eggs. I think five dozen will be enough for now, we need to get a lot of baking done before Matthew gets here, and you never know what company might pop in…what sounds good for dinner tonight?"

Karen continued to put various items into her basket until it was full, and Lilly was doing the same. By the time Waldo and John came over to see how they were doing, their baskets were heaping.

John slipped his arm around Karen's waist, and she knew that her life was complete now, even way out here in the middle of nowhere. She returned his hug and asked, "Were you able to order the parts for the seaplane?"

"I think so," he replied, "of course I won't know until I get it torn apart. It is pretty old, but if we can't find the parts Waldo said Jamie could fabricate them. So we'll be in pretty good shape. It would sure help the business if we can use the seaplane to get customers a little farther out than we can take them by 4-Wheel. Are you two lovely ladies ready, how about some lunch?

Edward looked up from sacking the purchases, "There's a real good diner around the corner. My wife is the cook there and as you can tell she's a mighty fine one." He laughed and patted his rounded tummy.

Waldo looked at Lilly skeptically, "I don't know, I'm afraid we might run into Elma again."

"Come on Waldo, we're hungry. I want to meet more of the local people, and I swear I'll be good," Lilly promised.

Thanking Mr. Bjorn for his hospitality and again complimenting him on his beautiful store the two couples took their purchases to the truck and then walked the short distance to the "Once in a Blue Moon" diner.

The small diner was clean and bright. The windows had blue gingham valances tied with grosgrain ribbons, and the tables had matching blue gingham table clothes. Fresh wild flowers graced each of the tables. The counter held glass containers of yummy looking pies and cakes. Lilly and Karen took notice of the large cinnamon rolls and apple pies and then looked at each other knowing that they both approved.

The four sat down at a middle booth next to a big window and opened their menus as they looked around. There was a couple at the back table, and one man sitting at the counter, but it was still a bit early for lunch.

"I wonder if Elma comes here for lunch," worried Waldo. Lilly replied, "Don't worry about her. If she does come in I'll be on my best behavior. I don't know what came over me anyway. After all I just spent the last two years of my life in the only part of the country where manners come first. Anyway, I want to apologize to all of you for allowing that disgusting woman to rile me up."

John reached across the table and patted Lilly's hand. "I saw it all. You were coming to Karen's defense. We all know the only reason you ever get that upset is when you're defending someone you care about. Now let's forget all that and get some lunch. And I don't mean to offend you Lilly, but those desserts look awfully good."

"No offense taken John, I get my best recipes from sampling someone else's cooking." Lilly smiled and squeezed his hand.

The four ordered seafood salads with the intentions of having room for dessert. John and Waldo got up to check out the old jukebox. It was full of golden oldies and it wasn't long before they were singing along to songs that were popular when they were born. The café was empty enough, and not being very shy they had no problem in hamming it up a little.

Patrick and Nona O'Callaghan entered the café with wide eyes. They had never seen such entertainment on the lunch hour before.

"Look," Nona said to her husband, "the Lansford's friends are here and they're entertainers. I know Lilly said they would be entertaining guests at the lodge, but this is not what I expected! I know you said that she mentioned needing help, and Lanie would need work, but I never imagined this, did they want her to sing with them?"

"No, no, they need help with the lodge," Patrick answered, "The men will be off fishing a lot with their clients, and there are a lot of rooms in that place. They need someone to help cook and clean."

Lilly finally looked up to find that Patrick and Nona were standing there watching them. "Oh, my goodness, we were having such a good time..."

Waldo still had enough composure to introduce John and Karen, and then he continued. "Would you two like to join us?"

"Well, being there's only room for four in your booth, and we can't sing very well, I think we'll sit right here," replied Patrick with a funny little smile on his face. "It's good to see life at the lodge again. Welcome."

"When does Lanie get home from college?" asked Lilly.

"Next week," replied Nona. "We're so anxious to have her back, and I told her you were looking for someone to help out."

"Good, we're all looking forward to meeting her. Please have her call when she gets here," Lilly replied.

They all settled back in at their tables. 'Blue Moon' started playing on the jukebox and the friends began speculating on how the diner had gotten its name. "I hope it's not how often fresh fruits and vegetables are delivered," Lilly said.

"No, maybe it's how often they get new customers," Karen suggested.

"No, I'll bet it's how often they get complaints about the food," John said.

"Hey, maybe its how often Elma Smith eats here a day," Waldo contributed, and they all laughed at the thought of that. They were still laughing when the waitress brought their salads.

Lilly and Karen groaned at the same time. The salads were so huge they could have easily shared two of them. When Lilly bit into a piece of crab and endive she groaned again with pleasure, "This is wonderful. The lettuce is just as fresh as the seafood. Well there goes that theory on the name."

By the time they finished their salads, with fresh sourdough rolls and creamy butter, they were all too full to even think about dessert.

"I wonder if we can buy a whole pie. We could have it tonight along with the left over chowder from last night. Does that sound good?" Lilly asked everyone.

After they all agreed, the waitress affirmed that they could purchase an entire pie and the price was less than they expected for the huckleberry creation that came boxed from the kitchen. Paying the bill, Waldo left a generous tip and the four friends made their way back to the truck.

"Here we are making a memory that will last a lifetime," said Karen. "These things seem so much more important now that our kids are grown. We have a new perspective now." Her heart welled up within her with her love for John, the satisfaction of having good friends, and the anticipation of living the rest of her life with her beloved.

"You're so sentimental, but you're right," answered Lilly as they climbed into the back seat. She then exclaimed, "Oh rats, we forgot to ask the waitress about the name of the diner. That's going to drive me crazy not knowing why it's called "Once in a Blue Moon."

Karen laughed back at her friend, "If we get bored we can do some more speculating. I sure liked the O'Callaghan's. I hope they didn't think we are too strange for their daughter to work for."

As they approached the valley once again they were awestruck at the view of the lodge.

"Oh no!" Karen said suddenly.

"What?" asked Lilly.

"The roof! Look at its slope!" Karen answered.

"Of course it's sloped, the snow slides off that way," Lilly said in a puzzled tone.

"No, I mean look at that peak. It must be an attic and it has to be massive…and we haven't cleaned up there yet."

"Oh Karen, you're right, I almost feel tired at the thought. Maybe we could just hose it out. Or maybe we'll find some real treasures up there? A bunch of stuff you only use once in a blue moon? Anyway, we'll worry about it in the morning. Tonight we have to put away all of this stuff," Lilly said

The lodge was feeling much more like home now that it was clean and organized. Karen placed the fresh wild flowers they had purchased on the table by the front door and promised herself she would pick some later in the week. Lilly quickly put away the supplies they had purchased and started supper. The men were busy planning their projects they had gotten supplies for, and they let Tyson run around for a while.

The evening went quickly with so much to do. Soon they were able to retire to their rooms. The two suites on opposite ends of the lower level of the lodge would be their living quarters, and there was enough space to add on a privacy deck for each suite later on when the guest rooms were ready for company. Karen was already missing her hot tub and asked John to put that on his honey-do list.

CHAPTER 3

After a lazy morning breakfast of coffee and French toast, with syrup they had brought from the south, the four started on their tasks for the day. Lilly and Karen were expecting a lot more dust, and readied with their hair tied up in scarves, the broom, squirt bottles, and supplies in hand.

"I'll open up the stairway," offered Waldo. "We need to get the cable up there for the satellite connections, and then when Matthew gets here all we'll have to do is install the dish and hook it up."

Waldo pulled the stairway down from the ceiling of a storage room, and they all ventured up in hopes of finding treasure. John opened the small windows to let in some fresh air.

Several light sockets were readily available with old-fashioned chains and pull strings. Two bookcases stood back to back in the middle of the floor, taking advantage of the higher ceiling area. Three old trunks were in one area, and a variety of interesting items filled the attic. Scattered around were boxes of papers, a spinning wheel, gold mining equipment, a couple of horse saddles, an old dog sled, and Christmas decorations. A large jar of buttons, a bottle of rum, and a first aid kit with sutures sat on the shelves along with many books.

Lilly and Karen went straight for the old trunks.

"Look at this," said Karen in amazement. The first trunk was filled with baby clothes, and two wedding dresses. "I bet these are a hundred years old! How long has it been since you played dress-up, Lilly?"

"About a million years, Karen. Look at the lace on this christening gown. It had to have been hand made," Lilly exclaimed, holding up a delicate white cotton and lace gown. "Can you imagine being pregnant a hundred years ago out here in this wilderness? I wouldn't want to go to through that here today, let alone then."

Karen had carefully lifted the wedding gowns out of the trunk and was practically upside down inside it. She dug into the trunk's depth and then squealing with triumph she suddenly sat back on her heals. "Look, it's a diary. Now we don't have to imagine. What do we know about the people that built the lodge?"

Lilly moved over to look at the book over her friend's shoulder. "Waldo," she called, "what do you know about the history of Wolf Creek?"

Waldo answered, "I know it was for sale when we were looking to buy and that's about it. Engelbert found the place, remember? We can call and see what he knows."

"That's OK, honey, Karen and I will do a little research on our own."

"Look, there's another access down here," John called from the far end as he examined the square piece of flooring with a handle on it. "I don't remember seeing anything on the ceilings of the upstairs area, where does this come out at?"

The two women were so engrossed in the treasures they had found that they didn't pay much attention to the men, and soon found themselves alone.

"Try this dress on," insisted Karen as she skimmed thru the diary. "You'll look adorable in it! And this hat…it will go with your outfit. And oh look, here's a part in this diary about a wedding in 1942."

"You know I don't look good in hats Karen…"

"This one is different Lilly, you'll look fantastic. Just try it…and here's a mirror over here as soon as I wipe the dust off."

Karen continued to read in the diary while Lilly put the dress on. The dress was ivory lace and looked like it had been made just for her. It had a high neckline, fitted empire waist and the sheer sleeves came to a lacy point just past her slender wrists. Lilly felt like a fairy princess and couldn't resist putting on the hat and then turned to catch her reflection in the mirror.

"This Ted guy asked Lois out about fifty times before she would go out with him, he had to buy her candy and flowers, and then she finally went out with him, and they went to church!"

"Come on Karen, you have to put on this other dress here, and help me with all of these buttons," Lilly pleaded.

Karen put the diary aside and came to her friend's aide, "Can you believe how many buttons there are on these dresses? What a pain to have to go through all this."

Lilly smirked slightly, "Yeah, I wonder if they had fun unbuttoning them?"

Karen laughed back at her friend, "Shame on you Lilly, these were proper ladies, I'm sure."

"Don't you think even "proper ladies" had a little fun? Especially if they had husbands like ours," Lilly replied.

"Oh, from what I've read so far in that diary, I guess they did have fun," Karen said as she slipped into the second wedding dress. "And It'd be just like you to wear that dress if you ever played strip poker," she added with a sly smile.

Soon the two were blushing, giggling brides again, and the hats accented their outfits to the tee.

The two were singing using their broom handles for microphones when Waldo and John returned to the attic to find they had stepped back in time a hundred years. Their eyes were wide with amazement as they viewed the site of their wives as brides again. They looked at each other, shrugged their shoulders, raised their eyebrows, then each look his wife in his arms.

The four danced lightly around the attic, knowing that they were living their lives very well, and loving it. It was one of those rare moments in time when both Lilly and Karen felt their lives were complete and both knew there would be special thanks in their prayers that night.

"When are we leaving for the honeymoon?" asked Waldo. Lilly blushed and swatted playfully at her husband, "Hush, Waldo."

"Hey, who are the newlyweds around here?" John asked and Karen answered, "Really hard to tell isn't it? Shall we leave them alone?"

"I wouldn't mind having you alone," John replied.

Just then the romantic mood was broken by the sound of the doorbell chimes in the front hall. "Could that be some more of our furniture already? Waldo, I didn't think it was due in until next week," Lilly said.

"Come on let's check it out," Waldo said grabbing her hand and dragging her down the stairs.

Tyson was doing his job barking at the stranger, and the look on the deliveryman's face was priceless when the slender brunette wearing an antique wedding gown answered the door.

"Uh, hello Ma'am we have a delivery here. I believe it's a bed?" the young man said, his face blushing all the way to the roots of his even redder hair.

"Well bring it on in, son," Waldo said pulling the massive double doors back and latching them on the sides.

The lodge had been built to accommodate large deliveries and the young man and his assistant had no trouble bringing the king size rough pine bed in through the main doors. Waldo led them to the Kodiak room where they had the bed set up in no time.

Introducing himself and Lilly to the young delivery man, Waldo explained that the ladies were playing dress up in the attic. The young man blushed again and said he understood even though the look on his face was one of skepticism. Waldo did manage to find out that he was a local resident who worked for the company that met the large ships at the dock in Anchorage and delivered throughout Alaska.

When Waldo and Lilly heard that his name was Scott Smith, their jaws dropped.

"Are you related to Elma Smith by any chance?" Waldo asked and Scott answered,

"Why sure, Elma's my Mom. Do you know her?"

Waldo pinched Lilly's arm when he heard her partial groan, "Of course we know her. What a great lady. Tell her hello for us will you?" he said ushering Scott and his assistant out.

182

Waldo came back in and pushing the great doors together behind him he found his wife collapsed. Not knowing if she was laughing or sobbing he joined her on the floor and putting his arms around her said, "Well my love, I would certainly like to see Elma's face when her son tells her about today."

"I'm hungry," complained John. "What's to eat around here?"

"Goodness, you'd think you never get fed," replied Karen as she led him to the kitchen to see if she could figure out what Lilly was planning.

CHAPTER 4

After lunch, Lilly and Karen went back to work and resisting temptation to play 'dress up' the rest of the day they actually made some headway on the attic. The two worked together all afternoon as they speculated and made up stories about the women who wore the beautiful dresses in the trunk. After a long afternoon they cleaned up and met again in the kitchen to fix supper.

"Karen, have you heard from Heather lately?" Lilly asked.

"No, and I've been thinking about her off and on all day…"

Just then the phone rang, and of course it was Heather.

"What's wrong?" asked Karen. "Is everything alright?"

"Oh Mom, I'm so confused. David is sounding so serious, and I just don't know what to do."

"Sounds like you're a little scared honey, but I know you'll do the right thing, and that's always been my advise…you'll always be happiest if you do what you know is right. And its okay to take some time, don't make any big decisions until you know in your heart that it's right."

"I feel better already Mom," Heather said.

"Good, just have a lot of fun and get to know him. After all you need to know if you'll be living the rest of your life with the toilet seat up or not. Now don't get me wrong, my love for you is unconditional but that doesn't mean that I think it's ok to live together. And have you ever seen him angry? How does he handle it? Is it something you can live with?"

"Mom, you're rattling on…and not making a lot of sense. I would never move in with him unless we were married," Heather stated.

"I guess I am rambling. I'm sorry, honey, I just want you to be happy…has he…uh, proposed or anything?" Karen asked.

John and Waldo had come into the kitchen shortly after Heather called and John had been quietly listening to half of the conversation. "Karen," John finally interrupted as he slipped his familiar loving arm around her waist and kissed her cheek. "Let me talk to her please?"

Immediately John and Heather were talking like he had been her doting father all of her life. Karen's heart knew her love for him as she listened to him give advice with love and friendship, not pushy, just what Heather needed. He was much more tactful than she was and Karen knew that she needn't worry that Heather would need a boyfriend, or any other man, to fill the void of a missing father figure as long as she had John. Feeling the comfort of the relationship, and blessed to have such an asset in their lives, Karen busied herself helping with the meal preparations.

Lilly started speaking Karen's own thoughts. "It's an answered prayer that Heather has a father/daughter relationship with John. I'm so glad, and it feels so "right" as you put it. Ever since her own father died, it's seemed that there's been a big piece missing in her life, and now she seems to be moving into the fulfilled life that she deserves. Even if David isn't the person she is meant to spend her life with, I'm so glad she's in a relationship and not alone down there."

Karen agreed with her friend, "I am too, and it's time I quit feeling guilty about her. I have always felt somehow that I let her and John Jr. down."

"Karen, don't even think that. You did what you had to do at the time. And just look at the amazing kids you raised in spite of that dork you were married to."

Karen laughed at her friend's reference to her first husband, "Lilly it isn't nice to speak of the dead that way."

"He knew what I thought of him when he was alive and I see no need to mince words now. But I'll give him credit for one thing—he gave you a beautiful daughter. And now she has a real father and you have a real husband. "

The two couples spent the evening quietly in front of the fire. Lilly and Karen had made chicken potpies and fresh fruit salads for dinner.

They talked quietly for hours as they watched Tyson chew contentedly on a bone. It was getting to be quite a ritual for Waldo to bring the puppy in for a while after dinner and they all enjoyed his antics.

"Lilly, where do you think Heather would want to get married? I've dragged her from one end of the states to the other, dropped her off in Louisiana, and now we're almost as far away as we can get. Maybe we could have a Christmas wedding here, no...the babies are due about then and her friends are in Louisiana. And we promised Jennifer we'd give her a big wedding, who knows how soon we'll have to go back for that one. Oh, what are we going to do? Anyway, as usual, I'm jumping way ahead of myself. As far as I know he hasn't even actually proposed yet." John patted his wife's hand and reassured her that the logistics of all the weddings would work out the way God intended them to.

The early morning air was still crisp even though the Alaskan summer was well on its way. With help from Waldo and Jamie to create the needed parts, John had the seaplane running smoothly.

"Smooth as a baby's butt," John said with a touch of pride in his voice.

"In just a few months you should have first hand experience at how smooth that is," commented Lilly. "Me too for that matter, it's been a few years and I think I've forgotten."

The four were ready to take off on their first flight, and in anticipation of viewing the land clear to the North Pole if the weather would allow them to go that far. So far it was looking like a gorgeous day with only a speckle of a cloud here and there.

After their not-so-long-ago tragedy in Louisiana, they were very particular to take extreme safety precautions. John had gone over the plane about a hundred times, and Lilly was especially thoughtful to every little detail. She had an emergency food supply, space blankets, extra fuel, rope, flashlights, etc. Plus food for later in the day in case they weren't able to land where there was the convenience of a restaurant.

"You'd think we were packing for a week long vacation," said Waldo as he packed the last of the supplies into the box at the back of the plane.

Karen sat in the co-pilots seat next to John, and Lilly snuggled close to Waldo in the seats right behind them.

As the seaplane rose above the valley, Waldo exclaimed, "Look, there's the O'Callaghan place."

The mountains in the distance were beautiful as they climbed up and out over the vast tundra, and the land seemed to reach endlessly into the horizon.

Unbeknownst to Karen, John had put the plane on automatic pilot. Taking his hands from the controls he crossed his arms across his chest. "Ok, you can drive now," he told her in a matter of fact tone.

Karen felt a pain in her chest as the panic struck her, not knowing if there was something essential that needed to be done here. There was no way she wanted anything to do with this. It was scary enough just being at this height in such a small plane. Suddenly it seemed imperative that there was absolutely nothing right outside the windows!

"Do you all want to end up flying sideways and upside down?" she said, her voice showing her panic.

"Oh no, you don't, none of that stuff," said Lilly from the back.

John took the controls again and apologized for scaring them. "We're going to have to give you some flying lessons though; you never know when it might come in handy." Waldo was still chuckling as they located the airport.

Soon they were landing at their first stop. The city was bigger than the village, but still much smaller than what they were used to. The first priority was to obtain the papers for their state license to run a business. Then they would pick up some of the things that they had ordered but hadn't been delivered yet.

The office was small, but had three employees busy at their desks. "I don't think they get much business here, but they do look efficient," whispered Lilly to Karen as they waited for the front desk secretary to look up from her busy typing.

"Hello, we're here to pick up our business license...Lynsie," announced Waldo as he read her nameplate on the counter.

"Your name please?" Lynsie Davis looked up from her computer.

Waldo told her the necessary information and a look of recognition came over the secretary's face. "Oh you're the folks that are going to operate the Wolf Creek Lodge, aren't you? My husband and his dad can't wait to go on one of your fishing expeditions. Aren't Engelbert and Angie Garner going to be a part of your business?"

"Talk about small towns," Lilly whispered to Karen as Waldo was bringing Lynsie up to date on their friend's latest ventures in Nashville.

"Wow, I always knew she could sing. I've heard the story of Engelbert falling in love with her when she was singing at the Golden Nugget Saloon, but I never thought she'd try Nashville. Wow, I can't wait to call Aunt Elma and tell her. Of course she lives near your Lodge so she probably already knows," Lynsie said as she handed the laminated business license over to Waldo. "Oh well, I'll give it a try anyway. Honestly, that woman knows everything. Have you all met her yet? My Aunt, Elma Smith?"

It was Karen's pinching that kept Lilly from exclaiming out loud. As usual Waldo smoothed things over.

"Oh yes, we know her well. And what a lovely lady she is too. We'll tell her we met you. Good day," he said with a smile and the four left the office.

As soon as they were outside Lilly demanded, "Karen, quit pinching me. Is everyone in Alaska related to that woman?"

John, Karen and Waldo couldn't answer her for the howls of laughter coming from the three of them. Waldo put his arm around his wife and hugged her close.

"I'm beginning to think so, Love. Better make the best of it and make friends with her when we get back. Maybe you and Karen could invite her for tea," he said wiping the tears from his eyes.

"Never", she replied, "I won't give her the satisfaction of seeing the inside of our home. Oh why do the Elma Smith's of the world always find me?"

Karen linked her arm though her friends and pulled her down the street, "Come on, let's do a little shopping and get some lunch. That will make you feel better."

As they rounded the corner, the Golden Nugget Saloon stood in front of them. Lilly gave a little gasp of surprise as the many stories about this place came to mind. She had never realized that it was such an impressive building. Her previous worries that had developed over the last few minutes melted away at the sight of the famous building.

It was very large with old-fashioned swinging doors accenting the red brick front along with wooden paned windows. The inside was decorated with antique gold mining equipment. A massive crystal and gold chandelier hung from the center of the large room, gold wallpaper accented the gold plated brass railing around the bar. A golden velvet curtain hung over the now silent stage where their friend, Angie, once sang. As they entered, the bar tender slid a beer down the counter to a customer.

"I could sure go for a big ole hamburger and greasy French fries," said John with a bit of excitement in his voice. "And then I challenge you to a game of pool," he warned Waldo.

The burgers were a good ten inches in diameter, brimming with lettuce, raw onion and tomato garnish. The large basket of crispy golden brown French fries looked like a mountain, and home made raspberry beer blessed their taste buds.

"Once again, we should have shared one of these," Karen informed Lilly. "I guess we'll learn sooner or later, maybe we ought to plan on really big portions for our business as this seems to be the norm here in Alaska."

"I don't think we've ever served small portions, but I guess we could really heap it on. After all this is a big land and everything should be proportionate. We'll have to work on some signature items, like "Wolf Creek Stew" or "Wolf Creek Cobbler" featuring what ever berry or fruit happens to be in season and in the winter it can be apple," Lilly answered dreamily.

They spent a couple of hours playing pool and relaxing, and soon it was time to be on their way. After doing a few errands, the four were once again in the air. A little further north, and then home again was the plan. John gently put his hand on Karen's to let her know that everything was under control.

Waldo was the first to pick out the polar bear and her cub in the ice and snow. It really was quite the sight, so typical of Alaska but yet so different than a picture in a book. Several polar bears could be seen, and they circled for a few minutes to watch.

As the seaplane touched water they were all glad to be home. The flight had been flawless and it was good to be back in front of the fire with Tyson again.

The four were still so full from the enormous burgers and fries that no one wanted dinner, not even John. Waldo and John poured over maps spread before the massive hearth and tried to keep Tyson from ripping them to shreds. The two were plotting possible fishing expeditions now that the seaplane had proved itself.

While the men had dreams of fishing, the two women were planning recipes and looking at mail order catalogs to complete the six remaining suites at the Lodge.

Lilly and Karen both stifled yawns and looked at each other. "Can you imagine we're thinking of bed at 9:00 PM?" Lilly asked.

Karen smiled at her friend and agreed, "My how we've changed."

Lilly patted her husband on the shoulder and gently reminded him to put Tyson out before he went to bed.

Distractedly he didn't look up but spoke, "Sure hon, and put a little ice cream on it too please."

"What, ice cream on what?"

"On the apple pie, didn't you ask John and me if we wanted pie?" Waldo asked seriously.

John looked up hopefully. "It has been a long time since lunch."

Karen laughed, "You go on to bed, Lilly. I'll feed these guys."

CHAPTER 5

After almost a month of decorating, planning, and a lot of muscle work, the lodge was looking magnificent. Pictures were taken for the web site, and reservations were now available.

"I think we're ready for customers," said Lilly with pride in her voice as she hung a polar bear wall hanging in the Polar Room."

"Yes, we are and that tapestry is the perfect finishing touch for this room," replied Karen.

"Thanks, I thought so too. You know Waldo bought this tapestry for me in Alaska before we were married. It hung in our bedroom at our first apartment and then we had it hanging in Jamie's room. When we moved south I put it in storage, it didn't seem to go with the décor in Louisiana. I'm so happy to be able to use it again."

They were interrupted by a very big noise that quickly grew bigger and louder. The two looked at each other in shock as they thought there was nothing in this part of the country that could make such a big noise.

Looking out of the window, they could see that a helicopter was landing in the strip at the far end of the valley.

"It must be Matthew!" exclaimed Karen.

They rushed to find John and Waldo. All four jumped into the truck and drove out to pick him up.

Matthew climbed down from the helicopter with a big grin on his face, knowing that he was welcome here, and also knowing that the gift he had brought Karen was priceless. Matthew wore Levi's, a faded t-shirt under his Levi jacket, and a modest attitude which disguised the famous, wealthy person that he really was. Being a welcome sight, he was greeted with the kind of a warm hug that only a mom knows how to give.

"Alright, close your eyes and hold out your hands," he instructed Karen.

"OK, but if you have to climb back into that helicopter and out again I'll have to wait too long," she complained.

John Jr. loved the surprised look on his mom's face as he took both her hands in his. Karen turned to her husband. "John, did you plan this?"

"No," he responded as he gave his son a big bear hug, "this one I didn't but I'm sure glad someone did."

"I knew Matthew was coming," explained John Jr., "and Melinda's mother is helping her out this week-end so I was able to get away for a couple of days. And you know we're all curious about the lodge here." As he finished explaining, his brown eyes met his dad's matching ones. Karen knew that the two would never really be separated again, no matter what the geography was. Her heart filled with satisfaction as she watched them connect, aware that they were growing close and enhancing each other's lives.

After being rewarded with another thank you hug from Karen, Matthew turned to Lilly. Catching her up in a big bear hug he whispered he was sorry that he hadn't been able to bring Jamie too. "I asked him but he didn't think he should leave Kelsi with all the work on the ranch. But they did say maybe Christmas."

Hugging him back Lilly replied, "That's OK, I understand. I'll just have to spoil you for a few days."

"I do have something for you though," he told Lilly with a twinkle in his eye. "I know you love to cook, but today I've brought lunch. I can't imagine not having fast food ever again, and you guys must be all going through withdrawal." He pulled a heated bag and a couple of six-packs of cold cola's out of the doorway of the helicopter. The aroma of the pizza was a little more than they could take, so not wasting any time they found a blanket to spread out by the creek and enjoyed a pizza picnic.

John Sr. and Waldo sat side by side. The only conversation they made consisted of taking turns saying "yum, yum," between bites. Just as the pizza had totally disappeared, the air was suddenly filled with a foul odor.

"Matt, what did you do?" teased John Jr. "You need to go for a swim in the lake!"

"It's not a lake, it's a creek and I didn't do anything, it must have been you."

"Dad…?"

"Not me," replied John Sr.

"Uncle Waldo…?"

"Look over there, the other side of the lake on the south side of the clearing," instructed Waldo in a concerned tone. "I do believe Sasquatch, also known as Big Foot, is keeping an eye on us."

The hairy man-like creature was exactly like the stories they had all heard. The stench in the air was strong now. They all sat watching his every move for a few minutes.

"He must have smelled our pizza," said Matthew in a nervous tone. The look on his face showed his fear. "I'll bet he's never had the pleasure, and I really don't care to meet him. Do you think he'll come over here?"

As soon as the tall creature seemed to realize they were all watching him, he disappeared into the woods, walking as if he were a man.

"We'd better get back to the lodge," said Waldo in a calm voice. "Tyson is probably hungry, I can hear him barking."

"Who's Tyson?" asked Matthew.

"Come on, we'll load the pickup with the supplies and then you can meet him," answered Waldo.

John Sr. and Waldo gave the boys a complete tour of the place while Lilly and Karen started dinner. They had already prepared everything in advance that they could, not knowing exactly when Matthew's arrival would be. Karen was flitting around the kitchen in total happiness.

Matthew poked his head in the back door of the kitchen. "What's for dinner?"

"It's cheeseburger pie tonight, and deviled eggs WITHOUT paprika," announced Karen, "and I made you a chocolate sour cream cake from scratch. The eggs here are so fresh they don't spread at all, they're just perky."

Matthew gave her a strange questioning look, not understanding about fresh eggs. "I'll show you later," she promised.

"Mm, that sounds great," said John Jr. coming in behind Matthew. "How's the business going?"

"We're not really open yet, but we should be soon. Waldo hopes to take the first customers out yet this fall before the weather gets bad. And we just got our license. So all we need are people," Lilly replied.

The conversation at dinner was lively with the addition of the two young men. Karen's eyes never left John Jr. and Lilly was doing her best to shower Matthew with the same amount of attention she would show her own son.

After dinner Karen and Lilly listened as Matthew explained the installation of the satellite dish, and the web site that he had in mind for the lodge. It was complete with fish jumping out of streams, bears peeping from behind bushes, and wildflowers sprouting before your eyes.

CHAPTER 6

The next morning Karen was the first one up eager to fix a special breakfast for her two young men. She was happily mixing the batter for waffles, using Lilly's special recipe that she would share only with Karen, and was surprised when John Jr. stuck his head through the door. "Mmm…I thought I smelled coffee," he said giving his mom a quick hug and pouring himself a cup of the fresh brewed French roast.

"Honey, what are you doing up so early? Is everything OK?" She had always been able to read his thoughts and knew when something was troubling him. John looked at her with somber brown eyes and finally spoke.

"I didn't want to tell you last night, Mom. And an extra day wouldn't make a difference. But you need to know that Mrs. Bartholomew passed away earlier this week. She died peacefully in her sleep."

Karen felt as if someone had taken all the breath from her lungs. Mrs. Bartholomew had been a mainstay in her life from the time of her first marriage to Dunston. Mom B, as Karen called her, was the mother of a childhood friend of Dunston's and was like a Grandmother to Karen's children. She had been a source of comfort to Karen after Dunston died and she was forced to raise the children alone. A simple visit to her modest home would comfort Karen and give her the strength to go on. Mom B was a widow and only one of her three children was still alive. Whenever Karen felt bogged down in the injustices in her own life she had only to look at the adversity that Mom B had lived through to put her life in perspective. The motherly woman never said anything negative about anyone, and was definitely a positive light in the world. When Karen and Lilly had first started talking about the New Orleans venture, Mom B had encouraged them to make the move and even tried to invest her modest income in the business.

Karen brushed the tears from her eyes and sniffed, "I'm glad John and I stopped to see her on our way here. She was so happy to meet him. You know she was the only other person besides Lilly and Waldo that knew Dunston wasn't your father. When is the service?"

"Not until next week. Mom, I'm so sorry I had to tell you like this. But there's no easy way to handle these things." John reached out and took his Mother's hand in his.

Karen squeezed his hand and replied, "We all knew she was getting up there. I'm just glad she was able to live at home until it happened and she was never sick or in pain. Does Heather know?"

"Yes, Melinda and I both talked with her a couple of days ago and decided that I would tell you here."

At that moment Lilly rushed into the kitchen. "Oh my goodness, I overslept. Karen, are you cooking breakfast this morning? What's going on?" she asked as she noticed the tears on her friend's cheek. "Are Melinda and the kids OK? Is it the baby?"

Karen rose from her chair at the table and put her arms around her friend and told her about Mom B. She was very special to Lilly also and Lilly had always been grateful that Mom B. was there for Karen during the times she couldn't be.

When Waldo, Matthew and John Sr. joined the group in the kitchen they found them telling "Mom B" stories and laughing together with their memories of this remarkable woman whom they would never see on this earth again.

Karen lovingly painted a verbal picture of a beautiful lady in the 1950's. The flowing skirt on her dress was covered with an apron. Her hair was perfect, and you could almost smell the bread and cinnamon rolls baking in her antique oven as the scene was described. Even the gray linoleum flooring came alive. They were all mesmerized in the moment as silence fell upon them for a few seconds.

"You know Karen, you really should write some of your memories down. That way she will always be remembered through our lives and the lives of our children too. You know memories live forever if they take the form of written words," Lilly said.

"Right after breakfast, I'll go work on that. Now let's get these men fed," Karen answered.

As soon as breakfast was over, Karen slipped her arm through her husbands and led him to their suite. "Just hold me for a minute?" she pleaded.

"Of course dear..." The comfort of his strong arms around her made everything okay again. He kissed her forehead as he lovingly brushed the hair from her face.

"Life comes and goes, and I just needed to treasure this moment of life here with you for a moment. Does that make sense?" Karen asked.

"Yes, it makes sense," he answered.

"And I really do need to write about this," she continued. "It's in my heart and spirit, I feel it."

An office had been put together in a small room next to the kitchen. The window held a pleasant view out over the back deck with the mountain and trees in the background. Matthew worked quickly to complete the hook up of the computer, printer, and a new monitor he had brought with him.

It wasn't long before Karen had her first draft finished. A phone call to Heather reminded her of things she had forgotten about, and the second draft was created.

Karen worked thru the day until Lilly had the evening meal prepared. As they gathered at the table John Sr. sensed Karen's mood of reverence and said grace, thanking God for the people in their lives along with the good food on the table.

At the end of John's grace Karen solemnly announced that she was finished with her story.

"Read it for us," coaxed Waldo.

"Of course," she answered. "I would love to honor Mom B and take you on an imaginary visit to her home." And she began to read:

"Driving down the gravel driveway, I turned around by the old garage that I knew housed an antique car of some sort. Parking next to the grassy hill that Dad always called the 'upper 40', I walked past the newer double garage. I smiled as I remembered the story of when they were building it. They had cut and cut the final board until it became too short and they had to order more wood at the end. I could almost picture Dad on the riding lawn mower as the doorbell chimes rang through the house and I noticed the pansies were back again this year like usual. A welcome was always followed by the climb up a few wooden steps, and the ringing of the bell, which was mounted by the top of the inside kitchen door to ring every time the door was opened or closed. Entering the familiar turquoise kitchen with a matching turquoise rotary dial telephone on the counter, I freely took a lemon drop from the dish on the table. She had just come in from her rose garden, and setting down her clippers she offered me a 7-Up. After insisting that she didn't need to bother, she would make a trip to the basement. Finding the green bottle among the bittersweet memories treasured there, she would soon return and fill a small glass with ice cubes and 7-Up. The ranger cookies came right from the freezer along with a story about the person that made them for her.

The newspaper lay open on the table, the word puzzle half completed as it had stumped her today. The Tiger cartoon was also on top for conversation, a laugh and a memory. Fresh roses from her garden graced the center of the table in a crystal glass vase. Once again, I glanced at the built-in china cupboard that held hundreds of bells and below it the counter that seemed to hold just as many birthday cards each February. Many times my children had tried to count the bells, only to find more in the windowsill or the cowbells on the bookcase that they had missed. It was a little like trying to count the stars. Then just when they thought they had a good count, she would tell them about the ones tucked away in the basement. We talked about what was new in our lives, and then went to the living room. I stopped briefly to put my glass in the sink and the used napkin in the burner of the antique stove.

The living room was also a very familiar room; it had textured wallpaper, a transparent lampshade with scenery pictures on it, and Dad's empty chair. The console television displayed pictures of her two grandchildren and family members. The television was off, but I knew it was not a stranger to the Lawrence Welk show. When my kids were younger, she would always find some Lincoln logs and other toys for them to play with on the hardwood floor. She showed me the Christmas stocking she was knitting. She was very modest, but I knew she was determined to force her arthritic hands to finish the project so that no child in her family would be left out. It was a large project, with a detailed picture and the child's name spelled out in the knitting. In our conversation, she happened to mention that she had drawings that she used to do. I didn't remember ever seeing them before, and hadn't realized she had such an artistic ability. Pulling them from her bedroom closet, she called them pictures of "pretty ladies." She had drawn the portraits from magazines that were at least fifty years old. I was very impressed to learn of her talent.

The hand made quilt on the bed was a beautiful Sunbonnet Sue, and obviously not to be sat on. So we carefully folded it up to protect it and to make room to open up her photo album. I had seen these pictures before, but this time it was different. Her life story was here. We viewed her childhood pictures, antique cars that were new at the time, old-fashioned bathing suits, and memories of her dating years. Her true love and three beautiful children completed the pages. As I viewed the pictures that had been carefully hung above the headboard, she again named each one, touching them with her heart. Only one of her sons was still living, yet her whole family was in her heart, and complete on the wall. I felt a touch of her pain as I thought about her loss of a daughter, son, and husband. This was the day she taught me a lesson about family. I will never forget the emotion we felt, and the love for family that she demonstrated as we viewed her completed collection.

As I prepared to leave, she pulled out a couple of unwrinkled $2.00 bills from under the pie plates in the stove drawer for me to give to my kids. I never left her home empty handed, so with an arm full of roses, snowdrops, and little pink bells, I returned to my car.

Returning her wave as she said good-by at the screen door, I knew I had just experienced something very special. As a single mother of two, I left that day feeling encouragement, and knowing that my children were my family. I had been given new insight, and a new appreciation. The value of life and family had changed for me. I will remember her every time I make Chicken Supreme, taste a cinnamon roll, or see a Butterfinger in a Halloween basket. I will remember her when I see her favorite color, turquoise. I will remember her when I drive by the home that she lived in. I will remember, and my children will remember.

I am not a blood relative, but Verna Bartholomew let me have the privilege of calling her "Mom" for almost twenty-eight years. The memory of this loving, generous lady will always live in my heart.

Lots of Love,
Karen

John Jr. had closed his eyes during the story. "Mom, it was just like I was there!" he exclaimed. "I never knew you could write like that, wow what a tribute."

Karen had tears in her eyes when she finished reading and towards the end her voice had quaked slightly. Composing herself she asked, "John could you take this home with you? Your dad and I have decided not to go to the funeral, but I would like for this to be read. I want everyone to know how she touched my life."

"Sure, Mom, I'll read it. I know it will mean a lot to her son to hear how she touched other people's lives too."

"Enough of this sadness," Karen exclaimed, "Lilly prepared this wonderful supper all by herself, and we better eat it before it gets cold."

"It wasn't a problem Karen, its only chili and cornbread," Lilly said.

"And apple pie?" Waldo asked hopefully amidst laughter from everyone in the room that knew how much Waldo loved his wife's apple pie.

"Yes, apple pie," said Lilly, "and Karen if it makes you feel better YOU can do the dishes."

"Don't worry darling, I'll help you," promised John Sr.

As it turned out everyone carried their own plates to the kitchen sink and the entire group helped clean up. Then they spent a lively evening playing charades to the complete puzzlement and amusement of Tyson, who probably thought that his rather strange "masters" had lost their minds.

They all retired happy and exhausted. As Karen nuzzled her nose into her husband's neck, he spoke softly. "I'm really glad you wrote and read that story tonight, I thought I knew you well, but I keep learning more about you that I never imagined. And we really learned a lot about each other playing charades, and I love spending time with my son, it's as if we've always been connected somehow. I think this is the happiest I've ever been."

"I know, I love you too," she replied as she ran her fingers through the curls at the nape of his neck.

Giggling, she continued, "Waldo really does do a good monkey imitation, and you and John Jr. are real hams."

Under the same moon at the other end of the lodge, Lilly was cuddled up next to Waldo. "Dear, do you think you could do that monkey thing for me again?" she teased.

CHAPTER 7

Saturday was to be a very busy day, and Matthew had the itinerary decided. By the end of the day the communication system in the lodge should be complete.

The men awoke to the scent of bacon and fresh coffee throughout the lodge. They arrived in the kitchen just as Karen was taking the steaming hot biscuits from the oven. Lilly was immediately taking orders for eggs.

"I'll have mine sunny side up!" responded Karen before anyone else had a chance.

"Me too," said John Sr. as he winked at his wife.

"Ok you two, we need some help with these plates," said Lilly. "And that reminds me, there's no reason why we can't all go to church tomorrow. When we were in town I noticed that the service is at 10:00."

Karen looked at Matthew to see what his reaction was. She knew that he hadn't been real keen on going to church growing up, and was curious as to how he would respond. She didn't think John Jr. would mind though, as Melinda was sure to have the kids at Sunday school every week.

"Sounds like a plan," said John Sr. "Looking forward to it."

It was obvious to Matthew that he would have to go along with this event; after all he was the visitor here, and he really didn't want to be left alone in such a big place all by himself. But giving it a try anyway he complained, "I didn't bring church clothes."

"That's ok, we'll all go casual. I don't imagine anyone around here would be all dressed up anyway," replied Waldo, knowing that Lilly wouldn't have it any other way.

The men prepared for a hike up the mountain with the satellite equipment. The plan was to mount the dish on a sturdy pole at a clearing they had determined would be an ideal spot for reception. Each of the four men carried their share of the load, and the parts would be assembled upon arrival.

Lilly and Karen packed them a lunch even though they promised to be back in a few hours, and the two women started to work on setting up the computer stations in each of the suites.

After seeing them off, Lilly and Karen decided to work their way from one end of the lodge to the other, starting with the Kodiak Suite. The highlight of this room was the duvet cover on the down comforter. A family of brown bears with the cub nestled up to its mother accented the cozy bed made of rough pine logs. Matching furniture gave the room a woodsy feeling, and the large print of a brown bear hung above the fireplace.

"This is just about like living in the woods," commented Lilly as she rearranged the placement of the tree shaped coat rack.

Each of the suites had a small desk with the facilities to give the guests access to their e-mail, and they would each hold a compact computer. The goal today was to unpack the equipment and distribute it to each suite.

"There, this desk fits great here, moving the desk over by the outlet was an ingenious idea, don't you think?" said Karen as she pretended to take the credit for the obvious good idea.

Lilly ignored the fact that Karen had just taken the credit for her idea, but promised herself that she would get even later, one way or another.

The next room was the Polar Suite. Lilly's tapestry hung above the large bed, and a polar bear print adorned the area over the fireplace. A faux polar bear rug lay in front of the fireplace, and a white oak sleigh bed, covered with a white down comforter, made you feel like you were right at the North Pole.

"I bet Santa would feel at home here," commented Karen.

"Yeah, I bet he's watching and listening right now so you better be good and tell the truth! I think I hear bells!" teased Lilly as they both laughed at their silliness.

The Homestead Suite was full of antiques, some found at the nearby village. Waldo had made a case with a glass window to show off his petrified tobacco plug that his grandfather had brought on the first cargo ship to Alaska.

A copy of a picture of that first cargo ship had been enlarged and framed to hang above the hearth. It had been quite a time consuming project, but very productive as the mat and the large antique wooden frame suited the print well. Simple furniture gave the room a rustic feeling. A row of large hooks took the place of the closet, and the bowl and pitcher set could make a person think there might not really be a bathroom adjoining the room. A large wooden chest held extra bedding and also served as a coffee table.

The Gold Mine Suite was decorated with the old equipment Lilly and Karen had pulled out of the attic. They had found a picture of Ted and Lois, the people in the diary, and had a copy enlarged to hang above that fireplace. The duvet and matching pillows were white silk flecked with gold.

The fifth room was the Husky Suite. Tyson himself graced the fireplace with his portrait. Waldo and John had crafted a table from the old dog sled they had found in the attic. The headboard of the queen size bed was made of metal, the design twisting and turning in a swirling pattern. The wool comforter and throw pillows came from the local mercantile.

The Fishing Suite had been easy to decorate since the mail order catalogs seemed to be full of fishing memorabilia. The table lampshade had fish on it; the fabric of the bedding had fish on it, throw rugs, even the flush lever on the toilet was in the shape of a fish. The papasan chair and love seat sat next to a window overlooking the creek, and went well with the wicker headboard.

"You could almost catch a live squirming fish from this room," commented Lilly.

The next room was decorated in knotty pine with a king size log bed and wardrobe. As you entered the room your eyes were instantly drawn to the massive moose head mounted over the fireplace. The wrought iron moose sculptures adorning the walls were creations of Jamie and Kelsi's as were the twisted iron towel racks and paper holders in the bathroom.

The eighth room was everyone's favorite, the Aurora Borealis Suite. Fiber-optic lighting, and shimmering taffeta and silk fabrics in shades of blue, green and gold made the room shine and sparkle.
"The kids will like this one," said Karen. "I think we'll leave the twin beds apart in here until after Christmas. We can always push them together later to meet the needs of our guests."
The last two rooms weren't finished just yet. One would have an Aleutian Indian theme, and hopefully Lanie would be able to help with that.

As they finished placing the last computer, the two women looked at each other, knowing that each of them was feeling the satisfaction of a job well done. Their stomachs had started grumbling long before the work was finished but the two had delayed eating until they had finished. Returning to the kitchen they were not surprised to find it was well after 2:00 PM.

Since the men hadn't returned, Lilly and Karen made their favorite chicken salad with cucumber sandwiches and Lilly checked on the chicken she had put in the crock-pot for dinner. As Lilly removed the chicken from the stock to de-bone it, Karen began preparing the vegetables for chicken potpie.

Karen asked if they had time to make orange, carrot and pineapple Jell-O that John Jr. and Matthew loved so much.

Lilly had already started taking the utensils out for the Jell-O and laughingly said they would have time if they used ice and didn't make jigglers.

Karen started grating carrots and laughed with her friend saying that maybe the two had outgrown the jigglers.

"I wonder how the guys are doing," said Lilly.

Suddenly the room became very quiet, and the two women looked at each other. The feeling of being watched overcame them, and this was the first time they had felt any fear here in the wilderness. The men were not here to protect them, and they were on their own.

"I guess we didn't turn the radio on yet," said Karen calmly, hoping for an easy solution to the quietness.

As both of them struggled to figure out what was going on, they looked over at the back window of the kitchen as a dark shadow crossed the room. A very large moose was standing there with his nose up against the windowpane. He must have stood nine feet tall.

"Well I'll be we have a peeping Tom!" exclaimed Lilly. "What should we do? I've heard that they can be real mean, and Waldo said they'll attack your car sometimes."

"I bet he smells the food and he's hungry," said Karen. "But I don't think we'd want to feed him, or he might want to move in!"

"Maybe he's been chasing the guys, maybe he chased them up a tree, maybe they're afraid to come home because he's here…maybe that big moose head upstairs is his grandfather and he's not very happy with us!" worried Lilly, not knowing whether to laugh or cry.

"Calm down, Lilly", said Karen, "I'm sure the guys are OK. He doesn't look mean, just curious."

As the two stood and stared at the gigantic animal staring in at them, they were startled by a loud noise. Both of them jumped at least a foot as the noise erupted in what could be an imitation of the band that Jamie, John Jr. and Matthew had started as teenagers. Rushing to the window they saw their men were shouting, jumping around, and waving their arms in an attempt to scare the intruder. Waldo's monkey imitation the night before appeared to enhance his performance quite a bit. The moose stared at them for a moment and then slowly sauntered away. He was there one minute, and not a trace of him could be seen the next. Lilly and Karen had the door open as soon as he left the porch and were running towards their husbands.

After each of them had shared their experiences, they settled down to finish their tasks for the day.

John Jr. came into the kitchen as his mom and aunt were finishing the meal preparations.

"Did you know you two kind of do a happy dance when you're cooking together?" he asked laughingly. "It's something I should get on tape some day…"

"You guys scaring off that moose is what we should have on tape! Just go wash your hands and be thankful we aren't having moose for dinner," instructed his mother.

After saying grace, Waldo cleared his throat and then apologized, "Matthew, I'm sorry we won't have time to go fishing while you're here."

"Oh that's ok; you know I don't like to be away from things that are digital and just basic technology for very long. And I don't think I'm ready to live among the Big Foot and bears, and moose."

"But you will come and bring Annie and Maggie for Christmas won't you?" asked Lilly.

"Of course, we wouldn't miss that for the world, and Annie would be very disappointed if we didn't make it," he replied. "When are the babies due?"

"Kelsi goes to the doctor on Monday, and then after that we'll know a lot more and be able to plan a little more definitely. Melinda isn't due until the middle of January now, so we're thinking they'll all be able to make it. And speaking of company," Lilly continued, "what do you say we invite the O'Callaghan's for dinner tomorrow after church?"

"That would be great. But I think Waldo should call Mr. O'Callaghan; I think they're kind of old fashioned that way. What do you want to fix?" Karen answered.

"How about turkey? I have cornbread in the freezer for dressing and we can make that and the cranberry relish tonight. Oh and how about a peach/raspberry cobbler for dessert? I still have peaches and raspberries in the freezer too. It will just take a jiffy to get things thawed."

"Sounds like you have our evening planned," Karen laughed.

Lilly frowned, "Oh, Karen, I'm so sorry. I forget sometimes that everyone doesn't share my passion for cooking and you have a husband now and your son is here. You go on and spend time with them and I'll do the cooking."

"Oh yeah sure, so you can claim all the credit for the dinner tomorrow. No way!" Karen replied.

The two were interrupted from their good-natured arguing by Waldo who agreed that the dinner was a great idea and left to make the call from the den. He was back shortly with the news that the invitation had been accepted and engaged the help of everyone. "Who says you women should have all the fun? Lilly, love of my life, you know my dressing is better than yours. Now move over women, I've brought the troops."

With that the men rolled up their sleeves and while Waldo began chopping vegetables, John Sr. mixed cobbler dough and John Jr. and Matthew cracked nuts.

Lilly and Karen attempted to supervise the preparations but their advice was mostly ignored by the men's intent on proving their worth in the kitchen.

So the evening was spent in the homey atmosphere of the large country kitchen as the friends and family prepared an early

Thanksgiving feast to share with their new friends in this new world they now called their home.

The next morning the entire lodge was busy with the buzz of getting everyone, and everything ready. The turkey was in the oven, the potatoes were peeled, and Karen had made deviled eggs again for Matthew. The massive table in the formal dining hall was set and everyone was dressed and ready to go.

Matthew had come down late for breakfast, but dressed for church. Karen and Lilly exchanged a look when he appeared. They had often speculated about his reluctance to attend church but cared too much about him to invade his privacy with a blunt question. After many hours of discussion they had remembered the words from the age-old song of their youth that stressed the importance of being known as Christians by your actions and not your words, and decided the best way to handle the Matthew church dilemma was prayer.

Almost surprisingly, the six fit comfortably in the pickup. As they arrived at the church, the parking lot was at least half full. The building was very different from the little chapel in Louisiana, and also different from any other church they had ever attended.

"This building must have been built by the Russians that migrated here," commented Waldo.

"Yes, I think that would be the history," replied John Sr.

The tall white Russian Orthodox building stood at the far end of the village. It was full of many shapes in its structure, and three large gold domes jutted from the top, all of them sweeping up into pointed tops like ice cream cones.

If the group thought that the outside of the old building was intimidating they were certainly not prepared for the interior. As they entered, the majesty of the golden cross at the front of the church brought them all to silence.

Lilly squeezed Karen's arm and whispered, "I sure hope you don't have any pizza in your pockets today, Karen."

Karen snickered and whispered back, "Did you bring the animal crackers?"

The two were shushed by Waldo who nudged John and whispered that they would need to separate their wives if they were to enjoy the service.

The six looked around, now recognizing a few people, and then sat in am empty pew.

Elma Smith sat with her husband and three children in the pews across the isle, and just ahead of the newcomers. Of course they recognized Elma and Scott, but her other son and daughter were quite a shock to see. The girl had tattoos on both shoulders, and wore a skimpy top showing her mid-riff a few inches above her hip hugging faded jeans. As she turned to look around, she showed off her pierced tongue when she smiled and made a face. Her hair was rather blue, and her pierced nose caught the light with a twinkle. Her brother's arms were full of tattoos, his black hair fairly dripped with the grease it took to create the spike style he wore. He seemed to carry himself with the same attitude of rebellion as his sister and for a moment Lilly was grateful she no longer had teenagers at home.

"I didn't know teenagers had such a case of rebellion out here in the wilderness," whispered Karen to Lilly.

"I wonder how she even got them here," marveled Lilly. "Now Karen, I know you always want to, but don't you go tugging on those oversized pants of his to see if they'll fall off."

As the O'Callaghan's arrived, they stopped to welcome the newcomers, and then sat ahead of them several rows. The room rapidly filled with more unfamiliar faces, and Lilly and Karen's minds were whirling with speculation of who each person was.

The service was fairly formal. The gray haired minister arrived through a side door at the back of the pulpit, wearing a black robe with a deep purple shawl. Candle lighters in white robes made their way down the aisle to light the candelabras just before the service started.

The service was surprisingly a lot like the services they were raised in, probably due to the variety of people attending the only church in the small town. The first hymn was one Karen and Lilly recognized from their youth. Looking at each other with smiles they raised their voices in praise and knew they both were re-living the same fond memory.

The pastor then preached a sermon on the story of the Good Samaritan…A lawyer asked Jesus how to get into heaven, and Jesus had him answer his own question, as the lawyer knew the law. The answer was; love the Lord thy God with all thy heart, and all thy mind, and all thy soul, and love thy neighbor as thyself. The lawyer pressed Jesus further, asking who is my neighbor? Jesus responded with a parable…There was a certain man who fell among thieves. He was wounded, and laid in the road. A high priest came by, but did not stop. A second man representing the law came by, but he did not stop either. Finally a certain third man came by who stopped and took care of the wounded man. He poured oil and wine into his wounds, and took him to the Inn. Before he left he paid for the man's care, and promised to pay any other expenses needed for his care the next time he came by.

After the offering was taken, the pastor welcomed the newcomers to the congregation and invited them to stay for the coffee hour after the service. The final hymn was Amazing Grace, a fitting end to a memorable sermon.

Karen and Lilly left the cathedral on the arms of their husbands and made their way with the rest of the congregation to the enormous meeting hall below the main sanctuary. There they met so many people that keeping names to faces was impossible.

After assuring Pastor Morgan that they would return, they made their way to the pickup eager to get home and finish the dinner preparations. Karen couldn't help but remark to Lilly that she must have taken the sermon message to heart since she went out of her way to be pleasant to Elma Smith.

"I felt so sorry for her when I saw her with those misfit teens. It's probably her fault that they turned out that way, but for today I will give her the benefit of the doubt," Lilly said with a sad smile.

"Thank you my love," Waldo said. "When you walked toward her I wasn't sure what you had in mind."

"When did you all learn to sing that way?" John Jr. asked.

"Oh yeah, I thought I was listening to the Mormon Tabernacle Choir," Matthew chimed in.

"Cut it out your two, the songs were familiar that's all," Karen said affectionately, "But thanks for the complement. I think."

Soon the lodge was busy with a buzz of excitement. The aromas coming from the kitchen was almost more than the men could handle.

"What's this?" asked John Jr. as he dipped his finger into a bowl of yummy creamy stuff.

Tyson's excited barking welcomed the dinner guests. Everyone went out to welcome them to the lodge.

Lanie really was as beautiful as Lilly had described, thought Karen. Her long dark auburn hair flowed around her smooth coffee colored skin. Her green eyes were almond shaped and surrounded by long thick black lashes. High cheekbones accented her face. She was petite and appeared very graceful. It was obvious from the start that she was a big help with her younger siblings and her mother depended on her a great deal.

Arnie and Earl were strong teenagers, probably still in high school. It wouldn't be long before they were put to work, Lilly guessed, as she observed their strong shoulders. She was already speculating about the help they could be to her and Karen when Waldo and John were out with fishing expeditions. They weren't helpless by any means but a couple of strong boys would certainly come in handy. Esther was a pretty little girl with her mother's dark hair and eyes, and obviously a "daddy's girl" as she clung to his leg.

Jimmie was the youngest. Probably about seven years old Karen guessed to herself as she was reminded of her own grandchildren. As he got out of the van it became obvious that he wore braces on his legs. He was very determined to do everything himself without a bit of help that was nearby.

Lilly met Waldo's eyes and she could see her own pain mirrored there as they both fought the urge to pick the young boy up and carry him into the house. It was only minutes before Tyson had Esther pulled away from her daddy. Tyson hadn't been around children yet, and seemed to identify with her youthful play. Jimmie joined them, not minding a bit that his face was almost licked off, and Waldo kept a close eye on him to make sure he wouldn't hurt anyone.

Waldo and John took Patrick and the older boys to check out the seaplane. Patrick gave Esther a piggyback ride and Arnie swooped up Jimmie to keep up with the group. John Jr. and Matthew tagged along.

Lilly and Karen welcomed Nona and Lanie with friendly hugs and it seemed like they were all old friends even though they barely knew each other.

"We'll give all of you a tour of the house after dinner," Lilly instructed as they headed for the kitchen.

Nona and Lanie fit right in and knew just what to do to help. "Do you want these napkins on the table?" asked Lanie.

"That would be great," answered Karen as Lanie began folding the white linen into fancy shapes. Karen and Lilly watched Lanie's creativity for a moment and then met each other's eyes. As usual they knew what each other was thinking and after a moment Lilly put the interchange into words.

"You're hired," said Lilly. "I mean it, we would like for you to work here. Would you be interested? Of course you can think about it if you want, but as you can see we have a lot of space to handle here. And when the lodge is full we'll have more chores than we can manage."

"I think that would be great," replied Lanie gently in her soft voice. "I've been offered a position at a massage therapy clinic in the city, but I'm not sure I really want to live there. Here I could be closer to home, and the therapy I've learned so far will help Jimmie if I'm here to administer it."

"Hey, lets set up a massage parlor in that little room next to the office," said Karen excitedly, her eyes wide with ideas. "I'm sure it would be popular with the fisherman and hunters."

"We'll explore that possibility after we eat, and it's about ready," replied Lilly. "How about you two go find the men while Nona and I get the last of these dishes on the table?"

The table was like a Norman Rockwell picture, and the aromas pulled the guests eagerly to the table. Jimmie was full of one hundred and one questions at the least.

"What are all of these forks for?" he asked. "And why do we have so many dishes?"

Waldo laughed at the young boy and whispered in his ear, "I can never figure out which one to use either so just pick one and hang on to it. That's what I do," he said with a wink.

Waldo gave John Sr. a go-ahead nod, and John Sr. said grace this time. As the "amen" was said, Jimmie immediately asked, "What are those?" As he pointed to the deviled eggs at the same time as he grabbed a fork.

"Those are deviled eggs," replied Karen proudly.

"Oh, we don't get eggs for breakfast very often any more, do they belong to the devil?" Puzzled Jimmie as his mother gave him a look that told him maybe he should be silent.

"Yeah, there seems to be a shortage of eggs at the store," offered Earl.

Karen's pride swiftly melted away, and her cheeks turned slightly rosy as she now realized she had been snatching all of the eggs she could on their trips into town. She was speechless as her mind tried to figure out why she had such a silly attachment to eggs lately.

Lilly came to her rescue by explaining that deviled eggs were one of Matthew's favorite foods, and he didn't get them very often.

Nona also saw Karen's embarrassment, and asked about their families to change the subject.

Lilly told them about Jamie and Kelsi's ranch, and all of the animals, trying her best not to show more pride than would be appropriate. Esther had to know each one of the animal's names, and it was a challenge, but with Waldo's help they named them all.

"And, the next new animals on the ranch are going to be the two legged kind," said Waldo proudly. "Lilly and I will be first time Grandparents around the first of November. And we also have a new Grandpa over there," he added as he looked at John Sr.

The O'Callaghan's learned about all of the family members, and the Mon Amie Famille in Louisiana. Karen and Lilly both caught the look of disappointment in Lanie's eyes as she learned that John Jr. and Matthew were both married and had children.

John Jr. told the O'Callaghan's' about seeing the Sasquatch and asked if they had encountered him also.

"Yes, we've seen him a few times," replied Mr. O'Callaghan.

"My Grandmother was kidnapped by them," offered Lanie. She loved to spend time with her Grandmother and hear the stories she told, and it was now easy for her to tell the story she had heard so many times.

"When my Grandma was a little girl, about eight years old, she got lost while picking berries with her mother and her sisters. They were not able to find her, and figured a bear got her. She was a teenager when she returned to her family. People have hunted the Sasquatch, and forced him north for many years. Their babies had all died due to disease and the cold weather, and they believed humans had power to heal. They stole my Grandmother to replace their children that had died. Grandma says they live under a big rock on a mountain, but Grandma could never remember how to get there. The reason they smell so bad is because they never bathe. When Grandma returned, they didn't even know who she was at first, but she remembered her family and had missed them greatly. The Sasquatch knew she missed her own family, and she never grew very big compared to them, so they finally returned her out of the kindness in their hearts. Not many are seen now, and it is believed that their species is dying off."

The group was mesmerized for a moment by the story telling. Finally Lilly broke the silence, "Wow, what a story, Lanie. Is it true?"

Lanie's laughter was as light as the ringing of a crystal bell. "Of course it is, isn't it Mom?"

Nona nodded in agreement, "That's just the way my Mother told me. We were never allowed to pick berries without my Father or Grandfather going along. As far as we know no one else was ever taken, but you can never be too careful."

The thoughtful silence was broken by Jimmie's small voice, "Excuse me, could I have that last "Egg from Hell"?" He asked to the complete enjoyment of everyone at the table.

Waldo speared the last deviled egg and put it on Jimmie's plate. "There you go, son. Save some room for pie, I think it's apple," he said looking at Lilly hopefully.

"Honestly Waldo, one day you're going to turn into an apple pie," Lilly said affectionately. "Karen and I made a Raspberry Peach Cobbler and we have French Vanilla Ice Cream." Lilly's heart melted at the smile of anticipation on Jimmie's face.

About the time the last drops of cobbler were devoured, Waldo and John Sr. had Arnie and Ernie hired to help cut firewood that following week. Lilly would have plenty of people to cook for, since both of the older boys had proven they could put away a lot of food.

"It's time for the tour," said Esther with her young enthusiasm.

Everyone joined in the tour and as the group trooped through the spacious suites, it would have been hard to say who was proudest of the accomplishments. Lilly and Karen began as the tour guides but it was Waldo and John Sr. who took over and pointed out every little detail that the two women had accomplished in their re-decorating.

Nona had heard of Ted and Lois and promised she would try to remember all the stories and would fill Karen and Lilly in on the details of the former owners of the Lodge.

Esther and Jimmie were very curious, asking many questions. Even though their parents tried to restrain them, they stole the attention of the lodge owners and were allowed to look in any of the drawers they wanted for inspection of their content.

"Wow, this was the best day ever," exclaimed Jimmie as the tour ended. "Can we come back for dinner again?"

"Of course you can," replied Waldo before his parents were able to speak a word of restraint.

"First, we need to help clean the mess we made," said his big sister as she guided the two younger children into the kitchen to help with the dishes.

Despite Karen and Lilly's protests the dishes were done and the food put away with the help of their company.

The men had gathered in the great room in front of the fire. Waldo had brought in Tyson and the younger men were attempting to teach the puppy tricks. When the kitchen and dining room were cleaned and everything put away the women joined them in front of the fire.

Waldo showed Esther and Jimmie how to pop corn in the antique corn popper hanging from the mantle over the fireplace. So the evening was spent with family, new friends and old, quiet conversation and lively antics of children and pet.

As Lilly surveyed the room and the people in it she was at once overwhelmed with a feeling of humble gratitude. Her life had been so richly blessed with a family that she not only loved, but also felt their love for her in return. As her eyes rested on her lifelong friend Karen turned towards her and their eyes met. As it so often happened to them they had read each other's thoughts and with a smile Lilly mouthed "Mon Amie Famille." And Karen smiled in return. It seemed no matter where these two women roamed they carried with them enough love to envelop and touch the lives of everyone they met.

CHAPTER 8

The next morning was busy with the now usual aromas and activities of the lodge. John Jr. and Matthew departed in the helicopter after warm hugs and wishes sent to their families. The O'Callaghan boys were to arrive soon to work on the firewood supply, and Lanie was to come with them so that she could verify her employment there and work out the details. Lilly, expecting a call from Jamie, had kept her eye on the phone all morning, and was cautious not to move too far away from it. However, when it finally rang, she jumped about a mile high in surprise. Karen listened as Lilly talked; attempting to put together any details she could prematurely. After all, their Christmas plans had become a big desire of her heart, and this was the one situation that might keep Jamie and Kelsi from coming.

"Yes, yes," Lilly said. "Just a minute…Waldo, get on the other phone, it's Jamie and Kelsi!" she yelled out the back door.

Lilly's unrevealing conversation continued and her excitement level rose to a peak. Her "yes, yes," now turned into an unbelievable "no, no." Then she was counting, and saying things that didn't really make much sense at all…"But there isn't enough room!" she said.

We certainly have enough room around here, Karen thought. Then at the thought of something bad happening, Karen could hear her heart pounding in her chest. There was no use putting together a speculated story yet, but something was sure happening.

Finally, the news broke…"It's triplets, it's triplets, it's triplets," said Lilly three times.

Karen's mouth dropped open in shock just as John Sr. stepped through the back door. He had been in between the shop where Waldo was and the kitchen where Lilly and Karen were and hadn't heard the news.

Fearing the worst he pulled Karen into his strong embrace. "What is it darling? Is Kelsi OK?"

Before Karen could answer, Lilly said goodbye and replaced the receiver in its cradle on the wall. For a moment her slender shoulders shook and her dark hair covered the face she placed in her hands. Just as she turned to face her friends Waldo burst through the door with a whoop and grabbed his wife up in an enormous bear hug. As Waldo swung Lilly around John and Karen could see that the tears on her face were tears of joy and Waldo's face mirrored that joy.

Karen and John watched their friends twirl around the room and laugh and giggle like five years olds.

Finally Lilly and Waldo composed themselves long enough to fill them in on the good news that Jamie had given them. Just coming from a prenatal doctor appointment their only son had called to tell them they were going to have three grandchildren all at one time.

"Hey Karen, I'm going to catch up with you all at once. Oh no, for about a month I'm going to be ahead of you! How about that?" Lilly giggled.

"That's the most wonderful thing I've ever heard. But that boy of yours always was an over achiever," Karen answered as she gave her friend a big hug.

Their celebration was interrupted by Tyson's barking which announced the arrival of the O'Callaghan boy's coming to work.

Lilly was flittering around the kitchen happy as a butterfly, planning a big meal for the noon hour.

"We're having triple-decker sandwiches, and three-bean salad," she announced. "And marbled chocolate, caramel and vanilla pudding for dessert."

Karen was enjoying her friend's excitement. This was the happiest she had seen her in years, and it had been a long time coming.

Lanie entered the kitchen, immediately caught up in the light dance of happiness. Karen and Lilly quickly filled her in on the news and as

Lanie started helping fix lunch she volunteered to work extra hours and even stay over if she was needed when Lilly and Waldo went to Washington.

Jamie and Kelsi had asked the new Grandparents to be to come for a quick trip so Lilly could help set up the nursery and Waldo could help out on the ranch until they had a chance to interview and hire some permanent help. Kelsi's doctor had given her orders to start taking it easy and it appeared her ranch hand days were over until after the babies were born.

"Oh, I'm going to miss you big time," said Karen, almost lonely at the thought. "But don't you worry. Lanie and I will keep things in order around here. Hopefully you two will be back by the time Dylan and Angie come for their stay."

"Who's that?" asked Lanie. "Your first clients?"

"Do you know Dylan Wyatt?" asked Lilly?

"Do I…he's my favorite and I have tickets to his concert! But isn't his wife's name Norma?"

"Yes, and she's coming too," explained Karen. "Angie is our friend that Waldo met in Alaska twenty some odd years ago, and she is going to open for Dylan. Her husband's name is Engelbert, and he'll be fishing with Waldo and John Sr. as soon as he gets here probably. The man has always been anxious to dip his line into the water."

Karen paused, "Lilly, do you think we're really going to be able to have Christmas here? With the babies and all?"

Karen's heart was sinking at the thought of not being together this year. She had so many dreams of Christmas lights in the snow, decorating the lodge, and plans to be with her grandchildren. But she also knew very well that there would be nothing either one of them would ever do to endanger the needs of the babies.

Lilly looked somberly at her friend. "I don't know. We'll just have to play it by ear. If Jamie and Kelsi and the kids…oooh…I love the way that sounds, can't make it for Christmas, Waldo and I will go there. You know we'll be together in our hearts if not in body. And this is just one of many Christmases we'll have with all of our grandchildren."

Karen smiled back at her friend, "I know. The health of Kelsi and the babies come first. Now when are you leaving? What do you want us to do while you're gone? What do you want us to do about the unfinished suite? We could make it into a nursery. We'll install baby monitors and make a comfortable place for their nanny to stay," Karen said hopefully.

Karen, Lilly and Lanie finished the lunch preparation amidst the conversation of babies and bear rugs and tapestry's. It was decided that the last suite to be finished would be a nursery since it was large enough for four cribs and a sleeping alcove for the nanny. Lilly suspected that Lanie would be applying for that job from the look of tenderness in her eyes when babies were mentioned. Lilly wondered again if there was a special man in Lanie's life and if not why such a beautiful, kind and loving girl was still single.

After lunch the boys went out with Waldo and John Sr. to start on the woodpile and Lanie started cleaning the kitchen. Lilly had gone to make airline reservations and for a moment Karen was at a loss. Once again her life was turning upside down, but this time she felt ready and eager to tackle whatever came her way. She knew that she and John could run the Lodge while Lilly and Waldo were gone. She knew that Kelsi and the babies were going to be fine and she was just as assured that her new grandchild would be born safely in the New Year. Karen would miss her friend greatly but after all she and John were still newlyweds and she was secretly looking forward to having that gorgeous hunk of man alone for a while.

Karen sat in the light of the kitchen window lost in thought, planning her rendezvous with her husband. She could take him "north" to one of the suites, maybe a treasure hunt? Or they could create a sunny place in the middle of Alaska, or maybe just a lot of candles, music, and a nice dinner…whatever she decided on it would be sure to create a memory.

She was so engrossed in her thoughts that she hadn't heard John come up behind her. He slipped his hands over her eyes and said, "Guess who?' I love the smell of your hair."

"I haven't heard that one for a long time," she replied as his rich voice penetrated her being and she pulled him around and slipped her arms around his waist. "It's my favorite person in the whole wide world, and you smell a little like the woodpile," she answered with a twinkle in her eye. "Did you know Waldo and Lilly are going to Washington for a few days?"

He began to nuzzle her neck with his beard, "Mmhmm Waldo just told me. I'm sure going to miss them, aren't you?"

Karen giggled and said playfully, "Do you think we can handle this business alone?"

"I was thinking we would close up shop while they're gone. Maybe continue the honeymoon," John said hopefully.

"Do you have any ideas of what you would like to do?" Karen asked. "I know what some of your ideas are and I have some of those ideas too. But I thought I would make a special candlelight dinner for just the two of us."

"How would you like to check out the Gulf of Alaska?" he asked. "We could make the trip in a day if you want."

"Oh, let's spend a night or two, and then maybe we can find some antique shops. I'd love to just hang out with you for a while," Karen responded with eager anticipation.

"That sounds spectacular my dear," he replied happily. "I'm just glad to have you to myself for a while."

The honeymooner's plans were interrupted by Lilly coming back to let them know she had scheduled her and Waldo's flight to Washington for the following Friday morning.

"That's four days. I think I can get packed in that amount of time. And I know there are just a million things I have to do before then. There's so much to do here before we officially open Labor Day weekend. I hate to stick you guys with so much of the work but Jamie and Kelsi are counting on us and I do so want to see them." Her voice trailed off wistfully.

"Don't think a thing about it, Lilly. If Karen and I are going to be partners we want to do our fair share. And you two were here weeks before us by yourself," John said.

"That's absolutely right," added Karen.

Lilly glanced back and forth between her friends and rested on John's strong arm around Karen's slender waist. "Uh huh, so you want to work, do you?" she said slyly.

Waldo had come in toward the end of this interchange and catching on to the tone of the conversation warned John about the wool cover on the new sofa in the great room.

Blushing Lilly swatted at him, "Waldo, stop that."

He laughed back at his wife and repeated, "Well after all we were here weeks before they were. You weren't going to let them think we were working the whole time were you?"

"Come on Lilly, I'll help you start your packing," said Karen.

"OK, but let's check on Lanie, I forgot we left her cleaning the kitchen," Lilly answered.

Upon entering the kitchen the two weren't really surprised to find it was spotless. The chrome fixtures and copper-bottomed pots gleamed and reflected the flames from the cozy fireplace. Lilly sniffed the air, "Mmm, is that bread baking?"

"Yes it is. I hope you don't mind, but you all seemed so preoccupied and the kitchen really wasn't dirty. I decided to bake a loaf from the sourdough starter I brought you and while I was at it I put beef and vegetables on for stew," Lanie answered.

Karen and Lilly looked at each other for a moment, "Wow, we're keeping her," they each said at the same time and laughed as they always did when they read each other's mind.

The two women went off to start planning their packing. "I think I'll take my blue cashmere sweater," said Lilly. "And my jeans of course."

"You'd better take your painting clothes," warned Karen. "Do you think Lanie has a date for the concert?" she continued all in one breath.

"Probably," answered Lilly. "That's not something you usually go to by yourself. You can scope that out while I'm gone. I just know there's a story there somewhere."

"John said we'd all go on the flight to Juno and see you off from there. We're going to check out the Gulf of Alaska from there, and maybe spend the night. I wish you could be there too, but on the other hand he said we would be continuing our honeymoon," Karen explained. "So while I'd rather go to the antique shops with you, I'm really looking forward to the adventure."

Lilly could still see that twinkle in her friend's eyes and thought once again how wonderful it was to see her so happy.

Lanie had out-done herself with the meal she had prepared. Not only had she baked the sourdough bread, she had also created a triple layer cake. The men had their eye on it the minute they walked into the kitchen, and Lilly could have sworn she saw a couple of marks where a finger had been dipped into the frosting.

Lilly and Karen arrived in time to help place the food on the table, but everything else was already done. Again they marveled at the gifted worker that God had blessed them with.

As the food was placed on their plates, excitement could be felt as everyone was thinking of the triplets and the future of the lodge. The boys were calculating the amount of wood needed for the winter, Lilly was thinking of decorating nurseries, and Lanie was elated to have such stimulation for her creative mind.

"Would it be okay if my little sister Esther came with me tomorrow?" asked Lanie. "I try to watch her while my mom volunteers at the hospital and takes Jimmie for his appointments, it makes a really long day for her."

"Of course you can," answered Karen. "We're used to having children around, and quite honestly we miss them a great deal, right Lilly?"

"Absolutely," Lilly chimed in.

"And Lanie," Karen continued, "Do you have any ideas for the massage room? You know we have a knack for decorating with a theme around here."

"Actually, I have been thinking about that," Replied Lanie, "how about a water theme? I love the tranquility of the water when we're kayaking, and I saw an indoor water fountain the other day in a magazine. We could set the mood with candles and special lighting."

"We'll paint the walls pale blue," Karen said as she was picturing the creation. "I wonder if we could raise the humidity enough for some tropical plants. Lilly, why don't you ask Kelsi about it? I'll bet she could give us some great ideas on what kinds of plants we could have."

"Of course, we'll create a tropical paradise inside of an ice palace. After a day out in the cold hunting or fishing our guests can unwind in a hot tub created to look like a babbling hot spring and then follow it up with a massage," Lilly suggested. "You two work on that while I'm gone and let me know if you want me to check out any suppliers in Seattle. I could do that on the way back."

The conversation continued as the cake was finally served. John and Waldo were now planning reconstruction of the massage room, opening it up into the back deck with walls made of glass that also would serve as a green house effect. Waldo knew of some large rocks they could haul in, and some good soil for the indoor plants.

They sat at the table long after the cake was gone and continued planning the ventures. Before they were done Waldo and John had finished a rough draft of a six-wheeled, three-seated stroller with wheels sturdy enough that it could easily be pushed around the ranch. Jamie would be able to create the parts in his shop, and it could be completed on their visit next week.

Finally the group got up to clear the table and start the clean up. "Lilly," Karen asked in a very concerned tone as she pulled her friend into the empty office, "do you think this massage room is really a good idea? I mean, well…I mean I'm wondering who's going to give John his massage?"

"Don't be silly. You are!" Lilly answered confidently. "And if we have guests that don't act appropriately, they won't be back and we have Waldo and John to take care of that. You know we're going to be protective of Lanie, and we'll just have to learn the techniques if we want to provide special services. I know that there are very reputable, therapeutic massage parlors, and that's the kind of service we want to provide."

"Ok, I feel much better now," said Karen. "I shouldn't have worried."

As they rejoined the group in the kitchen again, John was singing as he often did. The group chimed in and the magic of the night filled their spirits. The dishes were done and the kitchen was cleaned in quick order with so many willing hands. Lilly was reminded of her childhood when she and her sisters would wash the dishes and clean the kitchen after every meal. They grumbled about it then but their mother only smiled and said, "Many hands make light work." Now looking back on those days, Lilly realized how much of her mother's values had been instilled in her and she felt sad for a moment because of the confused lonely woman her mother had turned into. So hoping to brighten her mood a little she excused herself to go to the office and call her mother and sister and tell them about the triplets.

Karen awoke to a slight rustling sound at her bedroom door. She always had been a rather light sleeper and the least little noise from her children when they were young brought her wide awake. As she tiptoed to the door and peaked out, she found a wooden stand had been placed there. The aroma of vanilla and hazelnuts was seeping from the insulated covered mugs, and a small bouquet of wild flowers graced the small display.

Smiling, and wondering if it was Lanie who brought the aromatic treat, she brought the tray into the room. "John, look...the coffee fairies have left us a gift of vanilla and hazelnut."

Before making their way to the kitchen they left a note on the now empty tray in a Chinese fortune cookie style that said "May the blessings you give come back to you two-fold."

When John and Karen finally entered the kitchen they found Waldo and Lilly deeply involved in a conversation with Esther. They sat at the table, each with a cup of hot chocolate warming their hands. The melting marshmallows were oozing over the rim as they sipped.

Esther's dark layered curls softly framed her sweet face of innocence. She wore a necklace of little pink beads that matched her tennis shoes.

"Honey, you look as if you just came from heaven," said Karen.

Lanie was preparing what appeared to be Pecan Waffles. Karen sniffed slightly as she went over to the counter where she was working. "Now that's something I haven't smelled since we left Louisiana. Is it really pecan waffles? And are you responsible for our morning coffee?"

Lanie smiled and said, "I confess. I've been reading one of those southern magazines. When Mom wrote and told me about you guys and the business I went to the Library and found the magazines that featured your B&B in New Orleans." Lanie then ducked her head and added shyly, "Did I impress you?"

Karen gave her a quick hug, "You were hired already, and you didn't need to go to all this trouble."

Lanie smiled back, "No trouble. I like to do things well."

Karen's eyes met Lilly's again in approval as she joined her friends at the table and told Lilly that if Lanie ever wanted to go south she would fit right in with the subtle elegance of New Orleans.

"Speaking of New Orleans, Karen, didn't Heather say they were bringing David's brother, Pastor Jim, when they come for Thanksgiving?" Lilly asked with a nudge and a wink in Lanie's direction.

"As far as I know he's still planning to come," Karen answered.

Lanie had caught a glimpse of Lilly's wink and was curious.

"Who is this Jim guy? He's a preacher?" Lanie asked.

Lilly and Karen grinned at each other and Lilly answered, "Ohhh Baby! But he doesn't look like any preacher we've ever seen."

Karen jabbed her friend in the ribs and continued, "Be nice Lilly. Jim is very handsome and his equally handsome brother, David, is my daughter's boyfriend. Pastor Jim married John and I at a little chapel down the road from Mon Amie Famille. David and Jim's parents are gone and we've kind of adopted them both. At least we're secretly hoping that Heather will decide they can stay in the family for good. She had a bad experience with a former fiancé and is finding it hard to trust again. But I think leaving her alone in New Orleans has helped her sort things out for herself."

The fleeting look of sorrow on Lanie's face at the mention of Heather's failed love was not lost on Lilly or Karen. As Lanie moved back to the counter to check on the waffles Lilly nudged Karen and whispered, "Get to the bottom of this while I'm gone, OK?"

CHAPTER 9

The men had busied themselves with the firewood project, and the three women and Esther were getting to know each other better as they worked in the heart of the lodge. The buzz of the chainsaws was now expected, and the women were almost used to it. The hum from the laundry room could be heard with the fresh, clean smell of lemon soap drifting into the kitchen…life was good.

"I'm cooking lunch today," announced Karen. "I hardly ever get a turn anymore with you two for competition! We're having flautas. Shredded chicken with fresh salsa and pepper jack cheese, rolled into flour tortillas and lightly fried, topped with chipotle dressing and served with Lilly's sweet jalapeno jelly. How does that sound? Can't you just see the cheese oozing out?"

Before anyone had a chance to answer the question, a blood-curdling scream came from the back of the house. Lilly was the first out the door with Karen right behind her.

"Karen, we need the first aid kit," yelled John.

"We're going to need some ice and a baggie too," Waldo added.

Karen turned around to snatch the first aid kit off the shelf by the back door, then grabbing a tub of ice from the freezer and a zip lock freezer bag she ran across the back yard to where the men were huddled.

Lilly almost fainted at the crimson red blood staining the pristine white snow combined with the sight of Earl writhing in pain on the ground and Arnie getting sick in the bushes.

Waldo had a steady hand on Earl's shoulder while John was trying to stop the steady flow of blood coming from the stub of his pinky finger.

Grabbing the first aid kit out of Karen's hands John expertly packed the stub in ice and rolled the gauze padding and tape around it. Waldo took the baggie from Karen and scooping up the severed tip with a good helping of snow he calmly dropped it into the baggie and handed it to his flustered wife telling her to pack the baggie in ice. Then he sprinted for the garage and his pickup.

"I'll pull around front; John, you bring Earl around; Lilly, you bring the finger and I'll pick the three of you up." He shouted, "Lanie, call your parents. Let them know we're taking him directly to the hospital. You can bring everyone else in your car."

Lilly picked up the ice bucket and neatly tucked the baggie with the severed pinky tip deep inside surrounded by the ice. Then putting another arm around Earl she helped John lead him around to where Waldo was waiting in the Ford.

Esther was watching with wide eyes, but she didn't seem to be upset as Karen swooped her up and buckled her into the car.

"My mom is already at the hospital with Jimmie, she'll be waiting for us," Lanie informed them. Then handing the keys to Karen she asked her to drive. Satisfied that her brother and sister were securely buckled into the back of the SUV, Lanie got into the passenger seat next to Karen. It was only minutes before they were all moving at top speed out of the valley. Lanie's anxiety level rose to a peak as they neared the hospital. Her tension permeated the atmosphere until Karen sensing her anxiety patted her hand gently.

"What is it?" she asked. "Earl will be okay, I know he will."

"It's just that I have some sad memories here," she answered as the tears rolled down her cheeks. "I didn't ever want to come here again...and that's our song on the radio," she sobbed.

"We don't all have to go in if you don't want," soothed Karen.

"No, my family is more important than my foolish memories. I guess I have to face it," Lanie answered.

"Memories are never a foolish thing, and what do you have to face? If you don't mind me asking...we can talk later if you want." Karen said.

"Thanks Karen, maybe it would help. Sometimes things start going around and around in my mind and I can't seem to find my way out,"

Lanie said with a tremulous smile and then continued, "I'd like to tell you my story."

"It's a date, now let's get in there and see what kind of damage was done," Karen replied."

Arnie was waiting at the front door of the emergency room entrance. As they opened the door to go in Karen noticed the tears in Arnie's eyes. "Hey, he's going to be OK you know."

"I know, but it's my fault, I didn't put the safety guard back on after I used it," Arnie whispered.

"Now don't go blaming yourself. Accidents happen and that's why they're called accidents. You never hear of anyone having an "On Purpose" do you? Now go sit in those chairs over there and I'll see what I can find out," Karen said reassuringly.

Arnie smiled weakly and allowed Esther to take his hand and lead him to the waiting area. Lanie had gone immediately to the reception desk and asked about her brother. After feeling their efforts to obtain information were just about exhausted, the doctor finally came out to talk to them as a group. They had all expected surgery, but they hadn't expected such a long ordeal. It had been four hours since Earl was taken into surgery and the hospital waiting room was full of the entire O'Callaghan clan and John, Karen, Waldo and Lilly had stayed to wait for the outcome.

Everyone was getting restless by the time Dr. Seidel, the family physician, came to report that fortunately for Earl they were being visited by one of the best orthopedic surgeons in the Northwest, Dr. Thomas Ferguson. The doctors had reattached Earl's pinky and they had every reason to believe that the surgery was successful and his parents would be able to see him as soon as he was out of recovery. Dr. Seidel reassured them that Earl should be recovered sufficiently to compete in the Iditarod in March. Earl had been mumbling about it just before the anesthetic took hold. This was the first year that Earl and

Arnie would be eligible to compete and it seemed as if they had been preparing for it their entire life. They were all relieved at the words from the doctor; but no one more so than Arnie who was still blaming himself for his brother's accident.

CHAPTER 10

It was late morning by the time they woke. Still exhausted from the events of the previous day Lilly got serious about packing for her trip while Karen prepared brunch.

"You were complaining that you never get a chance to cook," said Lilly. "Now you have your chance."

"What do you have to pack that takes four days anyway? Do you need some help?" Karen asked.

"I'm sorry," Lilly replied, "I'm just a little antsy about flying and the weather's still warm in Washington so I have to dig some of our summer clothes out of storage and wash and iron. And I'm a little cranky from lack of sleep; you remember Jamie almost lost his pinkie finger the year he graduated from high school when he ended up upside down under Kelsi's horse. I think I had nightmares all night about it. I'm just so grateful that Earl's going to be alright, and I'll be OK, like you said I have four days."

Karen poured coffee for herself and Lilly and taking the coffee carafe along with them the women joined their husbands at the breakfast nook rehashing the previous day's events.

"You know," said John, "I hope we didn't scare Lanie off. She looked really upset yesterday. Do you think it was too much for her?"

"She was upset," answered Karen. "Yesterday was very emotional for all of us. Lanie seems to have some bad memories lingering at that hospital, and she said she would talk about it a little later. But I think she's okay. Lilly, let's call on my English roots, and invite her for four o'clock tea?"

"What a perfectly lovely idea," Lilly replied in the strongest English accent she could muster. "I suppose you want me to make crumpets too?"

Karen laughed, "No, apricot or blackberry scones would do just fine. And don't blow a gasket; we have those in the freezer. So you guys get to work, Lilly you start your washing and I'll call Lanie to find out how Earl is and invite her over this afternoon."

The morning passed quickly with everyone busy at their chores. Karen fixed the flautas for lunch that she had been about to prepare the day before when she was interrupted by Earl's accident. Promptly at 3:00 Lanie arrived with Esther and Jimmie in tow.

"I hope you don't mind, Mom was up most of the night with Earl and I wanted to give her a chance to rest," Lanie asked hopefully.

Karen was quick to reassure her that the younger children were always welcome. Fixing them some popcorn and pouring root beer for both they were soon settled in the family room watching a Disney DVD from Lilly and Waldo's collection.

The ladies retired to the sitting room just off the country kitchen where a fire crackled cheerfully and tea and scones were set out in a lovely bone china tea set Lilly had brought from Louisiana. At the time she wasn't sure she would ever use it in the wilds of Alaska but knowing that Karen shared her penchant for elegance she had hoped that the time honored tradition of teas would find their way here.

As soon as the tea was poured and with just a little urging from Karen, Lanie began.

"Larry and I knew each other pretty much all of our lives, but it wasn't until our last year of high school that we actually dated. He said he had a crush on me since second grade and I guess he did carry my lunch box for me once or twice," she said with a blush and a smile, loving her memory. "We both competed in the high kick competitions. He bought a pickup our senior year and we would go to town and dance until they kicked us out every Friday night. Our friends called us 'L&L'.

234

The plan was to get married as soon as we graduated and have a summer wedding, but I knew there wasn't very much money with us four kids. Daddy worked on the Alaska pipeline for several years, but then work was scarce and we didn't have very much for a while. I had dreams of a big wedding, but when I finally realized it wasn't going to happen, we decided to elope to Fairbanks." Lanie paused to take a sip of tea and then continued, "So that Friday night we took off for the city. Mama and Daddy thought we were going out dancing like we usually did. I wanted to tell them, but I just couldn't. I was so in love that I didn't stop to think about how they would feel. But now I know that it would have broken their hearts."

Lilly and Karen's hearts were torn with this information. Lanie paused to look at their expressions on her new friend's faces and then continued on. It was too late now to stop.

"A big storm was coming, but we thought we had plenty of time to make it back home. However, the storm came quickly and we had problems with the pickup. It stalled out and we weren't able to fix it. So we cuddled up in the front seat and waited. I woke hours later to the sounds of my dad and brothers digging us out. I was so cold I couldn't move, and then I realized Larry was still on top of me. The doctor said he saved my life with his body heat. His heart was still beating when we got him to the hospital, but they weren't able to save him. He had gotten his feet wet when he was working on the truck, and the cold took him." The tears were rolling down her cheeks at this point and Karen slipped her arm around her like she would have her own daughter.

Picking up her cup of tea, Karen inhaled the mint fragrance and took a sip. Carefully replacing her cup back in the saucer Karen asked, "The suspense is killing me...did you actually elope?"

"Yes," she admitted shyly and cautiously as she looked into Karen's eyes searching for her response. "It took a little bit of persuasion, but Larry talked a preacher into marrying us and because of the storm we immediately started back home. I found out later that Mama was remaking a wedding dress for me from her Mother's dress. She made a hundred and fifty little blue roses out of ribbon and was sewing them onto the gown. But she wanted to surprise me and I didn't know about the dress. I never told Mama that we had gotten married because when we got home the dress was lying in her chair, and the roses were spilled out onto the floor. I took one look at the dress and then swore to myself I would never tell her."

"It surely sounds like you've danced the dance," said Karen after another long silence.

"You remind me a lot of myself, only John was taken away by the war and I ended up pregnant." The look on Lanie's face gave way to the possibility of another story at these words.

"You know the picture you found of Ted and Lois?" Lanie asked.

"Yes, do you know them?" Lilly eagerly answered.

"That's Larry's Grandparents. Ted discovered gold in this valley and built this lodge. I'm sure Mama didn't want to tell you in front of me because she thought it would upset me. But to tell you the truth…it's actually a relief to tell the story. Everyone in town already knew what happened, and I've never actually put it into words before."

Lanie continued to pour her heart out and as a matter of fact it was flowing quite nicely. "I was very angry at first, and when I looked into the mirror I had no idea who the person in the reflection was. A big chunk of my heart was ripped out, and the healing hasn't come easy. Mama finally talked me into going back to school and I delved into the classes to lose myself there. But to tell you the truth, working here at the lodge is the first time I've ever felt a part of something alive since the accident."

"I'm so glad you're a part of our lives here," said Karen. She paused and then continued. "I have another question. You said something about you four kids? How long ago was this? Isn't there five of you?"

"Actually, it was our stay in the hospital that introduced us to Jimmie. Oh, that's right you probably didn't know he was adopted?"

Karen and Lilly looked surprised at this news. "Go on dear," Karen urged.

"Jimmie was in the waiting room that night, just sitting there in his little wheelchair. I had sat down next to him and when they brought us the news that Larry was gone I began crying uncontrollably. But through my weeping I suddenly became aware of a small hand patting my head. You see Jimmie's parents had deserted him in that waiting room and there had been several accidents that night because of the storm, so in the confusion no one realized for hours that he was all alone. He had to have been scared and confused himself, but he put his pain aside to try to console me. When we found out he had been abandoned I begged Mama and Daddy to bring him home with us. The last thing they needed was another mouth to feed but here he is today as much a part of our family as if he had been born into it. We never did find his parents and the adoption was final six months ago."

Karen and Lilly had been dabbing their eyes since Lanie had began talking and with this final revelation they were both sobbing quietly.

"Lanie, if there's anything we can do...," said Lilly though her sniffles.

"You already have," Lanie responded with a smile. "Like I said, this is the first time I've actually felt like I was among the living again."

"Here we are a bunch of blubbering females," said Karen. "I think we should all start living life and do something exciting."

"You can help me iron," said Lilly.

Karen replied, "No way, I'll do your washing but no ironing. Lanie, don't let her talk you into do her ironing either. She's impossible to please. Everything has to be starched and pleated, I suspect she irons the towels in the bathroom and Waldo has accused her of ironing his shorts but she won't admit to either one."

Lanie looked back and forth enjoying the easy bantering of her two new friends, "You two are the best. I'm so happy you've come into my life and there's probably nothing I wouldn't do for either one of you, but I really do hate ironing. And I need to take the kids home. I'm sure Mama has had her hands full with Earl all day and I want to fix dinner for the family."

Standing up to leave she approached Lilly and Karen and placing an arm around each one she pulled them close. "Thank you," she whispered and left the room to gather her brother and sister.

The three came back to say good-bye. "Thank you for the popcorn and root beer," chimed the two children together.

"You're so welcome," said Lilly.

"Would you two like to meet my Grandma?" asked Lanie. "She lives not very far from us. Perhaps we could see her tomorrow; that is if you have enough time with all of the packing and ironing you have to do," she said with a grin. "I'm sure she would love to tell you the Big Foot story, although she doesn't tell just anybody. And she has a lot of other stories and a sense of humor too."

"Of course we would," the two women answered together enthusiastically.

"We can't wait to meet her, and we wanted to visit Earl too. I should have time, my laundry is done and in spite of popular opinion I don't iron everything, only cotton. So there," she said sticking her tongue out briefly at Karen.

"Perhaps you could buy some polyester when you're in Washington to cut down on the ironing," teased Karen.

"My goodness Karen, do you remember the first time we went to the Apple Blossom Festival in Wenatchee? You were probably fourteen or fifteen and I told you we had to wear polyester dress pants instead of jeans."

Lilly laughed as she told this story from their past. "It sure didn't take us long to figure out Levi's were the only way to go."

"And we're still wearing them too," Karen added.

Karen and Lilly walked Lanie and the younger children to the car where their husbands joined them.

When Waldo and John heard there was a Big Foot story in the works they insisted on going with them on the visit. So the plans were made to visit Earl after lunch, and then take Lanie into the city with them to meet her Grandma.

CHAPTER 11

Waldo and John were excited about the plans for the sunroom and had been working on it all afternoon. Their excitement poured out and was contagious as they showed their wives the plans and the internet web sites they were ordering supplies from. Since Waldo had spent some time in Alaska before, he knew how the darkness of the winter could bring people down into depression. The room was designed with glass walls to let in the summer light, and tract lighting for the plants to thrive. Individual lights would be mounted above the hot tub and at various places throughout the room for light therapy. They had started digging for the foundation earlier, although the area was already a perfect layout for such a creation.

As the four settled down to a simple soup and sandwich supper the magic was alive. Not only did they have each other, the knowledge that their children were well and safe, and new friends to enhance their already full lives; their imaginations were rich with possibilities that in the past had only been dreams. As Waldo and John continued to discuss the plans for the sunroom and the work they were hoping John would continue while he and Lilly were in Washington, Karen and Lilly's eyes met across the table and they smiled. Any doubts they had about leaving Louisiana had disappeared and as usual the two were filled with an enormous gratefulness for the lives they had been given, the men they loved and the friendship they both valued.

After a busy morning of washing, ironing and packing, Lilly finally felt like she was once again in control of her life and escaped to the kitchen to bake chocolate chip cookies for Earl. The anticipation of the activities for the day drove her to perfection as she added a little extra smidgen of vanilla and cinnamon to the mix.

Both Waldo and John had already been in to dip their fingers into the batter, and now the aroma had them popping in now and then to see if the first batch was out of the oven yet.

"You know they'll have to cool when they first come out of the oven," Lilly scolded. "Now go get your work done. Karen's in charge of lunch today and I'm sure it's healthier than chocolate chip cookies."

Just then Karen entered the kitchen, full of energy with a basket full of blueberries. "I think the season is almost over, but I did find some good berries over by the woods, I haven't had the fun of picking berries for quite some time, did you get your ironing done?" she asked Lilly all in the same breath.

Karen looked up to see John and Waldo looking at her with stern concern like she had done something wrong. "What did I do?" she asked innocently.

"Why did you go that far by yourself? Did you think about what you would do if a bear charged you?" asked John as he possessively put his arm around her and kissed her forehead.

"Well, no...I guess I'd run like the wind," she replied.

"I don't want either of you to go that far, by yourself or together either one. And you might think you would run like the wind, but a Grizzly can run faster than that," said Waldo firmly. "And if it was absolutely necessary, you should take Tyson with you."

"Ok, I promise, I'm really sorry, please forgive me," pleaded Karen.

Lilly understood the importance of the warning, but tried to sooth her friend a bit..."I'm sure we'll all forgive you when we have blueberries on our cereal tomorrow morning."

Karen turned her attention to making lunch; going to all the extravagance she could think of to make up for what she had done. When her creation was finally finished, they sat down to hearty homemade chicken and dumplings and spinach salad with fresh cucumbers, mushrooms, and red onions in rice vinegar dressing. The salad was a work of art with vegetables arranged artistically around the side of the bowl and on the top of the lettuce, and the dumplings were a perfect golden brown. Not even Lilly could identify all the spices she had used.

Karen had felt the need to make up for her mistake, but also there was no telling where they would eat dinner or how long it would be until they returned home. She knew that John and Waldo would probably be hungry before they got back and wanted them to have something substantial before they left.

After the four had eaten their fill and had sampled the cookies Lilly had allotted them, they piled into Waldo's pickup and headed for the O'Callaghan's.

On their arrival they found Earl sitting on the porch giving his brother instructions on how to change the oil in the 1956 Chevy pickup they were restoring. From the look on Arnie's face it appeared he might do more damage to his brother if he was allowed. Nona appeared at the front door just as Patrick was coming from his shop behind the house and they welcomed their company warmly into their home. Pausing briefly to let Earl and Arnie know that she had brought cookies, Lilly followed her friends into the house. After a quick scan of the room Lilly's eyes met Karen's and they smiled. Although the native stone fireplace was definitely the focus point of the living room, the two women's attention was drawn to the hard wood pine floors that were scrubbed to a bright sheen. Brightly colored "rag" rugs were scattered throughout the room. The "art" on the walls were framed pictures of the children through the different stages in their lives. The living room flowed into the dining area at the opposite end of the large room where another native stone fireplace glowed brightly. A rough-hewn pine table, large enough to seat the entire family, was centered in front of the fireplace.

Lilly gave Nona a quick hug and said, "What a perfectly wonderful room. Did you do the rugs?"

Nona nodded shyly, "My grandmother taught me when I was a little girl to dye the rags and braid them into rugs. I use nylons now, they are much easier to work with and wash wonderfully. I could show you if you like."

Karen nodded enthusiastically, "These would be great in the hallways."

In no time at all the three were engrossed in their effort to learn to braid the nylons Nona had been working on, and were making plans for rugs for the lodge.

Waldo and John had pulled Patrick aside when they entered to discuss Earl's accident and reassure him that they would cover anything the insurance didn't.

Lilly's mind was put at ease when she heard Patrick's reassuring voice from the next room, "Don't you worry about it. He's going to be fine…"

At the promise of the cookies Earl and Arnie had followed everyone into the house, and now the men had gathered with Esther and Jimmie in the kitchen to consume the scrumptious treats.

Lanie entered through the back door slightly out of breath. Her cheeks were rosy and her long chestnut hair flowed down the back of the scarlet running suit she wore. "I'm sorry, I really thought I would have time for a run before you got here," she apologized. "Are those chocolate chip cookies I see?" She looked longingly at the plate. "I have to get a shower before we go. Can you save me some of those?"

"First come, first served," said Earl.

"I'll save you some," offered Jimmie.

"Ok, Jimmie, thank you. Why don't you put a couple on the counter on a plate and put my name on them, and we'll take a couple to Grandma too," instructed Lanie.

Lanie rushed off to shower and dress and it seemed like only moments before she was back announcing she was ready to go.

Waldo buckled Jimmie securely into the front seat between him and John and Lanie climbed into the back with Karen and Lilly.

Nona's mother lived in the same house she had moved to as a young bride. She had raised her children here and even though her husband had been gone for ten years she refused to move into something smaller. As they all entered the home, it was obvious that the large picturesque window was a pathway to her peaceful personality. The room was simple, but held the same bright colored rag rugs as her daughter's home, and her collection of family pictures on the walls.

Lanie handed her grandmother the wild flowers she had brought for her as she met her for a warm hug and introduced her new friends.

"My, you have a wonderful view of the mountain," exclaimed John. "And the river too, do you see many animals?"

"Yes, sometimes in the evening the bears come out of the woods looking for food. And sometimes I see an occasional moose or two. There's a rabbit that comes up to the window every morning for the carrots I put out for him. I named him Chuck, and he has a notch in his left ear."

"This is a beautiful dream catcher," said Karen. "Did you make it?"

Grandma Anna, as Karen and Lilly already thought of her, smiled sweetly.

"That was made by my Grandmother and I brought it to this house on my wedding night. It hung over the cradleboard of all my children. The legend of the dream catcher is an ancient legend and says: since dreams will never cease, hang this dream net above your bed, dream on, and be at peace. I keep it in this room now, since this is where I sleep most nights. I like to see my animal friends in the evening and when I wake up in the morning. One day I will join my husband in the great beyond and that is what I dream of most nights. So I know the dream catcher is still working."

Lilly and Karen smiled in spite of the tears that stung their eyes and immediately surrounded the lovely little lady with hugs and reassurances. Lilly suspected Grandma Anna brought more comfort to them in this time than they did to her.

After a few moments Waldo cleared his throat uncomfortably and Lanie laughed. "I think the men are looking for a Big Foot story, Grandma."

"Yes, yes," pleaded Jimmie.

Jimmie loved to hear his Grandma's stories over and over and he never seemed to tire of them. His eyes were big in anticipation.

"Ok," replied Grandma Anna as she sat back in her chair and took a big deep breath.

She straightened her apron as Jimmie got as close to her feet as he could in order to have the best seat in the house.

"I was about eight years old that summer. We survived on the land in those days, and always worked hard at gathering as many berries as we could find. They were a treat dried, and my mother made tea out of them too. The day was long, and the berries were plentiful that year. As I picked, I was determined to fill my bucket with the biggest and best berries. Before I knew it I had wondered quite a ways from my mother and sisters. Everyone was intent on filling their baskets and I'm sure they didn't notice how far away I was. The wind must have been either still or blowing away from us, because I didn't catch the scent of the big hairy creature until he was almost to me. It was his big feet I saw first, and then as I looked up at his height I started to tremble. The stench was almost unbearable. I had been taught not to make a lot of commotion when confronted by wild animals, so it wasn't until he picked me up in his arms that I called for my mother. I could see her running towards us, but the creature was so fast…we disappeared from the clearing in no time at all."

"Where did he take you?" asked Jimmie breathlessly.

"We traveled for a long time. It must have been at least two or three hours. He climbed up the mountain, along some cliffs, across some streams, and finally to the cave where they lived. When we arrived he set me down among his family who were very curious. They touched my smooth arms, and I knew they wanted to love me. We ate berries for supper that night. As time went by, I learned that their child had died the previous winter. I'm sure they took me to replace the child they had lost. And they believed our people had healing powers. I must have appeared a lot younger than I was because of the size difference. We prepared for the winter and although I longed deeply to go home, I had no idea which way I would travel and they kept a close eye on me.

"How did you talk to them, Grandma?" Jimmie pleaded.

Grandma Anna put her middle three fingers on her forehead. "There were no words Jimmy, we just knew. "

She paused long enough to take in the looks on her guest's faces before she continued.

"I stayed with them through the summer and fall. When the weather turned cold they tried to keep me warm but I had no winter clothing, and of course I didn't have the thick coats they did. I soon got sick. My adopted mother did her best; she held me close and rocked me as my fever raged. I can still see the concern on her face and feel her tears on my cheek. I don't remember the day they brought me home; my mother said I was delirious from the fever. My father and uncles had looked for me everyday since I was taken but had to stop when the snow closed the passes into the mountains. Then one particularly cold and snowy night, the dogs outside our home were going crazy when my parents heard a knock against the door. My father opened the door to find me lying there. As he picked me up to carry me inside he saw the male big foot peering around the side of the house. My father said he was close enough to see the tears in the big foot's eyes. He was so moved by the apparent concern over me that he did not seek revenge for the kidnapping."

The group was moved beyond words at the story.

Finally Jimmie broke the silence, "Did you ever see them again, Grandma?"

Grandma Anna pulled Jimmie close to her, "Only from a distance, Jimmie. My parents never let me out of their sight again. But sometimes through the years I have glimpsed them watching me and I know they have looked over me to make sure I was well and safe the same that my real parents did. In fact I have seen one of them from my window right here in the evening."

"Wow, Grandma, aren't you afraid?" The young boy asked.

"Never, Jimmie, never be afraid of something that loves you."

"Now that's just amazing," said John. "I've never heard of anyone being that close before."

John nudged his friend for a comment but for once Waldo seemed completely speechless.

Lilly and Karen were also at a loss for words as their minds tried to comprehend the reality of the story and the realization that a parent's love for a child did not exist only in human beings.

Lanie looked at her grandmother with pride. She was a stable "rock" in her life. The unconditional love she gave had brought her through some very hard times, and this was someone who always had time to listen to her.

"Well sunshine," Grandma Anna said giving Lanie a long searching look. "It looks like you've gotten some of that sunshine you used to have back into working order. What have you done?"

Lanie smiled lovingly at Karen and Lilly and then back to her Grandmother, "Just a little girl talk over tea, Grandma."

Waldo suddenly found his voice again, "Grandma Anna, I learned a long time ago not to keep anything from these two. If they have the slightest inkling that something might be wrong, out comes the teapot, and before you know it you're spilling your guts. Oh, excuse me, I probably could have found a more delicate way to put that."

Grandma Anna laughed with delight, "Nonsense, you said it just right. And I can tell my lovely girl is in good hands working for you people. Now how about some tea for all of us? Lanie would you mind?"

They talked over their tea and chocolate chip cookies for some time, and Grandma Anna seemed to delight over the questions they asked. Jimmie still had a curiosity to understand communicating with a Big Foot and periodically placed his middle three fingers on his forehead to test it out. He pretended to know what someone else was thinking, and Waldo and John played along with him.

It was much later than they realized by the time they finally left for home. After they thanked their elderly hostess for the tea and Big Foot education they drove Lanie and Jimmie to their house.

For the return trip to the lodge John insisted that Lilly sit in front with Waldo and he climbed into the spacious back seat with his wife.

"This was a perfect day," replied Karen as she snuggled close to her husband.

Pulling her under his arm he rested his strong jaw lightly against her forehead and softly murmured his agreement.

CHAPTER 12

Time seemed to fly as the final preparations were made for their trips. Lanie had been a tremendous help, and had promised to watch over Tyson and the lodge in their absence.

Once again Waldo wondered just how long they were really going to be gone by the amount of luggage Lilly had packed.

"We'll be back before winter sets in…I think," Waldo said to John as they loaded the gear from the truck into the seaplane.

John looked from the luggage and back to his friend and said rather skeptically,

"You'd better be. I'll need some help with those glass walls and besides; we have our first fishing expedition scheduled. You have to be back for that."

Lilly came up just in time to hear this exchange. "Quit fussing, Waldo. Two of those suitcases are practically empty. I have a new wolf figurine for Jamie and a horse print for Kelsi and the curtains for the nursery that Karen made. And I have to have suitcases to bring back goodies from Washington for everyone here. So calm down it's not all clothes."

Turning to Karen she whispered, "Don't tell him our winter coats are in there, OK?"

Karen whispered back, "They better not be, we need you two back here for the opening."

Lilly's anticipation of seeing Kelsi pregnant with triplets was growing, and she felt like she could hardly wait to get there. She was excited at the prospect of becoming a grandmother, but she was even more excited at the knowledge of the happiness that these babies would bring her only son. But for now she needed to be patient a little longer, Waldo had planned the itinerary to include a couple of hours to explore the coastal area before the connecting flight.

Soon after they took off John and Waldo began scouting areas where they would be taking their guests fishing.

Once again the view of Alaska was awe inspiring. The plane glided over the round globe with nothing but horizon in any direction that you looked. The flow of the continuous mountains surrounded them and a few clouds decorated the sky. The color of "sky blue pink" (as Karen's dad always called it) was painted above the eastern horizon. No signs of life could be seen as they started the travel south.

Waldo gazed out at the view, secretly wondering where the Big Foot lived. His eyes scanned the mountains as he tried to calculate the approximate area from what Grandma Anna had told them, but the area was so vast it was impossible.

By the time the ocean came into view they also had a view of the city and were able to easily spot their landing location. The sight drove the women to excitement and anticipation of antique shops and quaint hidden treasures they had been dreaming of.

John and Karen had reservations at a hotel close to where they would land that also served the local airport, so they would be able to make the most of their time and have a place to have their baggage ready to go.

Karen rested her hand on John's leg as her heart fluttered with the smooth landing. No matter how much she flew she never was comfortable with the landings, but having John's sturdy leg to hold on to helped immensely and she tried not to leave nail marks in his thigh. Before the baggage was even unloaded, the hotel help arrived with a cart and relieved them of the chore. After checking into the hotel and verifying the lunch reservations the four hopped into the SUV that John had waiting for them. As John pulled away from the covered portico Karen and Lilly were craning their necks to see the hotel from every angle possible. Here, as in most of Alaska, turn of the century Russian architecture was prevalent and the two friends were already anticipating what their rooms would look like and the elegance that awaited them in the dining room. The only planned destination was the sporting goods store. Lilly and Karen automatically visually scouted the area for other places of interest.

"That looks like an antique store over there," said Lilly. "Oh, Karen, look at that store," She said pointing at the small shop next to the antique store.

"Oh…" they both said at the same time as their eyes were drawn to a sign with baby lambs in pink and blue.

"If we don't find you two first in the sporting store, that's where we'll be," Lilly informed the men as she pointed to the baby store.

There was no time to waste, so after a quick peck on their husbands checks the two women were half a block away before either of the men had a chance to say anything.

"Ok…see you later," they called.

Lilly and Karen were tumbling out of the specialty store with their arms loaded with shopping bags as Waldo and John were just coming down the sidewalk.

"What'd you do, buy the store out?" asked John.

"You know we had to have three of everything," Karen reminded him. "And they had the preemie sizes which are hard to find, and we'll probably need those. I can't wait to show you what I got for Melinda too."

The men took the load of the packages and headed to the SUV to store them with their purchases from the sporting goods store.

To Lilly and Karen's surprise the back was already packed full of snowshoes.

"Wow, looks like we're going to have fun this winter," said Karen.

"You never know when we'll need to navigate, and you can't drive in the deep snow," said Waldo.

"I guess you're right, we have quite a bit of winter preparation to do, don't we?" said Lilly. "Enough about that though, here we are in the city and I'm ready to explore. Let's see what that antique store has?"

The SUV was safely locked and the two couples headed back down the street.

Lilly met Waldo's eyes with hers as she took his arm, knowing that they both had the same thing on their minds these days. They had done their homework, reading up on the risks of a triple pregnancy and the fear of a problem lurked in the back of their minds. Buying the tiny delicate clothing had made Lilly realize that all three of the babies were now a reality no matter what happened. Determined to be positive Lilly whispered, "You know…the circle of our love is going to be branching out, have you thought of it that way?"

Waldo patted his wife's arm and whispered back, "I sure have. We're going to be blessed with boys that can fish and hunt or maybe girls that can break horses and bake apple pies."

Lilly giggled softly, "What if the girls want to hunt and fish and break horses and the boys only want to bake apple pies?"

Waldo grinned back at her, "As long as they're healthy Lilly, my love, as long as they're healthy."

Karen and John had paused at the front door of the antique store to wait for their lagging friends, and picked up a brochure on the museum located just a few blocks away.

"They have an actual sample of the pipe line, let's go there too," said John.

"You two go ahead if you want to," Karen said rather wistfully, "you really don't have to go to the antique store with us."

John gave his bride a quick kiss on the lips, "I always want to be where you are," he reassured her.

Waldo agreed, "No way am I letting Lilly in another antique store by herself. The last time that happened we ended up with a complete bedroom set."

Lilly laughed and quickly answered, "It was a steal, Waldo, and you know it."

Everyone knew that Waldo had a hard time refusing Lilly anything and he was secretly relieved to see that antique stores in Anchorage did not hold the same charm as antique stores in New Orleans. What furniture they did have was rough-hewn and not in the best condition. Most of the dishes had cracks and chips and what lace there was appeared to be yellowed and tattered. But after an hour of browsing, Lilly and Karen had to practically drag their husbands away from the vintage gold mining equipment.

"Do you think they actually have the gold rush fever?" Karen asked Lilly.

"Probably," Lilly answered, "who knows what they'll try next. I wouldn't worry too much though because they know we have to finish the projects we have going first."

Deciding they had just enough time to visit the museum before lunch they were once again on their way to explore the exhibits. After a quick tour of the museum they went back to the restaurant at the hotel to eat lunch. Excited about their new education, the four settled in at their table with conversation of Alaskan culture, history, and Indian tribes.

Lilly and Karen had new ideas for the lodge, and Waldo and John were anxious to take their fishing expeditions to the next level.

They had been so involved in the conversation that they hadn't noticed the old Volkswagen Bug pulling an overloaded utility trailer that had come to a stop directly in front of the restaurant. The woman behind the wheel appeared to be in her mid twenties and she was frantically trying to start the ancient VW. As the ignition continued to grind the four friends inside the restaurant turned as one to see what was going on.

Lilly and Karen immediately noticed the little girl sitting in the front seat and what appeared to be a baby car seat in the back. Before they had even had a chance to comment, Waldo and John were quickly out the front door and sprinting towards the old car.

It was only a few minutes before John brought in the family of three and introduced them to Lilly and Karen and then returned to help Waldo with the disabled car. Waldo and John had pushed the car out of the travel lane and Waldo now had the hood up.

Lilly's graceful manner put their new friend at ease right away. The children were a bit shy but it didn't take much time for them to warm up. Karen caught the attention of the waitress for a child's menu and coaxed little Abigail to order whatever was her fancy. Mary couldn't believe someone would actually come to her rescue like this. She relaxed her shoulders and told her story as her hungry children ate and she sipped on the cup of coffee she had ordered for herself. Her husband was in the Navy and his ship had just been deployed to the Persian Gulf. She wasn't sure she could make it through the winter by herself with the children, so she was on her way to live with her parents for the winter months. She had packed all she could fit into the little utility trailer she was pulling and headed to her parents home in Skagway.

"That's such a long trip for you," said Karen overwhelmed with concern. "Do you plan on making a lot of stops?"

Mary didn't have a chance to answer as Waldo returned, pulling up an extra chair to the table. "I'm afraid we're going to need a part, and matter of fact it's available at the auto store in town here but it will probably take an hour or two to fix it," explained Waldo.

"Oh no, I wasn't planning on this," said Mary. "How, how much is it?"

"No one plans this kind of thing," said John as he joined the group. "How far are you going?"

Mary ducked her head shyly, "Not far, just to Skagway, the other side of Juneau."

Waldo practically exploded, "Not far? Girl, that's two days away."

"Now, now, Waldo. I'm sure Mary knows what she's doing," Lilly tried reassuring her husband.

"The kids really do travel well," said Mary trying to coax them into thinking everything would be all right. "We'll be okay."

"How attached are you to your car?" asked Waldo. "You know you could sell it for the price of an airline ticket and be there tonight."

Mary looked wistful as she pondered the thought and the possibility of something else going wrong with her car.

"I guess it would be nice, but where could I find a buyer at such a short notice? And I really do need my things."

"There's a used car lot not too far from here," John offered. "I saw it when we went to the museum today and we could ship your things on the train."

The men knew the dire state the VW was in and they were determined to do anything they could to convince Mary she needed to move on to another plan. There's no telling what could happen on such a long trip with two small children.

Lilly and Karen looked at each other thoughtfully. They certainly did not want to see the young mother take on such an adventure alone with the children but they understood and admired the stubborn set of her chin as she thought over her options.

"I don't know" she said wistfully, "how much do you think I would get for the car and trailer? Would it be enough for the plane fare and shipping our belongings?"

Waldo and John were contemplating their answer when Karen and Lilly nodded at each other. As usual they were on the same wavelength and it was Lilly who spoke.

"Mary, why don't you stay with Karen and me here at the hotel while the men take care of all the arrangements? They can fix your car, take your belongings to the train station, sell the car and get your airline tickets. If the sale of the car isn't enough we will advance you the rest and you can come up to the lodge next summer and work for us to pay us back."

"Oh no, I couldn't impose on strangers like that," Mary said wistfully as she looked at her two young children.

"Nonsense, we're going to need extra help at the Lodge when we get going. This will be perfect," Karen said. "And about us being strangers, I suppose we are now but not for long. You already feel like family, and that's what our business is based on…friends and family. I think you'll be able to see that when you read our brochure for the Wolf Creek Lodge. Besides, your husband is fighting for our country and helping you out a little while he's away is the least we can do."

"Well okay, since you put it that way, but I promise I will pay you back every penny one way or another," said Mary with a heart full of gratitude.

So with keys and a signed title in hand Waldo and John left to get what they could for the old car. The men both understood from the looks their wives had given them that the money they gave Mary after their dealings were done would probably be far over what they would actually get on the sale.

Karen and Lilly took their new friends back to Lilly and Waldo's suite where they put the kids down for a nap. Lilly ordered a pot of tea to be sent up to the room as they settled in with Mary for a real heart to heart.

"Would you like to see a picture of my husband?" asked Mary. After all, a lot of the generosity being offered her was because he was in the service. It would be the least she could do to share her treasured photo with these two, she thought.

"How long have you been married?" Karen asked.

"Oh my," said Lilly as she looked at the picture, "Your last name is Johansson? Your husband isn't related to a Ted and Lois Johansson is he?"

With a puzzled look Mary answered, "Those were his Grandparents names. But they've been gone for a long time. How do you know about them?"

"Was Larry your brother-in-law?" asked Karen.

"Yes…" Mary couldn't do more than look at the two women in amazement with her mouth hanging slightly open.

Lilly and Karen filled Mary in on the Lodge and the diary they had found in the attic, and how they knew of Larry.

As it turned out, Mary had taken some college classes with Lanie and they had kept contact for several years now.

"I guess we really are family," said Lilly as she sipped her tea and settled back in her chair and smiled at Karen. As usual their instincts were right on target.

"Lanie told you about Larry?" asked Mary. "She had such a hard time, and I've never heard her talk about it. I've been really worried about her. Have you met Jimmie?"

Karen answered filling Mary in on Earl's accident and their visit with Grandma Anna and then Lilly took over telling their new friend about the special place that Jimmie had in her and Waldo's hearts.

Mary's eyes were filled with tears as she told Karen and Lilly how relieved she was to have found them and the prayer that had been in her heart as she packed her belongings and her children for the trip that would take her to her parent's home in Skagway.

"Daddy didn't want me to try it but he hasn't been well and I couldn't ask him to come and get us and Mama needed to stay there and take care of him and I truly believed that God would provide safety for us and look, he has not only kept us safe, he also provided us with another family to love."

Karen and Lilly looked at each other and smiled, once again their list of friends and family was growing as it seemed to where ever these two traveled. Mary and her children may truly have been blessed but Karen and Lilly also reaped the benefits.

CHAPTER 13

Everything had worked together perfectly. Even though Mary strongly suspected that they had blessed her with more finances than she was worth at the moment, the smile on her face couldn't be wiped off and she knew she would be back. Her light and gentle spirit was evident as she practically danced down the ramp to the airplane. She even managed a last wave with her arms full of children and bags.

"Did you see that restaurant we passed on the way here?" asked Karen. "I'm absolutely starved. I think this emotional day has made me very hungry."

"I totally agree," answered Lilly, as she searched the men's faces for their response.

"Ok, what did you two eat this afternoon?" she coaxed knowing there had to be a reason why her husband wasn't starving. "You didn't find an apple pie somewhere, did you Waldo?"

Waldo smiled back at his wife, "No Lilly. Besides you know I live off of love, don't you?"

Lilly patted his slightly round stomach, "Living off love didn't get you this little pouch, honey."

"Oh yes it did, love of your cooking got me every bit of it."

As they entered the elegant restaurant they wondered if they would be able to stay without reservations, but due to a cancellation and John's charm they were given one of the best views overlooking the Inlet. The setting was outlined with fishing boats and seaplanes, and their full hearts took in the beauty.

Karen again felt the strength of her love as she sat close to her husband and slid her hand onto his thigh under the table. He slid his hand on top of hers as they viewed the menus and decided on the halibut macadamia. As much as she loved her friends, Karen was looking forward to the next few days when she and John would be alone. They had their own suite at the Lodge but it wasn't the same as being totally alone with the person you loved.

Waldo and Lilly both ordered the salmon with twice baked potatoes and Caesar salads. As the waiter was preparing the salads at the table, the conversation turned away from the events of the day and the four went back to where they had left off at lunch.

"What are your plans for the rest of the time here?" asked Waldo as Lilly lightly kicked him under the table and gave him a look he knew well.

"Tomorrow morning John has the meeting with his music producer friend, and then we're going to rent bicycles and ride along the Inlet path," said Karen. "We're going to shop in the open mall, and explore the city a little more and John wants to go to the airplane museum," she rattled on.

John just sat there and smiled as he watched his wife's rush of excitement, letting her ramble on all she wanted. After the years they had spent apart he considered each precious moment together a special gift and he was inclined to indulge her every whim.

As Karen wound down John reassured Waldo, "We'll be back at the lodge by the end of the week, so don't worry about a thing."

Waldo was quick to reply, "That Lodge is the furthest thing from my mind. Lanie is spoiling Tyson and the O'Callaghan boy's are taking care of the rest. You two just have a good time and we'll see you in a few weeks. Now, Lilly, my love, we've got to get an early start in the morning. What you say we hit the rack?"

"Sure," she answered as she gazed out the window, "but do you think we could take a walk along that path first?"

CHAPTER 14

It was good to be home again, thought Karen as she walked through the front doors of the lodge with her arms heaped full of packages.

"Lanie," she called, "are you here?"

Lanie appeared, coming from the kitchen. The smile on her face grew to a grin as she took in the sight of John and Karen in their new winter hats and mukluks.

"Wow, don't you two look great," she said giving Karen a quick hug. "Are you hungry? I've made homemade chicken soup from Lilly's recipe."

"The soup sounds great as soon as we get the packages unloaded and I have a chance to check on things outside," John replied.

Karen was equally anxious to unpack and then she couldn't wait to give Lilly a call in Washington. They hadn't talked since Lilly and Waldo had left Anchorage and she was eager to find out how Kelsi was doing.

"How about if we eat in about an hour?" suggested Karen. "That way I can get a few things put away and give Lilly a quick call."

"Sure, I'll put the rolls in the oven in a little bit," Lanie agreed.

The three talked over the steaming soup Lanie ladled from the soup tureen and shared about their encounter with Mary and the kids and their adventures in Anchorage.

Karen reported that Kelsi was doing well, and Lilly was getting ready to paint the nursery so everything was going according to schedule there.

"You know," Lanie said thoughtfully as she paused, "Scott Smith delivered some of the supplies for the tropical room. He really is a strange one."

"Were you here by yourself when he came?" asked Karen.

"No, Jimmie was here with me. I just don't trust that guy."

John was listening to the two women with a frown on his face, "If he bothers you, or you don't feel comfortable with him around, we'll just get our supplies from somewhere else. I know Waldo said something about the guy being a little off before he left. We don't want to take any chances."

Lanie smiled back, "I'm sure everything's OK. You guys are back now and it wasn't so much anything he said as just a creepy feeling I had when he was around. Don't worry you two, it's cool."

Karen smiled to herself at Lanie's choice of words. The young woman was so composed and capable that it was easy to forget how old she really was.

As the two women did the dishes and cleaned the kitchen Karen was thinking that she was grateful for the company. She wasn't really used to not having Lilly around, and even though she now had a husband to share her life with she hadn't really had time yet to adjust to married life either. They had a very strong love, and roots that went back over thirty years, and they had John Jr. and Heather; they just didn't have the memories and experiences in-between then and now. Sometimes it felt like they had been married for thirty years, and other times she felt like she was just around the corner from her single life.

"This big ole place must be awfully lonely when you're here by yourself," she said as she started to verbalize her thoughts.

"Yes it can be, but I just bring Jimmie or Esther with me. And it won't be long before the guests will fill it up and we won't even notice," replied Lanie.

"And we have so much to do, what time can you be here in the morning?"

"How about 7:00? Tomorrow is Jimmie's therapy so Mom will take him. But if it's OK I'll bring Esther will me?" Lanie answered with a question in her voice.

Karen was quick to reassure her that the kids were always welcome and as they finished the kitchen she told Lanie to run along home.

After John had checked on the progress the O'Callaghan boys had made outside he had disappeared in the den. Karen had heard hammering coming from that room and was anxious to see what he was doing. As soon as Lanie left Karen eagerly opened the den door and found John just stepping back from the painting he had hung.

Hanging above the mantle was a painting of the Wolf Creek Lodge. Karen's breath caught, "Oh, John, it's just beautiful, who painted it?"

John put his arm around Karen and quietly urged her toward the painting. "I sent the picture of the Lodge that's in the brochure to a painter friend of mine in New York. Go on, darling, read the inscription at the bottom."

Karen stopped just under the painting and read the small bronze plaque that had been added to the cherry wood, "All our worldly cares cease to be when we allow our hearts to be led by divine destiny."

With love and appreciation in her eyes Karen stepped into John's arms. "John, it's beautiful. Thank you."

John pulled her to him, "No, darling, thank you. And thank Lilly and Waldo for bringing us back together and for allowing us to live and work in this beautiful Lodge. But most of all, we need to always remember that it was God's divine destiny that allowed us to find each other after all these years. Without God in our lives and turning our hearts over to him completely we would never have known that it was his will that we be together. And my darling, for as long as I live I will thank God every day for bringing you back to me.

CHAPTER 15

The days had passed quickly, and it was time for Waldo and Lilly to return. John and Karen had found that they worked together very well, and had all of the groundwork in place for the tropical room. The glass walls were laid out to be placed in their frames, and an old fashioned "barn raising" was scheduled for Saturday. Lilly had already been planning the food even though she was miles away, and thanks to e-mails and telephones the plans were in place.

The day Waldo and Lilly were due to return was dark and dreary. Karen could tell that winter would come early to this barren land. She was always uneasy when someone she loved was flying, so to calm herself she planned an elaborate menu and threw herself into cooking a real feast for her friend's return. Lilly's last e-mail had said they expected to be back by 4:00 pm and Karen was determined not to start worrying until at least 4:05.

After spending an entire day in the kitchen she had sourdough rolls rising on the back of the stove, a fresh apple berry pie cooling on the kitchen table and the aroma of pot roast with fresh root vegetables wafted from the oven. As she left the kitchen at 3:55 to freshen up she heard the seaplane and knew her prayers had been answered. Lilly and Waldo had returned safe.

Karen's spirits lifted and she quickly slipped her hair into the ivory clip she had purchased in Anchorage and changed into her new baby blue short-sleeved sweater. "I wonder what Lilly brought me?" she mumbled to herself as she returned to the kitchen just as her friend came through the back door. Dropping her bag Lilly grabbed Karen and they hugged and hopped up and down as they often did when they were excited.

"I've got so much to tell you," Lilly continued; "You won't believe the babies' room. Kelsi has painted ponies all over the walls and the rugs on the floor in front of each crib are latch hook ponies and the light fixtures and lamps are covered in tiny cowboy boots. Oh you're just not going to believe it."

Waldo and John smiled at these two from the doorway for a moment and then John spoke, "Come on Waldo let's get your bags upstairs while these two play catch up."

"Wait just a minute," Waldo said sniffing appreciatively, "Karen is that apple pie I smell?"

Karen left Lilly and gave Waldo a quick hug, "You bet, and it's your wife's recipe too. Now get those things upstairs."

The lodge was filled with an air of excitement as the four were back into the swing of planning and brainstorming. The aromas of the pot roast and the freshly baked rolls mixed with the energy of these four, and their anticipation of the future events they were about to experience, filled the immense space.

Lilly and Karen spent the rest of the evening in the kitchen catching up on what they had missed and working on the preparations for Saturday. Every once in a while Karen would stop what she was doing and admire the antique aquamarine bracelet that Lilly and Waldo had brought her from Washington. Lilly had found the bracelet at a little antique store in the small town where Jamie and Kelsi lived, and knew that it would match Karen's blue cashmere sweater.

John had seemed equally pleased with the iron wolf silhouette that was from Jamie and Kelsi's latest line of metal creations.

CHAPTER 16

Waldo threw another log into the fireplace in the kitchen as he inhaled the promise of flavor to his taste buds and satisfaction to his stomach. He inhaled slowly again as he went out to feed Tyson.

Thanks to the time saving preparations from the night before, Lilly and Karen were putting the finishing touches on the buffet breakfast as John entered the kitchen and headed straight for the coffee pot.

"Honeymoon's over already?" teased Lilly.
"Oh no..." he replied as he took a sip out of his mug and then swung around to kiss Karen on the lips.

The sound of voices brought their attention to the back door at the O'Callaghan family's arrival. As Lanie entered Lilly and Karen took in the sight, then looked at each other as the grins grew on their faces and then back to Lanie.

"What in the world are you two grinning about?" Lanie asked.
"Well, it's just that we've never seen you with a tool belt on before," explained Karen.
Even John couldn't take his eyes off of her for a moment. Her beauty seemed to be highlighted by the morning light. Her long, dark hair was neatly braided, accenting her features and she obviously had no need to wear makeup. She was a perfect picture of health and life. Lilly knew in her heart that Lanie was a good catch for any decent deserving

man, and vowed to herself that she would do a little more plotting to get pastor Jim here on a visit.

"I didn't know anyone could look so feminine in a tool belt," stated Lilly. "I think you and I ought to try that Karen."

"I don't know, Lilly," Karen answered skeptically; "somehow I don't think we would achieve the same look, but it sure looks good on Lanie."

Waldo agreed that for Lilly to wear a tool belt, her slender frame would be weighted down with the necessary kitchen utensils.

"Hey now, do you think kitchen tools are the only kind I know how to use?" Lilly objected.

Waldo was quick to answer, "Lilly, my love, you can use any tool you want, it's just the kitchen tools are the ones you know the best."

They turned at the sound of another vehicle in the driveway and soon welcomed Edward Bjorn and his family to the day's event. They would only be able to stay for the morning though as he needed to open his store to customers for at least a few hours.

After everyone had filled their plates and gathered at the massive pine table Waldo said grace, thanking God for the food they were about to eat, the work they had been given to do and the ability to enjoy the many bountiful blessings in their lives.

Lilly received many compliments on her breakfast sausage casserole and Mrs. Bjorn was convinced that Lilly and Karen had stayed up all night cooking.

Arnie and Ernie felt right at home, helping themselves to second servings.

The food was devoured and then everyone was anxious to start the day's work. Jimmie was checking out the glass wall panels, unsure of how they would be assembled into a room. He had never seen such a project before and was pleased as punch when he was given the job of distributing the screws when needed. Waldo made sure he was a safe distance from the panels though.

Karen was slightly conscious that Lanie was giving her some competition as far as looking good in her Levi's. Even though she knew it was a silly thought and she had absolutely no need to feel jealous or envious, she promised herself that she would work hard today and refuse dessert at least once. She glanced at Lilly to check her friends' composure and guessed that she wasn't alone in feeling the loss of youth. However, it didn't take long before all of that nonsense was forgotten.

The men soon had the heavy panels ready to hoist into position, and Lanie and Lilly were ready with their power tools to put the screws into the framework.

John gave a big "heave ho…" and the structure quickly grew into the shape of a room. It took six men to position each of the panels into its framework.

By the time the last panel was set and screwed into place, Lilly was feeling every day of her fifty years. Her knees and calves ached from the strain of stretching and reaching and her neck and shoulder muscles were so tight she could hardly hold the drill upright.

As Waldo helped her down from her perch on the ladder she gratefully put the drill in his hands, "You were right, honey, I think I'll stick to kitchen utensils, if you don't mind."

Waldo laughed and gave her a quick hug, "Couldn't have done it without you, my love. You too, Karen, you gals did great."

Karen and Lilly stepped back to the doorway and admired their morning's work.

"Come on Lilly, we'll help you reach into the oven and carry your baking dish to the counter," teased Karen.

The two women were anxious to get to know their guests a little better and to do the job that they loved. Once in the kitchen again, Lilly seemed to forget about her aches and pains as she dusted the top of the lasagna with fresh grated Parmesan cheese. The garlic cheese French bread loaves were under the broiler and Karen was slicing fresh mushrooms to add to the green salad.

"I can't believe how easy the panels went up," exclaimed Karen. "But then again with all of the planning we did I would have been disappointed if they didn't. I really think we can get the roof on this afternoon with all of the help we have."

"What a treat!" said Mrs. Bjorn as she came into view of the massive table set with place settings of blue ceramic plates and filled with delicious food that looked like it belonged on the front page of a magazine. "And the best part is that I don't have to cook today."

After everyone had their fill Lilly brought out a tray of cookie bars. There were lemon, chocolate chip, and carrot, nut and raisin. In spite of the oohs and aahs Lilly felt compelled to apologize for the lack of a more elaborate dessert. Waldo agreed, under his breath, that an apple pie would have been awfully good.

As the meal ended Mr. Bjorn regretfully headed back to open his store for the afternoon and Mrs. Bjorn stayed to help clean the kitchen. This chore took most of the afternoon due in part to sore muscles but mostly because of the lively conversation between Karen, Lilly and Lena Bjorn. Lanie had returned to work on the sunroom with the men and her brothers, so Karen took this opportunity to fill Mrs. Bjorn in on their plans for their young friend and Pastor Jim from New Orleans.

Lena agreed that Lanie was a wonderful person and she didn't know of anyone around here that was a good fit for her.

With a half dozen caulking guns going at the same time, a well thought out plan in place, and strong knowledgeable workers, the rest of the structure took place easily. It was late in the day before the last of the roofing had been attached and they all gathered to view the creation.

"Wow," said Jimmy as he reached up and took hold of Waldo's hand.

"You said it," replied Waldo.

Nona O'Callaghan had left earlier to feed the sled dogs and now returned, calling Ernie to come and help her.

"Well bless your heart," said Karen as soon as she saw the large platter of sandwiches she had carefully packed into the truck of her car.

"I didn't think you'd feel much like cooking tonight," explained Nona. "So I talked Lilly into letting me make sandwiches. After all my family eats most of the food around here."

"Thank you," said Lilly graciously, "your family has worked very hard here and don't ever feel that it's a problem for them to eat here. However, tonight you've brought us quite a treat."

The following morning John and Karen were up early dressed in their paint clothes. Lilly cooked breakfast and then John and Karen gathered the glass painting supplies and went to work with the patterns John had designed. Karen was especially excited since she had previewed the drawings and helped to plan the supplies needed. As Waldo and Lilly watched the mural in the sunroom take shape; helping to move ladders and replenish the paint trays they were astounded at the picture forming before them.

The lower half of the glass held a mural around the three sides of the open room. The viewer's attention was automatically drawn to the left side that held a great whale with the ocean waves surrounding his majestic size. The mural then smoothly blended into the back panels, up onto an iceberg on which a polar bear and her cubs were pulling a fish out of the water. As the mural proceeded to the right the ice gradually turned into tundra and then to land. A pack of wolves stood back by a wooded mountain area in the back corner of the panel with one prominent wolf facing the middle of that side. The paintings were carefully planned to allow enough light for the plants that would be placed on the shelving around the bottom of the panels, and to allow light to give the ocean water a transparent look. At the same time the painting provided privacy to the room.

John was such a talented man it didn't really surprise Karen that he was an artist too. The glass paintings were awesome and held the attention of the group for quite some time. She was very proud of his work and was already planning to redesign the Wolf Creek Lodge brochure with pictures to show it off.

"When in your life did you have time for art lessons?" asked Waldo.

"Not even once, Waldo, but thanks," John said modestly. "I think it'll probably take us about two more days to finish."

"It's not finished?" asked Lilly.

"He has to put in the details," explained Karen.

"Goes to show what I know about painting," Lilly said. "I would have called it good after the ocean and tundra. I probably wouldn't have thought to put the animals in. And if I did they sure wouldn't have looked like that."

John laughed, "Don't be so hard on yourself, Lilly. Everyone has their special talents and we all know where yours are."

Lilly grinned back, "So you're telling me to get back to the kitchen? Ok, Ok, I'll get out of your way. Come on Waldo, you're not needed here either."

As Waldo and Lilly left the room John whispered to Karen, "I know where your special talents are too, honey."

Blushing Karen swatted her husband playfully, "Stop it John, they might hear you."

Lilly was up to her elbows in soapy water and Waldo had the dishtowel in his hands when they heard Karen yell, "Come here quick!"

Karen's tone definitely had an urgent note to it and the two sprinted to the sunroom in a flash.

They arrived to find Karen in John's arms.

As they entered Karen said, "Look!"

They had dimmed the lighting fixtures to reflect just enough light on the mural, and with the aurora borealis flashing and flickering through the skylights it appeared that the ocean waves were moving.

"Oh, it's just gorgeous," said Lilly gasping.

Regardless of the work that was still yet to be done the four friends spent the remainder of the day in the "Sun Room" admiring the mural as it changed with the lights outside.

Finally Waldo went out to take care of Tyson and Lilly forced herself into the kitchen to fix the evening meal. They had all been so caught up in the new room that no one had eaten since breakfast. Lilly pulled a beef stew from the freezer that she had tucked away for just such an emergency, and popping Ranch Parmesan biscuits in the oven, she had Waldo help her set up TV trays and chairs in the new room so they could continue to watch the changing scenery.

Later Karen took a turn in the kitchen to make popcorn for the show, sprinkled with white cheddar seasoning. "Might as well add an aroma to the memory we're making," she explained. "We're probably the only people that will think of the aurora borealis when we smell popcorn or eat beef stew. And just think, in a couple of weeks we'll be watching it from the hot tub. I can't wait."

CHAPTER 17

Karen looked up and smiled as Lanie came to the back door with her tool belt in her hand and a bounce in her step. "So you think you guys will finish today?" asked Karen.

"I sure hope so, your guests will be here in two days and Waldo says it's possible. Where's Lilly? We need the updated plans for the plants that were delivered yesterday."

"She's working on it right now with Kelsi; you'll find her at the computer in the office." Karen answered.

Kelsi wasn't able to do much work on the ranch these days, but she was an expert in the greenhouse and she could sit in front of a computer to plan the placement of the plants and their needs of light and moisture. She had done most of the ordering and with the help of digital cameras it was almost like being there.

Lilly looked up from her work to find Lanie's bright face. "Good morning, do you have the instructions for the plants?" Lanie asked.

"Here, I just printed out the blue print."

They heard a knocking at the front door and went out to see who it was. "Maybe it's the rest of the plants," said Lilly hopefully.

John was already by the door when he heard the solid knock. He was prepared to accept another delivery but opened it to find a young man about Lanie's age, well fed and a bit tussled.

"Hello sir," the young man said. "I understand Lanie O'Callaghan is working here and I wonder if I might see her for a moment?"

"Sure, I'll go get her. Wait right here," he instructed.

Lanie appeared and introduced her friend from school. Ken lived with his mother in town for the summer months when he wasn't in school. Lanie had gone to college with him, sharing rides home on occasion.

Karen and Lilly soon realized that he was her date for the concert, which was the reason he had come home. This brought a frown to Lilly's brow right away. "This might put a kink in our plan for Pastor Jim," she whispered to Karen.

"Whatever is meant to be will happen," Karen assured her. "Maybe Lanie really likes this guy, we really don't know and it is her decision."

"Just wanted to let you know I was in town, and maybe we could get together tonight," he suggested.

"I'll see you later," promised Lanie. "We have a lot of work to do today and I really don't know when we'll be done, so why don't I give you a call later?"

As soon as the young man left Lilly asked Lanie if she would like to review the plans Kelsi had e-mailed. Karen was not about to miss out on whatever Lilly had in mind and followed her friends into the office.

"Was that your date for the concert?" asked Lilly.

"How long have you been dating him?" asked Karen.

"Now, Karen, let's not be pushy," said Lilly. "Lanie has a right to her privacy. Do you like him?"

"It's okay you two," Lanie said calmly. "Like I said before he's just a friend from school. I was talking to him when we first learned Dylan Wyatt was coming and I needed someone to go with so we agreed to buy tickets and go together. Actually I think he might be dating someone, but then again I haven't figured out who it is yet. He's always asking me out and I usually turn him down, but I really wanted to go to the concert."

"He drives a nice car, does he have money?" Lilly blurted out.

"Lilly, you heard Lanie. Now just leave it alone," Karen admonished.

At the disappointed look on Lilly's face, Lanie laughed and answered. "Honestly, you two, he's just a friend. Just a friend to go to a concert with. And yes, Lilly, he comes from a very well to do family. Now can we please get to work?"

There was a new buzz of energy and the work began. Lilly's mind was more on how she was going to get Pastor Jim here and introduce him to Lanie than her work. Karen kept trying to get her back on track.

"Here, this plant goes over there in the corner," Karen instructed Lilly as she pointed to its designated place.

Later on that afternoon Lilly declared that the sunroom was finished. And it was a true masterpiece. The hot tubs were surrounded with plants and rocks and the artificial stream ran around them and into a pool under the polar bears. The pool was stocked with large gold fish and had a mist maker in one end. A few of the plants had blooms, and more unusual blooms were expected to appear soon.

Lanie had her massage station set up with privacy screens and mood lighting. The stream provided a tranquil atmosphere as it rippled by, and the lighting could be dimmed and re-directed any way she wanted. Her cart was stocked with a variety of scented oils, and a towel warmer.

The opposite corner held three tread mills, a stair stepper, a stationary bike and a weight lifting bench. There were comfortable reclining chairs positioned by the whale, and a couple of big overstuffed chairs where you could curl up and read a book. Speakers located throughout the room directed music to any location.

Karen, Lilly and Lanie stood together at the entrance taking in the view. "I'm really impressed," said Karen.

"Absolutely," said Lilly.

"I can't believe we're really finished," said Lanie.

"Oh…Angie is going to love this," exclaimed Lilly. "I can't wait until she gets here."

"When do you expect them, Lilly?" Lanie asked and then added hopefully, "Will Dylan Wyatt be with them?"

"Engelbert and Angie will be here sometime tomorrow evening and Dylan and Norma will come over after the concert for a few days."

Lanie perked up, "Do you think he'll need a little stress reliever after all the energy he puts out on the stage?"

Karen and Lilly looked at each other and grinned, "Girl, just what do you have in mind?" Lilly asked.

Lanie smiled mischievously, "Nothing, I'm just wondering if I might get a chance to massage him."

"Sure" Karen laughed and then added, "With Norma's supervision."

"And his bodyguard's supervision too..." added Lilly with a snicker.

"You know you don't have to worry about me, I've already had my one true love in life and that's all I need," said Lanie changing to a serious matter of fact tone, then she lightened up again. "There's no law that says I can't have a little adventure though, and from what I've read I really doubt that he'd ruin his reputation of being a gentlemen so I don't think we need to worry. Besides, I wouldn't do anything that wasn't professional, that's what I'm trained to do. It would be something to tell my grandkids about though..."

Her voice trailed off as she realized what she had just said; in one breath she would never love another and in the next she had an expectation of grandchildren someday.

"Never mind that last part," she corrected herself. "I'll probably have nieces and nephews some day."

Karen and Lilly's eyes met. Their hearts ached for their young friend and they wished they could find the words to explain to her that it was okay to love again. But they both knew from experience that this was something that Lanie had to work out for herself. Lilly strengthened her resolve to somehow get Pastor Jim to Alaska and introduce him to this extraordinary young woman. Despite Waldo's admonitions to mind her own business she knew in her heart it would be a match that could only bring good to everyone involved.

"I'm sure you'll have lots of nieces and nephews," Lilly reassured her.

CHAPTER 18

Karen was fluffing the pillows and Lilly was hanging fresh towels that still held the scent of the fresh summer air in the Husky room.

"I hope Angie likes this room and I think she will, knowing her love for dogs, but we could let her pick their room after she sees them all. She might prefer the Homestead Suite," said Karen as she finished straightening the pillows and then folded an extra blanket and hung it on the back of a chair. "What do you think Lilly?"

"I think she'll love them all and we'd better make the decision for her. If she fancies a particular one though, we'll move them. It's just that simple," answered Lilly.

Lilly had been planning Angie's favorite foods all week, and for breakfast tomorrow they would have the biscuits and sausage gravy that Engelbert loved. The table in the kitchen had been extended to seat the six of them comfortably, and it had been set with china and cloth napkins since right after breakfast.

Karen had collected what was probably the last of the wild flowers and made an arrangement for the centerpiece.

The evenings were very chilly now and Waldo and John had brought in a good supply of wood for the fireplaces, and also had their fishing gear ready to go.

Lanie was "on-call" for massage appointments, and would stop in later to meet the guests.

"We actually have a celebrity coming," said Lilly as she thought about how Angie's life must have changed. "She's come a long way since she sang karaoke at the Golden Nugget."

The large Navigator came slowly into the driveway as Engelbert and Angie took in the setting of the lodge. Lilly had been watching from an upstairs window and came running down the stair shouting, "They're here, they're here."

Karen and the men joined Lilly to meet their guests and welcome them to Wolf Creek. The two guests felt more than welcome with the reception they were given.

"My goodness," said Karen, "Look how thin you are Angie. You must be working out."

"And it looks like you've been pampered a bit," said Lilly. "Come on in and take your boots off and then we'll show you around. We have something really special to show you."

"You guys make me feel like a queen," she said. "But don't try to pamper me too much. I want to see everything and then I want to help you cook something yummy. And no, Karen, I haven't been working out. I just don't seem to slow down anymore and I never seem to have the time to enjoy eating."

"We'll certainly do something about that" Lilly answered, "I hope you brought your stretch jeans."

Angie was excited as they toured the suites and explored the lodge. Every room was her favorite, and Lilly had been right about choosing the room for her. She loved them all and wanted to try each of them. As a matter of fact she did try out most of the beds to see which was the most comfortable.

"Ok, we have one more room to show you," said Karen with a bit of pride in her voice. "Close your eyes for a minute…"

Lilly lead Angie into the sunroom and once again the aurora borealis was flickering through the glass panels. The song Angie had written and recorded could be heard throughout the room and the spotlights were on the whale and the polar bears. Angie opened her eyes and gasped at the beauty. Speechless, she wandered through the room taking in every detail.

The song told the story of a young girl who wanted to go to Nashville to try her hand at becoming a music star only to fall in love with a handsome fisherman and give up her dreams of fame for a life with him. The song goes on to tell of her chance meeting with a very famous singer and how thanks to encouragement from her husband and friends she had become a star after all. When the song first came out it had become a symbol of hope to young girls all over the world, a sign that if you followed your heart, you could find happiness, with or without fame and fortune.

Finally Angie returned to her friends and putting her arms around both of them she drew them close. "Thank you so much. No one else has ever seemed to understand just how beautiful this country is, but you two do, don't you? You have to or you couldn't have created this room." Turning to look back at the ever-changing scenes, Angie continued. "Just knowing this room is here is going to make it easier for me to go away. Now I know I can always come home again."

"Absolutely," said Lilly. "You know you're always welcome to come home to visit any time. And we have a reservation for you and Engelbert tonight with our masseuse. That is if you want to relax to the max after your long trip today."

"And that scrumptious scent coming from the kitchen reminds me that we need to check the oven!" Karen chimed in. "My mouth is watering already!"

Lilly continued as they made their way to the kitchen, "And maybe we can go to the village tomorrow while the men are fishing," she said with a spark of excitement in her voice. "Angie, do you remember ole lady Kelly in Louisiana?" Lilly asked as she grabbed a potholder to check the hot dish.

"Yes…how could I forget? How could anyone forget meeting that woman?" Angie answered.

"Well, she has a twin here," Lilly stated.

"No…you're kidding. Not really a twin?" Angie asked with astonishment.

"Well, she does look like her and we'll probably run into her tomorrow. That woman seems to be everywhere," Lilly answered

Both Lilly and Karen's eyes were twinkling with mischief as Karen continued, "Lilly's already had a run in with her. And she has beady little eyes and she wears large tent dresses, or house dresses, or whatever you call those things."

"Maybe we'll need to give you a disguise so no one will recognize you," Lilly added thoughtfully.

The three women chatted companionably through the dinner preparations, catching up on the different things happening in each of their lives. Their husbands had been in Waldo's shop all afternoon getting the fishing tackle ready for the next day and reluctantly came in to eat after Lilly's third call. However, their reluctance turned to gleeful anticipation when they smelled and saw the delicious dishes steaming on the dining table. The large platter holding the ham was garnished with pineapple and parsley. The steamed vegetables were fresh and flavorful. The black cherry gelatin salad was served in a crystal bowl and garnished with cherries and bits of pineapple, and the fragrance of the rolls in the wicker basket was unbelievable.

It was John's turn to say the blessing that night and his words of thanks for delivering their friends safely home brought a mist to the women's eyes and Lilly thought she saw Waldo secretly brush a tear away. The near drowning experience they had shared in Louisiana would not be forgotten.

During dinner John and Waldo told their stories of Big Foot and the moose that had visited the lodge. Angie's eyes were wide with amazement before they finished. Soon only scraps remained of the beautiful dinner and Lilly suggested that the men retire to the "Room of Lights" as she now thought of it. When Waldo started to protest that he hadn't had pie yet Lilly reassured him that dessert would be served to them where they could chat and enjoy the ambience of the new room.

Lanie was scheduled to arrive in an hour to begin the massages and that would give plenty of time to enjoy the dessert they had prepared.

Karen busied herself grinding coffee beans, making coffee to go with the dessert as Lilly sliced large pieces of tart apple pie and topped each with a wedge of extra sharp cheddar cheese. Angie carefully placed each piece under the broiler just long enough for the cheese to bubble slightly. Arranging the desserts and coffee on trays the women followed their husbands to the "Room of Lights."

"This is just like old times, only better," said Waldo. "And I think the pie gets better with time too."

"Tell us what it's like to be a big star," begged Karen as she sipped her hot coffee and inhaled the aroma.

"I'm sure you and Engelbert live a very different life since we saw you last," said John.

"Well, I still have the fisherman in me," insisted Engelbert just before he took another big bite.

Lanie arrived a little early with a bag of extra supplies weighting down her shoulder. After being introduced to Angie and Engelbert she was coaxed into having a piece of pie with them, and then Angie started to talk a little about her new life of stardom.

"It's so nice to be here," Angie said. "Really, all of the lights and glamour are great, but I need to have my personal time once in a while. I must say working with Dylan has been quite a pleasure though. And Norma is just wonderful. The country music scene is a lot like living in a small town. Everybody knows everybody and they're all so willing to help each other. It's nothing like what I've heard show business would be like. And the best part is making a difference in people's lives with the music. When you're passionate about a song, and you have lived it, people see that and relate to it."

Angie had always had a knack for bringing people into the open and her recent success hadn't changed her one bit. With a few tactical questions she soon had Lanie talking about herself. Angie took a liking to Lanie right away and when she learned that Lanie planned on being a teacher it wasn't long before she was telling Lanie about her teaching experiences in Hawaii. Lilly and Karen then learned a lot by listening as Angie pulled details out of Lanie about her education and her family history.

By the end of the evening they all had a better insight, thanks to Lanie, into the trials and joys of living with a special needs child. The group had so enjoyed the visiting that no one had gotten around to having a massage and it was decided that Lanie would come back early the next day to give Angie hers before their shopping trip into the village.

CHAPTER 19

The lodge was alive with a buzz of excitement that comes when family and friends are together. Lilly was mixing sourdough pancake batter and frying thick slices of ham for breakfast while Karen worked on the men's lunches. Angie had been up early to use the treadmill and then receive her promised massage. The men were making their last preparations for the day's fishing trip, and Tyson was in the midst of the action.

"I feel like a million bucks," said Angie as she entered the kitchen. "What is that I smell?"

"You look like a million bucks," said Engelbert as he entered the back door just in time to hear his wife's comment.

As usual Angie's eyes lit up when she saw her husband. Her adoration was mirrored in his eyes as he placed a kiss tenderly on her upturned lips.

"We're having pancakes," announced Lilly. "And they should be ready in about fifteen minutes or so."

"I can't wait," said Engelbert. "I don't get home cooked meals very often any more," he complained.

It wasn't long before the meal was devoured and the men were about ready to take off on their trip. With a smooth move Karen pulled John around the corner while everyone else was still taking the last sips of their coffee. She slid her hands around his neck and through the curls at the base of his neck as she gave him a good-bye kiss that he couldn't forget easily.

"That's so you don't forget what you have to come home to," she said with a twinkle in her eyes.

"Maybe I should stay home," he said with a yearning look in his eyes as he pulled her closer. "Not a chance," Karen said giving him a quick kiss and playfully pushing him away, "We all have plans today and you have a fish to catch."

"John, you ready?" Waldo called from the kitchen, "Daylight's a wastin'."

After sending the men on their way the women were now free to embark upon their adventures of the day. "I sure miss my car," said Lilly.

"Me too," said Karen.

"I'll never forget the ride we had to the church," exclaimed Angie.

The three friends laughed at the memory of Karen folding herself and her bridal gown into the front seat of Lilly's Volkswagen. The trusty old VW was the only vehicle that would start that day to deliver them to the church. Karen's dress had been so full that it was necessary for her to shift when Lilly hit the clutch.

That memory evolved into Lilly and Karen telling Angie more stories of the fun they had as teenagers when they would zip around their hometown in the VW. It was still undecided just how many guys they could cram into the back. The trip into town passed quickly and they were almost hysterical with laughter by the time they pulled up in front of Edward Bjorn's Mercantile Store. Composing themselves they entered the store and walked right into Elma Smith.

Elma put her hands on her large rounded hips, which made her purple and yellow tent shaped housedress rise just above her red knee socks. She took in the sight of the three gleeful women with her little piggy eyes, and opened her mouth to speak but Lilly quickly greeted her first. "How are you today, Mrs. Smith, don't you just love this fall weather?"

"Well I never!" exclaimed Elma. "Are you all goin' to do your grocery shoppin' today? Or maybe you're just goin' to fill this town with strangers?"

Karen quickly answered, knowing that Lilly's blood was probably about to boil and steam would come out of her ears any second now. "Yes Elma, we're going to get a few groceries. Looks like you've accomplished your shopping already today. And this is our friend that has come to visit for a few days. Goodbye, we hope you have a good afternoon."

With that the three were able to start browsing and ignore the grunting sounds Elma was making as she slowly moved to the door. She had already paid for her groceries so there wasn't much she could do but leave, although she obviously wanted to stick around so that she didn't miss anything.

"I can't believe it Lilly," whispered Angie. "She really is a twin to old lady Kelly."

Mr. Bjorn greeted the three with a big smile. "Good Morning, Mrs. Worthington, Mrs. Lansford," he said moving from around the counter as Karen spoke, "Good morning, Mr. Bjorn, we'd like for you to meet our friend..."

"Oh, I know Angie McIntosh," Mr. Bjorn said with a broad smile, "We have all of her CD's and the wife and I have tickets to the concert. Oh boy, wait until she hears that Miss McIntosh was actually in our store."

Holding her hand out graciously Angie demurred, "Mr. Bjorn, it's so nice to meet you. Karen and Lilly have told me so much about you. Just being in your store makes me homesick. My Papa had a store much like this one and after school I would play old records on his old phonograph in the back of the store. That's where I learned to sing."

Angie's eyes had become misty with this memory. Mr. Bjorn was still holding her small hands in his. Seeing the tears in her eyes brought a lump to the large man's throat. Smiling at Angie he gently said, "What a wonderful memory."

Lilly and Karen smiled with amusement at the sight of their large, new friend all misty-eyed, still holding the hand of the petite Angie.

"Mr. Bjorn, we wanted to show Angie your store. That is if you'll let her go," Lilly said with a teasing tone in her voice.

Becoming rather flustered Edward Bjorn suddenly released Angie's hand and stepping back behind the counter he cleared his throat loudly. "Ladies, let me know if I can be of any assistance," he said.

The three browsed until they came to the selection of scarves. Lilly tried on the deep wine red and Angie the vibrant blue. Karen was drawn to the one of purple and lavender shades.

"I think this will go with my dress I'm wearing for the concert," said Angie with enthusiasm as she made it flow around her neckline.

Not finding a mirror they modeled the scarves for each other. "Oh my…" said Lilly as she peered into the back corner of the store. "I didn't even know there was a photo booth back here. We have to get a picture! Anybody have quarters?"

After some digging in the bottom of their purses they came up with enough change for the old photo machine. While Lilly and Karen had been finding change, Angie had discovered a trunk of vintage clothing. Slipping into a sapphire blue taffeta low cut dress and draping a silver feather boa around her neck, Angie asked her friends for their opinions.

"You look great, just like a real dance hall girl," Karen said.

Clapping her hands excitedly as her eyes lit up, Lilly added, "Let's all dress up as dance hall girls then we can get photos for the guys."

In no time Lilly had discovered a scarlet silk dress cut so far up the thigh even she was a little self-conscious. Turning to get her friend's opinion she caught her breath. The emerald gown that Karen had picked out couldn't have been a better color for her friend. The fine silk material shimmered in the dusky light from a small window nearby, and brought out golden flecks in Karen's green eyes. Determined to accomplish the task, they dug a little deeper into the trunk and found boas and hats to match their outfits. The three of them fit easily inside the photo booth, and their laughter grew with each seductive pose.

Unaware that Elma Smith had returned to the store Lilly was suddenly caught off guard when she emerged from the booth and found the portly woman attempting to peak through a gap in the curtain. "Why, hello again, Mrs. Smith," she said still giggling. "We were just trying on outfits to wear to Angie's concert. What do you think?" Lilly spoke her words without thinking as she swung around and propped her bare leg up on the bench outside the booth.

Before Mrs. Smith had a chance to answer, Angie grabbed her friend's arm and drug her off to the changing room leaving Karen to explain they were only taking pictures for their husbands.

"Well I never..." said Elma, shaking her head in bewilderment. Not giving Karen a chance to explain, Elma left in a hurry. I bet she's determined to tell the town, thought Karen.

The three women purchased the scarves they had originally picked out and Mr. Bjorn shared a brief story of how he had picked up the old trunk of clothing from an auction when the Golden Nugget had been remodeled several years ago. He told the story with a large smile on his face, knowing that these women had given him enough entertainment for the month.

"I think we are safe to have lunch at the Once in a Blue Moon Cafe," explained Karen as they left. "Elma went the other way and besides I'm starving again."

Karen answered her ringing cell phone to find Lanie on the other end. "Dinner will be ready about 7:00 like we planned and everything is fine here, but do you think you could possibly take some oatmeal and canned peaches to my Grandma while you're in town?" she pleaded. "I wouldn't dream of imposing, but Mama is at the hospital with Jimmie and I didn't know that she needed anything until just a little bit ago. Once she gets her mind set on something she doesn't let go of it, and I know she'd love to see you if you have the time."

"Of course we will do that for you, Lanie," said Karen. "Does she like instant or the regular kind? Will it be okay if we go after we have lunch?"

After a leisurely lunch they went to the local grocery and bought the few items that Lanie had said her Grandma needed.

On the way to Grandma Anna's, Karen and Lilly filled Angie in on the details of the wonderful elderly Indian woman that had become their friend.

Their arrival brought a smile to Grandma Anna's face. She thanked them for the groceries and then insisted they stay for tea.

Glancing into the living room Lilly could see that Grandma had set the tea table next to her chair for company and accepted the invitation graciously. When they sat at the small table by the chair where Grandma Anna spent her days, Lilly's eyes were drawn to the lovely rose teapot with gold trim sitting in the middle of the table.

"Grandma Anna you shouldn't have gone to so much trouble. The table is just lovely and wherever did you find that teapot? I haven't seen anything like that since we left New Orleans," Lilly said.

The smile that had formed on Grandma Anna's lips grew as she settled into her chair. Karen and Lilly met each other's eyes and smiled. They knew they were about to be treated to a special "memory story" as Lanie called them. "Long, long ago when I was a young woman I fell in love with a handsome trader. My parents said that he would only break my heart. But of course I didn't listen. I had my heart set on that man and nothing would change it. So of course we were married. He had tried to warn me that life with a traveling man would be lonely, especially in these parts. Just before the wedding he built me this house and this is where we came on our wedding night and where I have spent every night since. All except one." Pausing briefly to take a sip of tea and settling a little farther into her chair, Grandma Anna continued. "The first three months of our marriage were pure heaven. We laughed and talked and planned for our future and," pausing shyly she continued, "we made love. We were so in love we couldn't see past those days. All too soon the honeymoon was over, as they say, and I saw the restless look in his eyes and knew he would be leaving. One day he was especially quiet all day and as we were eating supper that night he told me he would be gone with the dawn. I fell apart. I couldn't conceive even spending one night away from him. In my tears and hysterics I ran from the house, and I ran and ran, and found myself in front of the home of the new pastor in town, Ted Johannson. Ted's wife, Lois, saw me from her front window and seeing how distraught I was she came and helped me inside. Ted was away visiting another village and Lois sat me down and after fixing a pot of tea for us she started talking. She never once questioned why I was standing in front of her house crying. She simply shared, in her quiet way, some of the trials of her life and before long I was telling her about mine. We had come from such different walks of life but had so much in common. We had each left our families to follow the man we loved and both of us wanted nothing more than to live our lives with our husbands. Through the night we talked and drank tea. Lois served the tea in a beautiful china teapot that had belonged to her Mother. With the morning light I ran to the pier to say goodbye to my husband only to find he wasn't there. He had spent the entire night looking for me and was half out of his mind with worry." Taking a deep breath Grandma Anna paused to offer more tea.

Karen replied, "Please go on, Grandma Anna. What happened?"

Grandma Anna smiled to herself, "He left the next day. Thanks to Lois I came to realize how precious each moment spent with a loved one is and I cherished the time spent with my husband when he was home. Lois and I became the best of friends and saw each through spats with our husbands, the births of our children, and the miscarriages that Lois suffered. And then finally, with time, came the deaths of our beloved husbands. We were always there for each other, and I came to realize there is no pain that can't be eased with a good cup of tea served in an English china tea pot, shared with a friend," With a twinkle in her eye she continued, "But I suspect it's the friendship that actually eases the hurt, not the tea."

Lilly asked quietly, "So this teapot…?"

Grandma Anna quietly replied, "Yes, my dear, it belonged to Lois. She wanted me to have it when she died. And I enjoy telling the story from time to time."

Anna's voice had grown quiet and Lilly and Karen realized she was about to doze off. Speaking softly, they each murmured their thanks and kissed her gently on the cheek as they let themselves out.

"Oh…I barely spoke to the woman and I feel like I've known her for years," said Angie with emotion in her voice. Ted and Lois lived in the lodge, right?" She continued. "That means they had tea right there at your lodge!"

"It's absolutely amazing, said Karen. "And you know we've just made a memory that we'll always remember for the rest of our lives. We'll never drink tea the same again. And Lilly, do you think those wedding dresses in the attic belonged to Anna and Lois?"

"You know, they probably are," Lilly said thoughtfully. "Maybe we can show them to Anna sometime and find out. I'll bet the one with the trail of pearls down the open back belonged to Anna and wouldn't it look just wonderful on Lanie?"

"Oh, it would be just perfect for her," Karen agreed.

Angie looked puzzled at this new information, "Is Lanie engaged? Why didn't she say something yesterday?"

Lilly and Karen grinned at each other, "Lanie's going to marry Pastor Jim from New Orleans," Lilly said.

At the shocked look on Angie's face, Karen continued, "She just doesn't know it yet."

"She doesn't know it? You...you mean she hasn't even met him yet?" Angie stuttered.

"That's right, we're going to get him to come out for Thanksgiving, and then Christmas too," said Lilly.

"I was under the impression that she wasn't interested in a relationship from the way she talked," pondered Angie. "What makes you so sure this will work?"

"Just a hunch," Lilly said as she parked Waldo's pickup in front of the Lodge. "I'm going to let Waldo put the truck away and I'm going to ask him again if we can't have my car shipped up here, even if I only use it a few months out of the year it would be better than herding this monstrosity around."

Entering through the kitchen door the three women found their husbands gathered around Lanie who appeared to be guarding something on the kitchen table. "Thank heaven's you're back," Lanie gasped, "I'm not sure I could hold them off any longer."

Stepping away from the table she revealed a steaming blackberry cobbler. Standing behind her were three hungry men with spoons in their hands.

"Looks like it's too hot to eat, you'll all burn your tongues," scolded Lilly.

"Ah shucks," sighed Engelbert, "another five minutes and we could have actually had our spoons in it."

"I kind of doubt that from the look on Lanie's face," laughed Lilly.

"What else do we smell?" asked Karen, laughing at the little boy looks on the men's faces.

"I think it's a roast," said Angie as she took a peek under the lid of the crock-pot.

Deciding to take charge again, Lanie instructed, "It'll be ready in fifteen minutes, and so by the time you men get your fishy hands washed we should be ready."

"What do you need help with?" asked Karen.

"Just getting everything on the table before they come back and start eating out of the pots and pans," Lanie said laughing.

With the four of them working they succeeded in having dinner on the table by the time the men came back into the room. Lanie had cooked the pot roast with carrots, potatoes and onion in the crock-pot all afternoon. The mushroom and onion soups she had added for flavoring had made its own thick, succulent gravy. A carrot and pineapple salad arranged over fresh greens had been chilling in the refrigerator and buttermilk biscuits were being kept warm in the oven.

The men entertained them with fishing stories all through dinner. Engelbert had caught a fish big enough to impress everyone back home, and he was sure it would feed the two of them for at least a year. The techniques used to reel the huge fish in would provide stories for the years to come, and the men savored every detail.

CHAPTER 20

Karen was tucking the last of her things into her overnight bag when John objected.

"You're taking that blue swim suit? That's the one you wore in the Bahamas."

"Yes, is there a problem? Is it a fashion mistake to wear the same one twice?" she asked, detecting his tone of discontentment.

"Well, it's just that...well, you're really hot in that one and I'm not sure I want to share."

"How about this one then," she said as she opened the dresser drawer and traded it for the black one piece. "Is this better?" she asked holding it up next to her loving smile.

With John's approval Karen gave him a quick kiss and then zipped her bag closed. Taking a moment to thank God for the love she was now living with, she then hurried out to find Lilly. The two women were anxious to arrive at the reserved Hotel suites in plenty of time to primp for the concert, and hopefully they would be able to fit a bit of shopping into the day also.

Lanie and her friend were meeting them at the dock where they kept the vintage seaplane; there was just enough room for the six of them for the trip to the big city. Angie and Engelbert had left a couple of days prior to be sure they would have plenty of time to get familiar with the city and prepare for the concert.

"Lilly, where are you?" Karen called from the kitchen door.

"I'm upstairs," Lilly answered. "Just making sure everything is ready for Dylan and Norma."

Karen quickly ran up the stairs to help with whatever it was she was doing so that they could be on their way.

"Are we ready?" Karen asked, almost out of breath.

"Well if we aren't the guys will probably leave without us," Lilly said.

As they skipped down the stairs Lilly continued, "Waldo's had the truck warming up for at least fifteen minutes now." Grabbing her purse off the kitchen counter she took one last look around the kitchen, "OK, let's get."

When he saw them approaching, John jumped out of the front seat where he had been keeping Waldo company. Taking the overnight bag from his wife he helped her inside the large vehicle and then crawled into the back seat with her.

"Lilly, you go ahead and sit up front with Waldo. I think I'll harass my wife for a little bit," John said giving Karen a quick nuzzle on the neck.

"OK you two, none of that. Well…go ahead since we're only about five minutes from the plane. But no hanky panky in the airplane, John, you're the pilot remember?" Lilly said laughing as she climbed into the front seat with her husband.

In no time at all, the entire group had their gear loaded in the plane and after they were securely fastened in they were underway. Waldo was sitting in the co-pilot's seat and with Lanie and Ken in the rear that left the middle seat for Lilly and Karen. As the small plane soared up through the clouds Lilly reached over and took her friend's hand.

"If you'd like you can squeeze my hand, of course it won't be the same as John's thigh, but maybe it will help," Lilly laughed.

Karen lightly hit Lilly's shoulder with the back of her hand in a reaction to her comment, putting a look of shock on her face partially for the benefit of their guests and partially because it was easy to do with the rolling effect she felt in her stomach. Then she put her hand back onto Lilly's and smiled as she squeezed a bit. "I'm OK. I won't ever get used to flying but I feel very safe with John as the pilot."

"Remember that little shop we found last time we were there? It wasn't far from the Hotel and they had really cute clothes," Lilly asked. "Bet we'll find something there."

"What color did you have in mind? Did you bring your emerald earrings or ruby?" Karen asked.

"I'm kind of in a mood to try something different. Remember those peasant style tops that were popular in the '70's? They're back in style," Lilly replied.

Karen knew that her friend was trying to distract her from her fear of flying and it wasn't hard to get caught up in Lilly's enthusiasm for shopping. "Tie-dye is back in style too. Maybe we can find a white gauzy beaded peasant blouse for me and you can get a tie-dyed stretchy t-shirt?"

"Right, Karen. And maybe it will be the other way around too!" Lilly laughed.

As soon as the small plane had reached its cruising altitude Waldo began playing tour guide pointing out different sites to Lanie and Ken. John took the plane down for a smooth landing next to the Hotel dock. Once again the Hotel employees greeted them, and it was nice to see a couple of familiar faces this time.

After checking into their rooms, there was plenty of time for the shopping they wanted to do. Lanie didn't seem to mind at all that Ken went to the sporting goods store with the men. Lilly and Karen carefully took notice of how she seemed to keep her distance from him, but he was always trying to get closer to her.

"Come on Lanie, we're going to find you something new to wear too," said Karen.

"Are you going to dress me like a hippie?" she asked rather skeptically.

Lilly laughed at the look on Lanie's face. "Not unless you want to. Karen and I were just having flashbacks to the 70's. Did I ever tell you about the time she threw a cup of scalding hot coffee on my bare legs while I was driving about 70 mph down the highway?"

Lanie's eyes grew big as she turned to Karen, "Is that true?"

Karen giggled, "I was only trying to put out the cigarette she dropped between her legs."

Before Lanie had a chance to react to this information Karen and Lilly each grabbed an arm and headed her towards the store.

"Don't worry Lanie; we don't do things like that anymore," Karen said giggling and Lilly snickered, "Why, we're practically matrons."

"Lilly," Karen said as she paused a moment in serious thought. "I've never thought of us as being matronly. Do you really think we are becoming like our mothers?"

Lilly laughed and shaking her head she answered, "Not hardly! Now let's shop."

CHAPTER 21

The men were talking and watching TV in Lilly and Waldo's suite, and Karen had pulled both Lilly and Lanie into her suite so that they could help each other get ready. Lanie was making eye shadow suggestions to Karen while Lilly brushed out Lanie's hair. Lilly had secretly wanted to play with Lanie's hair for a long time, and now she had her chance. "Do you want it braided, or shall we just use the hot roller to give it lots of curl?" she asked.

"Go ahead and do whatever you want," replied Lanie.

Karen carefully tried the new shadow techniques as Lanie instructed. "Do you think I need more eye liner?" Karen asked.

"Ok," Lanie said, "It's your turn for the makeup, Lilly."

It wasn't long before they were ready to present themselves to their men. Still giggling, they made their way next door.

Little did the women know that their '70's flashbacks earlier in the day would actually play out in the store. Karen and Lilly had talked Lanie into a tie-died blue and green body shirt with low-slung hip hugger jeans and silver studded belt. Lilly swore that she had the same outfit when she was a teenager.

Karen looked like she had walked out of 'Style" magazine in a teal green sheer shirt with three quarter length sleeves over an ivory lace camisole tucked into faded green/blue Levi jeans.

Karen had insisted that the peasant blouse that Lanie had found for Lilly wasn't too young for her. The blouse was white semi-sheer gauze with black and turquoise beading around the flared sleeves and off the shoulder neck. She wore it tucked into black flared jeans with a black leather belt that tied and left fringe laces hanging over one hip.

At the look on the men's faces when they walked in the room the women knew they had made the right wardrobe choices.

Waldo's grin was a mile wide as he jabbed John in the ribs, "Hey, buddy, what year is this?"

John grinned back, "Man, I don't know, but I'm likin' it."

Ken looked a little puzzled at this interchange, "Lanie, you look great, are you ready to go?"

Grabbing their purses and checking for keys the group headed out the door to the limousine waiting downstairs.

John and Karen were the last ones out of the suite and as he shut the door behind them, John turned and brought Karen into his arms. Nuzzling her neck he whispered, "You're even more beautiful than you were the last time I saw dressed like that."

Blushing from the compliment, Karen kissed John lightly on the cheek and pulled him into the hallway.

"I've never ridden in a limousine before," remarked Ken.

"Me either," answered Lanie.

The restaurant was elegant, and the service excellent. The meal was superb, from the crisp salads to the succulent steaks and on to the strawberry cheesecake and full flavored coffee.

"I wonder what Angie is doing right now?" said Karen.

"She's probably working out," said Lanie.

"No, I think she's kissin' on Engelbert," giggled Lilly as she took hold of Waldo's knee under the table.

"And Dylan?" Karen asked.

"He's kissin' on Norma," Lilly answered still giggling.

Lilly paid no attention to the bewildered expression on Ken's face as they returned to the limo. She could tell from glances exchanged with Karen that a good "heart to heart" with Lanie was in the works. Ken seemed like a nice enough guy, but Lilly didn't think he was quite the brightest guy in the world. As Waldo had whispered to her last night, "the elevator doesn't go all the way to the penthouse."

"How in the world did you get box seats?" asked Ken.

"They have connections," explained Lanie, rolling her eyes slightly. Lilly caught the gesture and wondered how many times Lanie had told him they were friends with Dylan and Angie.

Engelbert and Norma joined them as they found their seats and the group started to sway and move as they clapped with the now familiar beat of rhythm. Anticipation of seeing their friend appear was mounting as the lights dimmed and the spotlights focused in on Angie's band playing for her entrance. The drummer was already putting on a show, and the fiddler played like he was pulling the notes from the depths of his soul. Angie finally appeared almost magically from the crowd, wearing a royal blue tea length sequined gown, which fit her perfectly and showed off her sleek, petite figure. The scarf she had purchased at Mr. Bjorn's store graced her neckline and flowed behind her as she moved. Her smile radiating out to her fans as her graceful form floated up onto the center of the stage and the hem of her gown and her hair swayed with her movements.

Lilly stole a glance at Engelbert to see the expression of pride and admiration on his face, and noted that Karen also had taken notice before she turned her attention back to the stage.

The emotion of the moment almost brought tears to Karen's eyes as she savored the moment and felt the pride of their friends' accomplishments, added to the atmosphere and life of the music.

Angie started out with her newest single and the crowd went wild as her golden voice penetrated the arena. A group of teenage girls had gathered as close to the stage as they could and were reaching out to give her flowers and to touch her hand.

Angie sang two new songs that she had written and then paused to introduce her band and interact with the audience. Everyone there knew she was one of them and that made her all the more popular. After singing five more of her songs she introduced Dylan Wyatt and the crowd went wild.

Karen was watching Lilly as Dylan came onto the stage. Lilly had never quite gotten over her idol worship of this man who had become their good friend. Honestly, if Karen didn't know better she would think Lilly was drooling. Due to the volume, sign language and yelling in someone's ear was all the communication possible at the moment. Karen nudged Lilly as she held up both thumbs and first fingers in the shape of a "W." Of course Lilly knew she was pointing out the emblem on the back pocket of Dylan's jeans. They laughed and then checked to see if Norma had noticed. She had, and to their relief she was laughing with them.

Dylan put on a professional show and as usual played and sang much longer than anyone expected him to. The evening ended with pie and ice cream in a private, secluded dining area of the Hotel's restaurant. It was good to visit with friends again, and to catch up on the events of the tour Angie and Dylan had just completed together.

Back at the Lodge, Lilly, Karen, and Lanie were still excited from the recent trip and as they prepared brunch, they revisited the events of the previous two days.

The four visitors were sleeping in a bit to recuperate from their strenuous schedule. Angie had requested the bear room this time, and Norma had wanted to stay in the room with the "most antiques and Alaska history."

"I can't believe Ken actually fell asleep in the restaurant," said Karen.

"I can," Lanie replied quietly.

"Did you see the look on Norma's face?" said Lilly. "I thought she was going to poke him with her fork or something."

"I almost felt like I should apologize for him," Lanie said, "but it really was funny when Mr. Wyatt poked him in the ribs and he almost fell off his chair."

"Would have too if John hadn't caught him," Karen said giggling.

Knowing they would have a long talk later about Ken, Lilly tactfully changed the subject. "Engelbert was so proud, he could have popped the buttons of his shirt if he hadn't been wearing a pullover," said Lilly.

"Norma is one classy lady," remarked Karen. "She looked perfect all night. I think I started to wilt about ten o'clock."

"I'm just so blessed to have been able to do all of this," said Lanie and continued, "Thank you so much for taking me along. I had a blast and I'll never ever forget the experience. Especially our wardrobe!"

Lilly was arranging steaming hot biscuits in the breadbasket and as she turned to set it on the table Engelbert and Angie entered.

"Why, good morning Mr. and Mrs. Garner, did you find your accommodations suitable?" she asked.

"Stop that Lilly," Engelbert said and Angie added stretching, "That was probably the best night's sleep I've had in a long time."

Dylan and Norma were right behind them and agreed that they had slept well also.

"Do we get to spend time in the "ice room" today?" asked Norma hopefully as she took the cup of coffee Lanie handed her. "Lanie, I want dibs on your schedule," she added as she gave Dylan a look that pleaded for him to join her.

"You can spend all day in there if you want," laughed Karen. "As a matter of fact we usually serve tea and coffee in the early afternoon and we'll set it up in the ice room if you like. Lanie will be here all day, so I'm sure you'll find what you want in her schedule, and if we're lucky the aurora borealis will grace us with its beauty tonight. Waldo is ready to go fishing at a moment's notice, and John has mapped out the trails for hiking. We can take you kayaking if you want, we can explore the local village, or you can kick your shoes off and do nothing."

"Is it true that you saw big foot?" asked Dylan.

"That's right," replied Waldo, "and we have some stories for you that you'll have a hard time believing."

Angie was impressed, "Wow, you really have the lodge up and running! This is a much larger operation than your New Orleans business."

298

"It's certainly more exciting. You know everything down south is so laid back and relaxed and up here in the frozen north it's just rush, rush, rush all the time," said Lilly showing just a bit of pride in her voice, "and we're actually booked until Thanksgiving. We even have some reservations for next year and we plan on being very busy. We are so fortunate to have Lanie here to help us out."

Lanie blushed at this comment, but Karen also saw the satisfaction in her eyes. She obviously loved her work and took pride in doing it well.

Lanie had been secretly hoping that Dylan would schedule a massage, so she was pleased when he said that he did have a kink in his neck as he sat down at the table.

CHAPTER 22

The Wolf Creek Lodge had taken on a reputation of first class accommodations with an air of excitement in just a few short months. "A one of a kind vacation that you will always remember," read John from the latest volume of a well know travel magazine. The cover featured a photo of the ice room with a picture of Waldo holding his biggest catch overlapping the bottom right corner of the photo. The suites were featured throughout the article promoting the Lodge.

The article had been written by one of the first guests that had come for a fishing trip with his family. He was the photographer for the magazine and had been so impressed that he did the photo shoot during his stay, and had the connections to have the article printed right away. Lilly and Karen huddled around John to see.

"What about the food, John? What does it say about the food?" Lilly asked excitedly.

"Calm down, Lilly, and let him read it," Karen admonished.

"OK, here you go," John began reading. "Traveler's who have tasted the fare at Mon Ami Famille in New Orleans won't be disappointed by the food at The Wolf Creek Lodge. While Mon Amie Famille features elegant full course dinners, guests at the Northern counterpart are treated to hearty stews and chowders. Karen Worthington bakes breads complimenting these dishes fresh every day. And you haven't lived until you've taste Lilly Lansford's blackberry cobbler."

Excitedly Karen and Lilly grabbed each other's shoulders and started jumping up and down. "We're famous, Karen, we're famous," Lilly said.

"We're going to have more customer's than we can handle, Lilly," Karen replied.

"We can handle it," said Lilly. "We'll just have to hire more help if need be, and it's actually a good thing if our schedule is full."

"May have to hire another fisherman too," added Waldo thoughtfully.

"Things will be busy enough here while Waldo and I make our next trip to Washington," Lilly continued. "Then we'll be able to focus on our families for the holidays. If Kelsi delivers early as expected, that should be about Thanksgiving time, then we'll have a month before Christmas and maybe, just maybe, we can talk them into coming here. Her doctor thinks we're crazy, but we'll hire extra help, and did I tell you my sister and brother are going to take charge of the ranch if they come for Christmas? And what better place to be than here; where the babies can get individual attention?"

"How is Kelsi doing anyway?" asked Karen.

"She's very frustrated. Says she can't see her feet, doesn't have a belly button any more, and can hardly waddle to the bathroom. Jamie hasn't let her even go to the barn for a month now and she only can see her horses from the front deck. She used to be able to use her tummy for a book rest when she reads, but now even that's getting out of proportion. She is so used to physical activity that this has been really hard on her, and she says she thinks she's going to be pregnant forever."

"Tomorrow we'll put together a care package to send her," declared Karen. "I have a couple of recent magazines, and we'll make some cookies and goodies. I think this would be a good time to send her the new night gown I got her too."

"No doubt, she probably needs something new to wear about now," Lilly commented thoughtfully, "Let's make those oatmeal, raisin, cranberry cookies that Jamie loves."

"And we'll send her the three little hats we found last week," said Karen as her ambition rose to a peak.

Lilly and Karen returned to their quilt project with a new ambition to finish the three pieces of art they had created. There was no telling how soon the babies would actually arrive, and they still had to finish the last of the quilting stitches and apply the satin trim. They had stayed up late many nights working on it and now that they were about to get busier they needed to devote every extra minute to the project.

"You know, this is three times the work and it will always be three from now on!" Karen warned. "Not that they can't handle it, and I'm sure we'll get used to ordering three of everything. We just haven't had to triple our work before."

Lilly answered thoughtfully, "No, we've only had to double our work with the two businesses and heaven forbid we should have a third one of those. But you know, the way Jamie and Kelsi put everything they have into whatever their current project is I always had an idea they would only have one child. So it really is a blessing I get three grandchildren at one time."

Karen smiled back at her friend, "Yep, you're going to catch up with me all at once…well you know what they say, "the more you have to love, the more love you have to give."

"Isn't that the truth, Karen," Lilly said yawning. "Maybe we better get to bed. Our husbands are probably getting tired of us staying up into the wee hours working on these quilts. And they have to get up so early for chores and fishing."

"Like they care about getting up soooo early when they're going fishing…Waldo's always ready to go fishing," said Karen. "And John loves it too, and it's really good to know they're happy with what they do."

As was their usual routine, Karen went to check the front doors of the Lodge and Lilly went into the kitchen to check the back doors. They both knew that their husbands had made sure they were safe before going to bed but this was a habit that they had picked up when their children were young.

Knowing her kitchen by heart, Lilly could move easily through the room with only the light from the range crossing the spacious hardwood floor. Just as she approached the large stainless steel sink, Lilly heard Tyson's low growl. Stopping abruptly in her tracks her eyes met the eyes of the young man peeping in the kitchen window. With her hand to her throat Lilly could not stifle back the scream that erupted. The scream brought Karen running from the front of the Lodge and John and Waldo at a full run down the stairs. Lilly's scream seemed to have used every ounce of breath she had and when everyone entered the kitchen all she could do was point to the window.

"Was it a bear?" Karen asked.

"No…a man!" Lilly finally gasped.

"We'll take care of him," John said as he grabbed a shovel on his way out the door. "Waldo, let Tyson loose!"

"OK, let's go," Waldo said pulling a small handgun out of the pocket of his robe.

"Honey, be careful," Lilly called.

"Oh great, now he has a gun! He didn't have one when we were chased by that moose," Karen said as the door shut behind their husbands. "Lilly, do you know who it was?"

Meeting her friend's eyes Lilly whispered, "I could swear it was that Scott Smith, Karen. Do you remember those beady little brown eyes sticking out from under all that red hair? I knew there was something strange about that guy. Remember the way he looked at us when he delivered the furniture?"

Just as Karen started to answer the women were startled by the gunshot. Their knees went limp, as they looked at each other frozen in terror. The unknown was more than they could bear and an emotional tear leaked from Lilly's eye.

It was only a moment before John busted through the back door with the shovel still in his hand. Looking Karen squarely in the eye he asked, "Are you two okay?"

"No," replied Lilly before Karen could say a word. "Not unless you can tell us nobody was hurt."

"That was just a warning shot, whoever it was ran and Waldo shot just to help scare him off," explained John.

"And just what were you planning to do with that shovel?" asked Karen. The way John had looked into her eyes had penetrated her being, and knowing within their unity that he would protect her to any extent possible for a human man; she had relaxed and now was able to tease about the shovel.

"I don't know," he replied still searching for an answer to Karen's question, "I guess I was ready to bury the body as quickly as possible."

The women burst into laughter at the look on John's face.

"What the heck is so funny?" asked Waldo as he returned to the kitchen.

He moved towards Lilly and slipped his arm around her small waist. His presence terminated her laughter as she looked into his eyes to search for the answer she wanted.

"Did you see who it was?" asked Karen.

"Nope," said Waldo almost too confidently. "He was already half way out of the valley before we could get a glimpse."

"Was he driving a vehicle?" inquired Lilly. She wasn't about to tell the men that she knew who it was. If she did they would never leave them alone and that would hurt their business. Besides, she and Karen had taken care of themselves for many years and she knew they were still very capable of handling whatever came their way.

"It's really late you guys, we better try to get some sleep," Lilly said taking Waldo's hand and leading him towards the stairs.

"I'm not sure I can sleep," Waldo protested. "But we do have to go fishing in the morning. Night, John. Night, Karen. Don't worry about anything, Tyson's on duty," Waldo reassured them as Lilly closed their bedroom door.

Stepping into his arms she looked deep into the blue eyes of the man she had been married to for almost thirty years, "Waldo, are you sure you're OK? Are you sure you didn't see who it was?"

Holding her tight he answered, "I'm fine and it was very dark. But you remember that little pistol I bought you for your 30th birthday? I'm going to take it out of the safe and we'll put it in a place that only you and I know about. Otherwise I'm not going to be able to leave you alone here."

Lilly nodded her head solemnly, "I know, now let's get to bed."

"I don't think I can sleep," Waldo answered.

With a gleam in her eye she answered, "Who said anything about sleeping?"

Karen carefully measured the coffee grounds into the filter. Her eyes felt a bit dry from the lack of sleep and she was purposely careful to be sure she counted the scoops correctly as she knew her mind wasn't really on the coffee, but rather on the events of the previous night.

Lilly returned the lid to the pan of steaming hot oatmeal she had just stirred and popped the oatmeal raisin bread into the toaster. "Did you say anything to John about who that was last night?" asked Lilly.

Everything was back in order for Lilly now, and she just had to be sure that Karen understood that they needed to keep this information to themselves for the time being.

"No," Karen said shaking her head, "I'm afraid of what they might do."

"I know me too. Besides he was probably so scared he'll never do anything like that again. But just to be safe let's ask Lanie if he's ever been known to do anything dangerous."

Their conversation was interrupted by John and Waldo coming in for breakfast at the same time. Waldo had been checking the fishing gear while John fed Tyson. The comforting breakfast was eaten in no time, and after several cups of coffee, Karen and Lilly were beginning to feel a little more energized. Kissing their husbands goodbye they quickly cleared the table and went into the small study to plan their tasks for the day.

As Waldo and John stepped off the massive wrap around back porch John remarked, "You didn't tell Lilly that we got a good look at that little weasel did you?"

Waldo grinned, "Nope, no need to worry her. After we get done with him he won't be around here anytime soon. Not even to deliver furniture."

CHAPTER 23

"The little table with the drop leafs that we ordered for the hallway should be here any day," remarked Karen thoughtfully. "Do you think we should ask the men to check for it so that they can pick it up on their way back through town tonight? I'm sure Mr. Bjorn would hold it for us if we asked him to."

"That's a good idea," replied Lilly. "And we do need it right away so that we can show off the flower arrangement Lanie put together last week."

The daily chores went quickly for the two women as they laughed together about the silliest things. The lack of sleep had affected their mood to a point that Lanie once again was surprised by their behavior, but she was getting used to these surprises by now and just joined in this time. She was very comfortable here and knew that she was getting a life experience to be treasured.

Lanie had looked shocked at the revelation of the peeping Tom, or peeping Scott as Lilly referred to him, the night before and reassured Karen and Lilly that even though Scott Smith was definitely strange she had never heard of him being dangerous.

Lilly had an apple pie in the oven and vegetables prepared for chowder by ten o'clock. Having the kitchen in order she returned to the study to make her daily phone call to Jamie. She knew that Jamie hadn't quite comprehended the reality of the life changes he was about to make. Of course he knew the facts and had made all of the appropriate preparations, it was just that this was a new experience for the two and it would be such an enormous change in their lives. The actual delivery of these babies would be phenomenal for him emotionally, and that part he wouldn't be able to prepare for. Both he and Kelsi had strong personalities that enabled them to accomplish anything they set their minds to doing, it was just that Lilly worried about Kelsi's well being during this intense time. She had lost control over her physical body and these babies would come when the doctor decided that the timing was right, not when Jamie and Kelsi wanted it to happen. And this was one thing the two had disagreed on. Jamie actually thought they wouldn't come for another month and hadn't accepted the actuality that they could be born any day now. On the other hand Kelsi was ready to be delivered yesterday and had been frustrated with Jamie's denial of the daily possibility of an immediate delivery.

Kelsi answered the phone on the second ring and quickly reassured Lilly that nothing had changed from the day before. The weather in Washington had cooled slightly from the Indian summer they had been having and Kelsi felt a little better with the relief from the heat. Kelsi's aunt and uncle, who boarded their horses at the ranch, were visiting for a few days so Jamie had felt comfortable enough leaving her with them to go into town to pick up fencing supplies.

Satisfied that everything was fine Lilly ended the call and went to find Karen and Lanie to share the daily news. The morning passed quickly doing the everyday chores. Lilly and Karen both had such high standards that it seemed the work was never ending.

Lanie entered the Kitchen to find Lilly engrossed in making a unique lunch of little sandwiches without the crust and fresh fruit cups.

"Look Lanie, I decided to revive my southern cooking skills since it's just us girls," Lilly said with a smile and then her intuition kicked in. "What's up? Did I hear the phone ring? Is something wrong?"

"Lilly," said Lanie cautiously, "Ernie just called me. I think Scott Smith has been confronted with his deeds."

"Waldo and John?" Lilly asked.

"Uh huh," Lanie answered.

"Are they OK? They're not in jail are they?"

"They're fine. I didn't really get the details."

"Well that should provide an interesting story over dinner. I should have known those two knew who the peeper was. They wouldn't have wanted to worry us."

It was after 7:00 by the time the men arrived home. The lodge was filled with the aroma of homemade bread and Lilly's fish chowder that was now her Alaskan specialty. The guests were thrilled and excited from a productive fishing trip, and wanted to hear every detail of Waldo's collection of fishing stories. It was plain to see that the conversation of the day's prior events would need to wait until later after the guests retired for the night.

It wasn't long however, before the subject came up. "I can't believe what you did to that kid in town this morning," said Mr. Becker. "I guess with the lack of law enforcement up her in the wilds you have to take things into your own hands sometimes."

John and Waldo each glanced at their wives to check for the reactions they expected.

Clearing his throat and looking uncomfortable Waldo spoke, "Actually Sheriff King was in on it."

"OK, Waldo, what did you guys do?" Lilly asked sternly.

"Not that much, Lilly, he did most of it to himself. John and I stopped in and let the Sheriff know about the peeping incident. We were in his office when we saw Scott walk across the street to Ed Bjorn's." Warming up to his story Waldo began to grin as he continued. "So we followed him across. What we didn't know was that a trapper had just dropped off a full head and skin of a thousand pound Bull Moose."

Waldo paused for a breath and John leaned forward and spoke. "Scott saw us coming just as he went through the door. Thinking he could split through the store and go out the back he took off like a bat out of hell." Pausing to chuckle John continued, "And ran right into the rack on that big bull."

Waldo's grin was miles wide, "Nope, don't have to worry about that young man anymore. He darn near castrated himself."

Lilly and Karen gasped at the same time, "No, he didn't."

"Yep, they took him away in an ambulance." Waldo continued, "Actually I was a little disappointed. I was kind of looking forward to taking care of him myself."

The two men settled back into their chairs with smiles on their faces that couldn't be wiped off. Mr. Becker had much the same look on his face, as did his friend and fishing partner of the last five years, Mr. Grant.

Lilly and Karen served warm apple pie with a big scoop of ice cream, which they knew would top off Waldo's night to perfection.

It was late by the time the kitchen was clean again, but Karen retreated to the ice room by herself rather than to her own suite. Karen pondered her thoughts as she sat comfortably in the white wicker love seat in the ice room. The bright yellow and blue fabrics of coordinating pillows and cushions accented the glass paintings and the tract lighting cast rays of light at her feet that were nestled in a light blue fluffy throw rug. Her heart was heavy and her thoughts were of her son John, and her daughter in-law Melinda. Something wasn't right, and all she could do for the moment was to pray. Melinda's pregnancy had progressed normally and no problems were expected, John's detective work was keeping him active and motivated. However the heaviness of her heart pushed a tear from her eye as it all welled up within her. She hadn't heard John come up behind her, but his comforting hands on her shoulders was a welcome touch of assurance.

"What is it Karen?" he asked. "What's wrong? Are you upset about Scott?"

"No, darling, I don't care about Scott Smith. I'm sure he got what he deserved. I really don't know what's wrong, it's just that I've been thinking about John and Melinda a lot lately and something just doesn't seem quite right. Did you sense the same thing?" she questioned.

"I'm kind of new to this father thing and Waldo and I have been a little busy today. Let's go call them. Or how about popping in to see them? You know we could be there in a few hours?"

"I don't know, honey," Karen said reluctantly, "You know Lilly and Waldo might have to leave at a moment's notice."

"So, Lanie and the boys can keep the place open," John answered.

"It's rather late, but why don't we call anyway," she agreed. "On the other hand I think John is working late and I would sure hate to wake Melinda, she hasn't been sleeping well…"

John had swung around and was sitting beside her as he absent-mindedly picked up the remote control and entered a command for the music to play. Music was such a part of his life it just came automatically to him, and he barely even thought about what he was doing. He stood up before his wife and took her hand. "May I have this dance madam?"

Karen was more than willing to dance with her husband. It seemed like an eternity since she had last been in his arms. And somehow the problems she had been pondering seemed to lessen as their graceful bodies flowed together. She slid her hand into the curls at the back of his neck and relaxed.

Lilly was making her nightly rounds to be sure everything was in order. She had a good idea where John and Karen were, but would check on them just to be sure everything was all right. Slightly opening the door to the ice room she took in the view of the two dancing as they often did in the late evenings. It was a beautiful picture and made her heart swell once again with gratefulness. Yes, everything really was in order now.

She quietly closed the door and went to find Waldo. Tonight she would light the ocean mist scented candles and get Waldo to start a fire in their fireplace too.

CHAPTER 24

The next day dawned gray and dreary. Waldo had told Lilly to expect snow any day now and from the looks of the sky it probably wouldn't be long. She had been up since before light preparing the sourdough yeast mixture that now sat rising on the back of the stove. Waldo had stoked the fire before he went out to do chores and it now blazed cheerily at the end of the massive kitchen. In spite of the warmth and coziness of the room Lilly felt chilled. Pulling her crocheted shawl a little tighter around her shoulders she carried her half empty coffee cup to the hickory rocker in front of the fire.

The moment Karen stumbled in half asleep; Lilly knew she was a little down. "What is it Karen?" She asked.

"Nothing, what do you mean?" Karen asked as she joined Lilly in the opposite matching rocker.

Feeling a bit down herself Lilly just shrugged, "Ok, nothing I guess."

Waldo came in from his chores and wasn't sure what was going on as the kitchen was never this quiet. He gently took Lilly's cup to refill it, and poured a cup for Karen. His generosity pleased them and he was starting to tease them out of their moods, but the feeling of the dark cloud still hung over them.

"It's snowing!" John said as he briskly entered the kitchen from the back door. "I just finished winterizing the plane, Waldo. Do you have any more of those plastic covers though?" Suddenly realizing that the kitchen was way too quiet, John gave a wink and a nudge to Waldo's shoulder. Before the two women could protest they were being dragged out into the midst of huge falling snowflakes.

311

There was no option other than to enjoy the beautiful white flakes floating gracefully around them. They held their hands out to catch as many as they could and giggled. Waldo gently kissed away the one that landed on Lilly's nose.

"Feeling better?" He whispered hugging her tightly.

"Uh huh" Lilly answered hugging him back.

"Good! Then fix me some breakfast, I'm starved," he said giving her a quick pat on the rear end as he pushed her towards the house.

"You're starved?" Lilly exclaimed pretending outrage. "What do you think I am? Your servant? Your wench to fix your meals and warm your bed?"

"Come to think of it I like that idea better," Waldo said with a big grin grabbing his wife's hand and heading towards the house.

"Oh no, you don't," Lilly exclaimed. "But on second thought, come on you can help with breakfast."

John and Karen had been huddled together under the eaves watching their friend's playful exchange. As Lilly headed past them into the kitchen she paused to tell Karen to take her time.

"Why don't we take a day off? Waldo, can we go into town today? I need some more turquoise thread to finish the quilts. Karen, John, you two wouldn't mind if we left you alone out here today would you?"

"Not a bit, Lilly," John said with a grin that matched Waldo's previous one.

"Come on, you're going to have to work for your breakfast too," Karen chided as she pulled John into the kitchen.

Waldo flipped the sourdough pancakes and John turned the sizzling bacon strips while Lilly and Karen sat at the table with their coffee cups watching and commenting. Although the men pretended to protest, they had a lot of fun clowning around and then did the dishes after the meal with a little bit more protest and additional encouragement from their wives.

As soon as Lilly and Waldo left for town, John handed the phone to Karen but asked if she wanted him to dial. Melinda answered on the first ring. She seemed pleasantly surprised to hear Karen's voice and after assuring her that everything was fine in their world she brought her up to date on the latest news. Melinda's pregnancy was progressing normally, the kids were busy in school and John Jr. had been working long hours on a case. Karen could read the underlying message that Melinda was not happy that he was gone so much in the evenings.

After John spoke to his daughter-in-law briefly he hung up the phone. Turning to his wife he asked, "Well, what do you think? Is everything OK?"

Burying her misty eyes in her hands and shaking her head Karen answered softly, "No, something is terribly wrong, but I don't know what it is. John, it's just a feeling. Call it mother's intuition or superstition or whatever, but I know our son is in terrible trouble."

"OK, enough of that just get packed. I'll call the airlines and Waldo's cell phone. We're leaving on the first flight out."

Karen was packed in no time at all. She threw clothes into the suitcase only half folded which was unusual for her. Waldo had turned the truck around as soon as John called him and now Lilly stood at the doorway watching her friend throw her clothes in the suitcase.

"I'm not going to tell you to calm down, Karen. But please at least slow down. I've never seen you pack like that," Lilly said quietly.

"Oh Lilly, I didn't know you were back," Karen said throwing herself in her friend's arms. "I feel so out of control. I don't know what's happening."

"Now, now, don't worry," Lilly said. "Sometimes we can't control everything in our lives, and that's OK. And I'm sure John and Melinda are fine too, but its best if you and John go find out for yourselves. I knew you were worried about something and I'm relieved that you're going. Call when you get there."

Composing herself long enough to zip the suitcase Karen wiped her misty eyes, "But we shouldn't be going. What about Kelsi? What if you and Waldo have to go to Washington while we're gone?"

"If we do, then we do. We'll leave Lanie in charge and everything will be fine. Or we'll close the place and lose a little money. Who cares? Family is what's important. Right, Karen?"

"Of course you're right, as usual," Karen said smiling through her tears. As she straightened her shoulders, Karen grasped hold of her fresh confidence and composure. "Lilly, I have John to share this with," she said as if it was a new realization. "My life is so complete with him…I think we could handle just about anything."

"I'm sure you can," Lilly said as she handed one of the packed bags to Karen and put the other on her own shoulder, "He'll have to handle this suitcase though, it's too heavy."

The trip to the airport completed the whirlwind day. Before they knew it Karen and John were airborne and for once Karen's emotions were too much in turmoil to mind the flight.

Lilly had somehow managed to get her turquoise thread after they saw John and Karen off and she had every intention of finishing the quilts as quickly as possible since there was no telling when they would have to up and leave for the deliveries. Maybe she could even get Waldo to help a little, she thought. It wasn't the same without Karen, but she would manage and she was full of determination.

Passing by the office she noticed Karen had left her things out on the desk and stopped to put them away for her. She picked up the notebook and couldn't help but to see the prayer written there. It was to all of her children, who would not only be John and Heather, but Jamie and Matthew and Lanie and all of their spouses and future spouses. She read…

> *Dear Lord,*
>
> *Thank you for these wonderful people you have put into our lives. Guide them and bless them beyond imagination. Saturate their hearts with righteousness. Show them the purpose in their lives and give them a vision to complete this purpose. Give them strength and wisdom and courage and may they live their lives with quality and fulfillment. Please wrap your loving arms around them and protect them from harm and evil.*
>
> *Amen*

The simple prayer touched her heart and she knew exactly what Karen was feeling. Their grown children were very independent, and yet so closely tied to them with roots that could never be destroyed. And the new branches that time brings were stretching out before her now as she viewed the nearly finished quilted projects. Lilly pondered her thoughts of the love a mother has for her children as the last of the stitches flowed into the three baby quilts that were made with this very love. The turquoise thread contrasted with the silver twine she and Karen had used to weave dream catchers into the quilt squares. Each of the squares promised only sweet dreams to the precious babies who would sleep under them. The wallpaper that Kelsi and Jamie had hung in the nursery was covered with frolicking ponies being chased by Indian children. The quilts were a surprise for Kelsi and Lilly couldn't wait to see how they would look spread out on the rough-hewn log cribs that Jamie had made.

Glancing at the clock Lilly was surprised to see how late it had gotten. Waldo had been in bed for several hours knowing that he had to be up early to complete the chores by himself. Karen had called as they were sitting down to dinner and they talked just long enough to reassure Lilly that they had arrived safe. John Jr. was at work and they hadn't seen him yet. Even with the miles distancing them Lilly could tell that Karen still wasn't satisfied that her son was out of danger.

CHAPTER 25

As the small plane circled over the Oregon coast John and Karen could pick out the neighborhood, and yes, the tiled roof, where John and Melinda lived on the hill overlooking the bay. They would stay at the beach house that Melinda's parents owned and rented out to guests when family wasn't using it.

John had a rental car waiting at the airport, and a quick call to Melinda gave her a pleasant surprise. Tyler and Kristin weren't getting all of the attention they were used to, and with their dad working late they had been in feisty moods and driving their mother slightly crazy.

"Can we bring anything?" asked Karen. "How about some chicken or sandwiches?"

"Actually, I'm just craving pizza," replied Melinda. "And I want pineapple, I don't care what else is on it, there's just got to be pineapple!"

"Guess you're having a craving?" Karen asked.

After feeding the group, John and Karen cuddled on the couch with their two grandchildren, Tyler taking up his Grandpa's entire lap. Karen read to them from one of their favorite books and the children drank in every bit of attention their grandparents could give. John was also keeping a close eye on Melinda at the same time, as she wasn't feeling very good after eating all of the pizza she could hold, and then some.

Finally the exhausted kids were tucked into bed, Melinda was relaxing in the lounge chair with a cup of tea, and most of the basic housework was completed before they heard John Jr. back into the garage. His dad went out to meet him and couldn't help but notice John Jr. looked tired and worn down as he got out of the Mustang, but his eyes lit up as soon as he saw his dad.

"I'm sure glad you're here Dad," he said with relief in his eyes.

"Are you ok John? You look like you've just seen a ghost, son."

"Well, maybe I have…I can't really talk about it yet though. Are Tyler and Kristin asleep?"

"There're supposed to be, but I think they're waiting for you, I heard them giggling just five minutes ago," his dad replied as they entered the house through the kitchen/garage door. John Jr. was met with a hug from his mother that reminded him of when he was just a child. The way she tussled his hair and then rubbed his back, brought back her familiar loving touch. He had been so busy he hadn't realized that he had actually missed her, and he responded by hugging her back harder than he realized. He then went to Melinda and kissed her on the forehead, checking on her pregnant condition by placing his hand on her rounded tummy. "How's the baby been today dear?" he asked with a smile.

"She ate a lot of pizza tonight," she replied.

"Did she save some for me?" John asked.

"Barely, but I think there's a little bit left."

"Are you telling us it's a girl?" asked Karen with big eyes of expectation.

"Yep," answered her son with a smile that couldn't be wiped off of his face.

Grandpa was sitting in the easy chair with a puzzled look on his face, trying to grasp the reality of a baby girl. He picked up a pink knitted blanket, touching the soft textures as he took in the concept. Karen smiled at the sight, knowing he would soon experience the miracle of new life.

"Daddy!" could be heard from the upper level and John Jr. quickly skipped up the stairs.

"Are my ragamuffins asleep yet?" he called.

"We're not ragamuffins Daddy, we're just children," they responded in unison.

Karen slid onto her husbands lap, searching his face and loving the responses she was finding to a house full of children and the concept of a baby girl becoming a reality for him. He welcomed her by sliding his arm around her waist.

Things eventually settled down for the evening and the adults were able to relax and visit.

"Dad," said John Jr. "We're out of milk, how about we check out your rental car and run down to the store?"

"Ok, we can do that you don't mind do you Karen?"

"Of course not," she replied. "Anyway I still need to finish in the kitchen."

As soon as they were out of the house John Jr. explained to his dad that he needed to drive by a certain location. He had thought the people he was watching had spotted his car and had followed him the previous day, but they wouldn't recognize the rental car.

As his dad drew near the address John Jr. slipped down in the seat, jotting down various bits of information. His eyes darted from one vehicle to another and to the names on the mailboxes.

Glancing at his son uneasily, John drove through the affluent neighborhood and kept quiet until they were well past the location.

"What's going on, Son? This is a pretty fancy neighborhood. Why I'll bet there isn't a house on that bluff overlooking the ocean worth less than half a million. You know your mother is convinced that you're in some kind of trouble? That's what brought us down here."

"I should have known," John said with a grin. "Mom could always tell when something's wrong. I think her and Aunt Lilly have some kind of ESP."

"Son, I'm only going to ask you this once. Are you OK?"

"Sure, I'll be fine and sorry, Dad, I really can't tell you what's going on. I can say that I'm probably in deeper than I've ever been before. But it's all about to crack wide open. I'm sure glad you're here though. How long can you stay? I don't think Melinda and the kids are in any danger but I sure feel better knowing you and Mom are there with them.

Smiling back at his son John answered reassuringly, "We'll stay as long as it takes, ready to go home?"

"I wouldn't be a very good detective if I forgot to bring the milk home would I," he answered with a sly smile. "There's a little convenience store right around the corner here, it'll only take a minute."

Karen and Melinda were visiting when the men returned. Karen had brought her daughter-in-law up to date on the happenings in Alaska. Melinda was laughing at the Scott Smith saga and insisted that Karen re-tell the story for John Jr.

John Sr. watched his wife closely and was relieved to see the look of contentment that had been missing for the last several days, return to her beautiful green eyes. Deciding that there was nothing else they could do for the time being, John and Karen stayed just two days. There would be a lot of work in Alaska when Waldo and Lilly went to Washington, and they hated to leave Lanie alone for very long in such a big place. And besides, Melinda's parents lived close and were always willing to help out with the kids and housework when she needed a little extra help. John Jr.'s late shifts weren't expected to last more than a few more weeks, and he promised to let them know if there was anything they could do. The visit had seemed to give all of them a renewed spirit and encouragement.

CHAPTER 26

Lilly was frantically packing her shoulder bag with the daily essentials. Her suitcase had been pre-packed for weeks now, but it had been so long since she had packed it that she honestly couldn't remember what all was in it. Now the babies were coming in just hours, and she had been ready for so long that she had the feeling that nothing was done.

Actually she had spent many hours planning ahead for the lodge guests; thoughtfully organizing prepared foods for the freezer to make meals easy for Karen and Lanie to put together quickly. The pantry was fully stocked as well, and Waldo had made sure everything was in order for John to entertain the guests with fishing and snowshoeing.

Thanksgiving was just around the corner, which created anticipation for the upcoming holidays. It was still unknown just who would be able to come. Obviously Kelsi and the triplets wouldn't be able to travel for some time, but Heather was anxious to make her first trip to Alaska. John and Melinda were still trying to decide if they would come in her pregnant state, or spend the time with her parents. The weather was colder now and the snow was accumulating in the valley around the lodge.

"Waldo, do you have your keys to the truck?" Lilly asked almost in a panic.

"Lilly, my love, you're about to blow a gasket," Waldo said calmly. "John's driving us. He has the truck running and parked right in front."

"Ok, ok, I'm alright, I'm alright," Lilly said trying to convince herself as much as her husband. "Where's Karen? I can't leave without seeing Karen."

"Lilly, I'm right here behind you remember? Now Waldo's right. You're not going to do Jamie or Kelsi any good if you don't live long enough to see those babies. Now calm down," Karen said rather sternly.

Lilly grinned back at her friend, "What would I do without you. I'm OK now. Waldo, quit dallying around. We have a plane to catch."

"Yes dear." He replied with a grin and a wink at Karen then mumbled under his breath, "She's baaack!"

Hugging her friends briefly at the door to the Lodge, Karen stepped back inside out of the draft. "I wish I could go to the airport with you but John is bringing the Smythson's from Boston back with him and I'm afraid there won't be room in the truck. Give those babies a kiss for me Lilly," She said brushing a tear back from her eyes. "Call me as soon as they're born. OK?"

"OK. Gotta go. I'll talk to you soon." Running for the truck Lilly turned and waved.

John had arranged for a limo to pick Waldo and Lilly up at the Airport and deposit them safely at the hospital. Even though it was their hometown he wasn't taking any chances on circumstances that could cause Lilly to miss the birth of her first grandchildren. There would be no living with her if that happened. Arriving at the hospital with little time to spare they barely had time to give Jamie a quick hug before he was allowed into the delivery room. Because of the nature of the delivery he would be the only family member allowed in the room. Lilly and Waldo joined Kelsi's family in the waiting room and while Waldo visited, Lilly called Karen to report in and then began pacing up and down in front of the doors leading to the small surgery wing.

After what seemed like an eternity, but was in reality only an hour, Jamie came through the door with the biggest grin on his face that his parents had ever seen. Grabbing his mom by the waist he twirled her around, "We have thirty toes and 30 fingers. Everyone's great."

Hugging her son tightly Lilly gasped, "Is Kelsi OK? When do we get to see them? You wouldn't tell us the names you two picked out, can you tell me now?"

"Whoa slow down, Mom. Kelsi's fine and so are the girls, Dallas Fay and Austin Rae, and your little grandson, Chase Edward, is just great too."

"Chase Edward, huh?" Waldo said slapping his son on the back, "Well at least you didn't name him Fort Worth!"

"I've got to call Karen," Lilly said unclipping her cell phone from her purse.

Lilly carefully relayed all of the information to Karen and was still trying to grasp hold of reality an hour later when Jamie informed them that they could see the babies.

Lilly and Waldo had been filling in Kelsi's parents on their plans for the Lodge. Lilly could tell that Leland would be tickled to death to be able to go to Alaska and fish but doubted that Ruth would ever let him venture that far from the family business. Now at the news that she could finally see the babies, she grabbed Jamie's arm and forgot all about Kelsi's parents. As usual, Waldo made up for his wife's bad manners and escorted the other new grandmother into her daughter's hospital room.

The doctors and nurses were amazed at how healthy all three babies were. Dallas Fay was the smallest but not far behind Austin Rae and Chase Edward had taken the lead in weight and height. Kelsi was already holding all three of them, determined to bond equally with her new family. Her face glowed with happiness and although tired, you could hardly tell she had just delivered the triplets.

Lilly was grinning as she started at one side and took each of the six little hands in hers, not knowing which baby to pick up and wondering how in the world she was going to hold all three at the same time.

"Go ahead," said Kelsi giving her the okay. "Why don't you start with Dallas Fay…you can tell which one she is because of a tiny birth mark on her right ankle."

"An Angel kiss," Lilly replied, taking her tiny granddaughter in her arms, and placing her own kiss softly on the baby's forehead.

Jamie picked up Chase Edward and carefully handed him to Waldo who reluctantly held out his arms in response. But the moment he had the precious bundle in the crook of his arm his heart melted and he lost all connection with the world as he sat in one of the rocking chairs to marvel over the miracle.

Austin Rae opened her little eyes and briefly cried a soft little cry as Jamie picked her up and handed her to Ruth.

Stepping back with his father-in-law after all the babies had been distributed, Jamie remarked, "Sorry Lee, we ran out."

"That's OK, son," Kelsi's father replied. "There will be plenty of time."

Lilly felt as if she had entered heaven. It took some time, but after taking a turn at holding each of the babies she found she had a special individual love for each one of them. She was practicing saying Chase, Austin and Dallas until the names were familiar to her and implanted in her mind. Already each of the babies had proved they had a difference in personalities, but they really did look alike and Lilly expressed her concern to Kelsi.

"You know, Austin and Dallas are going to fool people with their identities. Austin already has a mischievous look in her eye, how in the world are you going to tell them apart?"

Kelsi smiled serenely, "Oh, I doubt if I'll have much trouble. But I may be looking at their ankles a lot. And you're right; Austin looks like she's going to be a handful. It's probably a good thing Chase is so big, he won't stand a chance around his sisters."

Kelsi stifled a yawn and snuggled down contentedly in the bed. Lilly knew it was time to go but hated to leave the babies.

The nurses had all doted over the babies as they changed them and it was obvious that they would be well taken care of. They were all sleeping when Waldo finally slipped his arm around Lilly's waist, letting her know they needed to leave.

"Come on love of my life," he whispered in her ear. "Jamie and Kelsi need some rest and we'll be back in the morning," he promised.

The sound of crying babies could be heard all the way down the hall of the hospital's maternity wing. Lilly briefly greeted the nurses at the desk and then quickened her step as she made her way to the room. Throwing off her jacket she took a visual inventory. Jamie was attempting to change Chase's diaper, Austin was being fed, the nurse was trying to take Dallas' temperature and she didn't like that at all. Dallas and Chase were hungry and letting everyone know about it. Just as Lilly moved forward to help her son Chase promptly shot a stream onto Jamie's shirt as he fumbled with his diaper.

Lilly laughed at the look on her son's face. "You're going to have to learn to be a lot faster, son," she said laughing.

"The little heathen!" Jamie sputtered.

"Don't be so hard on him, Jamie," Lilly said, "You used to do the same thing."

"No way, Mom. I know I never did that."

Just then a young man poked his head into the room. "Is there a Chase, Dallas and Austin here?" he asked. "Oh, and a Jamie and Kelsi too," he added.

Jamie picked up the newly diapered Chase and stepped forward to be met with a large bouquet of flowers from John and Karen. In the center was a Trillium with pink and yellow baby roses nestled into the baby's breath around it. Miniature ivy was draped over the edges and there were three little lambs set into the floral design, and three helium balloons attached.

The young man set the arrangement on the table by Kelsi and then looked around the room. "So that's why I had to put three balloons on it," he said finally satisfying his curiosity. Kelsi laughed and thanked him for the delivery. As she held out her hand to wave good-by Lilly noticed the new ring on her finger.

Taking her daughter-in-law's hand she pulled it towards her for a closer look. The exquisite silver band was connected with two miniature mustangs; in between the horses was a horseshoe with three tiny opals.

"Why that's the triplet's birthstone isn't it? Where ever did you find such a beautiful ring?" Lilly asked looking first at Kelsi and then turning to look at Jamie. Her son had come up behind her to admire the ring on his wife's finger.

324

Giving his mom a quick hug he replied proudly, "I ordered it from Dad's jeweler of course. I did inherit a little of his sentimentality. You didn't think I'd give my wife horse blankets and truck seat covers all my life did you?"

"Well, actually…" Lilly said laughing.

Waldo came to stand beside Lilly and examined the ring also, "That's a fine piece of work," he said.

"Oh, I almost forgot," said Lilly. "I have something that Karen and I made for the triplets." She reached into the bag she had brought with her and took out a long narrow box. Inside were three little bonnets made from lace hankies, with ribbons and bows garnishing the pleats and corners. She handed one of the three enclosed poems to Kelsi who read it out loud.

"The Magic Hanky…
I'm just a little hanky as square as square can be
But ribbons and some stitching made a bonnet out of me
I'll be worn home from the hospital and on christening day
Then washed and pressed and neatly packed and carefully put away
You've heard that little saying
That every bride's been told
To have good luck she has to wear
Some little thing that's old
So what could be more fitting
Than to take me out and then
To snip some stitches here and there
And use me once again?
A wedding hanky I would be
And I would do my best
To hide a blush or wipe away
A tear of happiness
But if I'm given to a boy
I'm sure some day that he
Will find a lovely little bride
And she will carry me."

"My boy isn't going to wear a bonnet," said Jamie.

"Oh yes he is, just for the ride home," replied Kelsi. "This one has blue ribbons on it, so it's for a boy."

"OK, but no pictures," Jamie insisted.

"We'll see," Lilly and Kelsi replied at the same time, sharing a secret smile. They both knew that many pictures would be taken of that momentous occasion and that Jamie would be taking more than anyone.

The doctors were so pleased with the triplet's progress that they were anticipating letting them go home sooner than originally planned. Lilly knew that Kelsi was well prepared with diapers and supplies, but it would be interesting to see how the two new parents would adjust to their new family of five. Lilly knew her son and daughter-in-law well enough to know that they would adjust to their new life without too much trauma. She had told Waldo that God had known what he was doing to give triplets to strong healthy people like Jamie and Kelsi, and they were proving this to be true.

The living room was now a baby entertainment room full of baby swings, rocking chairs, and changing tables. The kitchen was over-taken with bottles and feeding supplies. Kelsi had finally agreed to hire a full time nanny to help out although she had been against it at first, insisting that she do everything herself. However, having a nanny would allow her to tend to her animals on the ranch again, which she had missed a great deal. Besides, soon the babies would be big enough to ride in the triple stroller Jamie and Waldo had created, and Kelsi's energy level was returning to normal.

The thought of leaving these three precious little grandchildren made Lilly's heart heavy, but she and Waldo did have obligations in Alaska to return to. She spent every moment possible with the babies, getting to know them as individuals and creating a bond that would last for many years to come.

"Jamie," Waldo said observantly. "You're quickly running out of room here. Have you thought about the future?"

"Sure have Dad, how would you like to help me build a new house in about a year or two?"

Waldo's eyes grew big with the idea. Lilly's thoughts were whirling around in her head.

"Have you also thought about a Bed and Breakfast here?" she finally asked.

Jamie grinned at the looks on his parent's faces. He knew well that they would want to be closer to their grandchildren and had been planning for some time now. "Mom, Dad, the babies are asleep and Kelsi's resting so let's take a little walk. There's something I need to show you."

Exchanging a puzzling glance Waldo and Lilly followed their son out of the house. Taking his mom's arm and with his dad following behind Jamie started the trek up the path to the hill behind.

Lilly's bad knee had prevented her from hiking the hills behind the ranch and now was surprised to see a road carved into the hillside. The hike was gradual and when they reached the top they saw what Jamie had been working on for several months. Leaving the perimeter trees and the meadow intact he had cleared enough property to build their dream home, pasture their horses and provide an enormous yard for the triplets to play in.

Waldo and Lilly looked at each other in surprise and finally Waldo spoke, "When do you want to start building?"

Jamie grinned proudly back at them, "Next year. We're hoping by the time we get this house built the Alaska Lodge will be running smoothly enough you two can come down here and start your dude ranch. You'll have to build on to the old house of course, but it shouldn't take much and it sure would be nice to have you two a little closer once in a while."

Lilly whooped for joy. It had long been her dream to live closer to her son and his family but she feared becoming a meddling mother-in-law and knew they needed to live their own lives, just as she and Waldo needed to live theirs. Jamie's plan fit her ideas perfectly and would still allow them to be as close to Karen and John as they needed to.

Strolling back to the old house they were filled with talk of the new house and Lilly's mind was already turning to western style dishes she and Karen would fix for their guests at the Bear Creek Ranch.

Just before sunrise Lilly silently left the bed she shared with Waldo. Jamie would be taking them to the airport at 10:00 AM and she needed quiet time with her grandchildren. Entering the nursery she silently took Dallas from her crib, crossing the hard wood floor quietly in her stocking clad feet with her precious bundle. She sat in the rocking chair Jamie had made for Kelsi. Careful not to wake the baby she began talking, telling her of the wonderful life that lay ahead of her, of her prayers that Dallas would grow up to be a self assured woman, humble yet never dependent on anyone, loving yet unyielding in her quest for truth and honesty.

With a kiss on the cheek Lilly put Dallas back in her bed and took Austin to the rocking chair and told her of the life that waited for her, knowing already that she would be the gentler of the two little ladies. She told her of her own fears growing up and striving to be heard in a world that could be overpowering to a small shy girl. Reassuring her that she would find her way, she then told her of the true love that awaited her and the children that God would surely bless her with.

Finally replacing Austin she took her grandson in her arms, bringing him close she smoothed his dark hair back from his forehead and kissed him softly. He looked so much like his father and Lilly could already see traces of her father in him. These features were a bit stronger than the ones in his sisters. Lilly told him then about the life ahead of him and how he would be as strong as his father and grandfather but cautioned him to never forget the source of his strength and never forget to humble himself before God and always be kind and gentle and watch over his sisters.

Replacing Chase in his crib she then lovingly folded the handmade quilts she and Karen had made at the end of each crib and then silently left the room.

After putting coffee on Lilly returned to the bedroom to get ready to shower and pack. But the sight of the large pine bed was too tempting and she crept back under the covers. Sighing contently Waldo slipped his arm around her, "Did you give them their life instructions, Lilly my love?"

"Uh huh." She replied and drifted back to sleep.

CHAPTER 27

The plane took off on time and Lilly was able to reflect on the events they had just experienced. She already missed her grandchildren with a new ache in her heart and yearned to hold them again.

"Waldo, we'll come back for Thanksgiving right? But they'll have to come to Alaska for Christmas or it will break Karen's heart. And I don't want to miss a minute that I could be with Chase, Austin and Dallas."

"I don't think they'll want to travel with the babies that soon," he replied softly, not wanting her to be disappointed.

"How can I tell Karen they won't come? I know she'll be understanding if it's not possible, but this could be the first Christmas we're split up and I don't know if we can do that to her. We could all go to Washington, but Heather has her heart set on Alaska and so does Karen, and John and Melinda are planning to be in Alaska too, that is if her pregnancy allows it but she's not due until January. Maybe Washington would be better for John and Melinda," she said losing hope as her voice dwindled in disappointment.

The truth was that Lilly had been dreaming about Christmas in Alaska as much as Karen had. They had ordered hundreds of lights and decorations to be delivered soon, and for months she had been organizing recipes and menus for the occasion. The nursery had been completed and there was no reason they couldn't accommodate the whole family for the holiday, no reason except for Jamie and Kelsi's decision not to come.

Patting his wife's hand comfortingly Waldo said, "Let's just take one day at a time. We will definitely come for Thanksgiving and the way those three are growing, why who knows? Maybe they will be big and strong enough to come north for Christmas. The way that Chase chows down, he might just be crawling by then." The pride in his grandson was unmistakable in Waldo's voice.

Lilly grinned at her husband, "Oh, Waldo, he'll only be almost two months old at Christmas. But you're right, as usual, and I'm worrying about something that might not happen. And the important thing is their health. We'll have lots of holidays together; I'm not going to work myself into a stew over this one."

Waldo and Lilly's senses were met at the front door of the lodge with the fragrance of blueberry pie. Lanie had been cooking and cleaning all day, she was determined to have everything absolutely perfect for Lilly's return. Actually Lilly had been the one that taught her to cook the prime rib on the barbeque to perfection, and Lanie had painstakingly hovered over it for hours.

Karen had made the blueberry pies mid-morning and the fragrance lingering was mixed with the homemade bread that had finished baking just a couple hours earlier and still sat on the cooling racks. John had the fireplace ablaze, with a fresh supply of wood on hand. And Tyson had been allowed to come in for a few minutes and lay stretched out in front of the fire. The puppy was enjoying the treat of being allowed inside, but John knew he would soon be back out again when he got a little warm.

The table was set with crystal goblets and the dishes had purple stripes and little tiny violets. Matching cloth napkins held the silverware. Crystal candleholders with purple tapers graced the center of the table next to a crystal bowl containing three purple floating candles. Tiny silver stars were scattered around the centerpiece on the linen tablecloth.

Lanie checked the baked potatoes again in the warming tray, and then turned on the vegetable steamer at the sound of voices at the front door. She had coffee beans ready by the grinder to make dessert coffee, and the serving dishes were all organized on the countertop, ready to be filled. She searched her mind for anything she might have forgotten.

"Lanie, you've created a masterpiece!" exclaimed Lilly as she entered the room.

"Welcome home," she said shyly giving Lilly a quick hug. Hugging her back Lilly looked around the lovely room and asked, "Where's Karen?"

"Right here, Lilly," Karen said entering the dining from the ice room. "Where are the pictures? You didn't pack them did you?" Grabbing her friend, the two hugged and danced around as they did when they were together.

"Of course not! They're all in my purse. But my purse is so heavy I left it for Waldo and John to bring in with the luggage. I've got 15 packets of 36 pictures each. That's one roll for every day we were there. Waldo's shopping for a digital camera for us and we're getting a new one for Jamie and Kelsi too so we don't have to wait for the mail." Pausing slightly to catch her breath Lilly hugged Karen again and with tears in her eyes she said, "Karen, they're so beautiful. It broke my heart to leave them."

Alternately patting and rubbing Lilly's back Karen replied, "I know, I know. But it's going to be OK."

Tyson had perked his ears up when Lilly came in and his hopes were founded when he heard Waldo and John talking as they brought the luggage into the kitchen.

Watching the dog barking and running in circles around Waldo, Lilly's heart was lightened. As much as she missed her grandchildren this is where they belonged.

Putting the bags down Waldo paused to give his dog a big hug and lifting his head he sniffed, "Is that pie I smell?"

"Yeah it is, but it isn't apple," said John with a teasing smile on his lips and slightly raised eyebrows.

"Here Waldo, I salvaged a couple of doodle socks for you," offered Karen as she uncovered her hidden stash.

"I thought I ate them all," said John in surprise reaching for the plate that Karen held out to Waldo.

"No you don't, you've had enough," Karen said waving her hand at his to move it away.

Grabbing the plate in one hand and a large suitcase in the other, Waldo told John to grab the rest of the bags and he might share after they were done. Lilly and Karen could see Waldo munching all the way upstairs and seriously doubted if any of the doodle socks would be left by the time John got there.

"I had never heard of doodle socks before today," said Lanie. "Jimmie and Esther were here this morning and they got to help too. Esther rolled out the left over pie dough and Jimmie buttered it and then they took turns sprinkling the cinnamon and sugar. They rolled them up and cut them like experts."

Lilly smiled fondly as she thought of the fun she had had as a little girl making these treats when her own Mother made pies. She had called them crusties. Doodle socks was the name given to them by Karen and her mother.

Waldo returned with the pictures and an empty plate. Karen couldn't wait another moment. "Let me see those," she commanded. Then added..."please."

The three women quickly poured over the best pictures Lilly had put on top of the pile. Lanie picked out her favorite ones and held them for a long moment looking longingly at the babies.

"Come on, we can take more time with these after dinner," said Lilly. "I'm starving and I can't wait to taste your cooking."

Pulling herself out of her trance Lanie rose to fill the serving dishes and Karen put the bread on the cutting board. "Could you please get that raspberry salad out of the fridge Lilly?" asked Lanie.

The meal was delicious, and Lilly once again knew that she was home. Lilly's face glowed as she talked about her grandchildren and told every little detail she could remember. Their little teeny tiny toes were her favorite part, well, one of her favorite parts. And she described each of her grandchildren so well that Karen felt like she had been able to hold them herself.

"Did Kelsi like the quilts?" Karen asked.

Lilly filled her in on Kelsi's excitement over the quilts and could have gone on and on all night about the three babies, but looking around at the lodge she asked, "Anything new around here?"

"No, not really," answered Karen.

Lanie perked up, "What about our guest, Mr. Wilson?"

"Go ahead," Karen said with a smile.

"Well," Lanie started with a giggle. "I about died when he came to the table with foamy anti-acid juice coming out of the corners of his mouth. Then when he lifted one cheek at the table and smiled like he had just done something cute I about died again. I know we're up here in the boonies somewhat, but please…"

"You think that's bad," said John. "I was confined in the boat with him, and that's enough said about that."

"Oh—and he fell asleep on the sofa in the front room and we had to wake him up and ask him to go to his room," added Karen.

They all laughed and chuckled at the memories of their interesting guest.

"Heather called," Karen said changing the subject. "She's still madly in love and can't wait for Thanksgiving. We figured you and Waldo would go to Washington for the holiday. She wants to stay a few days and is asking when you'll be here so she can arrange her schedule to be sure to see you."

Lilly paused for a moment and then replied, "We will probably go down the day before and come back on Sunday, but of course a lot depends on the weather and I'm not ready to give up hope that they will be here for Christmas. Is Heather coming by herself?"

Nodding her head Karen replied, "She is, but plans on bringing David for Christmas."

Glancing at Lanie, Lilly satisfied herself that their young friend was so absorbed in the baby pictures that she wasn't paying attention to Karen and Lilly's conversation.

"Just David?" She asked quietly.

Karen smiled in return, "I believe his brother might be paying us a visit also."

"Yes!" Lilly exclaimed.

"What are you two up to now?" Waldo asked

"Nothing, honey" Lilly was quick to answer.

"Just planning the Holidays," Karen added as they both giggled.

"I think I want one of those babies," said Karen.

Lanie perked up, "I do too," she said without thinking.

Lilly and Karen exchanged their knowing look as Karen got up and started the coffee to go with dessert, but Lilly put on the teakettle. She had seen the look of yearning and confusion in Lanie's eyes, and it was about time that they had a heart to heart talk about Ken.

John and Waldo were feeling ambitious about the new dude ranch. Waldo described the acreage and told John all about the land that had already been cleared. They were planning the new stables and Waldo was saying that Lilly wanted at least ten suites in the Ranch House, and maybe individual log cabins to supplement the area.

Karen had been excited about the news too, but hadn't quite gotten past the cowboy hats and boots in her thinking yet.

Knowing they all had important things to talk about, Karen eased the men into the other room with their blueberry pie and ice cream so that they could dream and plan to their hearts content. The china teapot would be used tonight. Without a word Lilly carefully took the tea cups from the cupboard and Karen got out the step stool to reach the china teapot that was kept on the higher shelf.

Lanie's face perked up at the sight of the teapot, knowing something special was happening. Karen and Lilly rarely got it out, and she had only seen it used once before, when "Mom B" had passed away. Her heart felt a heavy weight tonight, and somehow the thought of these two with their teapot medicine was a great relief. Maybe tonight she would be able to share all of her feelings. Or maybe she should just keep them to herself? Maybe it was those babies that had stirred up her maternal feelings.

"How's Ken doing?" Karen asked casually as she filled the tea sieve with a blueberry and lemon flavor they had just decided on. Ken was actually the furthest thing from Lanie's mind right now, but Karen was right, how else would she ever have a relationship? No, I don't need a relationship, she thought.

Doing her best to put aside the thoughts popping in and out of her mind Lanie finally answered, "He's fine. We went to the movies last weekend and he'll be going back to school at the end of September. That's just two weeks away."

Lilly slid the pie server under the next piece of warm pie and carefully placed it on the matching china desert plate. "And how do you feel about that?" Lilly asked softly as she passed Lanie the piece of pie.

"I'm not sure," Lanie replied. "Oh you know he's a nice enough guy and my parents really like him and he has hinted that he wants more from our relationship. But every time I kiss him I see Larry's face. I know it's silly but I feel like I'm being unfaithful. My arms ache for a child of my own, so maybe I should just marry him. Do you think I would come to love him with time like you and Waldo do? I mean what else do I have to pick from up here?" Lanie had tears in her eyes as she finished speaking and looked solemnly at her uneaten pie.

"Maybe I'm not the right person to give advice," Lilly said. "After all I married the love of my life almost twenty nine years ago. But one thing I do know is that marrying a man you don't love just to have children is wrong. Those children are not always going to be with you. Then when they're grown up and on their own all you have is an empty shell of a life."

Karen blinked back tears of her own and began. "I do know what it's like to marry for convenience rather than love. And my story is not unlike yours, Lanie. You see I thought John was dead and Heather's father offered me the security I needed. Not that I regret marrying him, after all he was a decent father to John Jr. and I can't even imagine my life without Heather, but you're not pregnant, and you don't have to get married. Don't give up on love, honey, it will find you again."

Not really believing that she could actually find love again Lanie responded. "Maybe I could adopt, I know a single lady who adopted two children, and she does just fine."

"I guess that's a possibility," said Karen. "But you have a whole world to offer someone. And…I happen to believe that you will find someone. You can't change your past, and there's a part of your heart that will always be with Larry, but that's the past and it can't come back to you. You'll have to tuck that away in your treasure chest."

"Lanie," said Lilly. "You have the beauty and charisma of a gracious queen. If there's a man worthy of having you we'll search the ends of the earth until we find him. No, on second thought he's probably looking for you and hasn't gotten to Alaska yet."

Lilly and Karen giggled at this image. Yes, Pastor Jim would have a lot to live up to when he visited, but they had a feeling he could handle it just fine. And if that didn't work out, something else would.

"You know, I was just wondering if Anna and Lois sat at this very same table to talk," said Karen.

"Of course they did," said Lanie as she picked up her fork and savored her first bite of the pie, and then she continued. "I remember it. Sometimes Grandma Anna would let me come with her. I can remember playing with my dolls right there in that corner," Lanie said pointing with her fork to the corner by the antique cast iron cook stove. "They would pour a little tea in my teapot and my dolls and I would have our own party. I just loved watching them sip tea, nibble cookies and talk about their children and their husbands. I think it was then that I realized how much I wanted to be a wife and mother some day."

"What a wonderful memory," Lilly said softly.

"You two are just like them," Lanie said laughing. "Solving everyone's problems with a cup of tea."

Karen and Lilly smiled at each other and Karen answered, "Well maybe problems don't really get solved, but I think everyone who leaves our table feels a little better."

Waldo and John, coming through the kitchen to put Tyson away for the night, interrupted the moment. Lanie glanced at her watch and was startled to realize how late it was. As John offered to see her to her car Lanie threw her arms around Karen and Lilly for one last hug. "Thanks, you two. I really don't know what I'd do without you."

CHAPTER 28

After taking quite some time in the bathroom, Karen finally came out in her purple print bathrobe and her hair on top of her head ready for a soak in the hot tub. Taking Johns hands in both of hers she pulled him to a standing position from the chair he had been waiting in and looked directly into his mesmerizing brown eyes. Seeing the concern and bewilderment in her expression he finally asked, "What is it Karen?"

"John…well…um…do you think I could be pregnant?" she blurted out.

"Wouldn't you know that better than I?" he asked after taking in a moment to register her question.

"I can't be, I'm too old," she said in a matter of fact manner.

"How old is too old?" he asked.

"I'm not sure," She answered, "I know it's not impossible at my age it just seems so improbable. Would you mind?"

Taking her in his arms he pulled her close, "Darling, as long as it's not physically dangerous for you then I would be just fine with it. In fact we seem to be going through a baby boom anyway. Why not have another one of our own?"

"But, what about our life style, a baby would totally turn that upside down," She worried.

"Nonsense, Lilly would just convert the ice room into a nursery and it would be business as usual," John replied laughing at that thought.

"No way, not that room!" Karen answered joining in his laughter. "Oh well, I'm probably not. More than likely I'm starting menopause. You know I'm the same age Lilly was when she started and she's only two years older than me. So that's probably it. Are you going to join me in the tub?" She asked hopefully.

Grinning John replied, "You couldn't keep me away."

As they relaxed in the bubbly water the thoughts of a baby overtook them.

"What would you want to name a girl if we had one?" asked Karen.

"I would have to change diapers, wouldn't I," he said thoughtfully. "How long does it take to have a baby anyway, I mean…when would it be due?"

"I guess that would be late spring or early summer," Karen answered.

Karen giggled the night away enjoying the new unity they shared. She loved the new light in John's eyes and treasured the moments, and the gift of his love was greater in her heart than it had ever been before.

It was later than usual when John and Karen arrived in the kitchen for breakfast the following morning. Karen floated by Lilly to the coffee pot and poured two cups.

"Well don't you just have a glow about you this morning," commented Lilly.

The "glow" comment brought her back to reality and Karen couldn't wait to get Lilly alone to get her opinion on this situation.

When the time finally came Karen blurted it all out in the form of ten different questions all at once. Lilly patiently and thoughtfully listened to her friend unload her thoughts. "And I know John would whisk me off to the doctor tomorrow, but I checked this morning and I can't get in for another two weeks. I don't think I can wait that long Lilly, the suspense is killing me!"

"We could just go into town and pick up one of those 90% accurate things at Mr. Bjorn's store," suggested Lilly thoughtfully. "We'd have to make sure Elma was busy elsewhere and maybe we could just slip it into our things without him noticing."

"Do you think he'd let us ring up our own groceries?" asked Karen.

"I doubt it, but we could ask Lanie to get it for us…no, on second thought we couldn't do that. We couldn't ask her to do anything that would start rumors for her."

"What are you two in a huddle about now?" Waldo asked coming in from feeding Tyson.

John had followed him in and after exchanging a look with Karen he knew that she had told Lilly. With a grin on his face he filled Waldo in on the suspected event.

"Way to go," Waldo said slapping John on the back and giving Karen a careful hug.

"You don't have to worry about hurting me," Karen said hugging him back. "Now our problem is if we go to Mr. Bjorn's store and buy a pregnancy test it's probably going to cause a lot of nasty rumors about Lanie. And we certainly don't want that. So what do we do? I just can't wait two weeks, can you honey?" She said appealing to John.

"Nope, not me, and I have just the answer. Waldo and I have to go to town this afternoon. We'll pick up the test and I'll tell Mr. Bjorn the truth. He's a good guy and won't go spreading any gossip."

"And if that old busy body Elma Smith is in the store we'll just tell her it's for Lilly," Waldo said ducking to avoid Lilly's playful slug in the arm.

By the time Lanie arrived at the back door Lilly was just finishing the breakfast dishes, Karen was in the office paying bills and the men were outside preparing for their trip to town.

After a cheery greeting to Lilly, she quickly found Karen, relieved to find her alone. "I want to ask you something, Karen." Lanie's face held a look that Karen didn't recognize and she was immediately curious.

"What is it?" Karen asked.

"You know what you said the other night about tucking away my past in the treasure chest?" Lanie said

"Yes, I do…what do you have in mind?"

"Do you remember what I told you about the wedding dress my mother was making for me? And how she was making the little ribbon roses that never were put on it?"

"Yes…"

"I hope you don't think I'm totally crazy, but I finished the dress and I have it in my car. I was hoping maybe you and Lilly would let me put

340

it in the old chest in the attic with the other dresses that were Grandma Anna's and Lois's. That is if it wouldn't impose on you or anything."

The hopeful look in Lanie's eyes went straight to Karen's heart. She was surprised and yet pleased that Lanie had taken this literally. She knew from experience how important it is to complete the grieving experience, and now she would have the privilege of helping Lanie come to terms with her past.

"Of course we can put it in the trunk," Karen said. "We'll do it this afternoon when John and Waldo are in town. And don't you give another thought to "imposing" on us. You're family and if that's where you want your dress we would be honored to have it there."

The three women busied themselves with the daily chores. The lodge was once again full with of the sounds and scents of cleaning and cooking.

It was Karen's day to make homemade bread, and she also made a batch of cookies as she sometimes did. These were usually stored in the freezer in preparation for the holidays, or a special desert for their guests.

Lanie was in charge of the laundry and Lilly was ordering supplies and making the grocery list for John and Waldo to take care of on their trip to town.

Karen shared the plan of putting the dress in the attic with Lilly, and they immediately knew what they had to do in preparation. Lilly carried the broom to the attic to be sure the cobwebs hadn't taken over, and Karen joined her as soon as her bread was in the oven. It didn't take them long to have the attic area cleaned up and prepared for the afternoon event.

Lanie had busied herself all morning in the laundry room. So she hadn't paid much attention to what her two friends had been doing and really didn't have a clue. It was noon before they knew it, and Lilly served a light lunch to the men just before they took off for the rest of the afternoon. The men were hanging around the fresh cookies as long as they could get away with it, but Lilly soon had them on schedule again.

Karen walked John out to the truck just to get in an extra hug. Knowing he would accomplish the purchase she was waiting for, she finally let him go with anticipation in her heart. But there were other things to think about now, and she hurried back to the kitchen.

"Ok Lanie, we're ready to have our ceremony," said Karen.

"Ceremony…oh, you mean the dress?" Lanie started to protest that she had to go get the dress first and then was taken by surprise as Karen took her by the hand and led her to the attic. Lilly followed with a tray that held the notorious seeping teapot.

Lanie's mouth dropped open as soon as they reached the top of the stairs.

The little round table was set with a lace tablecloth and a centerpiece of pink roses with a silver string of pearls woven through it and draped down onto the tablecloth. A silver plate held an assortment of fancy shaped cookies; some decorated with frosting of pastel colors and some with sparkling sugar crystals. An assortment of chocolate dipped strawberries was intermixed with the cookies, separated by little bits of silver confetti. Lavender candles were cradled in crystal holders, which reflected the light as soon as Karen lit them.

Lanie looked up from the table setting to find her dress was hung next to the treasure chest. The light from the windows gave it a heavenly touch and she gasped at its beauty. The three stood around the dress and admired it in silence.

Finally Lanie spoke. "Wow, and I was worried that you would think I was crazy…"

Lilly opened the trunk and they took out the other dresses. The individuals that had originally worn them were real people with real lives to them now, and somehow there was comfort and inspiration in imagining what the past had been like.

The tea was served and they nibbled on the cookies and chocolate dipped fruit as they talked. The afternoon was spent remembering, imagining, laughing, and shedding a tear or two together.

When they were finally ready to put the dresses away Lanie carefully tucked her dress into the trunk with the others. "Good-by to the memories I'll never have," she said.

"May the memories that you do have always be treasured," responded Karen.

"And may you make many more beautiful memories in your lifetime," added Lilly.

Peace flowed through and over the broken pieces of Lanie's heart and she knew that a healing of her wounds had taken place. Feeling the inspiration to live the rest of her life she turned and hugged her friends.

The importance of the afternoon's activities had somehow lessened the focus on Karen's curiosity of knowing whether or not she was pregnant. But the sound of Tyson's bark signaling the men's return home brought back her feelings of anxiety and her yearning to be with the man she loved. She quickly straightened the crisp collar of her baby blue cotton shirt and ran her fingers through her hair giving it more fluff to go with her rosy cheeks.

"Maybe I do have a glow," Karen whispered to herself. "And I look good in baby blue." She laughed at herself, totally enjoying the new self-confidence she had grown to have in the last few months.

She took just a moment to inhale the delicious aroma as she passed the kitchen and then hurried out to meet John with happiness saturating her being. Rushing into his arms John caught Karen up in a big hug and twirled her around. "Did you get it?" She asked breathlessly.

With a big grin John pulled the brown paper wrapped box out of his parka jacket. "Only one they had. But I didn't think we'd ever get out of that store. I'll swear Waldo dawdled hoping we would run into Elma so he could tell her it was Lilly's."

Looking deep into his wife's green eyes John continued, "Are you going to do it right now? Right this very minute?"

"What do you think, John? Should I? Or should we wait until after dinner?"

"Whichever you prefer, darling. I just want you to know that I love you regardless of the results. Having a child at our age isn't exactly what I had planned but it sure wouldn't make me unhappy," John answered.

Standing on her tiptoes Karen placed a tender kiss on her husband's lips. "I know. That's exactly the way I feel. So I'll do it now. OK?"

Grabbing the box she turned and headed for the Lodge. Glancing back over her shoulder she smiled again and said, "Just give me a few minutes, OK?"

The two huddled around the testing device in anticipation of the outcome.

"It's strange," Karen said. "In the next couple of minutes we're going to have a glimpse into the next twenty years of our lives."

"As long as the next twenty years includes you in my life then there's room for twenty more kids if you want," John said bringing his wife into the circle of his arms.

"I know, darling," Karen said leaning back against his arms to search his deep brown eyes. "But I don't think twenty is physically possible. In fact I would have said one would be improbable. What will Heather think? And what about John Jr. and Melinda? John's youngest would be older than his aunt or uncle?"

"Don't worry about them Karen. If it's positive they will be thrilled for us. And you know what Lilly always says, "the more people you have to love, the more love you have to give." Pausing to give her a tender kiss he continued, "Now look at the little stick."

Drawing a deep breath Karen picked up the testing wand, "Oh, John, it's negative," she said with a sigh. "I guess in a way I'm relieved, but I have to admit I'm a bit disappointed too. And you know this means I'm probably starting menopause and I have to face the fact that there will be no more children in my life."

Drawing her close again, John soothed, "We have our grandchildren, Karen. We're about to be blessed with a new grandchild, and I'm sure Heather will have children. And don't forget about Lilly and Waldo's triplets. No, darling, there will be many, many more children in our lives."

'I'm OK. Let's go tell Lilly, I'm sure she's pacing, wearing a path in front of the kitchen sink by now." Karen smiled weakly and slipped her hand into his as they headed towards the kitchen. John's hum soon turned into a familiar favorite as he starting singing one of Dylan's songs about his unconditional love, making her dreams come true and spending a lifetime in love and laughter. It was easy for Karen to harmonize with him and any disappointment she had just experienced was washed away and replaced with what was now a very special memory.

Karen stretched the fresh smelling sheet over the corner of the mattress in the aurora borealis room. Heather had dibs on this room ever since she first heard about it and Karen had put every effort into making it unique for her. Never having had a daughter of her own, Lilly loved doing extra special things for Heather and had been helping Karen all morning prepare the room for her. Lilly placed the little candy and dried lavender, tied with a ribbon, onto the pillow as they finished.

"You've always spoiled her," Karen teased as she picked up the lip-gloss and nail polish in the guest basket to check out the colors. "Lilly, where did you find these colors? I don't mean to be critical but aren't they a little dark for Heather's fair skin tone?"

Lilly paused, "Don't you think she's darkened up a little after being in the south for so long?"

"No, you know she never goes out without sunscreen. But I'm sure she'll love these colors just the same," Karen said replacing the nail polish in the basket.

"OK, OK, I confess!" Lilly said laughing as she pulled out the bottom drawer of the nightstand. The entire drawer was full of nail polish and lip-gloss in the pastel colors that went well with Heather's fair beauty.

"I've been collecting these for Heather for a long time. The polish in the basket is my color. I'm hoping to talk her into a manicure. You know I haven't had a decent one since we moved up here."

Laughing with her friend, Karen picked her favorite color out of the drawer and put it in the basket. "Good idea. If you don't mind I think I'll do the same. Oh, oh I think I hear Waldo's truck. And Tyson just barked, come on Lilly, she's here!"

Karen practically skipped down the stairs and out the front door. It seemed like forever since she had hugged her daughter, and it felt so good to see the familiar face that she had missed so much.

"Mom, I'm really glad to see you too and I'm not exactly breakable, but I don't think you should squeeze me any harder," Heather pleaded.

"Sorry dear, but I guess you'll have to put up with me for a week or two anyway," she replied with a teasing smile and a happy giggle as she lessened her grip and touched the layered wispy hair away from Heather's face. "I'm just so glad to see you."

She stood back a step and took in her daughter's new look that was a bit more refined and elegant. The changes were very becoming, and the subtle eye makeup and lipstick complimented the highlights in her hair.

Heather turned to her Aunt Lilly and hugged her. "I missed you too, Aunt Lilly, Louisiana isn't the same without you. And are you sure you have to leave for the holiday?"

"I'll show you the pictures of the triplets, and then you'll understand," promised Lilly. "And I just love your new hair cut, who did it for you?"

Karen turned to David, and before he had a chance to offer a handshake she gave him a big welcoming hug. "I'm so glad you could make it, and we're so glad you're here too," she said as she greeted Pastor Jim. "You know you're always welcome, and we wouldn't have dreamed of splitting up brothers for Thanksgiving."

"We're glad to be here, and it looks like marriage suits you quite well Miss Karen," Pastor Jim answered with his southern drawl.

"I'll just take my favorite daughter's luggage to her room," John said with a wink as he lifted the biggest one from the back of the truck.

"Thanks Dad," Heather said with a warm smile. "I think that should be the aurora borealis room, isn't that right mom?"

Karen was guessing that the two had had a pleasing conversation on their way back to the lodge. Ever since her father had died, Heather had felt bad about the fact that he wasn't in her life, like a big piece was missing that everyone else seemed to have in their lives. As a mother Karen had struggled for years with the emotional needs that Heather had as a result of her father's absence, and even though Waldo had been a wonderful uncle and male role model, something had always been missing in her life. Now that John had come back into Karen's life, not only did John Jr. have his dad for the first time in his life, but Heather also was able to reap the benefits. Karen knew it was a blessing that Heather and John got along so well, and was very thankful that John's personality seemed to fit right into that empty spot of her daughter's life. Not that he could ever literally replace her father, but her emotional needs were being met for the first time in ten years.

"I'm so blessed," Karen said so softly that hardly anyone noticed. She took an extra moment to appreciate the relationship scene in front of her. Pastor Jim took Heather's extra bag to carry in for her, and they all headed for the front door. Karen gently ran her hand over John's shoulder as he passed her, his arms loaded with Heather's luggage.

David was looking a bit shy, but relaxed when Waldo handed him one of the suitcases and Heather took his arm. Heather's eyes definitely held a new sparkle; I guess that's love, thought Karen.

"Welcome to the Wolf Creek Lodge," Lilly announced as they entered the large front doors. A cozy fire was crackling in the main room with an arrangement of fall leaves and dried flowers above it on the mantle. Fall colored throw pillows, figurines and candles decorated the room, and the smell of homemade bread filled the air.

David inhaled deeply. "What is that? Is it homemade bread?" he asked hopefully.

"That's right," answered Lilly, "would you like to start your tour with the kitchen?"

"I'm ready for the kitchen," Pastor Jim said eagerly. "I hadn't imagined such hospitality existing so far north in the wilderness, but I should have knowing you two."

Lilly led the group through the swinging French doors but stopped short when she saw Lanie. Only a few minutes ago she had left her rolling out crusts for pumpkin pies, and now the girl stood there covered in flour. She looked like a white ghost.

The surprised look on Lanie's face matched the one on Lilly's.

"I...I...I dropped the bag of flour," Lanie stuttered. Looking around at the group staring at her she murmured, "I'm so embarrassed."

Then dropping her flushed faced into her flour covered hands Lanie's slender shoulders began to shake.

Recovering rapidly Lilly and Karen rushed to their new friend and putting their arms around her they began to console. "Honey, don't cry it's OK," Karen began while Lilly reassured Lanie that she had done the same thing herself.

To their surprise when Lanie dropped her hands they saw tears mixed with laughter and the entire group began to laugh too. John howled when Waldo commented that Halloween was over and maybe Lanie should have dressed up as a Turkey instead of a ghost. Leaving Lilly and Waldo helping Lanie clean up the mess Karen and John continued to show their guests to their rooms.

As they climbed the stairs still giggling, Karen overheard Jim ask David if he knew anything about the beautiful girl covered in flour. It was all Karen could do to continue showing the young men to the Polar Bear suite before she ran back to the kitchen to pull Lilly aside and let her know that their matchmaking was working better than expected. Finally the guests were situated and Karen was able to return to the kitchen. She grinned as she picked up a dishtowel and gently wiped some flour from Lilly's cheek that she had missed. "Is Lanie ok?"

"Oh she's fine," replied Lilly. She's just cleaning up, maybe taking a shower?"

They were still laughing as Lilly placed the large soup tureen on the table and Karen got out the breadboards.

"She was asking about Pastor Jim," said Lilly in a whisper. "She wanted to know if he was really a preacher."

"I overheard Jim asking David about her on the way up the stairs," Karen whispered back. "Lilly, I'm so excited I can't stand it. Those two would be just perfect for each other."

"I know, so make sure they're seated next to each other," Lilly replied. "Rats, I almost wish I wasn't leaving, but we have to go and I know you'll do everything possible to point them in the right direction."

The smell of Lilly's beef stew brought Waldo in from the workshop where he had been getting the fishing tackle ready for the next day's fishing trip. John would be taking David and Jim out since Waldo and Lilly were leaving early the next morning to spend Thanksgiving with their grandchildren. Sniffing the air, Waldo asked hopefully if dinner was going to be early that night. Lilly replied that since the kids had been traveling all day they would eat early and then later on in the evening they could make smores and popcorn in the great room's large open hearth.

Lanie entered the kitchen to Waldo's whistle. She blushed as she stood there in Lilly's new deep red wine sweater and black tailored slacks. The borrowed outfit showed off Lanie's tall slender figure. She had braided her hair and the silver clip holding it in place accented the sophisticated look she had created. Her makeup was perfect; a little glitter on the eyelids, rosy cheeks and a rich shiny wine lipstick. Her look was completed with a simple silver necklace and matching earrings.

"Oh stop it Waldo," she scolded. "Thank you Lilly for letting me borrow your clothes, I didn't bring a change today like I usually do."

"That's ok Lanie…thank goodness I haven't had time to shorten those slacks. Otherwise they would have been capri's on you. I think you better keep the sweater…it sure looks a lot better on you than it does on me."

"I couldn't do that," replied Lanie. "I'll wash them and have them back to you tomorrow."

"No, I'm serious, I want you to keep it," argued Lilly.

"It really does look good on you Lanie," Karen confirmed as she joined her friends in the kitchen. "Actually, it's the perfect sweater on you…no offense Lilly."

"None taken, I love jewel tones but sometimes they wash my color out," Lilly agreed as they both stood back and nodded their heads in approval.

Karen's heart was about to burst with the anticipation of love for Lanie. She held her tongue from any further words in fear of saying something stupid or inappropriate. Lanie was a very beautiful woman, and Pastor Jim had even seen that though the flour. Lanie looked as though they needed to have her portrait painted to preserve the moment of perfection and to document her beauty for future generations to appreciate. Heather's chatter could be heard as she escorted her guests down the stairs. She obviously felt right at home in the surroundings that her mother and aunt Lilly had created.

Jim was tall and muscular, and held his broad shoulders in a confident way. His white, straight teeth accented his large warm smile, and he had a personality that people loved. People were drawn to him…he always had something positive to say, never a negative word. His haircut was clean and neat; not long but leaving wavy lengths of chestnut brown that one could run their fingers through if they were allowed.

As Jim entered the room his blue eyes went straight to Lanie. He stared speechless until Lilly finally broke the silence. "Lanie, this is Heather, Karen and John's daughter. And David, Heather's friend and Jim, David's brother. Everyone this is Lanie. Lanie helps out here at the Lodge and her family has become very good friends of ours."

Watching the young people greet one another Lilly met Karen's eyes as they saw Jim approach Lanie and envelope her tiny hand with his large one. As they smiled at each other Lilly asked brightly, "Who's hungry? We're eating in the kitchen tonight so everyone grab a bowl and I'll serve the stew. Lanie would you get the sourdough rolls out of the oven?"

"Let me help you," Jim offered.

"I'm absolutely starved," admitted David. "It's been hours since we ate on the plane, and this smells very, very good." Heather smiled at him and handed him the first bowl.

Lilly and Karen watched Jim and Lanie interact through dinner and smiled knowingly to one another when Jim insisted on helping Lanie clear the table. However, Lilly insisted that it was the young people's night and roped Waldo and John into helping her and Karen clear and cleanup. The two women smiled again and giggled when they overheard Jim insist that Lanie be his partner for a game of charades.

John and Waldo just shook their heads knowing there was no stopping the matchmaking that had taken place right in front of their eyes. As they went outside to take care of Tyson for the evening Waldo remarked to John that probably the only thing in the world that could take Lilly away from the Lodge right now was the promise of seeing her grandchildren.

The next morning John stood watch over the waffles while Karen cooked the sausage and set out the plates and juice glasses. Taking after her aunt Lilly, Heather had experimented adding bananas, nuts, flavorings, and various other ingredients to the waffle batter. John was helping her imagination along with suggestions of his own, and they already had a pile of waffles warming in the oven that was big enough to feed an army. David and Jim were working out in the ice room, and then planned on taking advantage of an early soak in the hot tub. John Jr. and Melinda had arrived late the night before with the kids and had been exhausted with the long day traveling. Today's breakfast would be the mini-Thanksgiving celebration with Waldo and Lilly before they took off for Washington.

Lilly finished packing the last minute things into her suitcase and headed for the kitchen to find the busy life that she loved. "I'm sure going to miss you all," she said as she looked around the room. "Heather, did you put the secret ingredient in the waffles?"

"Sure did Aunt Lilly," Heather answered.

"Is Lanie here yet?" Lilly asked.

"I don't think she ever left," Karen replied rather softly.

This revelation stopped Lilly in her tracks. Looking from Karen to Heather she stuttered, "What...what's going on? Where is she?"

Heather giggled, "Oh, Aunt Lilly don't worry, she slept on the couch in my room last night. It was late when we finished the movie and we didn't want to see her drive home so late so we talked her into staying. Right now she's upstairs making beds."

"Whew, well alright now that my heart is beating again. When are we eating?"

"Just as soon as John and Melinda get out of bed. I've already pounded on their door," replied Heather.

When everyone was finally together and seated Waldo said grace. Karen slipped her hand into John's under the table, her heart feeling complete and satisfied in the midst of her family and friends. John responded with a little squeeze as he took in the view of his family and grandchildren with a grateful heart.

John Jr. was a bit grumpy as he often was when he was too tired and Heather began teasing him a bit, knowing that he would get even with her later. Melinda had survived the trip ok but could feel the effects. She kept shifting to find a comfortable position in her pregnant state. Tyler and Kristen were full of questions about the lodge, not quite familiar with their new surroundings yet. Karen promised them that she would explore the lodge later in the afternoon with them.

David was trying to encourage a fishing excursion, including Heather and Lanie. Jim was all for arranging some time with Lanie included, relieved that it was David who suggested the women come with them. Lanie had appeared at the breakfast table wearing jeans and a t-shirt but even this casual attire didn't dim her classic beauty. As she boldly took the vacant seat next to Jim, Lilly and Karen exchanged a knowing look. Lilly was glad to visit with all of them, and of course anxious to watch the new romance, but in her heart she was thinking of her grandchildren. She was looking forward to being in Washington for Thanksgiving, but at the same time she was wishing she wouldn't have to miss anything here.

As the young people started to scatter about their various activities Lilly insisted on hugs from everyone. With tears in her eyes she threw her arms around Karen just as she heard Waldo's diesel engine roar to life. "Ok, I've got to go. You know how antsy he gets when we have a drive ahead."

Returning her friend's hug, Karen replied, "Go on, we'll be fine. Give those babies a big kiss for me and call when you get there. OK?"

"OK. All I can say is we better figure a way to get them here for Christmas. I don't think I can handle another Holiday away from everyone I love. I just have this feeling that it's important that we all be together this year."

"I know, Lilly, I have the same feeling. Now get out of here before Waldo goes to Washington without you."

CHAPTER 29

Karen was going through the checklist in her head for the Thanksgiving dinner. Turkey, dressing, mashed potatoes, rolls, Waldorf salad, Chinese cabbage salad, six pies…

"Did Aunt Lilly let you have her dressing recipe?" asked Heather.

"Yes, and we have all of the ingredients ready to go," answered her mother.

"When are you going to start the rolls?"

"I'm not; Nona is bringing dinner rolls and the cranberries. All we have left to do right now is finish setting the table. In the morning we'll get the turkey in the oven and peel potatoes. We can do everything else in just a couple of hours."

"The china looks really classy with the centerpiece Lanie made," commented Heather. "Lets fold the napkins special…I learned a new way, let me show you."

Karen struck a match and lit the cinnamon scented candle that Lilly had given her. Somehow it seemed to help fill the missing piece Karen felt in her heart. And it was only appropriate that the scent of cinnamon be in the kitchen…if Lilly were here she would have created a new aroma by now. Maybe that's why I have the feeling that I've forgotten something, she thought.

"I can't even remember a Thanksgiving that Lilly and I didn't spend together," said Karen with a longing look in her eye. But her thoughts were soon busy with the day. All afternoon was spent with Tyler and Kristen making little turkeys with a mound of colored construction paper, scissors and glue spread out over the kitchen table. Each place setting at the table would have a little turkey with each persons name on it.

"Aunt Heather wants to sit by David," said Kristen in a matter of fact way. "And I want to sit on the other side of her."

"Ok," agreed Tyler, "but I want to sit next to Grandpa and Grandma will want to sit on the other side of him."

"No, you dummy. Don't you know anything? Grandma and Grandpa have to sit at the ends of the table."

"They do?" Tyler asked with a puzzled frown on his face.

"Uh huh. That's because they are the oldest," Kristen said with a superior attitude.

Heather had to choke back a laugh with this revelation and calmly corrected her niece, "Honey, they sit at the ends of the table because they are the head of the family."

Tyler was silent for a moment then asked, "Well it's a good thing Uncle Waldo and Aunt Lilly aren't here. We would have a pretty strange looking table."

Karen smiled to herself, listening to their interactions reminded her of when John and Heather were young.

"Don't forget Esther and Jimmie will be here," Karen suggested just as the phone rang. Picking it up Karen answered brightly, "Happy Thanksgiving!" And she wasn't a bit surprised to hear Lilly's voice echo back the greeting. Karen had been waiting for her friend to call all morning. It seemed like a week instead of two days ago that Lilly and Waldo had left and the brief call Lilly made to let her know they had arrived safe and sound wasn't long enough to fill her in on everything going on.

"How are the babies?" Karen asked before Lilly could get another word in. As she listened to her friend rave on about how bright and smart and beautiful the triplets were Karen was busting to tell her the latest about Jim and Lanie. "What's the name of the love hormone…serotonin?" asked Karen. "Well anyway…the stuff is bouncing off the walls here. I don't think Lanie has admitted yet that's she's falling, but it's really pretty obvious to me. Oh Lilly, I wish you were here to see the look on her face. I've never seen her like this before. The four of them went into town exploring yesterday and Lanie and Heather couldn't stop talking when they got back. They were non-stop through dinner and way into the night. They brought back pictures from the photo booth at the store. The guys were dressed as trappers and Heather and Lanie dressed up as dance hall girls and were sitting on the guy's laps. And Jim had his arms completely around Lanie and they looked pretty comfortable. Other than that, John Sr. and John Jr. got to spend time together, and the kids and I finished the holiday baking so Melinda could rest. David really is good to Heather...I like him a lot. And I've never seen Jim act like this. He was very reserved when we lived in Louisiana. Except for the time he wrestled that alligator anyway."

Lilly giggled at the memory of their usually calm pastor jumping into the bayou and rescuing the little girl that had fallen from the dock. As the alligator roared at the loss of his anticipated snack Jim had pulled the massive beast under the churning water. When Jim had been pulled from the water his white shirt was in shreds and Lilly and Karen both had admired the muscles that rippled with each ragged breath he took.

Revived again after sharing everything with her best friend, Karen busied herself with the dinner preparations. The guys were whooping and hollering in the main room with the football game, and Heather and Lanie were playing hide and seek with the kids. Melinda squeezed into one of the stools at the center island and began slicing celery for the veggie tray.

"I really like David and Jim," commented Melinda. "I think they're both family material." Pausing briefly she smiled at her mother-in-law, "Lanie doesn't stand a chance does she?"

Karen laughed, "Nope, not when Lilly and I both are working on it. Now what's happening with you, honey? I haven't had a chance to really talk to you since you've been here. You look healthy, but I still have the feeling something's wrong. Tell me if I'm meddling, OK?"

"You know me too well, Karen. The baby and I are fine, but I'm worried about John. He won't tell me anything but I know something is up at work. I'm so glad he agreed to come here for the Holiday. Maybe..."

The doorbell chimes interrupted Melinda and the Lodge was filled with the laughter of children as Kristen and Tyler greeted Jimmie and Esther.

As Nona came into the kitchen carrying a basket of fragrant rolls Karen gave Melinda a quick reassuring hug, "We'll talk more later. Try not to worry." Then she rushed to greet her guests.

Karen's eyes met John Sr.'s from across the room and she once again felt that her heart was so full it could burst. Her soul was content with the knowledge that comes from living life, loving and being loved, and the appreciation for the family and friends that surrounded her. She smiled as she took in the aromas, the laughter of children, and the spark of new love that filled the lodge. Picking up the video camera she pointed it towards Lanie who was introducing her Grandma Anna, knowing that Lilly wouldn't want to miss a single thing.

CHAPTER 30

"I've missed you so much," Karen admitted to Lilly. She hugged her and then took her coat to hang it on the coat rack for her. "It just wasn't the same without you here," she continued excitedly as she helped her pull her boots off and almost fell over before she succeeded in shaking the remaining snow onto the throw rug.

"I have pictures…" teased Lilly.

"Oooh give them to me. I can't wait to see how they've grown," Karen said practically snatching the large packet from Lilly's hands as she took them out of her bag. Flipping through them rapidly Karen grew silent and when she looked up at Lilly again there was no mistaking the glimmer of tears in her soft green eyes. "Lilly, they are so beautiful. I know you said they were but I had no idea…I want to hold them and rock them and touch them."

Smiling serenely back at Karen, Lilly replied, "They are unbelievable. They have Jamie's dark hair and eyes. Chase has Kelsi's disposition but Austin and Dallas are Jamie through and through. Chase is going to have his hands full keeping up with those two."

The two friends spent the next hour quietly looking at pictures until Lilly had answered every question Karen could possibly think to ask about the triplets, and the ranch and Lilly's family in Washington. Finally as they came close to exhausting the baby topic Lilly asked about the Thanksgiving romance and Karen slyly answered. "We videotaped the whole day, Lilly, want to watch it?"

"Are you kidding, of course I do! Do we have time before making dinner? Never mind…we'll make time."

"I have everything ready for dinner anyway," Karen answered.

The whole morning, while waiting for Lilly and Waldo to return, Karen had worked diligently putting together her special lemon cake with cream cheese frosting. As soon as that was in the oven she thawed out steaks to marinate in a mesquite flavor. The twice-baked potatoes were made and ready to go into the oven about the same time as the steaks would go on the grill.

"Where is everyone anyway?" asked Lilly.

"The four of them went out snow shoeing. They should be back any time," answered Karen.

The two settled in on one of the couches in the main room, huddled close to the TV. They giggled like little girls as they watched Heather and John make faces into the camera. The special smiles and looks that passed between Lanie and Jim were not lost on these two and when Jim watched Lanie carry the potatoes to the dining table from the kitchen the camera caught a look of pure passion in his eyes that had nothing to do with potatoes or turkey, or thanksgiving for that matter.

"Oooh, did you see that Karen? Did I imagine that or did our good pastor undress that girl with his eyes?"

"Yep, Lilly, that's the second time I've seen it. I was coming in behind her with the turkey and if John hadn't been right there I probably would have dropped the platter. I'll swear the dining room windows steamed up and it had nothing to do with the weather outside or inside," Karen replied giggling at the memory.

"Oh what have we done?" Lilly giggled in reply.

"I can't believe you two." The deep scolding voice came from behind them. They quickly turned around to find John Jr. standing there with a shocked look on his face.

"Oh, it hasn't been that long since you were in those shoes," replied his mother.

"But this is our pastor," he argued.

Lilly and Karen exchanged a mischievous grin.

"Ok, we'll try to be good," soothed Lilly.

"Would you be a dear and light the barbeque?" asked Karen. "We're almost done watching our video tape and I know how well you can barbeque a steak."

John Jr. headed for the kitchen with his eyebrows raised, shaking his head.

Karen and Lilly continued giggling conspiratorially as they turned the TV off and then followed him to the kitchen and began putting together the dinner that Karen had prepared earlier.

"Karen...I really think the triplets could make it for Christmas," whispered Lilly with a hopeful look as she took the steak from the refrigerator.

The steaks and potatoes were eaten with relish and David and Jim split the last piece of lemon cake even as Waldo looked longingly at it himself.

The weather had turned colder on Thanksgiving Day and Karen was glad she had talked John Jr., David and Jim into putting up some of the Christmas decorations on Friday. The winter snow drifted deep around the lodge. The colored lights lining the roofline reflected onto the new snow, almost creating an aurora borealis of its own. And the inside of the lodge was now filled with new fragrances and familiar Christmas music. But best of all, it was filling up with the people that Lilly and Karen loved and their hearts were fully blessed with the presence of each one there.

Lilly was busy in the kitchen preparing for the next meals, and Waldo sat in the rocking chair in front of the fire reading his latest fishing magazine.

Karen and John had retreated to the back of the ice room and sat cuddled up in the love seat, talking about how it was rather ironic that they were here in the tropical atmosphere of the "ice room" but the ice was on the other side of the windows. The sky was dark most of the time now, but the lighting in the firewood shelters allowed them to watch the flakes gather on the branches of the larger trees and form their own unique work of art.

The scene suddenly reminded Karen of a childhood memory. "John, every year my aunt would create snow sculptures in the back yard of her rural home in Idaho. Aunt Mae had gotten quite good at the project over the years, and often would have her picture in the local paper next to the sculptures she had created...I wish you could have seen them."

"Wow..." he answered thoughtfully.

"Look," Karen said, her eyes filled with the delight of a child. "The A-frame roofs you and Waldo built to protect the firewood almost looks like a stable for a nativity."

Karen shared the details of her memory and it wasn't long before the two had their creativity in full bloom. The paths to the firewood shelters had been kept clear, and the first shelter was almost empty now. Waldo had installed lights in the rafters, and it would make a perfect place for a nativity scene. All tummies were filled with hot soup and rolls. Down coats, warm boots, and hats and gloves were located for everyone as Karen urged everyone out into the cold snow.

"I hope everyone went potty before they came out here," said Lilly as she shivered with the first blast of the snowy chill. John and Karen's enthusiasm was catching, and it wasn't long before the scene took on its basic shapes.

Teamwork was the key, and the first step was to pile big snowballs on top of each other where Mary, Joseph, and the other characters would be. The women directed the placement of the bases for the wise men and the animals. The men lifted the larger snowballs and placed them according to the heights they needed. Lanie and her older brothers hung branches just under the edge of the roof to give it a more rustic look, and Waldo helped them string clear Christmas lights through the branches to accent the roofline. Jimmie and Esther spread more braches out on the floor, and found a piece of rope for the donkey's tail. When Mary's character toppled over, Jimmie decided that she should be able to sit down anyway, and found a wooden box for her character to sit on. Karen and Lilly found a large piece of blue fabric to drape around Mary, and a tan color for Joseph. The wise men were draped in royal shades of red, blue and purple, and Esther had found some large jewels for them to wear. John sprayed the faces of the characters with a little bit of water to give them more stability and then sculpted their features, arms and legs. Jim helped Lanie shape a lamb while Heather and David created another donkey. After several hours of intense labor the scene came alive. The characters took shape and became almost life like from a bit of a distance. Waldo and John adjusted the lighting so that a spotlight was on the cradle. Tyler and Kristen reverently placed Kristen's baby doll wrapped in a soft blue blanket, in the manger. They all helped each other with the finishing details and then gathered as a group a few feet back so that they could take in the whole scene. Lilly and Karen once again shared their familiar looks of gratitude.

Jim didn't even realize that he had slipped his arm around Lanie as they all stood back to admire the creation…it just came so natural.

Lilly's hot chocolate hit the spot. Each cup was topped with whipped cream and a sprinkle of toffee crumbs. It warmed everyone's hearts as well as their half frozen fingers. Lilly and Waldo had brought back several boxes of the special applet candy that was made near Jamie and Kelsi's ranch. The sweet confection went wonderfully with the hot chocolate.

"Heather, why don't you just stay until Christmas?" asked Karen. "It's not very far away now, and then we wouldn't have to worry about the weather causing travel problems for you."

"I'd love to Mom, but I can't. David has a nursery full of poinsettias and I promised him I would help deliver them this year."

"Ok, it was worth a try," Lilly replied. "You will bring David back with you for Christmas. And Jim too, won't you?"

"There's no way we'd miss out on it," David replied. "We'll be here. And I understand Santa stops at each and every chimney in this place?"

"He sure does," said Waldo.

The four younger children looked at Waldo and David with wonder in their eyes, trying to imagine such a thing.

"You'll see," Waldo promised with a twinkle in his eyes.

With all her heart Karen was hoping Melinda's pregnancy wouldn't keep them away and Lilly had actually said that she thought the triplets could make it. She couldn't wait for her and Lilly to decorate the suites for Christmas. Each suite would have its own Christmas tree in varying themes. The polar bear suite had a white faux fur comforter and pillow shams and its Christmas tree would be decorated entirely with miniature polar bears. Karen's personal favorite was the Angel suite. The oversized down comforter was white satin with pale blue celestial beings embroidered throughout. That particular Christmas tree would be flocked white and would be adorned with tiny crystal angels. As much as she loved having her family here; she was looking forward to catching up with Lilly and working at the job they loved. Catching Lilly's eye across the room she was drawn to the corner where Jim and Lanie had retreated to talk.

Jim knew he had only a short time to find out if Lanie felt the same way he did, and he had to ask her if she wanted him to come back for Christmas.

4

CHAPTER 31

The glow of the lights on the lodge could be seen from the village. Waldo and John had reluctantly installed another two generators to accommodate the whims of their wives. After a bit of begging, and promises of an endless supply of Christmas cookies, the lodge was brimming with decorations and Christmas cheer. The hope of having all of their family together for the holiday had driven the two women to all lengths of extravagance.

Karen finally was able to carry out her fantasy for gingerbread boys and girls. She had dreamed of the project for years, and this was the perfect large kitchen for the decorating project. The theme was carried out though the room with fabrics and scents and ornaments of every kind. Gingerbread garlands graced the windows, and a great gingerbread house sat on a small table close to the fireplace.

The main room was filled with the scent of pine from the ten foot tall Christmas tree that was placed in front of the main windows. Even though each suite had it's own tree this one was THE family tree and was decorated with the Christmas balls that commemorated each year Lilly and Waldo had been married, numbering twenty nine this year. They were joined by the ornaments that Karen had collected, the glass nativity and angels that were a gift from Lilly's oldest sister before she died, and various ornaments made by Heather, John Jr. and Jamie over the years.

The office was being used as a wrapping station, and it seemed that a new delivery arrived almost every day. Packages had arrived from Heather so that she wouldn't have to carry them with her, and it was driving Karen and Lilly absolutely crazy with curiosity. They carefully checked each package before placing it under the tree.

Esther and Jimmie visited with Lanie every day that their mother would allow it. The lodge turned into a very magical place for them, and they spent hours examining each ornament and decoration. Of course Lilly had a tendency to spoil them with hot chocolate and cookies, and Karen always seemed to have a game or art project to entertain them.

Esther had Jimmie convinced that little Christmas elves came out every night and added to the decorations, and so the first thing he did when he arrived was to go on a treasure hunt, looking for something new. Of course Waldo went along with the game, making sure that Jimmie would actually find something. Esther was participating to the point of believing it too even though she had been the one to make it up.

To Lilly and Karen's delight, Lanie was e-mailing Jim every day. It was pretty much guaranteed that she would head straight for the computer at 10:00 every morning and as Lilly hung the mistletoe over the back door she dreamt of the romance that would come to life here this Christmas.

Arnie and Ernie were very busy training their dogs for the Iditarod, but somehow they had found time for an extra project. With Waldo and John's help they had created a heated cabin to fit onto a special sled. This was already being used to entertain the guests, and next year they would have a second sled to accommodate the demand that was anticipated. The tips tended to be substantial, and definitely added to the boys motivation to expand the business.

Everything seemed perfect, and there was no reason at all to think that the events they hoped for and dreamed of wouldn't come true.

CHAPTER 32

After an early meal of potato soup and corn bread, it was movie time. Excitement was in the air and everyone gathered in the main room to watch the old classic they had seen so many times.

As Bing Crosby's voice filled the large room Karen thought she heard Waldo's barely imperceptible groan. Glancing his way she saw Lilly snuggle into Waldo's arms a little closer. Smiling to herself, Karen remembered that Waldo always said he hated this show but never failed to watch it with Lilly every year. As a matter of fact they would probably see it a few more times before the holiday was over, but this was the first traditional viewing.

The fireplace crackled and the tree glimmered, enhancing the perfect environment they had created. Large bowls of popcorn had been distributed and as Karen settled down with John in the overstuffed recliner she glanced around the room and once again the feeling of awe came over her as she tried to contemplate how blessed her life was.

Just as the movie ended the phone rang and Karen ran to answer it. Lilly could hear the frantic undertones in Karen's voice as she tried to sooth and calm Melinda on the other end of the phone line. John Jr. hadn't been able to share any details about the trouble that had been happening in his world, but now it seemed to be reaching a new level of danger. The phone calls and e-mails had been giving hints of the trouble for quite some time, but now a new level of urgency had been reached. Both Karen and Lilly knew something was very, very wrong. The feeling had been growing stronger every day, and now with this phone call it was impossible to ignore the fact that it was entering into the perfect little Christmas world they had created.

After Melinda promised they would call back in an hour when John Jr. came home from work, Karen hung up and confided everything she knew to her friends. Lilly brewed a pot of coffee and the four sat around the kitchen table to review the facts that they did know, and the possible solutions to protect their family.

Melinda had shared that she wasn't willing to leave Oregon without her husband, who insisted he had to stay and finish his job. She was torn between the safety of her children and the need to keep her family together. The conflict between the two of them was more than she could take...and she needed to take action now. She hadn't been able to convince John to leave, and neither had he been able to convince her that she needed to leave without him. But the one thing she knew for sure was that her children's grandparents were capable of protecting them in another location more than she and John Jr. could ensure their safety at home. And that's why she had called out of sheer desperation. Finally it was decided. John and Waldo would go to Newport as quickly as possible and bring back Tyler and Kristen to the safety of the lodge. Besides, it was only another two weeks until Christmas and they would be coming anyway. With matters decided, Waldo put Tyson out for the night and John double-checked the locks on all the doors and windows. Waldo and John went to bed for the night knowing they had to get up early to head for Oregon.

Lilly, sensing that Karen had not told them everything kissed Waldo goodnight on the stairs and then returned to where her friend sat gazing at the glowing embers in the fireplace.

After a few moments Karen began to speak, "A stranger approached Kristen in the school play yard just the day before last. He asked what her name was and what her parent's names were and she had started to answer just as her teacher took notice and asked him to leave. The man left and disappeared quickly. When the teacher had reported this to John Jr. he had Kristen looking at pictures in the police station that same day."

Karen shivered slightly in spite of the warmth of the room, and finally Lilly spoke trying to reassure and comfort her friend.

"Karen, they're going to be OK. Waldo and John will bring the kids back here tomorrow, and Melinda too if they can pry her loose. And as soon as John Jr. can come he'll be here too. We're all going to be together for Christmas. I know it in my heart. And Karen, I also know in my heart that your son is going to be safe. You raised a smart young man and he's not going to take chances with his family."

"You're right, Lilly. He wouldn't do that." Drawing a deep breath Karen continued, "I'm OK now. We better get to bed; we've got more wrapping to do tomorrow before those kids get here."

In an effort to cheer each other a bit, Lilly lit the candles and Karen made sure all of the Christmas lights were on. Music played throughout the room as Dylan's smooth voice sang familiar carols. However, it just wasn't the same as it had been the week before. Jimmie and Esther weren't there to distract them, and Lanie was off doing errands of her own. Usually there was no problem at all to find things to do when Waldo and John were gone, but now the lodge seemed strangely empty. Tyson had been in the kitchen for a while, but now he had been put back in his pen for the night.

The wind beat against the windows and doors, and the two shivered at the same time, listening for the unusual. Lilly put another log on the fire.

"We have one more present to wrap," suggested Karen in an effort to change the atmosphere. "I finished the crocheted blanket for Grandma Anna earlier today."

"This is the first time I've actually felt alone in the wilderness," admitted Lilly, as she went to get the wrapping paper for the large box that contained the ivory and mauve blanket that Karen had been working on since she met Grandma Anna.

"I know Lilly, I'm jumpy too," Karen replied. "Let's get this present wrapped then we'll make some tea and after that we can bake gingerbread cookies. That should take our mind off things."

"Getting a little bossy, aren't you? Isn't that my job?" Lilly said as her laughter lightened the mood in the room.

"That must be where I get it from," Karen laughed in return.

"What time is it anyway?" Karen inquired.

"Oh my…it's midnight already," replied Lilly.

"Do you remember when we used to stay out until around three? We only went home then because we had to be there before your mom got up for work. Then we would take the back road so that we could coast down hill into the driveway. You'd turn off the motor and quietly coast your little VW into your parking spot and then we'd tip toe into the house and down the stairs to your room."

"And do you remember the night Daddy moved the coffee table into the middle of our path?" Lilly asked slyly with a new twinkle in her eye and a giggle.

"The part I remember is his deep voice coming out of the pitch black calling me clumsy," Karen said with a bit of embarrassment on her face.

"You know, I really don't want to go to my room by myself tonight, let's make a pizza and have an old fashioned slumber party! We can put on our jammies and make pop corn and watch a movie and eat buck eyes all night."

"Great! I think we have some hot dogs in the freezer," Karen suggested.

"Oh, no you don't…Pepperoni, black olives, mushrooms, and that's all. And don't try to hide a wiener under the mushrooms either like you used to!"

Karen smiled but didn't answer as she reached for the box of pizza mix.

After getting their fill of pizza and laughs, the two settled down to nibbling on popcorn and watching the movie. It wasn't long after they started a second movie that Karen looked over to find Lilly sound asleep in her down sleeping bag.

"I always could stay up longer than anybody else," Karen whispered right before she drifted off herself.

Lilly shivered from the cold she felt on her arm that was outside of her sleeping bag. She pulled it inside and snuggled in the warmth, missing Waldo. Tired of waiting for Karen to wake up she started making a lot of noise to encourage her. Besides, it was her turn to make coffee.

"Ok, ok…" Karen finally said sleepily. "I'll get up and make the coffee. But can you push my slippers over to me please?"

Karen got up and paused in front of the window. "Lilly, it snowed a lot last night! Come and look."

"You just want to get me out of this warm sleeping bag, I'm not falling for that one," Lilly said.

"No, really…" Karen insisted.

Grabbing her wool robe from the back of a chair Lilly stumbled to the window, brushing her dark hair from her eyes. As her eyes widened she turned to Karen, "There must be five feet, Karen. What are we going to do?"

"Lilly, the guys can't get in with this much snow. Do you know how to drive the snowplow?"

"Are you kidding, that's Waldo's baby. He wouldn't let me touch it," Lilly answered.

Standing and looking at the winter wonderland in awe they were both brought back to reality by the sound of sleigh bells. As the elegant red sleigh pulled up in front of the lodge Lanie, Arnie and Ernie waved at them. Arnie and Lanie hopped out and began shoveling their way to the Lodge door while Ernie drove the sleigh to the shop where Waldo's snowplow was kept.

Lilly pulled her robe tighter around herself, feeling slightly embarrassed to be seen in her pajamas.

It wasn't long before the roar of the diesel engine could be heard making it's way down the driveway to the main road.

"Karen, I think we better get some breakfast going," Lilly said. "Those kids are going to be hungry."

"Sorry, Lilly, but I think we probably ought to make lunch, or maybe brunch? It's almost noon."

"No, I don't believe it," Lilly said in shock. "The dark hours have really messed up my sense of time."

As Lanie and Arnie reached their destination, Karen and Lilly pulled open the massive log doors that graced the entrance to the lodge. Pushing Lanie inside along with a good helping of blowing snow, Arnie pulled the doors shut behind him and began shoveling his way to Tyson's kennel beside the garage.

Lanie unloaded her bags onto the kitchen table and pulled a steaming casserole out of her heat bag. She took off the lid and the aroma filled the room. "Somehow I didn't think you two would be cooking today without your husbands around. Hope you like lasagna," she said with a comforting smile. "Then if the snow lets up a little we'll take you for a sleigh ride."

It had been hours since they had last heard from Waldo and John. A massive amount of snow had fallen, and apparently there had been some trouble. But once again they had been denied the details, and waiting and praying was all that they were able to do. They had spent the day doing the usual chores and enjoying Lanie's company. It was a lot easier to focus on the holiday preparations when they could put their minds on the romance they were expecting to happen. At their gentle urging Lanie had disclosed that she was receiving two e-mails from Pastor Jim each day since he had returned to New Orleans. From the wistful look on Lanie's face they were assured that the e-mails were not going unanswered. The wind outside had picked up considerably and Lanie and her brothers returned home before the promised sleigh ride.

Lilly had insisted that Tyson stay inside with them for now even though Ernie had assured her that he would be fine. She not only wanted the protection and company the dog could provide but also worried that she and Karen wouldn't be able to make it to the kennel to feed him.

"Maybe we'll be stuck here by ourselves for Christmas," commented Karen with a bit of fear in her voice.

"Now don't be so dreary, you know we'll hear from them any minute now," replied Lilly confidently. "Your mom always said where there's a will, there's a way. And besides, if we had to be by ourselves for Christmas, you know we'd make the best of it."

Lilly had sounded very convincing, but they both shivered at the thought. The two had spent enough hours in worry that they both felt tired and worn out. Mixed with the lack of sleep, they felt the stress in their shoulders and a pulling sensation in their stomachs.

"My eyes feel dry," complained Lilly as she closed them and tried to relax.

"I know, I almost feel dizzy," said Karen.

Now that the symptoms had been identified, they knew what they needed to do. Lilly made grilled ham, cheese and tomato sandwiches and Karen prepared a grated carrot and apple salad. They settled on the chairs in the ice room and made sure all of the lights were on. They had heard about the cabin fever people got in Alaska, and had every intention of warding off such a dreadful thing.

"I feel better already," said Karen as she finished the first half of her sandwich and poured another cup of tea for her and Lilly.

CHAPTER 33

Lilly stretched out under her down comforter, halfway expecting to encounter Waldo's always-cold feet. "That was the best sleep I've had for a long time," she mumbled to herself, "I wonder what time it is." She rolled over to look at the clock but stopped still as she listened to a strange sound coming from outside the lodge. Jumping up and slipping her feet into her slippers at the same time she pulled her robe on, she hurried to the window just in time to see Waldo and John hop down from the sleigh. Rushing down the hall she knocked loudly on Karen's door. "They're back," she called excitedly.

Tyler and Kristen had had a grand time in the sleigh. They had pretended they were the king and queen parading through the town giggling and waving as if they were the most elegant children in the world. Waldo and John had gone along with the imaginary story, adding to it by appointing themselves as the guards. Lanie had equipped them with warming bags, blankets and hot chocolate. The children were all bundled up in the down blankets and Karen pulled Kristen out of her little nest while Lilly helped Tyler down from the sleigh. The children's eyes were wide with amazement. The lights of the lodge could be seen for miles, and they had pretended they were traveling to the castle. Now it seemed that they had arrived at the grandest place in the world.

"Are the babies here yet?" asked Kristen.

"How long will it be until mom and dad get here?" inquired Tyler.

"Don't you worry," soothed Karen. They'll all be here soon and do we ever have a surprise for you!"

"Will there be a banquet?" asked Kristen.

"We promise," Lilly answered hugging Kristin tight, "There will be a banquet fit for a King and Queen, or at least a Prince and Princess."

Turning to Waldo she threw her arms around him, "We were so worried. What happened? How are John and Melinda?"

"One question at a time, Lilly my love," He said hugging her tightly.

That evening, the children ate the hearty chicken and noodle soup that Lilly had been saving for such an occasion. Karen's homemade bread complemented the meal, and then they topped it off with gingerbread man cookies. They all settled in the main room in front of the fire, and John read the Christmas stories from the Bedtime Story Book Lilly had had since she was a child herself. Tyler and Kristen were exhausted and asleep before the second story was finished. John and Karen each picked up a child and took them to the Aurora Borealis room, which was the closest to theirs and tucked them in. Returning to the main room Lilly and Karen were all over Waldo and John with questions.

"What happened?" demanded Lilly.

"Are John and Melina ok?" Asked Karen.

John spoke with careful words. "We did our best to talk Melinda into coming with us, but finally we gave in when she promised to stay with her parents until John Jr. would be able to stay with her. "

Waldo couldn't stand it any longer and started to tell more of the story. "John Jr. happened upon some illegal activities last year, and since it involved some pretty important people in Oregon politics he had to be especially careful who he trusted. Karen, it seems that for over a year your son has been working with the FBI and now that we've taken his children out of harms way and Melinda is safe at her folk's house there's going to be no stopping him. He is going to bring all that corruption crashing down around those crooked politicians. He's probably making the arrests this very minute!"

"We just might see it on the news in the morning," agreed John.

Lilly's brown eyes mirrored the fear in Karen's green ones as they looked to each other for reassurance. Their hearts knew they would be saying extra prayers tonight.

"He's going to be alright Karen," John said with confidence as he took her hand in his and looked into her eyes.

Karen got up and softly went to the Aurora Borealis room. She found her grandchildren sleeping peacefully with sweet innocence on their faces. With a gentle touch she softly moved Kristen's hair away from her face, and lightly touched her cheek. As she turned to tuck the blanket around Tyler's feet, Lilly tiptoed in to join her.

"Aren't they just amazing?" whispered Karen. "These precious, sweet children are the result of the love John and I have. I can hardly comprehend it."

"I know exactly what you're feeling," Lilly whispered back.

CHAPTER 34

Lilly finished stacking the last of the disposable diapers on the closet shelf of the nursery. She straightened the blankets that hung on the ends of the cribs for the hundredth time, and grinned at Karen.

"They're going to be here today, but I can't wait another minute," Lilly said as she inhaled and held her breath for a moment.

"It looks like we have enough diapers for a whole year, are you sure they're just staying a couple of weeks?" Karen replied as she smiled back at her friend.

"I would keep them here for the rest of their lives if I could," Lilly answered smiling at her friend, "No, I take that back, Jamie and Kelsi have built a wonderful life for themselves and the babies and I wouldn't take that away from them for anything. I just wish they lived closer." Lilly's voice trailed off as she lovingly patted the soft huggable fluffy dog that Karen had just placed at the head of Chase's crib.

The two friends were interrupted then by the blare of the horn on Waldo's big diesel truck. Grabbing Karen by the hand Lilly pulled her toward the door and down the stairs, "They're here, Karen, they're here."

The front door was thrown open just before Karen and Lilly got there and John swept Karen up in his arms, hugging her tightly he twirled her around and exclaimed, "Do we have a surprise for you! Look who hitched a ride on the same plane as Jamie and Kelsi."

John had barely set her back on her feet when she was caught up again in the strong arms of her son. Laughing and hugging John Jr.,

Karen paused long enough to make sure Melinda was with him. Then pulling her daughter-in-law into their embrace she burst into tears. "This is the best Christmas present I've ever received. When Heather gets here tomorrow we'll be complete," Karen declared as she wiped away her tears and said a prayer of thanks in her heart for the safety of her son and daughter-in-law.

"Can I hold one of the babies, Grandma?" asked Kristen as she clung to her mother's leg.

"Maybe, honey, but Aunt Lilly gets to see them first," Karen answered.

Lilly was already cooing to her three adorable treasures as she unbuckled the belts on the car seats. "You've changed so much...just look at you. Let's get you in where it's warm and get this cute little snow suit off of you," she said as she picked up Austin and cradled her in her arms.

Ushering everyone in out of the cold and blowing snow, Karen took Chase from Kelsi and tried peering over Jamie's shoulder to get a look at Dallas.

"They all need to be changed, Mom," Jamie proclaimed rather loudly to Lilly as he juggled his daughter and the oversized diaper bag.

Coming in from putting the truck away, Waldo took Dallas from his son and seeing the frazzled look in Kelsi's eyes, he asked Kristen if she could show Jamie and Kelsi to their room while the rest of them entertained the babies for a while. He knew that once Karen and Lilly got their hands on the triplets they weren't likely to let them go for the rest of the day.

Reassured that the babies were in good hands, Jamie helped Kelsi unpack.

"Wow, I haven't been able to sit down in a quiet room forever," commented Kelsi to her husband as she relaxed and closed her eyes for a moment. "I think I'm going to like it here, but we'd better check on the kids to see if everything is alright."

"Of course they're alright. Mom's got them so you just relax," Jamie coaxed as he massaged her shoulders.

CHAPTER 35

Jamie and Kelsi opened the door to the nursery to find a lived in look, but no one was there. Curious, they made their way to the kitchen.

Lilly and Karen had the triplets on the table, each in a baby seat on a lazy susan. All three were bright eyed and cooing, loving the entertainment and the twinkling lights in the windows.

"Santa's coming," Lilly told them as if they could understand. "And he's bringing lots of toys for you, well…clothes anyway, but lots and lots of toys next year for sure." She looked up to see the surprised looks on her son and daughter in-law's faces.

"Mom, what are you doing with my children?" Jamie exclaimed, "If someone bumps them they could fly right off that counter."

"Calm down, Jamie. Your dad built this, come take a look," Lilly replied calmly.

When Jamie took a closer look he could see that the over sized solid wood lazy susan had been bolted to the top of the counter top from inside the oak cabinet and each baby seat was double bolted to the lazy susan.

As Waldo explained the materials and tools he used to build the contraption, Jamie looked up at him and grinned, "Good job. Guess you were paying attention to me all those years, weren't you Dad?"

"Who was paying attention to who, Jamie?" Waldo questioned.

Lilly interrupted their good natured bantering about who had trained who in the art of building and construction, "We have a schedule made out…you can have any slot you want, but I think we have it all covered with everyone here. Heather wants the first late shift and Lanie wants the early one. If that's OK with you, Kelsi? The Polar Bear suite on the other side of the nursery has two queen size beds and the girls thought they would bunk in there together and take care of the babies through the night. Then Waldo and I can get them up in the morning and John and Karen can have them through the day."

"But when's my turn?" Kelsi asked with a worried look in her eyes.

Hoping to reassure her daughter-in-law that she only had her interest at heart Lilly spoke urgently, "Kelsi, honey, you can have them whenever you want them. We just thought since you're here with us we can help and take some of the load off of you. You and Jamie can rest and go snowmobiling or sleigh riding."

Kelsi looked relieved and had perked up considerably at the mention of the sleigh, "Sleigh, do you mean dog or horse drawn?"

"I knew that would get her, Lilly." Waldo said, "It's a horse drawn sleigh and the horses actually belong to Lanie's brothers Ernie and Arnie, but I'll bet they would let you drive if you ask."

"OK, when do we go?" Kelsi replied suddenly looking bright and refreshed.

"They should be here in about half an hour," answered Lilly with a new twinkle in her eye.

"Where's Karen anyway?" asked Kelsi.

"I don't know, but she's around here somewhere," answered Lilly.

Waldo had a thoughtful look on his face as he asked, "Where's John?"

"I don't know but he's around here somewhere," answered Lilly again as she gave Waldo a knowing look.

John Jr. entered the kitchen and gently tickled each of the six little feet in the baby seats and threatened to twirl them around.

"Oh no you don't, if they spit up you're going to clean it up," said Kelsi knowing his playful nature.

"Where's Mom anyway?" asked John Jr.

"She's around here somewhere, why don't you sit down and try out this cheese ball," coaxed Lilly as she placed the platter on the table.

"Where's my cheese ball?" Jamie asked

Lilly feigned exasperation, "Can't you two share this one?"

"OK" Jamie said grudgingly as he sat down across from John and pulled the platter to the middle. "Just remember, Mom, I have to have my own on Christmas Eve. What's for dinner tonight anyway?"

At the mention of dinner Waldo's ears perked up as Lilly replied, "Stew, sourdough rolls and apple pie."

Seeing the grin on his dad's face Jamie couldn't help but reply, "Why do we always have to have apple pie two days before Christmas?"

"Because the pumpkin, mincemeat and pecan pies are for Christmas," Kelsi answered for Lilly. She had heard this discussion for the last eight years and knew Jamie's grumbling over the apple pie was a time honored family tradition as was the cheese ball Lilly would make special just for him for his Christmas Eve dinner.

Assured that her babies were in safe hands Kelsi went to get ready for the promised sleigh ride.

Waldo sat down at the table with John Jr. and Jamie and attempted to share in the crackers and cheese ball.

Finally getting his fill John Jr. pushed away from the table and asked again, "Aunt Lilly, where did you say Mom and Dad were?"

"I'm right here," Karen said as she came in the room with John Sr. right behind her.

She almost had a skip in her step and looked refreshed, but Lilly refrained from making any comment. She just smiled at the two.

"I understand Kelsi is going for a sleigh ride," said Karen. "Don't you think we better give her that one present a little early?"

Lilly replied, "Definitely. I'll go get it."

As soon as Kelsi came back she was presented with the gift. "Why do I get one early?"

"Just open it and you'll see," said Lilly.

She ripped open the package to find a beautiful wool scarf and hat set, "Oh Lilly, it's just perfect." Pulling the hat down over her silky brown hair and looping the scarf around her neck she snuggled into the warmth of the wool. "Thank you too, Karen. I know you had a hand in picking it out, I can always tell."

"Where's mine?" asked Jamie as he looked around for another package.

"Oh no, you don't. You have to wait for Christmas Eve just like everyone else."

"Oh, Mom, can't I open just one?" Jamie pleaded.

"No. If you get to open one then we have to let John and Melinda and Heather open one and if they get to open one then so do Kristen and Tyler and everything will just get out of hand. So…no one is opening early this year," Lilly answered sternly then seeing the hopeful look on Kristen and Tyler's faces fade she whispered to them, "Maybe just one later, OK?"

"Woo hoo did everyone hear that? Aunt Lilly said we could open all the presents right now," Tyler said with a shout as he ran for the mountain of presents waiting in the great room.

Seeing the grin on Jamie's face Lilly couldn't help but smile to herself, "Now see what you did, Jamie. You go straighten him out right now."

The sound of sleigh bells filled the air and before Lilly knew what was happening her only child had kissed her cheek and grabbing his wife's hand they were out the door and running for the waiting sleigh.

Lilly busied herself with the bottles for the next feedings, and Karen helped while they took turns entertaining the triplets. Kristen was given a promise that she could feed one of them in just a few minutes, and she was trying to choose which baby she wanted.

Lilly and Karen's eyes met and smiling at each other Lilly spoke, "Did you have a nice "nap" Karen?"

Giggling in return Karen blushed and replied, "I'll never tell, Lilly."

"I suppose you're going to tell me you were only talking?"

"Actually we were. John was filling me in on what John Jr. has been up to. I really need to talk to him. He told his dad that everything is OK now; they are no longer in danger. But I'll feel better when I hear it from him myself. Do you know where he is?"

"I think he went upstairs to check on Melinda," Lilly answered.

"Hmm," Karen mused, "I think I'll wait for him to come back down. They might be 'talking'."

Giggling at each other they began humming their own rendition of Jingle Bell Rock as the triplets watched with wide-eyed wonder.

Feeding triplets was quite a process. Chase would only let Kristen feed him, Dallas had spit up on Karen, and Austin just gulped hers down without a problem.

John Jr. and Melinda entered and surveyed the scene. "We thought maybe we could help with dinner tonight," Melinda offered.

"That would be wonderful," answered Lilly. "The stew is in the crock pot and the pies are in the warming oven, but we still need to have the biscuits made and a salad. Karen has to change her clothes and all three of these little people need to be changed now. We have to have everything in order before Kelsi gets back or she'll think we can't handle this."

As Karen and Lilly whisked the babies from the kitchen, Lilly with one in each arm, John and Melinda smiled at each other.

"Do we know how to make biscuits?" John whispered.

Shrugging her shoulders Melinda giggled and said hopefully, "Maybe there's a box of Bisquick here somewhere."

CHAPTER 36

Thinking she was up early enough to be the first one up, Karen slipped on her jeans and a warm sweater. Expecting to make coffee and start breakfast, she gave John a light kiss on the cheek and then quietly slipped out of the door. But to her surprise the little hallway table held a thermos pot of fresh coffee.

"Huh," she mumbled to herself. "Someone else is up earlier than I, and I think I know who it is!" Sure enough, she entered the kitchen to find Lanie putting another log on the fire. Lanie looked beautiful, as usual, and the firelight behind her outlined her beauty. She was wearing the wine red color again that looked so good on her, and she was in a warm energetic mood.

Karen smiled at her knowingly. "Expecting company today?" she teased.

Lanie blushed and then smiled back at her friend. "So are you."

"You're certainly up early," Lilly said as she joined them and poured three cups of coffee. She motioned for Karen to join her in the rocking chairs in front of the fire. "Karen, I'm so excited I can't stand it. We have always been so fortunate. Waldo and I have had a very happy life together and after John came back into your life, I finally saw the light of happiness in your eyes that had been missing for so many years. And now with this Lodge we have two successful businesses, and I didn't think it was possible to be happier. But now, just leaving those precious babies up in the nursery my heart feels like it's going to burst from happiness."

"I know, Lilly, every time I look at my grandchildren I somehow feel completed, especially now that their grandfather is in our lives. And

Heather's coming this morning, and tomorrow is Christmas Eve. And I'm so happy for you. Chase, Austin and Dallas are the sweetest, best babies I've ever known. I can't think of a better Christmas present for you."

Wiping the tears from her eyes, Lilly took a sip of coffee and with her usual energy declared, "Enough of this sadness, even if it is sweet sadness, it's Christmas!

"What's on the agenda for this morning? How early did you get up anyway?" asked Karen.

"You know babies…Lanie and I fed them about 4:00 and then we rocked them to sleep again. And Lanie was a natural." Lilly answered.

As they got up from the comfortable chairs the two women each took notice of the look on Lanie's face. The yearning was plain to see.

Lilly and Karen took their places at the kitchen counter. As Karen began cutting thick slabs of bacon Lilly started taking out the ingredients for her famous pecan waffles.

"Let's see, Waldo and John are going to the airport first thing to pick up Heather, David and Jim," Lilly said as she looked to see if the mention of Jim's name affected Lanie. "Oh, by the way, Waldo asked if we thought it would be OK if he and John Sr. took all of the younger men on a fishing trip tomorrow morning. What do you think? It is Christmas Eve but he said they should be back by noon."

Pausing briefly to take in the logistics of this last minute fishing trip, Karen finally nodded. "Sure, why not. We can put the finishing touches on the meal preparations and have a real teatime with our girls. Besides, when I talked to John Jr. last night he had his heart set on it. He seems like a different person here than he did in Oregon, and he could use some good fishin' fun. Do you think they'll take Tyler?"

"They would have a real battle on their hands if they tried to leave him again, and I don't think we need to worry about their safety this time," said Lilly. "Waldo and John have taken every precaution to satisfy our worries."

Heather's arrival was very festive. Her raspberry red coat and creamy white fur hat and mittens brought cheer to the season. It was obvious that she adored David and that he felt the same way about her. A few flakes of snow had settled on the blond hair that escaped her hat and her black boots were stylish to say the least.

"Oh, I found the mistletoe," she said as she pulled David directly under it, closed her eyes, and waited for the magic to happen.

Pastor Jim had already greeted Lanie with a friendly hug, and looked longingly at the mistletoe. Lanie blushed when she realized his intentions, but never the less allowed him to pull her under the mistletoe. Looking briefly into his eyes she stood on her tiptoes and boldly planted a kiss lightly on his lips. Lilly and Karen couldn't help but notice that Lanie's hand lingered just a moment longer in Jim's and Lilly was sure that she had seen Lanie squeeze his hand before she pulled away.

"Aunt Lilly, where are those babies?" Flustered but happy for the distraction, Lanie grabbed Heather's hand. "Come on I'll show you."

Heather and Lanie tip toed into the nursery and hovered over the sleeping babies.

"This one has to be Chase," said Heather. "He's the only one with a blue blanket."

"And this is Austin and over here is Dallas," continued Lanie.

"Can we wake them up?" asked Heather. "Will Kelsi be mad if I do? They are absolutely the most perfect, precious, babies I've ever seen in my life. And how do you tell them apart?" She whispered.

"See the little angel kiss on Dallas' ankle?" Lanie explained as she pulled the soft pink blanket slightly off of her foot to show her ankle. "They should be hungry in about another hour or so," Lanie informed her.

"Well, I guess I can let them sleep a little bit longer," Heather said reluctantly as she touched Austin's tiny little toes and continued to ponder the idea of waking them up.

"Come on let's get your stuff to our room. We're sharing the room right next door so we can take care of the babies at night and give Kelsi and Jamie a break."

Giggling to herself Heather added, "Mom and Aunt Lilly are pretty smart aren't they? Babies make great chaperones."

Blushing at that remark Lanie asked quietly, 'I don't want to put you in an awkward position Heather, but does Jim ever talk about me?"

"A better question, Lanie, would be does he ever STOP talking about you!"

Relieved of her worries, Lanie lightly skipped out of the room. Not paying much attention to where she was going, she stumbled into Jim, his arms full of suitcases.

"Oh I'm so sorry!" She said as she observed his muscular build that had held his load together.

"I brought Heather's luggage up, where would you like it?" Jim asked.

After taking a moment to pull herself together she stammered, "Heather and I are staying next door here in the Polar Bear room. Which one do you have?"

"The Kodiak suite?" Jim looked questioningly at Heather, "Or is that the one we had at Thanksgiving? Are we staying in the same one?"

Heather laughed in reply, "Nope the one you had at Thanksgiving is right across the hall from us. There's no way Aunt Lilly and Mom are going to let you two stay right across the hall."

"I remember now, I'm sure they intend for you to stay in the Moose Suite," said Lanie still flustered from her near collision with Jim. She had taken hold of his arm in the encounter, and the touch still penetrated her being as she tried to gain control and show them to their room. She wanted to touch him again and pondered what would be appropriate.

David put Heather's luggage just inside the Polar Bear room, and then Lanie led him down the hall to the Moose Suite. Opening the door she stepped back to allow Jim to enter the room first.

The Christmas magic that Lilly and Karen had sprinkled throughout the Lodge dominated this room as well. The Christmas tree sparkled with multi colored mini lights and the moose head above the fireplace wore a Santa hat. The specialty chocolates on the pillows were inside of miniature candy cane stockings.

"Wow," Jim said as he put the bags down and turned to Lanie, "They sure get into Christmas don't they?"

Lanie laughed in return, "Lilly said the other day that they had so much to be thankful for that they couldn't help but spread the joy of Christmas to everyone they knew."

Taking Lanie's small hand in his Jim asked rather urgently, "And what about you, Lanie? Do you have a heart full of Christmas joy?"

"I do now, Jim," she replied shyly. As he leaned closer she tilted her head back to search his eyes for the answer to the questions she had in her heart. Leaning even closer they were startled to hear the giggles coming from the hall and Tyler's voice whisper, "I don't see any Misseytoes do you Kristen?"

"I hear bells," said Heather as she came up behind them. "I think Santa is watching. Are you two snooping?"

"No, Aunt Heather, we were just watching," replied Kristen as she giggled again. "It looked like Pastor Jim was going to kiss Lanie."

"Oh really?" Heather said attempting to shoo the children away and sneak a peak herself at the same time.

The sound of a baby's cry stopped them all in their tracks. Then a chorus of three little cries filled the hallway. Heather made a beeline for the nursery.

CHAPTER 37

"Karen, have you checked the babies schedule lately?" asked Lilly with her eyebrows raised and her eyes big.

"No…let me see it," Karen answered as she grabbed the schedule and her eyes scanned down to the next early morning feeding.

"Oh, so it takes four people to feed them now? Those sneaky little love birds!"

"Mom!" Heather said as she entered just in time to hear the last comment. "We need three people to feed and one to be the gopher. It never fails, you get all settled in and then you realize you forgot the burp rag or you wish you had a blanket or something."

"It's OK, honey, we understand. Don't we Lilly?" Karen answered.

"Of course we understand. We've all had our turn at taking care of the triplets," Lilly said soothingly and then added with a grin; "We've also had our turn at being young and in love too. Heather would it be prying too much to ask you what's going on with Jim and Lanie?"

"Not at all Aunt Lilly, he's crazy about her. And I know she feels the same way about him, but there's something holding her back. Has she been hurt?"

"In the worst way, Heather," Karen replied. "Her fiancé was killed in a snowstorm. He actually died saving her life so she blames herself and I think she's afraid of falling in love again."

Heather looked earnestly at her mother and aunt, knowing some of the pain that Lanie must be feeling. "We can't let her lose out on happiness, sometimes you have to take a chance," said Heather.

"I don't think Jim knows about this yet…" Her voice trailed off as she pondered the possibilities of Jim's reaction to this new information.

"No," Lilly and Karen answered at the same time, and then looking at each other for a moment, Karen continued, "And it's not up to any of us to tell him. If their relationship is going to evolve into something permanent then she needs to be open with him about her past."

Nodding her head in agreement Heather answered, "He won't hear it from me. And I won't even tell David about it. Well at least not as long as we're here. Will that do?"

"Of course it will, honey. We just want so badly for Lanie to be happy and have a family of her own someday," Lilly said.

"We want you to be happy too," said Karen. "And it seems like you are."

"Oh Mom, I couldn't imagine living the rest of my life without David. And we want lots of kids too, that is if he doesn't change his mind after taking care of triplets for a while," she said with a giggle.

"Where is he anyway?" asked Lilly.

"He and Kelsi are in the ice room taking care of the plants. I heard her mumbling something about a miracle though. Do you know what she was talking about?" Heather asked.

Lilly and Karen giggled at the same time and Karen answered, "Kelsi considers it a miracle every time any plant lives longer than three months with Lilly."

Karen went to the kitchen to start dinner. Everyone had been too busy taking care of the babies to think about the usual meal routines, so it was good that they had prepared for this. She went to the pantry for another bag of flour to fill the canister. Pulling the pull string on the light and closing the door, she pulled out Lilly's step stool to reach the back of the top shelf. Before she could re-open the door Jim and Lanie had entered the kitchen and Lanie was checking on the dinner preparations also.

I love the way your hair smells," said Jim. "And I love the way you look at me like that."

Karen paused to peek through the pine knothole in the door after quietly replacing the step stool. Feeling like an intruder she wondered what she should do next. "Should I wait and let their moment happen? Or should I let them know I'm here?" she asked herself.

Jim looked like he was going to really kiss her this time, and she just couldn't bring herself to interrupt the moment so she sat down on the stool to wait.

Soon though, it was evident that Lanie had pulled away and taken his hand.

"Jim, there's something in my past that you need to know. Let's go sit in the ice room and I'll tell you about it," Karen heard Lanie say as they left the room.

After a fulfilling meal the evening was spent in the main room in front of the fireplace. The triplets were lined up, cradled in their seats on the floor, as they cooed at the twinkling Christmas tree lights. Jamie and Kelsi sat nearby marveling at the miracles in their life.

Jim sat close to Lanie on the couch and Lilly and Karen each took notice, secretly wishing he would move even closer.

Melinda had settled herself into the overstuffed chair, and Heather sat close to David on the love seat.

Kristen and Tyler were anxious for Christmas and the whole family sat around talking. "Daddy, tell us again about the time Santa visited you when you were little," begged Tyler.

John Jr. took his children onto his lap and started to tell the story he had told them many times, with a flare for drama that held their total attention. "Ok now...I was about five or six years old. Heather was little too, and we were ready for bed and kind of tired. It was a quiet evening, just a couple of days before Christmas, and Mom told us that Santa was going to visit. I couldn't believe it, because I had heard that Santa wasn't real and I didn't think he could do that. I thought he just came on Christmas Eve. Well anyway, there was a knock on the door and sure enough, it was Santa himself with his elf! His elf was taller than I had imagined, and Santa's bells jingled and his belly jiggled just like the storybooks say. He stepped into our house with his shiny black boots. And you know what?"

"What?" they both asked with wide eyes.

"He already knew my name, and he knew Heather's name and he knew our dogs name too. The Santa at the shopping mall would always ask what our names were but not the real Santa! We talked about what we wanted for Christmas, but he already knew that too! When he was talking to us I reached up and pulled on his beard to make sure that it was real. That was when I knew for sure it was the real Santa. He didn't seem to mind that I pulled on his beard though. Then he gave us candy canes and left. I ran outside to see if I could see his reindeer, and followed him down the driveway as far as I could. He was really fast though, and disappeared between some cars and a black van. It was dark and hard to see very far that night, but there was nowhere for him to go, he just disappeared. I got a look around that black van, but couldn't see any sign of him anywhere...and then we saw a red glow in the sky."

Tyler and Kristen were totally silent, searching the serious face of their father as they considered the facts of the story.

Lilly and Karen smiled at each as they were both transported back in time to that night over twenty five years ago when two days before Christmas, Waldo and Lilly had secretly come to visit. Waldo had been concerned that John Jr. was growing up too fast. As a child he had always taken care of his mom and Heather and never seemed to take the time to play and be a young child. Waldo had wanted him to believe in Christmas miracles. After a visit to a professional cosmetician he and Lilly had arrived at Karen's house in costumes designed to make believers out of anyone. Entertaining the kids and playing Santa and his elf was the easy part, getting away with it was the hard part. Lilly had simply slipped around the corner of the house but Waldo had not been expecting John Jr. to follow them. Running down the driveway Waldo stopped behind a large black van and peeking around the corner saw John Jr. hot on his trail. Running from car to car down the street he had finally eluded the small boy and then spent the next half hour making his way back up the street to where Lilly waited for him in their rental car. Her worry turned to laughter when he slumped exhausted into the driver's seat of the car. Waldo had taken a moment to catch his breath and then threw his arms around his wife, "Lilly, did you see the look in that boy's eyes? He's going to be telling this story to his kids one day. Just wait and see."

John's Santa Story, as they had come to call it over the years, came to a close and Lilly felt Waldo's arms tighten around her. Looking into his eyes and then back at Karen the three of them shared a secret smile. The conspiracy that had been necessary to pull off the Santa visit would be safe with these three for the rest of their lives.

"I believe in Santa," said Heather in a very convincing manner.

"Me too," said Waldo with a straight face that didn't give away a clue.

"I bet Santa's sleigh will slide real slick down the length of the roof on this lodge," commented Jim with confidence.

Tyler and Kristen's eyes were wide with wonderment as they listened to the confirmations that Santa would be there tomorrow night.

John Sr. had been left to wonder about all of this, and actually he was wondering himself if Santa was real. And he knew he would ask Karen about it later.

Pulling them back to reality John, Jr. announced that it was snowing outside.

Rushing to the window to take a look, Jamie asked, "Mom is it safe to make snow ice cream in Alaska?"

Making this winter treat had been a tradition when Lilly was a child but being concerned about pollutants in the air she had made it only a few times for her son when he was growing up.

"I don't know Jamie, what do you think, Waldo? John? Is the ozone safe this far north?"

"It's as safe as it gets, Lilly," Waldo answered. "Let's make it!"

Lilly grabbed her largest bowl from the kitchen and sent Waldo and John out the back door to scoop the freshest untouched snow from the drifts just off the enclosed porch. They returned, brushing the snowflakes from their hair after delivering the bowl with as much snow as they could fit into it. Lilly began mixing fresh vanilla and sugar in the snow quickly before it melted. In just a moment she had flavored the snow sufficiently and scooped the delicacy into small bowls.

"We're having another one of those memory moments," Karen whispered to Lilly with a twinkle in her eye.

"I know, Karen, the blessings are flowing," Lily whispered back with a smile.

Lilly snuggled closer to Waldo under the down comforter to take in his warmth. Her heart was full and happy. She and Melinda had helped Kelsi rock her three grandchildren to sleep, and the joy of being with them was still with her. Now she listened carefully as it was her turn to have the baby monitor for the night. They were expected to sleep most of the night, but she left her slippers and housecoat out ready to jump at the first sound.

Waldo held her close and they quietly talked about Chase, Austin and Dallas. Jamie had brought up the idea again of expanding their business into a dude ranch on his property in Washington. The very idea of watching her grandchildren grow up had Lilly so excited she couldn't sleep. As much as she loved her other two businesses, being close to the triplets was first in her mind and as long as John and Karen moved with them then her life would be complete.

Waldo's thoughts moved on to the fishing trip that was just hours away and Lilly finally slipped off into a light sleep as she listened to the sound of his voice. It seemed like only an hour or two had passed when she awoke to the sound of a little cry. She smiled and again tucked away the memory of such an experience with her own son in her heart. She quickly made her way to the nursery to find Lanie in the rocking chair soothing Dallas, totally consumed in her little world of wonder and amazement.

Lanie and Lilly had the babies changed and in the kitchen ready to be fed before Kelsi was even up.

"You're spoiling me," Kelsi complained as she tried to help with the bottles. "I won't know what to do with them when we get back home."

"I'm not worried," Lilly said confidently. "Your nanny is as good as they come, and I've seen you handle all three of them by yourself."

"This is so wonderful, though. To have help and know everyone who comes in contact with them up here loves them," Kelsi said.

"Who wouldn't love them?" Lanie asked, "They are just the most adorable babies ever."

"I know," agreed Lilly as she happily sang Christmas jingles to the triplets and started breakfast.

The men entered the kitchen nearly dressed for the morning of ice fishing. Jim and David had their boots on already, and Heather was teasing John Jr. about the ski mask he was planning to wear.

Waldo went over to check on his grandchildren and started talking to them like they were able to understand every word he said. All three of the babies looked solemnly at their Grandpa while he told them all about the fishing trips he had planned for them when they were old enough.

After a breakfast of sausage, hash browns, eggs, and buttermilk biscuits with honey, the men gathered their things for the fishing trip.

Lilly and Karen automatically went to their husbands to give them a kiss good-by, and Kelsi, Melinda and Heather followed suit.

Jim stood their watching for a few moments, then shrugged his shoulders and said, "why not?" He slipped his arms around Lanie and gave her a big kiss on the lips. When Jim finally released Lanie her cheeks matched the jewel-toned sweater she was wearing.

Grinning broadly at Jim, Waldo and John each took an arm and ushered him out the kitchen door.

Lilly and Karen smiled at each other in delight.

Lanie just stood there in a daze, suffering the confusing after effects of the passion.

CHAPTER 38

Excitement was in the air as last minute Christmas preparations were put into order.

Lanie was floating around on her cloud of happiness to the enjoyment of the others while she prepared the different flavors of tea for the party.

The triplets were down for their nap. Tyler had been allowed to go on the fishing trip and Kristen was helping her mother make divinity for their Christmas Eve gathering. Heather and Kelsi were decorating the sugar cookies Lilly and the kids had made the day before. Knowing that everything was on schedule, Lilly and Karen made their way to the attic to find the gifts they had hidden there.

"You know, John and Heather never have figured out where I hid their presents when they were growing up," said Karen thoughtfully. "I think I'll wait a little longer before I spill my secrets though. Just remind me to tell them before I die of old age," she laughed.

"You really need to tell them before you forget," Lilly laughed with her. "But I think you have a few years left before that happens."

"You don't think John suspects that I got him a fishing rod do you?" Karen worried.

"No, but he's sure been hinting. Waldo said he thought he was going to have to give it to him this last week. He was catching more fish with Waldo's rod than he ever has before."

"Karen, let me see Waldo's watch again before you wrap it," Lilly asked.

Karen handed her the watch box and Lilly lifted the lid to gaze at the Rolex enclosed.

"He's going to kill me for spending this much money," Lilly murmured. "But I also know he's going to love it. Did I ever tell you that I bought him one of these the first year we were married? It was while he was working for the government up here in Alaska and I went Christmas shopping one night and a smooth talking jewelry salesman talked me into charging it. You know if they would have let me put it on lay-a-way I probably would have bought it, but instead I took it home that night and I didn't sleep a wink. I was sure someone was going to break into the apartment and steal it. I also knew we couldn't afford it at the time and Waldo would have been furious. So I took it back the next day. Unfortunately I made the mistake of telling him about it a few years later and he's bugged me about getting him one ever since. So, thanks to John's contacts this is the year."

"He's going to absolutely flip," Karen assured her.

They had been near the middle of the attic area where the gifts were hidden. As Lilly turned around and took in the view of the far end of the room, she suddenly stood there in a frozen stance as she stared at the second opening to the attic.

"What's the matter?" asked Karen.

Then she saw what Lilly was looking at. The wooden trap door at the far end of the attic was ajar.

"Maybe John Jr. and Jamie got curious," offered Karen. "They always did like to explore. And leave it up to men to not put things away when they're done with them."

"Maybe," Lilly replied skeptically moving to the open door and pulling it tight.

Turning to look at her friend she continued, "You might as well know I've had a feeling all morning that something isn't quite right."

"No, Lilly it's not the guys is it?" Karen asked.

"No, I wouldn't have let them go if I thought it was. I'm just uneasy for some reason." With a slightly nervous laugh she gave her friend a quick hug, "Oh, don't pay any attention to me. It's probably just the holiday jitters or one too many hot flashes."

Karen had seen too many of her friend's premonitions come true to dismiss them that easily. She pondered the idea of trouble for a moment. It did seem like John Jr. had been extremely cautious lately, and he was still a little nervous even though he was now far from the danger that he had been in. What could happen way out here in the middle of nowhere anyway? The moose could come back? Scott Smith could show up again?

"I don't think Scott Smith would have the nerve to bother us again, do you?" Karen asked out loud.

"I doubt that very much," replied Lilly with a light laughter of the memory. "Besides, I think we would hear Tyson making a ruckus before he got near."

With her family near and the excitement of Christmas at hand Karen found it was easy to push her doubts into the back of her mind.

"Let's finish wrapping these and get started on our tea party," suggested Karen as she successfully pushed the uncomfortable thoughts away.

"And I'm going to let Kristen use the mini tea set with her dolls today. She's been dying to do that and we haven't had the opportunity yet. I think she's old enough," Lilly said as she handed Waldo's watch to Karen to wrap and placed one of her handmade bows on John's fishing rod.

Doing these simple things with her best friend brought calmness to her soul and as her spirits rose she began humming "Oh Holy Night."

Karen smiled and murmured, "That's the spirit, Lilly." and began humming softly along with her friend. The two moved on to "Silent Night" as they finished the wrapping. They lovingly tucked their gifts deep behind the others under the tree in the great room before heading for the kitchen.

Both Lilly and Karen caught their breath as they entered their rustic lodge kitchen transformed into a room that would compete with any they had known in the south. The fragrance of cinnamon completed the ambience of southern romance and their eyes were immediately drawn to the table in front of the fireplace. The theme was poinsettias. Heather and Lanie had set the table using Karen's poinsettia china with a gold rim, and each place was set with a wine red placemat over the white linen tablecloth. Gold napkin rings held poinsettia-fabric napkins, which were folded to fan out at the top of the setting. The centerpiece Kelsi had made was of deep red poinsettias with gold garland in the greenery surrounding an ivory pillar candle. A dozen wine colored candles in small crystal votives had been placed on the table and surrounding the centerpiece. Melinda had taken cotton fabric printed with deep red poinsettias and created covers for the backs of the chairs. The rose teapot had been carefully set out on a tray, and the simmering cinnamon tea penetrated their nostrils. Two of Kristen's dolls were already seated at a second smaller table of equal southern elegance and Lilly's miniature tea set had been unpacked and washed for the occasion.

"Grandma," Kristen called excitedly as she took her hand and led her to her little table. "See, Amy and Hunstabuns are all ready for tea." Kristen then took a step back, folded her arms and surveyed the perfection of her table exactly like Lilly had just done with the larger table.

Covering her mouth with her hands and with tears suddenly springing to her eyes Lilly sighed, "It's lovely. Absolutely lovely."

Kelsi, Melinda, Heather and Lanie beamed at the look of surprise and delight on Karen and Lilly's faces and finally Lanie answered, "I've never been down south, but Heather assured me this is just the way it's done."

Lilly came back to her senses and asked what else needed to be done.

"Lilly, you and Karen just sit down. We're waiting on you two today," Kelsi replied as she was lighting the candles.

Heather and Lanie pulled out chairs for the two older women and when they were seated Lanie brought the tray of chicken salad sandwiches to the table. Melinda waddled to the counter for the plate of delicate cookies and placed them on the table. The group seated themselves and Heather poured the tea.

Kristen had found a pair of large white gloves that covered her forearms to her elbows to wear for the occasion and was having an extensive conversation with her imaginative company.

Karen started to speak as the tea was being poured. "I'm just so thrilled that we have all of our family here this year, and Lanie…we love having you here too." She looked at every face there, and then locking eyes with Lilly, Karen knew she was feeling the same things in the depths of her soul. "I feel so blessed to have given birth to the two most wonderful children in the world and see them living fulfilling and satisfying lives and be further blessed by the partners they have found to share their lives with and the grandchildren that have so enriched my life. And how fortunate I was to have my true love come back into my life and to be involved in two financially successful businesses doing what I love every single day with my best friend."

Lilly squeezed Karen's hand but when she tried to talk the words wouldn't come but the tears flowed. Sniffling softy she murmured, "Me too! I just love you all so much."

Kelsi and Heather began giggling and Kelsi whispered loudly, "I've never seen Lilly speechless before have you, Heather?"

"Nope, don't think so," Heather whispered back. "They planned this tea party to get us to spill our guts and look what happened."

At that everyone broke into gales of laughter and when the laughter had subsided, the somber mood of the group had broken and a lighter teasing tone had begun.

"I know what you're getting for Christmas, Lanie," Heather teased.

Lanie's eyes lit up and no one could wipe the deserved smile off of her face.

"What?" Lanie asked.

"Can't tell," answered Heather.

"Would you like one lump or two?" asked Kelsi with a giggle.

"Excuse me," Lilly said laughing as she got out of her chair. "I need more Kleenex from the pantry."

As she crossed the large room to the walk in Pantry, Kristin ran to catch up. "Aunt Lilly can I see the secret pathway? Uncle Waldo told me the stairs go all the way to the roof."

"What secret pathway?" asked Melinda, "I haven't heard about that one?"

"We discovered it when we first moved in, but we never use it," explained Lilly, "Waldo says that they must have used it to clean the chimneys. Now we just use ladders because the old stairway is pretty rickety."

"Uncle Waldo said it's where the pioneers hid. He said the pioneers were afraid the Indians would scalp them so they hid up in the stairway and then escaped out over the roof," Kristen stated with eyes as wide as the teacup saucers.

"Kristen, you'd better stay here," instructed Melinda.

"Oh Mommy, please…I've never seen a secret pathway before but we read about it one in that book I got for my birthday. And it's Christmas Eve!"

"It's OK, Melinda," Lilly soothed, "Kristen, honey, nothing like that ever happened here. There were only friendly Indians in Alaska and the pioneers got along very well with them. In fact they helped each other out all the time. But if you want to see someone get scalped, just wait until I get my hands on "Uncle Waldo." Imagine telling you children stories like that! It's a wonder we haven't been up all night with you and your brother having nightmares. But if it's OK with your mother we could just check it out from the pantry," suggested Lilly as she sympathized with Kristen's anticipation.

"I want to see too," Kelsi and Heather called as they got up from their chairs to join in.

"I'm afraid you're going to have to wait your turn," replied Lilly. "There's only room for one person at a time back there in that little corner.

Lanie sat there and smiled as she remembered her own curiosity as a child. Lois Johansen had hung a thick velvet curtain over the opening to keep a draft out, and when Lanie was about seven she had discovered it. Her brothers had dared her to climb the scary stairs after they had heard different stories about its purpose, and she remembered the fear in her racing heart as she secretly attempted the climb while Lois and Grandma Anna were busy talking and having tea.

"Come on Kristen, I hear Tyson barking so we'd better hurry before Uncle Waldo gets back," Lilly said as she took Kristen's hand. "We won't be long, but don't say anything interesting until I get back."

Pushing the pantry door closed behind them for more room, Lilly pulled out a little stool and stood on it to reach the chain hanging from the light fixture in the ceiling. As the light came on she pointed out the little opening in the far back corner. Kristen's eyes went from the opening to Lilly's eyes to see if any of the fear of the unknown she was feeling was in Lilly's eyes too.

"Aunt Lilly, if anything jumps out of there I'm going to just scream," Kristen warned with a slight shiver.

"Come on there's nothing to worry about. We'll only go up a few steps," Lilly said.

Still holding back Kristen replied, "Bbbbut its dark in there."

"Not really. It only looks dark from here. See, when I turned this light on it shot a stream of light all the way up the stairs." As their eyes adjusted to the darkness Kristen could soon see that Lilly was right. She gazed up to the top and found her curiosity for adventure returning.

Lilly helped Kristen through the small opening, allowing her to ascend the first few steps. Suddenly they both stopped short, startled to hear a blood-curdling scream.

"That wasn't me was it?" whispered Kristen with wide eyes.

Pulling Kristen tight against her Lilly whispered for her to be very quiet. Leaving the small girl safe inside the opening to the stairway with instructions not to move, Lilly returned to the Pantry door. Her instincts warned her against opening the door and instead she peered through a knothole in the pine.

When Tyson had started barking everyone assumed the men had returned from their fishing trip. So when Karen heard heavy footsteps on the back porch she immediately went to the back door and opened it wide expecting to see her husband or son. To her surprise three strange men in dark parkas met her. Still not suspecting any danger she opened the door wide to allow the strangers in. After all this was a Lodge in the frozen north and opening your home to strangers was not unusual.

The first man entering the kitchen pulled the hood back from his face as Melinda looked up from her tea. Her eyes met his and she reacted with a scream, spilling her tea as she pushed away from her place at the table in an effort to get away from him. Her initial instinct was to run to Kristin, but Lanie took hold of her arm and simply said, "No," as she looked into her fearful eyes for a clue of what had just happened.

The man was large with broad shoulders and long dark hair that hung just past the bottom of his collar. His penetrating cold gray eyes shot ice sickles into the depths of Melinda's heart. As his eyes took in her pregnant state his bushy eyebrows rose slightly.

Karen tucked her left hand with the diamond sapphire ring deep into her pocket as she ached for John's comforting presence and protection. Then she remembered that Lilly wasn't far away and her heart rose hopefully. Lilly had the common sense that could make all the difference in this desperate situation.

The second man was tall and slender. His rough manner told Karen that he wasn't the type she wanted to be close to and she took a step back as she realized this.

"Don't mind if I do," he said as he walked over to the table and stuffed a cookie into his mouth.

Kelsi assessed the situation and knew she had to get to her children. The baby monitor had been knocked into her lap when the tea was spilled, and she clung to it in an effort to protect them. She remained outwardly calm, but as she gripped the device her thumb went to the volume control and she suddenly realized that she could protect them by hiding them. Turning the volume down, she slipped the remote as far under the seat cushion as it would go.

Heather was frozen in her place. She couldn't take her eyes off of the third man who looked like the devil himself. This man was small in stature but had the same cold slate gray eyes as the large man. Goose bumps could be seen on her arms and she started to tremble. As his eyes surveyed the women in the room they lingered on Heather and slowly traveled up and down her slender frame. When his eyes met hers he grinned licking his lips and her blood ran cold. It was all Karen could do to keep her composure with this man looking at her daughter like that. She quickly reviewed in her mind...Melinda, the precious mother of her grandchildren, Kelsi and her babies, Lanie's new love, and Heather's future life. There was no way that she would ever compromise or mar what she had given to her husband. She relaxed her left hand in her pocket as the worth of her ring dwindled to nothing. With a heavy ache in her heart, in that moment she knew without a doubt that if these men were going to bring evil into this house, they would have to make it past her first. Stepping forward with more courage than she actually felt, Karen spoke, "Who are you? What do you want? If it's food we have plenty, if it's money we have none. And you should know our husbands will be home any minute..."

The large man surveyed her up and down. "She knows who we are," he said pointing to Melinda. "Now shut up, I'll do the talking. Where's the other one? The small brunette?"

"Oh you must mean Lilly Lansford, my business partner. She went fishing with the men," Karen answered.

The man eyed her skeptically, "Naw, she wouldn't do that."

"She would too, used to fish all the time with her husband when their son was growing up and it's something she wanted to do again. And they really will be back any minute."

"Well we'll just wait. Joe, Mac, search the place. Make sure there isn't someone hiding out up there."

Kelsi half rose from her seat but Lanie quickly pulled her back. Gripping her arm she tried to convey reassurance that Lilly had the situation under control. And in fact she did. After quickly assessing the situation she had taken Kristen up the stairs to the opening in the suite she shared with Waldo. From there they crept down the hall to the nursery. She quickly stuffed supplies and the bottles ready for the next feeding into the diaper bags and tossed them onto her shoulders. Then she gently tucked Austin into Kristen's arms and carried Chase and Dallas in her own. Soon her grandchildren were secure on the second floor landing of the secret stairway with Kristen watching over them, ready to feed them when they woke. Lilly made her way back down the rickety staircase being very careful to step lightly and avoid creating any squeaking noises. She returned to the pantry in time to hear the two men returning to the room and report that no one else appeared to be in the lodge.

The smaller man was apprehensive about the nursery with three cribs, "All those beds, boss, but no babies. Look's pretty suspicious."

"You, dolt, can't you see the Mrs. is pregnant?" The man in charge replied.

"Yeah, but three, boss."

"I'm pregnant too," Kelsi spoke up with relief in her voice at the word that her children had not been found.

"Me too," Heather added.

"Well, well, looks like we'll have lots to barter with when Johnny comes marching home, won't we now?" He said grinning. His tone turned harsh and rough as he demanded; "Nobody leaves this room!"

"Melinda, who is this man?" Karen asked.

Looking him straight in the eye Melinda replied, "Karen, let me introduce you to Bill Smithson. Bill is the former Police Chief of Newport. His wife is the daughter of an Oregon State Senator and he just happens to be the man John busted for dealing drugs out of the department."

"Oh my," Karen said as she took in the new information.

"That's right, and now Johnny Boy's gonna get what's coming to him," Bill Smithson said with a smirk as he patted the side pocket of his coat.

"You can't get away with this," Melinda stated, "If something happens to us…"

"Lady, I don't care. I've already broken out of jail, I can't go home, and my wife and daughter won't even speak to me anymore; my father-in-law has taken care of that. So I've got nothing to lose. I just want to make sure that when I go down, John Randleman goes with me. It's going to be up to him just how many of you end up the same way." As he glared at Melinda with his gray eyes Karen's blood ran cold and she felt a shiver down her spine. This man's demeanor showed signs of danger that were beyond her ability to soothe, and his threats cut to the center of her heart. This was much worse than she had thought. Now she not only feared for the lives and safety of the women in this room but also for their loved ones that may be walking into this trap. There just had to be a way to stop them.

The three men settled in to wait for their prey. Bill placed himself in the rocking chair next to the fireplace.

Karen pondered the decision of whether to try to take control of this situation, or if that would just make things worse. She turned slightly and stared at the pantry door praying for an answer and willing Lilly to communicate with her. As she stared her prayer was answered when she saw the slightest movement in a knothole to the right of the doorknob. She had no idea how they were going to accomplish this feat, but she felt a reassurance in her soul that they would find a solution.

With her new found hope she stated, "If nobody minds, I'm going to make a pot of coffee." She moved to the coffee pot with confidence and pulled a fresh filter out of the cupboard.

CHAPTER 39

The fishing trip turned out to be very prosperous, as promised. David and Jim glowed with pride as they posed together for pictures with their large catches in front of Waldo's bright red pickup. Tyler stood proudly next to them as Waldo held up his catch. Tyler was convinced the fish was his even though it was actually slightly bigger than the small boy.

"We should have had these pictures for our Christmas cards this year," commented Jim.

"There's always next Christmas," David answered.

"Actually, I had another picture in mind for next year's Christmas card," Jim replied with his biggest grin.

Waldo was eager to get the fish cleaned and packed for the trip home, knowing that Lilly would be anxious to start the evening activities. The large catch had taken a little more time than he had planned on. Jamie and John Jr. also were ready to get home to their families and helped move things along quickly. Besides, if they were going to finish getting the two by fours ready to pull through the yard by morning so that it looked like Santa had touched down, they would need some time to test it out.

In no time the fish had been packed in the back and rods securely stored behind the seats. The men piled into the pickup for the trip back to the Lodge.

"I don't remember seeing that rig there when we came through," said Waldo, with a concerned tone, as they passed a dark green four-wheeler.

"You're right," said John Sr. "I wonder what human being would leave their truck out in the middle of nowhere?"

John Jr. had been in the back playing around with Tyler, but when he heard the conversation his ears perked up and he strained to get a look. "Go back, Uncle Waldo. Let's get the license plate number."

Jim had heard just enough bits and pieces about John Mr.'s recent troubles to know that something was going on with him. He felt the thick tension as they pulled close to the vehicle to check it out.

John Sr. and Waldo both saw the color drain from John Jr.'s face as he walked around the Land Cruiser. Bending down he examined the Alaska plate on the back of the vehicle. He pulled the plate away from the bumper and his worst suspicions were realized when it appeared that the plates had recently been changed. Not wanting to worry Tyler he motioned for his dad and Waldo to come closer and solemnly told them that the vehicle was identical to one that disappeared from the Newport evidence yard a week ago. "Dad, Uncle Waldo, I'm betting that if I have these plates ran they're going to turn up stolen. But we don't have the time to check that out. We need to get back to the Lodge as soon as possible."

Returning to the truck, Waldo had it in gear and tires spinning before John Sr. closed his passenger door.

"Buckle up," he barked, "This could get rough."

CHAPTER 40

The simple chore of making a pot of coffee worked to still Karen's nervous hands. With possibilities churning in her mind and knowing the same scenarios were coming to Lilly she turned and asked the men if they were hungry.

Licking his lips the smaller man, now known as Mac, came closer to the table where a few finger sandwiches remained. Popping one in his mouth he mumbled, "Blaaah, don't you have any real food? What's that I smell?"

Bill Smithson was an evil man, but Karen thought she detected a hint of weakness as he inhaled and looked towards the oven.

"That's the Christmas Eve ham. I need to baste it if that's OK?" Karen asked Bill.

"It's Christmas Eve?" asked Joe with a dumbfounded look on his face.

Bill nodded his consent and Karen slowly put on the oven mitts. Turning toward the pantry door she willed Lilly to read her mind and then slowly turned back to the oven. As she opened the oven door the smell of the succulent ham wafted through the kitchen and lured Joe and Mac closer to the source of the aroma and potential satisfaction of their taste buds. Karen carefully removed the cover from the roasting pan and set it on the counter top behind her. As she did this her eyes slowly met those of the women still seated at the table.

Lanie's hand suddenly tensed on Kelsi's forearm and they knew the time had come.

Turning back to the oven Karen's expectations were met when she saw Mac and Joe attempting to carve a chunk of meat out of the large steaming ham with the basting tools.

"Here, let me help you with that," she said as they peered even closer into the oven.

Suddenly, with her hands and forearms safely protected from the heat, taking a very deep breath and saying a prayer, Karen grabbed the back handle of the roasting pan and tipped it sharply sending the meat and boiling juices directly into the laps of the two men. Screaming in pain they both fell to the floor just as Lilly burst out of the Pantry door and laid a cast iron skillet alongside Bill Smithson's head with a force she had never known she possessed.

Moving just as rapidly, Heather and Lanie ripped away the strings of lights that Waldo had secured around the kitchen island and began tying Mac and Joe's hands behind them.

Karen yelled at Melinda not to move, worried that she would try to help and end up harming the baby.

Kelsi rushed to Karen's side to help tie up Bill Smithson before he regained consciousness. As Kelsi finished hog tying the man, like she would a small steer, she stood and paused for a moment to look him over. At that moment all of her fear and frustrations came to a head and she kicked him solidly in the ribs. "That's for endangering my children!" Breathing raggedly she turned to Lilly, "Where are they, Lilly?"

"On the second floor landing of the secret stairway, Kelsi. Kristen's with them."

Kelsi had just gone through the small opening when the back door burst open and Waldo and John Sr. came through at the same time closely followed by John Jr. and Jamie. David and Jim came next with Tyler and all six men stood in shock and stared at the scene before them.

"Where's Kelsi? Where's my children?" demanded Jamie in panic.

"They're fine," Lilly informed him. "You'll find them upstairs with Kristen." Jamie sprinted up the stairs.

John Jr. went to Melinda to see if she was ok. Kneeling in front of her he took her trembling hands in his.

"You should have seen them," Melinda said drawing comfort from his strong hands.

"What did those creeps do to you? Did they hurt you or Kristen?" he asked looking deep into her eyes for the truth.

"No…I mean Lilly and Karen and Kelsi and Heather and Lanie. You should have seen Karen dump that ham on the men and Lilly whacked that big man with a skillet. John, I'm pretty sure she had to stand on her tiptoes to reach his head." Drawing a ragged breath, she continued, "And I couldn't help at all. I just had to sit here."

"We can see that you obviously took care of the situation," said Waldo as he looked around and searched for his words after being totally speechless.

"Tyler, I want you to take Mommy upstairs and find Kristen," instructed John Jr. as he lovingly touched her cheek and then took her hand in his.

"But Daddy…"

"I need you to help," he instructed softy but in a firm tone. He looked at Lilly to be sure things were really ok upstairs and received a confirming look.

"Come on Tyler," Melinda said. "Help me up out of my chair."

"Ok, let's clean up this mess," said John Jr. going to the phone to call the nearest law enforcement to take over.

David directed the obvious question to Heather…"What happened anyway?"

While Heather told a short version of the story, Karen couldn't help but to be drawn to John. She needed to feel his strength and to look into his eyes. There she found a new connection that somehow bonded them deeper than before. There were no words for the feeling she held in her heart, and she laid her hand on his chest to feel his heartbeat.

Lilly was anxious to get the "trash" out of her kitchen. She needed this as bad as she needed time with Waldo and to see her grandchildren again. When John Jr. hung the phone up he reported that it would be about an hour before the local police could get there and asked what Waldo and John thought was the best thing to do with the men. Lilly was in favor of dragging them out on the porch until the police arrived but Waldo suggested that they escort them out to his workshop where at least there would be heat and tie them more securely and keep a close eye on them until they could be turned over to authorities.

In all the commotion no one seemed to notice or find it unusual that Jim and Lanie were sitting quietly on the loveseat in the dining room with their arms around each other. Lanie's head was buried in his neck as Jim murmured comforting words of reassurance.

Jamie and Kelsi had the triplets back in the nursery. They changed them and finished feeding them with Kristen's help while Kelsi explained to Jamie what had happened.

Melinda sat in the rocking chair and added her viewpoint of the intrusion whenever she felt it necessary. Tyler sat on the floor at his mother's feet; his eyes growing rounder as every detail came out.

As soon as the story was completed told, Jamie announced to Kelsi, "We're going home and I mean now. Where's the suitcase?"

"Jamie, you know we can't. We can't do that to your Mom. Just calm down, everything is OK now," Kelsi soothed. Giving him a hug and rubbing his back reassuringly Kelsi laughed softly, "Besides, we took care of the bad guys so there's nothing more to worry about."

Grudgingly Jamie agreed but also insisted that for the rest of the visit the triplets would not be out of their sight.

"Fair enough," Kelsi agreed. "Now, it's Christmas Eve so let's get the kids downstairs and see what Lilly has in mind for dinner."

Jamie laughed with his wife, "I'm betting it won't be ham. Did Aunt Karen really dump the ham on those men?"

"Full force, Jamie." Melinda added giggling, "They won't be hungry for a while, or able to do anything else for that matter."

"I think your Mom's going to need a new skillet too. I think she put a dent in it."

"Nah, it's cast iron so that's not possible."

"We'll see," Kelsi said skeptically. "She hit him pretty hard."

They entered the kitchen to find Karen washing the last of the dishes and Lilly just finishing mopping the floor. With everything back in order the two smiled at each other as Jamie asked, "Mom, what are we going to have for Christmas Eve dinner?"

"Pizza, honey. Homemade pepperoni pizzas." Lilly paused and then catching Karen's eye she laughed, "And no, Karen, you cannot put hotdogs on them."

"Bet I will," Karen murmured under her breath.

CHAPTER 41

"Hey…you want to lasso me that piece of pizza over there?" John Jr. asked Kelsi with his deep contagious laugh.

"Kelsi, hog tie one of 'em for me too," Waldo said with a laugh.

"OK, that's enough," Kelsi said with a giggle.

"Hey, Kelsi, if you ever get tired of ranching we can use you on the force," John Jr. added then seeing the scowl on Jamie's face, "OK, we're just joking."

"I know, but someone could have been hurt really bad," Jamie said.

The three captives had been turned over to the Alaska State Police for safekeeping and the mood in the kitchen had turned to playful levity. However, Jamie still appeared to have a dark cloud hanging over his head. He would not let loose of his fear of the danger that could have come to his wife and children. Patting her son's back reassuringly, as she put a basket of Parmesan bread sticks on the table, Lilly said, "The fact is no one did get hurt." Then giggling she added, "At least none of us."

"Aunt Lilly, do we still get to open presents tonight?" asked Kristen almost timidly.

"Of course, honey, we're not going to let a little thing like that spoil our Christmas. But you know the rules. We have to wait for dinner to be over, the dishes washed and the kitchen cleaned, then we can open." Lilly answered.

Seeing the sparkle that came into the children's eyes at the anticipation of gifts, Waldo couldn't help but comment, "We've already received the best gift of all this year. This is a little hard for you and Tyler to understand, Kristen, but I know that every man here will agree that having our women and children safe is the greatest gift we will ever receive."

"Here, here." John Sr. said raising his glass of root beer, "Let's have a toast."

As everyone raised their glasses John stood and continued speaking, "Here's to our family and friends and this wonderful Lodge where we can all come together to celebrate this holiest of seasons, here's to Lanie, Heather and Melinda for their courage, and here's to Karen and Lilly for having the strength and wisdom to defend themselves and their children this afternoon. Here's to Kristen, the bravest of all babysitters. And last, but definitely not least, here's to Kelsi and her hog tying abilities."

Sitting down amidst giggles John saw the scowl on Jamie's face, "Sorry, Jamie, better get used to it, she's our hero."

"Were you scared Kristen?" asked Jim.

"Not really," she answered. "Aunt Lilly said that she was going to take care of it, and I knew she wouldn't let anything happen to Mommy because she said so. Besides, I knew Daddy would be home before long."

"You were given a very big important job, and you did great," Kelsi complimented her. "You can come to the ranch and help take care of the triplets anytime you want."

The scowl on Jamie's face softened as he took a moment to look into Kristen's trusting and honest brown eyes and realized the part that she had played. A flashing thought into the future brought an image of Austin and Dallas when they would be that age and his heart softened.

Kristen cuddled up into her daddy's side and as she pulled on his sleeve she whispered, "Aren't you done eating yet Daddy?"

Hugging his daughter tight, John Jr. placed the last crust of pizza in his mouth, "I am now. You know the rules, dishes have to be done."

Stacking as many plates as he could carry, John Jr. headed to the kitchen sink as Jamie rushed ahead of him and pulled out the garbage can. "Here you go; we'll get this place cleaned in no time."

"Jamie, John those are my Christmas dishes, and you aren't throwing them away," Lilly gasped.

"Gotcha Mom," Jamie laughed as the cloud lifted from above his head and for a moment he and John Jr. were twelve years old again pretending to throw the Christmas Eve dishes away to speed up the process of opening gifts.

Tyler joined in by threatening to throw the silverware in the garbage and then they all got down to business.

Karen just happened to see Heather show her left hand to Kelsi like she was expecting to see a ring on that finger before the night was over.

John and Waldo went out to tend to Tyson, but had been gone a little too long for that. Lilly strongly suspected that they were up to something.

David and Jim disappeared upstairs for a while and Lanie made a trip out to her car.

Magic and the excitement of secrets were in the air and Tyler and Kristen were dancing around the tree as they picked out which present they thought they would open first.

John Sr. returned to the kitchen and seeing that all of the rules seemed to be met, he called for everyone to go to the ice room.

Poinsettias lined the base of the windows. John and Karen had arranged pillows and chairs around the window, which viewed the manger scene. The aurora borealis glimmered and flickered around the ice sculpture scene as he started telling the Christmas story of how the baby Jesus was born in a stable. Christmas in Alaska had definitely proved to be very unique and special. To Melinda's pleasant surprise her father-in-law's strong voice and theatrical ability had captured her children's full attention.

415

Karen's heart swelled as her husband portrayed the story to her loved ones in a memorable way like they had never heard it before.

Lilly relaxed and leaned back into Waldo's arm as her head rested just under his chin. She had not been this much at peace with herself in years. All of the anxiety of the past months had disappeared and there was no longer any doubt of the safety and well being of her family and friends.

Catching Karen's eye she smiled as John finished telling the Christmas story. For a moment no one spoke and then John softly began singing Silent Night, knowing it was her favorite. As the rest of the group joined in the chorus a new peace and fulfillment came over the two friends that could only come from the saturation in their faith mixed with the experiences they had bonded in.

"This is true happiness," Lilly thought to herself and sighed contentedly.

"Now, Daddy?" Tyler asked hopefully

"Who wants to play Santa?" John Jr. asked boisterously, not wanting to reveal the emotion he had just felt.

"Me!" Tyler exclaimed and Kristen joined in, "Me too, Daddy. Can we please?"

"OK, why don't you two each go get a present for everyone here then get one for yourself and we'll all open together?"

As the children and their parents rushed into the great room where the mountain of presents waited under the tree, John pulled Karen aside. Sliding his arms around her back he pulled her close and nuzzling her neck he said softly, "What do you want for Christmas?"

"John, I have everything I've ever wanted. I'm sure I'll love whatever you've gotten me," Karen answered.

Kissing her lightly he answered, "Let's go see," and made her close her eyes as he led her into the room and placed her in front of the large present.

"Ok, you can open them now," he said. "Why don't you sit right here Karen and watch the kids?"

To Karen's delight she opened her eyes to find a delicate but sturdy oak rocking chair with a big red bow across the back. Running her hands over the ornate carving on the armrests and then the homemade brocade seat covering Karen grinned back at him as she sat down to try it out.

"For me? John it's so beautiful. Where on earth did you find it? And it's so comfortable!"

"Right here in Alaska, my dear. I know how much you and Lilly admire the former owners of the Lodge. This chair came from Michigan with the Johansson's. Grandma Anna told me that it originally belonged to Lois' mother. Do you really like it?"

Rising to her feet Karen threw her arms around him; "Like it? I love it and I'll treasure it for the rest of my life! Nothing could have made me happier." She held him back at arms length to get a good look at his face. The joy of giving was throughout his being and radiated from his face, surrounded by some wispy curls of hair and highlighted by his brown eyes. Her love for him swelled in her heart.

"Now let me get your present." Turning to the tree Karen was met by Waldo carrying the wrapped fishing rod that had just been put behind the tree earlier that day since it couldn't be disguised.

"Oh boy!" John exclaimed, "Is this what I think it is?"

Karen delighted in the look of surprise and youthful glee that came over John's face,

"Waldo picked it out for me."

"Just think how much fish we can catch with two of these babies," Waldo said.

Karen was sitting contentedly in her chair watching John admire her gift to him when John Jr. and Heather approached. "Mom, this is for you," John announced with pride and anticipation.

Heather stood at his side expectantly as he handed their mother the slim jewelry case.

"What? What have you two done?" She exclaimed as she held the small box in her hands savoring the moment.

"Well open it!" Lilly exclaimed.

Slowly taking the gold bow off and laying it carefully aside she pulled the paper off and opened the box to reveal a brushed yellow gold link bracelet with a white gold heart centered in the middle of the links. Holding one end of the heart was a small diamond and the other side was held with a garnet.

As tears sprung to her eyes Karen clasped the bracelet to her breast, "It's just beautiful. You know I've always admired Lilly's Mother's ring and now I have a Mother's bracelet. Where on earth did you two find something this original?"

"Heather designed it, Mom, and Dad's jeweler made it. Do you really like it?" John Jr. asked.

Rising to her feet Karen pulled each of her children close, "I love it and there's nothing you could have given me that could have pleased me more." Brushing the tears away Karen held the bracelet out for Lilly to admire.

"Lilly haven't you opened a gift yet?" She exclaimed.

"Got it right here in my pocket," Lilly said pulling a small box from the back pocket of her Levi's. "I snatched this baby up first thing from that mountain of packages so it wouldn't get lost."

Waldo watched his wife with modest curiosity.

Lilly ripped the package open to find a familiar teal colored box with gold trim on the raised pattern from none other than Walter Lindy's jewelry store in Louisiana. She took a big breath and held it in as she opened the box. Her eyes grew big and she fell into a speechless state. The gems sparkled as she tipped the box around to catch the rays of light.

"Ok, you can breathe now!" said Jamie.

Karen and John leaned forward to admire the ring. "It's gorgeous! And you can wear that with anything," said Karen.

Colored gems represented each of her family members. The center stones represented her and Waldo. Several diamonds on one side lead to a group of three opals, and a matching flow of diamonds on the opposite side lead to the stones representing Jamie and Kelsi. The band swirled around to hold each of the stones in a very sophisticated setting.

Lilly turned to Waldo to confirm its meaning. "Look inside," coaxed Waldo.

Lilly lifted the ring from its place in the cushioned box and turned it to read the inscription. "Family…with my never ending love, Waldo," she read.

"It certainly can be called a ring of many colors," said John.

Lilly kissed Waldo on the cheek as she let a tear of joy roll down her cheek. He gently took the ring from her and placed it on her finger.

"I could never have imagined such a beautiful ring," she said as she began to come out of her speechless state.

"Now where's my present?" Waldo teased.

"It's under the tree, Tyler would you hand me that box right there? It's the one with the big red bow. That's it honey, thank you," Lilly said handing it to her husband. "Waldo it's been a long time coming. Hope you like it."

John, Karen, Jamie and Kelsi stood looking at Waldo expectantly while he turned the small box over and over.

"What could it be?" He questioned. "I wonder, just what could it be?" He pondered again.

"Dad, if you don't open it I'm going to do it for you," Jamie exclaimed in exasperation.

"Open it, open it!" chimed in Tyler.

Pulling the bow off the small package and popping open the hinged lid of the small box, Waldo's mouth dropped open and for probably the first time in his life he was the one to be entirely speechless. He carefully took the Rolex watch out as if it might break just touching it.

"Just how many years have you had this anyway? Never mind, it's this year's model," he marveled knowing that 30 years earlier Lilly had bought him a Rolex and then had returned it to the store concerned that they really couldn't afford it. Now here at last was yet another dream come true.

Soon Waldo and John Sr. were in a deep, serious conversation about watches.

"Oh look!" cried Tyler. "I got the walkie talkies I wanted! I can't believe it!" He ripped open the package with no mercy for the condition of the box.

Kristen was carefully taking a beautiful bride doll out of its box. From the glow in her eyes Lilly knew that the gift she and Waldo had picked out on their last trip to Washington would be one treasured by the little girl for the rest of her life. Looking around the room she noticed Jamie and Kelsi opening gifts for the triplets and showing them to the babies as if they could really understand what was going on.

Melinda was opening a small box that John Jr. had given her.

Drawing Karen aside Lilly pointed out that Lanie was also opening a very small present with Jim looking on.

Heather seemed to be looking for something as she collected the remaining presents from under the tree and designated Tyler and Kristen to deliver them. She looked at David with a bit of puzzlement in her eyes, and he responded by pulling a small box out of his pocket.

"You know how these things can get lost in the hustle and bustle," he said as he smiled and handed her the small burgundy and forest green present.

Heather opened it carefully with expectation. As she took the lid off of the box her face fell into disappointment and then bewilderment as there was just a piece of paper to be found. "Read it," encouraged David.

"Ok..."Will you be my honey? If your answer is yes, go to the appliance I love the best."

"You can't cook so it has to be the refrigerator? Oh David, you know I love scavenger hunts, but you make me suffer so," Heather said as she ran to the kitchen and opened the large side-by-side chrome refrigerator. There, sitting on the front shelf was a small box tied with a bright red bow.

"How did I miss this?" Heather wondered pulling the bow off and opening the lid to find another note. "Aaaagh"

"Read it!" begged Kristen who had shadowed Heather to her destination.

"You warm my heart; go see what you might find by the warmth in the great room." Heather read and then hurried back and began searching the fireplace mantle. Sure enough, tucked into the poinsettia garland there was a small red envelope with another note.

David came up behind her and slipped his arms around her waist as he watched over her shoulder.

She read; "Roses are red, violets are blue, I have something next to my heart that belongs to you."

Turning in his arms Heather placed her palms flat against his chest and felt the small package inside his vest.

Heather's eyes grew big and she reached into the pocket to pull out the box as she looked into his sapphire blue eyes. "I'm so glad you didn't make me look a hundred thousand places before we got here," she said with relief and a giggle.

David took the box from her and opened it. Heather gasped at the sight. Here was the moment every girl dreams of and the sparkling gem was more than she had ever hoped for.

"Will you marry me, Heather? Will you make me the happiest man on earth?"

"I will, David." Pressing her lips gently against his a small tear trickled down her porcelain ivory face. Her blond hair had been pulled back in a French braid and everyone in the room was awed by her delicate grace and beauty.

Leaving the couple alone for even just a moment was hard for Lilly and Karen and probably wouldn't have been accomplished if it hadn't been for their husbands holding them back. Finally Waldo and John let go of their arms and they rushed to the happy couple with open arms.

Heather reluctantly moved out of David's arms and held her left hand out for all to admire the platinum band with a two-caret heart shaped diamond surrounded by tiny pink sapphires.

Even though David had told her he was proposing on Christmas Eve, after getting permission from her father, the ring's design was a total surprise to Heather. Karen hugged her daughter and then taking her hand she admired the lovely ring and was struck by the realization of the depth of David's love for Heather and the fact that he could not have found a ring that better mirrored Heather's delicate fragile beauty.

"Champagne, this calls for Champagne," Waldo shouted. After Lilly reminded him that they didn't have Champagne at the Lodge, and as a matter of fact there was no alcohol of any kind other than cooking sherry, they decided on sparkling apple cider for the toast.

It was well past midnight before everyone was settled down. Kristen had finally fallen asleep in her grandma's lap as the comfort of the new rocker soothed her tired little body. Tyler tried to keep up with the adults but finally fell asleep on the couch curled up against his grandpa.

Jamie, Jim and David took a turn with the triplets and changed them with a bit of coaching from Kelsi and Lilly.

Heather, Melinda and Lanie decided to have a cup of tea in the kitchen. It just seemed right to have tea and visit after such a memorable evening.

Later on David and Heather would spend some time in the ice room after the babies were down for the night.

Jamie, Waldo, John Sr. and John Jr. then disappeared outside, as if it would take all four of them to tend to Tyson, while Lilly and Karen made sure everything was in order for Christmas morning.

Exhausted from the late night, every guest in the lodge cuddled into the warm down comforters and peaceful sleep was throughout the lodge.

It was Tyler who woke first to the anticipation of the morning. "Kristen, wake up!" he pleaded on his new walkie-talkie. "I think Santa came and Dad always says we have to make coffee before we wake him up...ten four good buddy? Are you awake yet?"

"I'm right here, Tyler," Kristen said from the next bed feigning exasperation, "You don't have to yell into the walkie talkie."

"Can we go down, now?" He pleaded.

"Race you down." Kristen giggled as her eyes popped wide open and she scrambled for the door.

"Ok, I know Grandma uses this coffee for the breakfast stuff," said Tyler knowingly as he pushed the step stool to the counter and pulled the big can down from the cupboard shelf and took the lid off.

"Do you know how much to put in?" questioned Kristen.

"Of course I do, Grandma always does it like this," he answered as he scooped coffee into the filter.

"I don't think Aunt Lilly uses that much," warned Kristen. "And I want to help too. I'll put the water in."

The two managed to get the coffee made with a minimal mess and then returned upstairs to wake their parents.

Tyler carefully carried two cups of the freshly made coffee on a tray. Kristen carried a tray of gingerbread cookies like the ones they had left out for Santa.

"Daddy, Daddy…wake up! Mommy wake up," they called as they climbed into bed with their parents.

"Is the coffee made?" mumbled John Jr. as he struggled to open his eyes.

"Yep, we made it just like Grandma and aunt Lilly do," answered Tyler.

"I think Santa came," exclaimed Kristen.

"I know he came," added Tyler as he pulled on his mother's hand and readied her slippers for her.

When John Jr. finally took the first sip of his very strong coffee his eyes popped open and sure enough, he was instantly awake.

The commotion woke Jamie, and he joined John Jr. in the task of being sure that everyone else didn't have the option of staying in bed.

"Well I'll be," said Waldo with total surprise in his voice when he entered the great room. "Santa did come and there's something in those stockings."

"Look…" called Jamie as he looked out over the yard. "Over there…that's Santa's sleigh tracks. He must have touched down before he took off."

"Of course," said John Sr. "I left treats out for the reindeer last night."

Tyler and Kristen's eyes were wide with amazement as they ran to the window to carefully examine the sleigh tracks.

Suddenly they both dashed for the stockings as they realized they could look now. In their stockings were various treats and goodies, and the end of a ribbon was tucked into the stocking.

"What's this?" questioned Kristen.

"Why don't you follow it and find out?" suggested Melinda.

The ribbon seemed to be endless. Tyler's ribbon was yellow and Kristen's was purple. They each followed their ribbon around the furniture, thru the table legs, behind the bookcase, under the rug, into the kitchen and back to the hallway. Finally the end was found underneath large stuffed animals that were waiting for them.

"I got a panda!" squealed Kristen in delight.

Tyler picked up the monkey at the end of his ribbon to check him out and giggled.

Lilly and Karen, helped by their husbands, picked up the remains of the wrapping paper destroyed by the children and adults, and restored things once more to order before their Christmas dinner company arrived.

John and Waldo had been grinning at each other all morning like they shared a secret and finally Lilly couldn't stand it any more. "What's up with you two? Are you hiding another present for us?" She questioned.

Grinning at Waldo again, John took his wife's hand and told her she needed to sit down for this one.

"You too, Lilly," Waldo said.

Perching expectantly on the end of the sofa they waited as John took an envelope out of his shirt pocket.

"Here you go," he said handing it to Karen.

Karen opened the envelope and found five airline tickets. Lilly leaned over to look at the tickets in her friend's hand.

"Five tickets! Where to, Karen? Why five?"

Waldo cleared his throat, "With Heather getting married, we thought you two were over due for a little shopping trip."

John continued, "Two tickets are for you two to fly to Louisiana, you can spend a few days there and then the three of you are headed to New York to pick out the most beautiful wedding dress my money can buy. I only have one daughter and her wedding is going to be everything she wants it to be."

Astonished, Lilly and Karen stared at each other and then Lilly protested. "But what about the Lodge? And who's going to cook for the guests?"

"We will," Waldo said proudly. "And Lanie will be here, we're not exactly helpless, my love."

"When are we going?" Lilly asked hopefully, looking at the tickets again.

"You leave on April 8th," John replied. "Those are the dates Heather can get away.

"You mean she knew about it?" Karen asked.

"She was in on it from the beginning," John replied.

"We're going shopping!" Lilly exclaimed as the ideas whirled in her head and the reality of a shopping trip set in.

After hugging and thanking their husbands, Karen and Lilly rushed to the kitchen with a new super energy to put the finishing touch on Christmas dinner and begin planning their shopping trip. These two had secretly been longing for an adventure such as this one for months.

"They're here, they're here, Jimmy's here," called Tyler excitedly as he ran to the door.

The lodge was full of the scent of Christmas dinner and everything promised to taste as good as it smelled. Heather and Melinda were in charge of the table settings. Kelsi had worked her usual magic on the centerpieces and lights from small votives twinkled amidst white poinsettias, lilies and greenery on the side table.

Lilly carefully took the prime rib from the oven and set it out to cool a bit while the stuffed baked potatoes warmed. Once again they had created the perfect meal that would be pictured in some magazine in a few months. Lilly and Karen couldn't have been happier. The picture of life they saw was one of family, energy, tantalizing aromas, new love and romance in the air, the sound of happy children, and the friendship that they shared.

CHAPTER 42

Everyone was gathered around the fireplace in the great room, letting the tasty food settle before dessert. Even Waldo said he wanted to wait for a piece of pie, and there would be plenty of time for that later. Tyler, Kristen, Esther and Jimmie were setting up the new monopoly game Tyler had gotten for Christmas. Esther was elected to be the banker and busied herself organizing the bills.

"I want the boot," called out Jimmie.

"I want the car," said Tyler.

John Sr. and Jim had found a couple of guitars and were strumming some tunes together. Grandma Anna was rocking gently in Karen's chair and the peaceful smile on her lips strongly suggested to Karen and Lilly that she was lost in memories of other holidays spent in this lodge. They both took note of the way she lovingly caressed the stitches on the quilt they had made for her.

"Grandma Anna," Lilly finally asked, "have you spent other Christmas's here?"

"Oh yes," she replied. "But it was much different than today. Lois and I cooked the wild turkey that our husbands hunted down. Every year we thought they'd never catch the critter. And then sure enough, it took them all day but they did it. We cooked it in that wood stove sitting in the corner of your kitchen. I do miss the good times we had," she said as her voice drifted off, "I miss the conversations we had over tea and the lovely quilts we used to make." Then perking up she called, "Lanie, would you be a dear and bring in that bundle from the car?"

"Sure, Grandma," Lanie replied.

Lanie returned with a package about the size of a basketball, wrapped in brown paper and tied with a piece of twine. She handed it to Grandma Anna who held it with care, touching it in the same way that she had the quilt.

"Lilly," she said softly with a loving look in her eye. "This is for you. I want you to have it." She held the package out to Lilly who hesitated to take it. After receiving an encouraging look from Karen, she finally reached out and took it into her lap.

"Go ahead, open it," coaxed Grandma Anna as she slowly rocked and nodded her head in a slow even motion.

Slowly pulling one end of the twine, the bow became untied and Lilly pulled the paper away from the gift. Expecting it to be a hand braided throw rug, Lilly let out a gasp of surprise as the gift was revealed.

"Oh Grandma Anna, you can't give me your teapot!" Lilly protested.

"Oh yes, I can. I don't know anyone that would take better care of it, and I had Lanie's permission. I won't be around forever you know."

"I just reserve the right to have tea with you two at any spur of the moment," said Lanie with a loving smile that reflected her grandmother's.

Grandma Anna's heart was filled with the joy of giving as she watched Lilly's face turn from protest to acceptance. Lilly ran her fingers over the hand painted roses on the teapot as if she was examining it for the first time. Blinking back tears Lilly handed the teapot to Karen and went to Grandma Anna. Kneeling next to the elderly woman she gently placed her arms around her. "I will cherish it for the rest of my life," she promised.

Grandma Anna patted Lilly on the shoulder, "I know you will my dear. You and Karen know the value of friendship and the magic that comes from sharing a good cup of tea from a very special teapot."

"Thank you," Lilly replied brushing the tears off her cheek. As Lilly rose, Grandma Anna reached out and took her hand once more, pulling her close she whispered, "You do know that Lois gave me that teapot don't you?"

Lilly continued to brush the tears away as she nodded.

"I have cherished it for many years because it belonged to her," Grandma Anna said.

Squeezing Lilly's hand tightly she continued, "To keep the chain of loving friendship you must give it to your friend someday."

"I will Grandma Anna, I promise," Lilly said.

"Not today, my dear. You will know when the time is right," Grandma Anna prophesized. "Meanwhile, enjoy it as it was meant to be enjoyed."

Nodding Lilly excused herself. Rushing to the bathroom she blew her nose and dabbed at her eyes trying desperately to not disturb her makeup. Taking deep breaths she was soon composed enough to return to the Christmas festivities. Kelsi had just brought in the bottles for the next feeding and Lilly jumped at the chance to help. She picked up Austin and one of the bottles, but as she started to sit down she suddenly changed her mind.

"Grandma Anna, would you like to feed Austin tonight?" Lilly asked.

"Oh, could I? I haven't held a baby for years."

After getting her settled, Lilly went back for Dallas and sat next to Kelsi who had Chase well on his way to finishing his dinner.

As she sat down she caught Karen's eye and her nod at the four that were sitting in front of the fireplace at the other end of the room.

Nona and Patrick were talking intensely to Jim with Lanie sitting calmly next to him. Lilly thought sure that she saw Jim wipe a bead of sweat from his brow and Lanie continued to smile calmly.

Karen couldn't help but to remember her own father's concern when she first wanted to marry John. Likewise, she was sure Patrick O'Callaghan wanted the best for his daughter. Smiling back at Karen and nodding, Lilly was also reminded of her own father's interrogation of the young sailor who came into their lives over thirty years ago. Her eyes then wandered to where Waldo was giving John instructions on the new fishing rod and then met Karen's eyes again. How blessed they were, she sighed contentedly.

CHAPTER 43

The children were tucked in for the night with their prayers said and questions from the day answered. "Sweet dreams," said Karen softly as she left the Aurora Borealis room.

Lilly was checking on the babies even though Jamie and Kelsi had them tucked in for the night. She softly touched the cheek of each baby as she whispered, "Good night Chase, good night Austin, good night Dallas."

The two women met in the hallway and went down the stairs together in silence, but with knowing smiles on their faces.

"Are you guys going to stay up all night again?" Asked Karen as she returned to the great room where everyone still sat. Lanie's family had left for home, and she was going to spend the night with Heather again. Nona had relaxed when Lilly assured her that Lanie was sleeping in Heather's room and that she also had baby duty in the morning. When Patrick O'Callaghan had said his good-bye's Lilly was sure she saw approval in his eyes when Jim shook his hand.

Jim was now telling Lanie about his travels in South America, and they both had a desire to visit Europe and maybe even Africa.

Their intelligent conversation was pleasant to Lilly's ears. "A relationship with substance," she thought to herself.

"I don't feel so good," said Melinda.

"Me either," said Heather, "I think I ate too much."

"No, I mean I really don't feel so good," said Melinda again as she tried to support her back with a pillow and wiggled around in an effort to get comfortable on the couch.

"Are you ok?" asked John Jr.

"I've been trying to tell you…" she said in frustration.

"Come on, I'll rub your back for you," he promised as he pulled her to her feet and guided her to the stairs.

"Honey, I don't think I can make it up the stairs," Melinda said with a bit of panic surfacing in her tone. She returned to the couch and looking directly into her husband's eyes she asked, "How far away is that hospital?"

"Oh my gosh, Melinda, you don't mean…" John stuttered.

"I'll get the truck," Waldo yelled heading for the door. However, as he opened the back door he was met with a swirl of snow blowing in all different directions. Determined, he fought his way to the truck.

John Sr. was immediately searching for an up to date weather report. The men usually kept a close eye on it, but with the holiday they had been distracted from their regular routine.

"Maybe it's just false labor," Karen said calmly.

But as she saw the first contraction take hold of Melinda's body her hopes dwindled.

Waldo returned from his attempt to make it to the truck and Lilly saw the worry in his eyes as he joined John in the office.

"It's a blizzard," he said confidentially looking over John's shoulder to see the report. "I don't think we're going anywhere until it slows down and then we'll have to plow before we can make it out. Maybe we could use the snowmobiles?"

"Ernie and Arnie can go anywhere with their sled dogs," offered John Sr.

"Too risky," Waldo stated.

Karen entered the office where the men were glued to the computer screen.

John sat there in his new t-shirt with a proud, "I'm a Grandpa," on the back, and a picture of buttons bursting open down the front of it.

"We could try," Waldo answered.

Karen and Lilly looked at each other over their husband's heads. As their eyes met they knew they were having the same thought.

Nodding at Lilly, Karen said, "How about a mid-wife?"

"Grandma Anna," Lilly added.

"Honey, I don't know," Waldo said skeptically. "She's pretty frail."

"Let's ask Lanie," Lilly said leaving the room.

It wasn't long before Lilly returned with Lanie.

"The boys are already getting the sled dogs ready," Lanie announced. "Grandma will be fine in the cab they have on the sled, as a matter of fact she loves to ride in it. And the dogs never get lost in a blizzard," she reassured them.

Karen went to her son to explain the plan. "That darn Bill Smithson," he muttered under his breath. "We probably wouldn't have even come here if we hadn't been trying to get away from him, and now he's caused all of this extra stress." He wrung his hands as he paced back and forth in front of the couch.

Knowing her son's response to anger and frustration, Karen put her hands on his shoulders and turned his face so that he had to look at her. "It's no one's fault. You probably would have been here anyway. Melinda said her doctors have reassured her all along that everything is perfectly normal. The baby and Melinda will be fine. After all, babies are born every day all over the world without doctors and hospitals. And besides, God put us all here together and things might have turned out a whole lot worse if you had stayed in Oregon."

Drawing a ragged breath he nodded, "You're right Mom. It's just I don't know what I would do if anything happened to her."

Karen took in the emotion of her son's face before reassuring him again. "Well nothing's going to happen. Now you go help Jamie move the furniture out of the way in the office. Waldo and your Dad are taking apart one of the big spare beds upstairs and we're turning the office into a hospital room. I don't want Melinda to have to climb the stairs."

Jamie led him to the office room as he also started reassuring him. "You've gotta admit we have a little experience. You've had two already and Kelsi and I just did a triple batch. Kelsi delivers the colts every spring and knows just as much as the vet does. Mother nature takes care of most of it you know."

Karen went to the kitchen where she found Lilly giving Lanie and Heather instructions on sanitizing everything in the office. As they left the room she pulled out her heaviest Dutch ovens and started filling them with water.

"What are you doing now?" Karen asked.

"Boiling water, of course!" Lilly answered. "That's what they always do in the movies! There has to be a reason why and I'm going to be prepared when Grandma Anna gets here."

"Well ok, I've got the new shoe strings, and I actually know what they're used for. You need something clean and strong to tie off the umbilical cord," Karen said.

"We'll get together some blankets and bedding," offered Heather and she and Lanie sprinted up the stairs.

"Don't touch me," Melinda demanded, as John Jr. and Jamie attempted to help her off the couch.

"We're just going to get you into bed," promised her husband lovingly.

"Ok, give me a minute and then I'll try to move," she said trying to muster up enough oomph to accomplish the task. "You two will pull my arms out of the socket the way you were trying to drag me up."

"Here let me help," Kelsi said, sitting next to Melinda and gently supporting her back, she helped her rise to her feet just as another contraction made her wince in pain.

The mother to be was finally situated in her new sterile but comfortable room. Heather and Lanie had made sure the blankets were warmed, and Kelsi was feeding her ice chips as she coaxed her out of her fears.

Back in the kitchen Lilly had three pots of water about to boil. She took a couple of steps back to observe her creation just as she heard the comforting sound of sled dogs in the distance.

John Jr. and Waldo barely got their down coats zipped up and their gloves on before they were out the back door.

"Maybe we should have strung a rope from the house to the shed," suggested Waldo as he blindly made his way to the sounds of the sled.

"It's a good thing the lodge is well lighted," replied John Jr. as he checked to be sure they would be able to find their way back.

Arnie stopped the dogs as close to the Lodge as he possibly could. When Waldo opened the door to the small cab on the back of the sleigh, Grandma Anna bustled out of a mountain of furs.

John and Waldo each took an arm and they carefully escorted the elderly lady over the porch and into the kitchen of the Lodge.

Grandma Anna's eyes grew big as she viewed Lilly hovering over her pots of boiling water.

Rushing to her Lilly hugged her tight, "Thank you so much for coming, Grandma Anna. The water is just about to boil. What do I do next?"

Smiling secretly to herself, Grandma Anna patted Lilly on the back and replied, "Just take me to the mother. We'll talk about the water later."

"She's soft as butter," Grandma Anna said smoothly with the charm of her Indian accent giving Karen and Lilly a new delightful memory.

CHAPTER 44

John Sr. and John Jr. competed for their time with little Allison. Karen loved to watch as they doted over the baby, but was secretly anxious to find a slot of time when she herself could have a turn. As much as she enjoyed watching John hold his granddaughter, her arms ached to hold the baby herself.

"Look, she's no longer than my forearm," the proud grandfather boasted as he tried to measure her length. "She's so tiny...and I can't believe you actually named her after my mother."

"Yep, Allison K. Worthington. Our new last name should be legal in just a couple of weeks now," John Jr. said with pride and satisfaction.

Karen squeezed herself into the loveseat next to her husband, her slender hips just fitting into the small space available.

"Hey there sweetie, are you tired of these men yet?" she asked hopefully as she took Allison's small hand in hers and touched her cheek. "Is this part of the witness relocation plan?" Karen asked, "For the entire family to change their name?" Karen asked.

"Yes and no Mom. I want to have my real father's name. And if that's my name then it has to be everyone else's too. Besides, there probably isn't any need for us to be in the witness protection plan, thanks to you and Lilly." John Jr. answered and then continued, "Mom, aren't you going to ask what the K. stands for in Allison K. Worthington?"

Looking surprised Karen said, "I just assumed it was K-a-y. Isn't that right?"

"Nope, your new granddaughter's name is Allison Karen Worthington. It was Melinda's idea," John Jr. answered.

"I don't know what to say," Karen stammered. "I have a little namesake; now will someone please let me hold her?"

"You bet," said John Sr. "I think it's your turn now, I hear a peculiar little noise."

"I think whoever is holding her when that happens is responsible," Karen replied with a giggle.

Karen and John left together with baby Allison to change her diaper, fussing over every detail.

"Mom," Jamie said as he sat down beside Lilly. "Do you think we could have hamburgers tonight?"

"Jamie, I think that's just what we need. Some basic comfort food. How about French fries too?"

"Not frozen?" He questioned.

"Nope, the real thing. Do you want to help?" Lilly answered.

"I guess. Just don't tell Kelsi that I know how to cook," Jamie cautioned.

Laughing Lilly answered back, "Honey, I think she knows."

"To tell you the truth, I'm looking forward to having you in the ranch kitchen…I can almost smell the food now. Do I have to peel the potatoes or do you have one of those machines that does it for you?"

Lilly hopped to her feet, delighted that she was going to spend the next few hours with her son, and knowing it would be quality time to treasure. Jamie's mention of her cooking abilities brought to mind the one single doubt Lilly had about living on the same Ranch property as her daughter-in-law and there was no better time than the present to question him about it.

"Jamie are you sure Kelsi's not going to resent having another woman around? I mean she won't resent Karen and me taking over the cooking?"

Grinning, Jamie answered his mother, "Mom, don't worry. I think she's looking forward to it more than I am. Well at least as much. And we will still have a separate house; she won't be able to get out of the kitchen entirely."

Breathing a sigh of relief Lilly swung open the kitchen door and was reminded of her latest embarrassing act by the sight of large pots of water still steaming.

"What in the heck are all of those big pots of water on the stove?" Jamie asked as he entered the kitchen and started to roll up his sleeves. "You're not sterilizing bottles are you?"

"No, but that does sound like a better explanation than the real one. When Melinda went into labor all I could think of was the pioneer books where they always sent the husband to boil water. Grandma Anna just told me they only did that to get him out from under foot." Giggling to herself, Lilly continued, "Who knew? Help me get rid of them, Jamie. Then we'll get dinner going."

"How are you going to keep this place going?" asked Jamie as he carried the biggest pot to the sink.

"I'm not sure," answered his mother. "We've always thought Lanie would fit right in but now I'm not sure what her future holds. It wouldn't surprise me if she fits right into Louisiana too."

Karen entered the kitchen and picked up on the last of the conversation. "How about Mary?" she contributed.

"Who's Mary?" asked Lilly.

"You remember Mary. The gal in the broken down Volkswagen we met in the city. Remember Waldo and John sold her car and got her plane tickets home to stay with her family until her husband came back from Iraq. She said she would make it up to us and we told her she could work for us."

"Lanie knows her, remember? And her husband was the grandson of the Johansson's. I'll ask Lanie if she knows her number. What's for dinner, I'm starving," Karen continued as she collapsed onto a stool at the breakfast bar.

"Jamie and I are making hamburgers and French fries. Why don't you go get a quick shower and maybe you'll have time to lie down and rest for a few minutes? You look exhausted."

"Lilly, you're a lifesaver. Are you sure you don't need my help?"

"We've got it under control, Aunt Karen. You go get some rest. Mom, how big do I cut the potatoes?" Jamie asked.

Karen left with a smile on her face, remembering the times that Lilly's sister, Lawanda, would make homemade French fries on a Sunday afternoon. Usually they would talk her into making them when they were too broke to buy taco burgers and chocolate milk shakes at their favorite hangout.

CHAPTER 45

"Mary's coming to visit", announced Lanie. "I talked to her last night and she's really excited. Her husband Randy just got home from Iraq and they need a place to live. She said you two were an answer to her prayers."

"He's coming too, isn't he?" Lilly asked.

"Of course, they're all coming. I hope you don't mind, but I knew we weren't booked next week, so I said they could come for a few days to meet everyone and decide if they want the job."

"They?" Waldo questioned.

Lanie ducked her head and nodded shyly, "He is a fisherman, Waldo, do you think you could use him too?"

"If he's any good, of course we can use him. Lilly, this sounds like just the ticket to free us up so we can get started on the Ranch. What do you say, John?"

"How in the world do you ladies get everything to fall in place like that?" he replied. "I'm impressed, and now we can go fishing or rope a calf any time we want."

"Don't forget about sitting under a magnolia tree and sipping mint juleps, John. We can do that too," Lilly said nudging Karen in the ribs and nodding at Lanie.

Karen giggled and added, "Lanie, have you ever sat under a magnolia tree and sipped mint juleps? Do you have any desire to?"

Laughing good naturedly while attempting to hide the blush that covered her cheeks Lanie replied, "Who knows, maybe I will someday. Now quit teasing me you two."

Lilly busied herself with the dinner dishes. A smile of deep satisfaction grew on her lips as she noted the passion in Lanie's eyes. She wiped up the ketchup drips that the children had left on the table and then sat down next to Lanie. "Lanie," She said seriously. "Why don't you meet us in Louisiana after Karen and I visit New York? Maybe you would even like to stay there for a while?"

"You'll just love the gazebo," added Karen with excitement brewing in her tone. "And we're going to need lots of help with the wedding preparations."

"Let's just wait and see how Mary and Randy work out," Lanie said as she took the last of the dishes to the sink. "I need to take things a little slower than they have been the last few days. Let me finish cleaning the kitchen, Lilly."

"Nope, Jamie helped cook and Waldo's going to help clean. I want the rest of you to get on out of here and enjoy the time you have left before everyone goes their separate ways tomorrow," Lilly said.

"Lilly, my love," Waldo said coming up behind and slipping his arms around his wife. "Are you sure it's the dishes you want help with?"

"Stop it, Waldo," she said slapping at him playfully, "or I'll send you out of the kitchen too."

CHAPTER 46

Lilly and Karen could already feel the emptiness of the lodge even though the Holiday guests hadn't actually left yet. Suitcases and bags gradually accumulated by the front door. Waldo had been on the snowplow since the break of dawn, and Grandpa John had pretty much taken over the care of baby Allison as he graciously took instruction from Melinda. Karen could see the bond they were building and her heart was full.

Lanie had disappeared to the ice room for the last hour and a half with Jim to no one's surprise. And Heather was obviously anxious to get home to start planning her life.

Lilly was spending every second she could with the triplets, not wanting to miss a single detail even though she knew she would see them again very soon.

"Look," Lilly said to Karen as she entered the nursery. "Chase is going to roll over!"

"He sure is. Just look at him," Karen answered grabbing Lilly's arm excitedly. "He's so strong."

Lilly smiled reminiscently, "He's just like his Daddy. Remember Jamie was doing pushups at one month and at six months he was using Waldo's hair to escape the playpen."

"Yeah, he was all muscle and no baby fat, and he used to hide his crackers under the playpen mat. Didn't you say he was saving them for later?"

"That's right, and we went through three crib mattresses before he moved to a regular bed!" Lilly said wincing at the memory.

The two friends laughed together and stood for a minute enjoying the sight of new life, remembering their own children as babies. Strangely enough, in spite of their ages, it was hard to comprehend that they had actually grown up and become mothers, let alone grandmothers.

Later on that night after a simple supper of beef stew and salad, Karen and Lilly snuggled with their husbands in front of the fire in the great room and reminisced about the holiday events and listened to Waldo and John brag to each other about their grandchildren.

The lodge would be quiet now for a couple of days before the next guests arrived, and it seemed to be a nice change before the spring events. Tomorrow the four of them would go on a snowmobile trip, and perhaps Lilly and Karen would have tea with Lanie later in the day.

"I love my life," commented Karen, stifling a yawn.

"Me too," agreed Lilly, "And it seems to get better by the day, doesn't it?"

"Uh huh," Karen agreed just as she slipped into sleep snuggled tight against John's side.

THE END